THE ANGEL

Kathy Shuker was born in north[...] working as a physiotherapist, sh[...] freelance artist in oils and watercolours. Writing took over her life several years ago and *The Angel Downstairs* is her seventh novel, the third of the Dechansay Bright Mysteries, each a standalone story featuring art restorers Hannah Dechansay and Nathan Bright.

Kathy lives with her husband in Devon. Art is still a major passion as are the natural world and music. Sadly, despite years of trying, (and the tolerance of both husband and neighbours) mastery of the piano, guitar and fiddle remains as elusive as ever.

To find out more about Kathy and her other novels, please visit:
www.kathyshuker.co.uk

Also by Kathy Shuker

Deep Water, Thin Ice

Silent Faces, Painted Ghosts

That Still and Whispering Place

The Silence before Thunder

Dechansay Bright Mysteries:

A Crack in the Varnish

By a Hand Unknown

THE ANGEL DOWNSTAIRS

Kathy Shuker

Kathy Shuker (signature)

A Dechansay Bright Mystery

Published by Shuker Publishing

All enquiries to kathyshuker@kathyshuker.co.uk

ISBN: 978-1-9168930-5-4

This book is written in UK English

Cover design by Lawston Design

Cover artwork: *Place du Tertre, Paris*, by the author

Prologue

Paris, December 1991

A dimming pink light filtered through the studio windows. It caressed the brushes, paints and mediums cluttering the tables, glinted sleepily off a glass jar and a palette knife and gave a rosy hue to a primed white canvas drying against the wall.

Oblivious to the charm of the crepuscular light, Eric stepped back from the easel where he was working and sighed heavily, eyeing up his progress with a critical eye. It wasn't going well and he hated these short winter days. Before long he'd have to put the lights on and it wouldn't be the same. Whatever the manufacturers might claim, no light bulb quite replicated natural light – not to his eyes anyway. Especially when he couldn't quite figure out what was wrong with the damn painting.

He tossed his brush on the table nearby in irritation, stretched his shoulders back and ran his hands through his thinning hair as he eyed up his canvas resentfully.

As if his employer's restive movement had given him permission to talk, Mark, the senior of Eric's two studio assistants, looked across and cleared his throat.

'Angélique has been a long time,' he remarked.

Angélique was the junior studio assistant. She had been sent out to get brioches, preferably chocolate. When work wasn't going well, Eric often had a sudden craving for a

1

chocolate brioche. Then, when he got engrossed again, he promptly forgot about it.

'Hm?' he said now, dragging his eyes away from the canvas. Mark was English but spoke French pretty fluently. Even so, his accent sometimes made him hard to understand. Eric, whose English was very good, often thought he'd follow him better if he spoke in his native tongue.

'Angélique,' repeated Mark. 'She's been gone ages. How long does it take to find a brioche in Paris?'

Eric glanced at the big clock on the wall, pointlessly, because, immersed in his work, he had no idea what time it had been when the girl left.

'It's probably the Christmas crowds,' he offered, and shrugged. 'It's getting crazy out there now.'

As if to emphasise the point, the sound of a police siren wailed in at them through the open window as the car tried to negotiate its way through the traffic on the Boulevard de Port Royal a couple of blocks away.

Eric frowned, glared accusingly at the window then turned his attention back to the painting. Neither of them spoke again till the phone rang some twenty minutes later.

'It's for you,' said Mark, handing Eric the handset with a strange look. 'It's the police.'

'The police? For me?'

*

Angélique's body was stretched out at the bottom of a short run of steps which ran down to a recently abandoned basement restaurant at the end of a nearby street. Apparently a couple of Eric's business cards had been found on her but nothing that could identify her, so the police had rung Eric in an effort to establish who she was. She had been covered with a blanket

2

but the police officer in charge told his second in command to pull the top down so Eric could see her face.

'You know this woman?' demanded the officer.

Eric couldn't speak, both chilled and magnetised by what he saw. The girl's face was heavily bruised on one side which only accentuated the extreme pallor of her skin; she looked like a waxwork. Her sweatshirt, marked in places with paint and pastel, was now soaked in blood as was her jacket. He cleared his throat and swallowed.

'She's my studio assistant: Angélique Paumier.' He paused and swallowed again. He felt slightly sick. 'She'd just popped out for... to do some shopping. I... Sorry, I'm shocked. What happened to her?'

The police officer raised his eyebrows as though the answer was self-evident.

'She's been mugged. Maybe she tried to fight back. She's been stabbed. It was a senseless and savage attack. There's no purse on her, nothing. Just your cards in her pocket.'

'My cards,' muttered Eric, his eyes still glued on the body as the junior officer replaced the blanket. 'Yes, yes, I see. My cards.' He pulled his gaze away and looked round, wild-eyed. 'But all this for a few francs?' He spread his arms in disbelief. 'She can't have had anything much to steal. I can't understand why...'

'So she works for you?' The officer picked up the plastic bag which now held Eric's business cards and read one of them again through it. 'Eric Dechansay. You're an artist, I see. Did she live with you?'

As if every artist slept with the girls he worked with, thought Eric. That's what everyone thought, wasn't it? Not that he never had, obviously, but Angélique had been little more than a child. He glanced back down at the shrouded shape.

3

Look at her: such a slight thing. He felt another wave of sickness.

'*Monsieur?*' prompted the officer. 'She lived with you?'

Eric forced himself to concentrate. '*Non, non*, she had a flat which she shared with another girl.'

'I see. Do you have the address? Is there a relative we could contact?' He was direct and business-like. Professional. Eric tried to pull himself together.

'I've got her address back at the studio. I think her parents live somewhere near Fontainebleau. Her flatmate might know.'

'If you'd like to go back to your studio then...' The officer glanced at the business card again. '...we'll come and see you shortly, see where she worked, find out more about her.' And you too, his tone implied.

Eric nodded and moved away, ducking under the yellow and black police tape, escaping. Was he being implicated in some way with this dreadful event? The police always made him nervous.

A crowd had gathered to gawp ghoulishly at the covered body and the comings and goings of the police and the forensic investigators. As Eric picked his way through the press of bodies, several pairs of eyes followed him with undisguised curiosity. It wasn't until he was free of them and able to turn for home that he saw the man standing on the corner, motionless, looking his way. Looking directly at him.

Their eyes met and Eric felt his heart skip a beat. There was something horribly familiar about the man, especially those black eyes, boring into him. Eric remembered those eyes; it was like seeing a ghost. Bad memories playing tricks on him.

Eric turned his head resolutely away and walked briskly back to the studio.

4

At the time he was too disturbed to see any connection between the man and Angélique's death.

That would come later.

Chapter 1

It was just past mid-day when Natalie turned up at her father's address on a bustling back street in the Latin Quarter. The old double wooden doors, their varnish peeling, were closed, a blank, anonymous entrance squeezed in between a *tabac* and an electrical goods shop. She ignored the intercom and the security keypad on the wall, turned the handle on the right-hand door and slipped inside. The doors were never locked anyway.

Immediately the noise of the city fell away. The archway supporting the apartments above led her to a rectangular courtyard, paved with small stone slabs. Two four-storey blocks faced each other and looked out on casual seating, stone troughs and an array of ceramic pots where greenery and flowers enjoyed the weak spring sunshine. The wall at the far end of the courtyard was blind and covered with Virginia creeper. The apartments behind her only looked towards the street. The courtyard was private and secluded, a vestige of a forgotten old Paris, hiding behind a façade of modern buildings.

The clunk of the gate brought an elderly woman into the doorway of one of the ground-floor flats to her left. She peered at Natalie, expressionless.

'*Bonjour Madame Février*,' Natalie called out. The old woman nodded and disappeared again.

There were six dwellings here: three small ground floor apartments and three larger ones occupying the upper floors. Eric Dechansay, Natalie's father, occupied part of the ground floor and all the upper floors of the block to the right. It was both his home and his studio. Once upon a time these had been convent buildings but they had been reused and remodelled many times over. A successful and well-known figurative painter, Eric had bought his block cheaply years ago when it fell into disrepair and he had slowly adapted it again to suit his needs, renting out one small flat at ground level and using the rest of the space himself. It was a good size by Paris standards; he'd done well for himself.

Natalie walked to his door at the far end of the block and let herself in, passing the storerooms and utility area on the ground floor and climbing the stairs to the studio. She paused by the door at the top and put a hand to her forehead. She felt fragile and her head ached; she wished she'd moved more slowly.

She pushed the door open and went in.

'*Salut*,' said a bright voice to her left. It was Florence, the young studio assistant who had replaced poor Angélique. Beyond her, Mark, the more senior one, fixed Natalie with a warning gaze.

Natalie glanced across to where her father worked on the other side of the studio. Normally a genial man, he did not like his work being interrupted. And maybe it wasn't going well today.

The studio took up the entirety of the first floor. Opened up to make a large, bright space, it had four large windows looking out onto the courtyard below and, in the middle, a low dais for a model. A number of work tables were dotted around the room. Against one wall in the corner a kitchenette had been installed next to a small cloakroom.

On the dais stood Jeanne, Eric's occasional model and current lover. Today she was dressed, wearing a silk taffeta, high-necked dress in a rich midnight blue, a colour which contrasted strikingly with her amber hair, neatly coiled high on her head. Her body faced a half-turn away, but she was looking over her shoulder towards the artist, chin raised, an enigmatic expression on her face, at once disdainful and yet vulnerable. In her hand she held a single white rose pressed ardently against her chest. She was a good model; her father had often said so. And he was staring at her intently now, as if trying to understand exactly what she was made of.

Then, as Natalie looked at her, Jeanne winked and Eric immediately turned. He looked at Natalie a long moment before appearing to register who she was.

'Natalie. I didn't hear you arrive.'

'Is this a bad time?' She walked over to join him and they embraced. 'Am I disturbing you *Papa?*'

'Yes, yes, you are.' He frowned, looking back at Jeanne and then at his canvas. He squeezed Natalie's shoulder. 'Leave me alone for a bit, will you, Nat? Go upstairs and I'll join you later.'

'Where did you find the rose – in March?'

'This is Paris. If you know the right people to ask…' He lightly shrugged one shoulder then waved her away dismissively. 'Now go.'

Natalie wandered away but didn't go upstairs. She had spent the first few years of her life living here until her parents divorced and she still found a certain magic in fingering the art materials and props arrayed everywhere around Eric's studio: palettes and brushes, tubes and bottles, charcoal and pastels and oily rags. And props, loads of props. And then there was

8

that smell: oil paint and white spirit. Unmistakeable. Part of her father.

She watched Mark starting the underpainting on a primed canvas on which Eric had already marked out his composition. Mark had been a studio assistant for two years already and was slowly progressing to more responsible tasks; he was even allowed to paint backgrounds sometimes – with Eric's supervision of course. Her father wasn't good at delegating.

Natalie walked to the window and looked down into the courtyard. Her father's eccentric neighbour Violette Février, wrapped in a huge cardigan, was now sitting having her lunch at the little table outside her flat. The sound of piano music drifted up from the flat Eric rented out below.

'You've been through my things again, haven't you?'

Natalie turned to see Mark standing by a chest of drawers, one angry finger pointed at Florence.

'No, of course not. What do you keep in there that's so important anyway?'

'I think you already know. And they're my things, my materials and my art work. My personal stuff too. You've got your own cupboard. Stay out of mine.'

'I haven't touched it.'

'There's a tube of cobalt blue missing.'

'So? It's nothing to do with me.'

'For God's sake,' shouted Eric. 'Will the two of you stop it? How can I concentrate with you bickering like six-year-olds?'

'Are you sure about the cobalt?' remarked Jeanne mildly. 'Maybe you used it Mark, and forgot. Is there anything else missing?'

'Stop moving, Jeanne,' Eric protested. 'You keep fidgeting.'

Jeanne promptly left her pose and walked across to him.

9

Beneath the long, elegant dress she was barefoot on the boarded floor. She studied the painting a moment then sniffed, leaned in and gave him a kiss on the cheek.

'I'm fidgeting because I'm getting tired and you're taking forever. Anyway, I need a pee and a coffee.'

Eric threw his brush down in a fit of temperament. 'Fine, fine. If no-one can concentrate, let's take a break.' He looked up at the clock on the wall. 'In fact, since Nat's here, let's make it a lunch break.'

Jeanne walked away, already undoing the fastenings of her dress. She stepped behind a folding wooden screen where her own clothes had been tossed in a pile.

Natalie came back to her father's side.

'Can we go out for lunch? I need to talk.'

'Talk?' Eric frowned. 'We can have lunch upstairs and talk there. I'm working, Nat.'

The first floor was given over to sleeping accommodation and a bathroom but the top floor housed a kitchen and an open-plan eating and living space with a small balcony. There was a tiny cloakroom up there too. Eric insisted that they eat before any talking. He liked his food and objected to being distracted from it. They sat either side of a big oak table eating dried ham with crusty bread and salad.

When they'd finished, Natalie cleared the table while he made coffee.

'*Maman* is driving me mad,' she said, leaning against the kitchen unit and facing him.

'Why, what's she doing?'

'What she's always doing: criticising, interfering, giving advice I don't want. I mean, I'm twenty-four now. I think it's time I had my own place. Don't you think so?'

'I thought you were planning to rent somewhere with Philippe?'

10

'Not any more. I finished with him. It's over.'

Eric watched her face. 'Why?'

'We had a row. I mean a serious row.'

'About what?'

'Everything. It kind of snowballed.' She shrugged. She didn't want to talk about it. 'Anyway the thing is, *Papa*, apartments are so expensive to rent. Nice ones anyway. And the restaurant doesn't pay a lot. I thought if you could see your way to giving me a helping hand I'd manage to find something. Just to start me off, I mean.'

He blew out impatiently between pursed lips. '*Ciel*, Natalie. I've given you so much money over the years and it just disappears: clothes, holidays, nights out and I don't know what. You never save. How do you manage to spend it all? You've got to learn to budget. And I've said before: you could get a better paid job than a restaurant. What about trying the big hotels?' He poured the coffee into two small cups and handed her one. 'I'm not made of money. I have expenses too you know.'

'I know,' she said peevishly, 'like white roses for your models.'

'Don't be childish. That's my work. The work that you are so keen to profit from.'

Chastened, Natalie fell silent. Eric led the way through to the *salon* and sat on one of the two sofas which faced each other across a low cherrywood table.

Natalie sat on the other, pouting. 'But I like my job. It's a smart restaurant with a cocktail bar and music. You know that. It's special. A hotel wouldn't be much fun.' She brightened. 'Perhaps I could come and stay here with you for a while instead?'

'No.' Eric's incisive reply came almost before she'd finished speaking. 'No, that won't work. I... I keep odd hours.

11

You'd affect my work. And Jeanne spends a bit of time here too. No. You've got to learn to manage Nat. Anyway, I'm cranky and I'm getting old. You don't want to be living round old people.' He grinned suddenly and his face lit up. 'Did I tell you about the old guy I did a commission for once who insisted I paint him wearing a Roman toga and a laurel crown? God, he looked a sight. He was eighty if he was a day with skinny ribs and legs like a chicken. Strange things can happen when you get old. Though I haven't started walking around the studio wearing a toga yet.' He chuckled.

Natalie smiled in spite of herself. She drank a gulp of coffee. It tasted good though her head still hurt and she automatically put a hand to her forehead and rubbed it.

'Heavy night again?' remarked Eric blandly.

'A bit.'

'You really should moderate it a bit, *chérie*.'

'You can't talk,' she protested angrily. 'You like to party too.'

'That's why I know how much it can hurt.'

'Look, *Papa*, I'm due some holiday. You couldn't see your way to lending me a bit of money just to tide me over to the end of the month, could you?'

'You should ask your mother. I am not a bottomless pit of money, Natalie.' He knocked his coffee back. 'I need to get back to work.'

She sighed.

Back in the studio, Jeanne was smoking a cigarette by an open window. Now in her early forties and not quite as much in demand as she'd been in her youth, she was still a striking woman with a good figure. 'I haven't had children,' she'd once replied to Natalie when asked how she managed to look so good. 'Not for me, girl. Anyway, children make life complicated. And a girl's got to make a living while she can.'

12

She'd paused and looked at Natalie meaningfully. 'I haven't had a husband either. You can't rely on men.'

Standing there now, her carefully coiled hair and large pearl earrings looked oddly out of place with her sloppy sweater and jeans. When she saw Eric and Natalie re-enter the room she quickly extinguished the cigarette in an ash tray on the window sill and went behind the screen to change back into the silk dress. Natalie went over to join her.

'Hi Jeanne,' she said lugubriously.

'Hello Nat.' Jeanne studied the girl's face. 'What's the matter?'

Natalie glanced round the screen to where her father stood staring at his canvas again. She dropped her voice to a murmur.

'I wanted my father to lend me some money but he won't.'

'Lend you?' Jeanne murmured back with a smile.

'Well, you know...'

Jeanne stepped into the dress, pulled it up and shrugged her arms into the sleeves. It fastened up the front with a line of tiny silk-covered buttons and she began slipping the loops over them.

'Perhaps you chose the wrong moment. He's very preoccupied with this painting. You know how he gets. Though I do wonder if there's something bothering him. Not that he's said anything.' She paused half way up the buttons, beckoned Natalie closer and dropped her voice to a barely audible whisper. 'But he's been getting letters.'

'What kind of letters?' mouthed Natalie.

'I don't know. He's had two that I've seen. Just short notes they look like. He reads them, then gets an odd kind of expression on his face and rams them out of sight.'

'Rams them where?'

'In his back pocket, folded up. I think he took them upstairs.'

'Are you coming to do some work or not?' shouted Eric impatiently from the other side of the room. 'You've been smoking again, haven't you?'

'I'm coming.' Jeanne quickly finished fastening the buttons, examined her reflection in a mirror on the wall and, with another wink at Natalie, padded back to the dais.

'Letters?' muttered Natalie to herself. What kind of letters? But there was no point asking him. Eric could tell entertaining stories till the cows came home but he never gave much of himself away.

Maybe she'd come and have a poke about another time and see what was going on. When he was out. Inquisitive by nature, she hated to feel excluded. And she knew where he kept the spare key.

*

At the Oxford base of Blandish Fine Art Conservation, Hannah Dechansay, one of the small band of restorers on their staff, came down from the first-floor workshops and into reception. It was just after eleven on the Tuesday morning, the twenty-fourth of March.

Daphne, who was both secretary to Timothy Blandish and receptionist for the small independent business, sat behind the reception desk, grappling with her new computer. Hannah put her elbows up on the counter and leaned forward to look down on what Daphne was doing.

'How's it going?' she asked.

'Slowly. I thought these things were supposed to make life easier.'

'I still can't believe you talked Timothy into it.'

Daphne sat back, always happy to have an excuse for a chat. Timothy, the owner and director of the business, was not

14

a bad employer but he was both penny-pinching and demanding. The atmosphere was always more relaxed when he wasn't there.

'I persuaded him it would make us more efficient. At this point, I'm not convinced.'

'You'll figure it out.' Hannah hesitated. 'Daphne, you said Timothy was away. When do you expect him back?'

'Not till Thursday. He's up in Scotland, assessing a potential restoration job. Some big, imposing castle or other. Why, did you want to see him?'

'No. I want to keep out of his way so he doesn't give me any more work before my holiday starts. I'm trying to eke out my present job to finish neatly on Friday.'

'Are you going away?'

'I'm going to stay with my sister for a few days in the first week. I don't see her very often.' Hannah grimaced. 'But even that might be too long. I think I've mentioned before that we don't have much in common.'

'Elizabeth, isn't it? And she's older than you?'

'Three years. And thinks that gives her the right to point out all the inadequacies of my life.'

'Ah.'

Hannah turned to go.

'I haven't seen much of you lately,' Daphne said quickly. 'Is everything all right?'

Hannah turned back. 'Yes, fine. Why?'

Daphne examined Hannah's face solicitously.

'You and Nathan. Are you still dating? Are you still, you know...? Only you don't seem...'

'No, we are *not* dating. We never were *dating*. Not really.'

Nathan Bright was the senior restorer. He was also a thorn in Hannah's side.

'But I thought...' began Daphne. '...you know, that you

15

were. And he was taking you out for your birthday, wasn't he? Just before you went on that job in Yorkshire? I've hardly seen you since you got back and you never told me how that went.'

'Really Daphne,' Hannah said crossly, 'I don't have to give a blow-by-blow account of my love life, do I? Not that you could describe it as my love life. We had three dates. Three, that's all. That doesn't count. They didn't mean anything. I suppose we were at a loose end or something.'

Daphne was silent. She looked wounded and Hannah felt bad. Daphne was a genuinely caring person. She didn't deserve to bear the brunt of Hannah's spleen.

'I'm sorry,' she said. 'That was unfair. It's just that it was... Look, I'd rather not talk about it. You do understand?'

'I do. It's all right, Hannah. But I'm sorry too, I mean sorry that it didn't work out for you.'

'Yeah, well... You should never date someone you work with. Everyone knows that.'

Hannah walked slowly back up to the first-floor studio and the painting by Watteau which was waiting for her. Her examination of it had suggested it was going to be a straightforward cleaning job; it was in remarkably good condition. She rammed the earplugs of her portable stereo in her ears, switched it on and allowed Beethoven's fifth piano concerto to wash through her head. Music generally helped her concentrate, but as she picked up a clean cotton swab, wrapped it round the tiny stick and dipped it in the cleaning solution, the conversation with Daphne still lingered in her mind.

And so did her brief romance with Nathan. The first date they'd gone on – the first proper date and not some convenient meal together because they happened to be working in the same place away from home – had gone well. After the two years of bickering they'd indulged in from the moment she'd started working in Oxford, everything seemed to have finally clicked into place. They'd been on the same page. The attraction they'd both tried to deny had finally blossomed. Or so she'd thought.

And the next date had been good too: a good meal, a good atmosphere, laughter and a lingering spine-tingling parting. Neither of them had wanted to rush into spending the night together. Perhaps because they'd both been there before and knew that getting too intimate too soon just piled on the pressure. They'd been taking it slowly.

Then it had been her fortieth birthday and Nathan had insisted that he'd take her somewhere special to celebrate it. But there had been something in his manner from the outset, something taut, pulled tight as if one more stretch and it would give. And it did.

Looking back now it was easy to see how it had happened. Their first proper date had been just before Valentine's Day. On the day itself she had received two cards in the post along with a couple of bills, post which, as usual, she had grabbed before leaving the house and not opened until she got to work. One of the cards had been a valentine from Nathan; funny, sweet, signed with his initials and a kiss. The second card had been a valentine from an ex-boyfriend, someone she'd dated for a long time before it all went wrong and she'd moved to Paris to work at the Louvre. Inside, a message had been elegantly, and not a little ostentatiously, hand-written:

Never got you out of my heart even after all this time.
Hoping you feel the same. I find I'm living your way now.
Time to try again? I hope so.
Nick

Of course Nathan had seen her reading it and wanted to know who it was from. He'd wanted to read it too so she'd handed it

17

over, thinking nothing of it.

'Who's Nick?' he said, looking up.

'Someone I knew years ago. I can't imagine how he got my address. But he was always resourceful, knew how to meet the right people and get on.'

'What does he do?'

'He's a graphic designer.' She took the card out of his hand and replaced it in the envelope.

'He's given you his address and phone number, I see. Seems a confident kind of guy.'

Hannah snorted. 'Oh yes, he's not short of confidence, Nick.'

There'd been a pregnant pause.

'Will you ring him?' said Nathan in a low, prickly voice.

'Ring him? Why on earth would I do that?' She'd rolled her eyes at him, got on with work and immediately forgotten about it.

But a card had arrived from Nick the day before her birthday and again she had opened it at work, not really thinking about it. This time a letter had fallen out. It had winged down and sideways, like a paper aeroplane, coming to rest on the floor not far from where Nathan was working. He bent to pick it up and recognised the writing. It was distinctive; Nick prided himself on making his script part of his creative output, as he put it - an advertisement for his graphic skills.

'It looks like Nick again,' he remarked, handing it back to her. 'Persistent, isn't he?'

'Yes,' she said with a sigh. 'That's Nick.'

She read the letter then, smiled at some of the things he'd said – Nick, for all that they had often fallen out, had a way of making her smile – and put it away with no further comment.

And she and Nathan had been sitting, enjoying a super meal at a smart Italian restaurant, when the whole Nick situation finally got out of hand. Maybe she should have seen it coming but she hadn't.

Nathan gave her a present – a pretty gold necklace – but he was quiet and introspective. Over the meal he kept looking at her then would look away when she caught his eye. By the time they finished their main course, she'd had enough.

'So what's the matter?' she said.

'Nothing.'

'But there is. Is something worrying you?'

'No.'

'Good.'

Nathan drank a mouthful of wine and put the glass down very particularly as if it required all his attention.

'So what did Nick have to say yesterday?' he said.

Hannah frowned, paused and sat back. 'In his letter? Nothing special. Usual Nick stuff.'

'Meaning?'

'Meaning...' Her frown deepened. 'Meaning why are you asking? It's not important.'

'Because you seem reluctant to talk about it. I noticed the words *on the phone* in his letter. Did you ring him?'

'So you even read some of my letter? You do understand the principle of privacy I assume?'

'I did *not* read it. I just noticed the words.'

'As you were scanning it.'

'I don't see why you're being so secretive.'

'Secretive?'

'Yes, secretive. You get a valentine from him. Then you phone him. Now he's written. At length it looked like. Of course I'm curious about him.'

She stared at him, completely taken aback.

'I told you it was nothing,' she said.

'So why won't you talk about it?'

19

'Because it was nothing and I expect you to trust me. I could tell you that yes, he rang me. I guess finding Dechansay in the telephone directory isn't hard. And yes, he referred to that conversation in the letter. Does that make you feel better? No, of course not. You'll want to know exactly what was said and I'm not going there, Nathan.'

He had accused her of wilfully blocking him, of keeping a secret life. She had retaliated, accusing him of behaving like an adolescent. The argument had spiralled out of control and they'd both said things in anger. Foolish things.

He'd called for the bill and refused Hannah's attempt to pay her share so she'd stalked off and rung for a taxi. They'd hardly spoken more than a handful of words – all work-related – since.

She glanced across at Nathan now. He'd watched her return from her conversation with Daphne downstairs and for a moment she'd thought he was going to speak but then he'd turned away, his attention fixed on the Constable oil sketch perched on the easel in front of him.

She longed for her holiday and to get away. She needed to think through where her life was going. Maybe it wasn't here. Yes, maybe she should be glad that she'd got out of the relationship before she'd got trapped.

*

Eric Dechansay was a mercurial man. Passionate about his art, he could also be stubborn, funny, difficult and charming. But for all his artistic traits, he was a creature of habit: he mostly worked daylight hours on his paintings; he usually gave himself at least one day off a week; and he always let his studio staff have the weekends off.

And on a Wednesday evening, just before seven, he would

get a metro to the Place d'Italie then walk the short distance to his friend Jacque's apartment in the thirteenth arrondissement where four of them would spend the evening playing poker, drinking and putting the world to rights. Would he do it tonight? Bound to. Natalie had an evening off which gave her the ideal opportunity to do a little exploring.

At seven o'clock, she let herself into the courtyard and walked calmly to his door, paused and looked around. Lights twinkled in a few windows but on-one appeared to be watching. She tipped one of the flower pots arranged outside and felt underneath it. Nothing. She tried another one, found the key and let herself in.

She'd brought a hand torch to avoid putting the lights on. It wasn't the first time she'd called when her father wasn't there. She thought she had a right – she used to live there, after all – but as soon as his ex-wife Virginie had moved out, taking Natalie with her, Eric had become protective of his personal space. He welcomed his daughter's visits and he often took her out for a meal, but he didn't like her nosing around the apartment and he refused to give her a key. He especially didn't like her reporting back to Virginie.

She climbed the stairs to the first floor and paused by the door to the studio. So where would these mysterious letters be? Jeanne thought he'd taken them upstairs. Would he have put them in his bedroom? More likely in the *salon,* in his bureau where he kept his bank statements and bills, photographs and general paperwork. She carried on up to the top floor.

Eric didn't care much for fashion. There was nothing here of the sleek pale sophistication of so many Parisian apartments. His furniture was old and didn't match. If he liked it, he bought it. The *secrétaire à abattant* – the drop-leaf bureau - in the *salon* was a prime example. It had been built out of flame mahogany back in the late eighteenth century and boasted a

21

two-door cupboard at its base and a glazed-front shelving unit at the top. Separating the two was a deep drawer. It had been knocked and scratched over the years but that only made Eric love it more. 'Lived in,' he called it.

Natalie pulled on the fake drawer handles and the drop leaf came forward and down to reveal an ink-stained leather writing surface and a range of pigeon holes and shallow drawers. He'd written cheques for her here. She could see his cheque book in one of the pigeon holes now. There were five ten-franc notes there too. After a moment's hesitation she pocketed two of them.

So, the letters... She rifled through each section in turn and eventually found two folded sheets of paper, pushed together and slightly crumpled. She unfolded the first one. It was handwritten in ball-point pen on cheap white paper.

Feel you're being watched? You are. You can't run away from your past, Eric. No-one can. It's a long time ago but you still owe me. You know you do.

It wasn't dated and it wasn't signed. Natalie stared at it, frowning, then unfolded the second sheet.

You've done well for yourself. I suppose you thought no-one would find out what you got up to all those years ago. But if you don't play ball, they soon will. Don't go anywhere.

Natalie could make no sense of them. They were threatening, there was no doubt about that, and something to do with her father's past. The time he spent in England maybe. Her mother often made waspish remarks about his 'other family' and 'old allegiances'; she resented the fact that he kept in touch with one of his children from that previous life, made worse, she claimed because he was so secretive about it. In Natalie's mind

22

it had become a dark time, something that was never talked about. So what had happened exactly?

After a few minutes' reflection, Natalie pulled a couple of envelopes out of one of the pigeon holes. She searched through the pictures till she found what she was looking for: a photograph of a woman with a young girl either side of her, one a little taller than the other. The clothes were old-fashioned, probably dating back to the fifties. The next picture was of a young woman of maybe twenty with short dark hair and big challenging eyes. Over a red check shirt she wore denim dungarees, her hands pushed deep into the pockets. On the back, written in pencil, was *Hannah, 1977*. Natalie had met this woman once. Going with her father for lunch – she'd been maybe nine or ten – they had bumped into Hannah by chance. She'd been working at the Louvre at the time. A picture restorer or something. The brief encounter had been tense, with Eric clearly reluctant to prolong it. And Hannah? Natalie remembered those big eyes, examining her.

She picked up her father's address book and found the entry for Hannah Dechansay. She was the only one Eric kept in touch with as far as Natalie knew. There was a barely legible address in Oxford and a phone number, scribbled in to replace a previous one, which he'd labelled *work*. Natalie wrote it down on a piece of scrap paper and put it in her pocket.

Chapter 2

'Hannah, you're wanted on the telephone.'

Daphne's voice crackled through the ancient intercom system on the Friday morning, prompting all heads to lift. There were three of them working that morning in the first floor Oxford studios. Nathan had been called out somewhere on a job. Hannah was glad.

Daphne was waiting for her, holding the handset of the phone and covering the mouthpiece with her other hand.

'Sounds like someone French,' she mouthed to Hannah. 'A woman. But she spoke in English.'

Hannah frowned as she took the receiver. 'Hello. Hannah Dechansay speaking.'

There was a pause, long enough for Hannah to wonder if whoever had rung was still there.

'*Oui,* yes. 'Ello. My name is Natalie,' the voice said in highly accented English. 'Natalie Dechansay. My father is Eric Dechansay.'

Hannah hesitated. 'Yes?'

'You know who I am? We met once, a long time ago.'

'Yes, I know who you are.'

Hannah dimly thought she ought to be more courteous, more welcoming maybe, but found she couldn't. There was too much going on in her head and she couldn't process it.

'Can you talk?' said the taut voice in her ear. '*Je veux dire:* does someone listen?'

Hannah glanced at Daphne who was trying to look completely absorbed by her computer, staring at the screen and tapping occasionally on the keyboard. She didn't doubt that Daphne was hanging on every word. She was a delightful person and kind to a fault, but Daphne did like to gossip. And Hannah was pretty sure that this was going to be a conversation she wouldn't want spread around the staff.

'*Oui. Mais on peut parler en français si vous préférez.*' Yes. But we can speak in French if you'd prefer.

'You speak French?' Natalie said in her native tongue, clearly both surprised and relieved. 'That makes it easier.'

'Makes what easier? Why have you rung me, Natalie?'

'Because... because my father has received some strange letters – just notes really – talking about something that happened in his past. I don't understand them. I thought you might know what it was about.'

Her tone was accusing and not a little aggressive and Hannah bridled.

'Me? Why should I know?'

'Because his past, it was in England, wasn't it? I think perhaps something happened there, something he doesn't talk about.'

'Have you asked him?'

A hesitation. 'No. He doesn't know I've seen the letters. He hid them away.'

'I see. Well there's no point asking me. I was eleven when my parents divorced and he'd left us years before that. I saw very little of him. And he didn't live in England that long anyway. Most of his life has been lived in France. I don't see why you assume it's something that happened here.'

25

'Because... because he never talks about England. Because my mother says he's always been secretive about his life there, that it was clearly a dark chapter that he preferred to forget.'

'Oh she does, does she?' Hannah struggled to keep the sarcasm out of her voice. 'And yet she knows nothing about it.'

'What was she supposed to think when he wouldn't talk about it?'

'Maybe that it was something he wanted to keep private? That he didn't think it appropriate to discuss his first marriage with her?'

There was a brief, tense silence.

'Perhaps your mother would know what it might be about?' Natalie said eventually. 'Would you ask her for me?'

'That would be difficult,' Hannah replied coolly. 'She died two years ago. And even if she'd been alive, I could hardly have passed on a message from you. She was very upset when my father left her. And then he married someone else.'

'Oh. Yes, I see.' Another pause. 'I'm sorry.'

Hannah relented. None of that was Natalie's fault. 'Look, I'm sorry I can't help. I have no idea what the letters refer to. If you're worried you'll have to ask him.' She hesitated. 'How is he?'

'He's fine. I think.'

'You think?'

'How can you tell?' said Natalie. 'He paints and he jokes and he drinks with his friends. He never talks about how he feels. But I've read the letters and they threaten him.'

'Threaten him? In French or in English? What kind of threat?'

There was a noise echoing somewhere in the room behind Natalie. The girl's voice fell away to a mutter.

26

'My mother has just come back. I'll have to go.'

The line went dead. Hannah stared at the handset then handed it back to Daphne.

'I'd forgotten you spoke French so fluently,' said Daphne. 'But that sounded very earnest. Problems?'

'I think French is an earnest kind of language,' Hannah responded with a smile. 'Just my half-sister wanting to chat.'

Daphne looked at her reproachfully. 'To judge from your expression, that was no ordinary chat.'

'No, well, true. But I'm not sure what it was really, Daphne. It was kind of strange. Anyway…' She produced a smile. '…just one day to get through, then two weeks off. I can't wait.'

Hannah raised her hands in the air in mock celebration and, before Daphne could pursue it further, went back upstairs.

*

It was nine forty-five that evening when Eric left a restaurant on the Rue Mouffetard and started for home. He'd eaten alone that night; Jeanne, when he'd rung her, had claimed a headache and the need for an early night. It was a shame. He'd have appreciated her company this evening. As well as being a smart and pretty lady, she was sensible and practical. There were no histrionics from her, no emotional blackmail. He didn't doubt she occasionally saw other men; they had a tacit kind of agreement about that: no ties. She'd be OK with him seeing other women too, though he rarely did these days. He liked Jeanne.

Before leaving, he glanced around the surrounding street and peered into shadows but he'd seen no-one waiting, no-one watching. He felt as alone as you could feel in Paris on a Friday night. *Feel you're being watched? You are.* The line from the

27

letter ran through his head again. He laughed at himself. Being watched. It was a wind-up, wasn't it? One of his friends was having a joke again, trying to get him going. Laurent was the most likely culprit though he was out of town at the moment and the letters had been franked in Paris. He could have got someone else to post them though. Or maybe it was Claude. Either way, Eric was determined to act as if nothing had happened. That was the way to rattle whichever of them it was.

It had rained while he'd been inside and, though it had now stopped, a chill vapour still lingered in the air and the damp pavements seemed to suck at his footsteps, deadening the sound. Shop lights twinkled in the darkness, cheery and enticing, but he wasn't one for window shopping and he kept a steady pace. Once or twice, aware of people walking behind him, he looked round but each time they were couples, out for the evening, innocent diners like himself. He couldn't pretend the stupid letter hadn't rattled him a little but it was foolish to let his imagination take hold, even for a moment. It's a game, he reminded himself; don't let them win.

He had been taken aback when the first note arrived, he couldn't deny it. And the second had bothered him more. He'd reread them several times over the last few days. Just checking, trying to feel their weight, their veracity.

You can't run away from your past, Eric. No-one can. It's a long time ago but you still owe me. You know you do.

It felt very personal but of course it was intended to. Laurent was a writer of thrillers. He was good at this sort of stuff. It must be him.

The problem for Eric was that he did have a past. But that was foolish too, wasn't it. Everyone had a past, though perhaps his had been more colourful than most. There were things in it he preferred not to think about.

You've done well for yourself. I suppose you thought no-

one would find out what you got up to all those years ago. But if you don't play ball, they soon will.

He was good, you had to admit that. Laurent had taken a wild guess, assumed that Eric had been... let's say, wayward at some time and played on it. Very clever. Of course, they'd all joked when they'd been drinking, he and his friends, describing the things they'd got up to as youths. A lot of it had been hyperbole, alcohol-induced bragging about their exploits, mostly with women. And Eric had done his fair share though no amount of alcohol would ever encourage him to speak of the darker things. And there was no way anyone else could know now. Not here, among his circle of friends.

He reached the gates to his home courtyard and went inside. A little light spilled under the archway from the courtyard and, after a second's hesitation, Eric ran a hand round the interior of the post box behind the gate. It was empty. What did he expect? The post had long since been delivered. Still he strolled more happily into the courtyard and across to his door. As usual, he'd forgotten to leave a light on but several windows in the other apartments were lit and it was easy to find his way. He pulled the key out of his pocket just as piano music started up at Gabriel's. The man wasn't working tonight then.

But the key didn't turn in the lock and when he tried the handle it opened anyway. He must have forgotten to lock it. *Ciel*, he must be getting absent-minded.

He flicked the lights on and turned to hang his jacket on a run of hooks by the door, then wandered up to the studio where, inevitably, his feet led him across to his work station and the painting standing on the easel. From a distance and, yes, from close to as well, the image was starting to come together. He nodded slowly, moving to view it from different angles. Definitely. Every time he painted he wondered if it would

29

come out right, would match the image in his head, and when it did he always felt the same relief: he could still do this.

It wasn't until he started to turn away that he saw it: a piece of folded paper, propped up on his work table against the jar holding his brushes. An icy hand gripped his stomach. He hadn't left that there. And there was something else on the table too: a very old tobacco tin. He recognised the brand and his hand trembled slightly as he reached to pick it up. It was empty but still exuded a faint smell of stale tobacco. He picked up the note and read the brief lines of script.

Salut Eric. A little bit of proof that I am the person you think I am. I'm going to ring you soon and tell you what I want. Be ready.

Again it wasn't signed but that tobacco tin was seriously unnerving. What was going on here? Someone had waited until he'd gone out and then let himself in. Eric lifted his gaze and slowly scanned the studio. There was no-one there, yet it felt polluted. It can't have been long since someone had been in there – Eric hadn't been out that long. But how had he done it? Did he find the spare key? Could he pick locks? Walk through walls? Eric felt his grip on reality shift a little.

An image came into his head unbidden: a staring man with dark eyes, standing at a remove from the crowd circling Angélique's body. Eric looked down at the tobacco tin again and turned it over in his hands, checking that it was indeed solid, that it was real. He shook his head, frowning. It didn't make sense. That man was dead and how could Laurent have possibly known?

But this tin was cold and hard. He sure as hell wasn't dealing with a ghost.

*

30

'Tomorrow? But I thought you were arriving later today. I was hoping we'd be able to spend most of the weekend together. I'll be back in school on Monday and I've got so much on this week.'

Elizabeth's voice in Hannah's ear was strident, peevish. Hannah pulled the phone handset away from her ear for a second and quelled a sigh.

'I told you I wasn't sure if I'd make it before Sunday,' she replied. 'I finished work late last night and I've still got things to sort out before I can leave. But I'll be sure to get there as soon as I can tomorrow morning.'

'We'll be in church probably.'

'Never mind. I'll wait in the car till you get home.'

'Nonsense, I'll leave a key under that stone at the back. You remember the one? I showed you last time. Make yourself a drink and we'll get back as soon as we can. You're in the same bedroom. By the way, watch the electric kettle: sometimes steam escapes round the lid and it can scald you. I think we need a new one. Oh and Hannah?'

'What?'

'We thought we'd eat out tomorrow night and we've invited some friends over on Wednesday. You will pack some tidy clothes, won't you? I mean, you know, normal things.'

Hannah rolled her eyes.

'I wear normal clothes, Elizabeth, just not your normal.'

'Well that's what I mean. You're so much like your father. Can't you be conservative for once?'

'*My* father. Really? Has it ever occurred to you that my clothes are just part of me? I'm not the same as you and I never will be.'

There was a hurt silence.

'All right,' Hannah sighed. 'I'll see what I can do.'

'Thank you.'

31

The call ended. Elizabeth was a teacher and she led a very regulated life. The problem was, she expected everyone around her to live in a similar way. 'Creative expression' weren't words in her vocabulary. And now apparently she had taken to referring to Eric as Hannah's father. Presumably she had disowned him because he didn't fit into her neat scheme of life, any more than Hannah did.

It was Saturday afternoon. Finishing late the night before had been a white lie – Hannah had managed to organise herself to finish almost exactly on time – but what she wanted most at this moment was a bit of space to regroup and relax. She wanted to potter round her little semi-detached house in north Oxford, tidying up, doing a bit of cleaning and taking her time to pack. She didn't want to rush and she couldn't face spending her Saturday night being preached at by her big sister.

She made herself another mug of tea, got her suitcase out and started sorting through what she would take. Normal clothes? For Elizabeth that meant blouses and fitted skirts or formal trousers, with either a nice cashmere sweater or a jacket, all very subdued and 'tasteful'. Whereas for Hannah normal was bright and cheerful, gaudy even, preferably casual and, above all, comfortable, and she knew Elizabeth would be weighing up her choices – and commenting on them – like she did her pupil's homework. This was going to be a long week.

Halfway through packing her case, she gave up, sat down on the side of the bed and ran a hand through her short, spiky hair. Elizabeth's remark *you're too much like your father* had sparked her thinking about Eric again and her thoughts had inevitably moved on to the strange phone call she'd received from Natalie.

Natalie. Hannah had only met her once, completely by chance, when she'd been working in Paris and for all that it was years ago she remembered it well. Eric had looked

32

embarrassed, put on the spot, and Natalie had still been a kid, curious, surprised, maybe put out. Hannah remembered searching the girl's features, looking for something familiar, still confused at the idea of having this young half-sister living in Paris, a relative and yet a stranger.

In Hannah's teens, a rare letter from her father had informed her perfunctorily of his remarriage and the birth of a daughter before swiftly moving on to another subject. He'd never told her anything about the girl and had studiously avoided any questions about her. And in truth Hannah hadn't wanted to know. She hadn't tried to look him up when she moved to Paris. How awkward would that have been? She'd heard later that his second marriage had failed too but she hadn't known that at the time. Either way, Natalie was the child Eric had chosen to spend time with and Hannah couldn't pretend she hadn't been a little jealous. She had doted on her father when she was a kid. Then he'd left.

But why would Natalie call her like that, out of the blue? And she'd sounded so confrontational. There was no reason why she should resent Hannah. Eric's first wife and her daughters had been left behind years ago. None of them had made any great claims on him. So maybe Natalie was genuinely concerned about her father, and that was worrying.

Hannah sat for a moment, thinking, then leaned over and searched in the drawer of her bedside cabinet. She pulled out a couple of photographs. The first was of both her parents with their two young daughters; it was a sweet image but gave the erroneous impression of them being a normal family. United. The second was a more recent picture of Eric which Hannah had taken on one of his occasional visits to London when she had been working there. She regarded it pensively. Her father was like no-one else she'd ever met. He was in fact just the sort of person to get into trouble. Maybe she'd been expecting it for

33

years. He was a brilliant artist, an engaging personality with an almost boyish optimism when things were going his way, and he was generous when he had money to spare. But he was also a chancer, a flirt and a compulsive teller of tall tales.

He'd received some strange letters, Natalie had said, ...*talking about something that happened in his past.* So? It had nothing to do with her. She knew very little about her father's past and they lived in different countries now for God's sake. When people asked, she told them that she saw her father occasionally but even that was an exaggeration; it was once in a blue moon.

But still the conversation replayed through her head.

How is he?

He's fine. I think.

You think?

How can you tell? He paints and he jokes and he drinks with his friends. He never talks about how he feels. But I've read the letters and they threaten him.

Maybe Natalie was overreacting. Maybe she was the kind of girl who exaggerated and dramatized things. It was surprising that she'd rung Hannah of all people but that was certainly no reason for her to get involved. What could she do anyway? She put the photographs away and resumed her packing.

But the conversation stayed with her, teasing at the corners of her mind all night long. The next morning, she rang Elizabeth to say she'd woken with a temperature and a sore throat. Not feeling well, she had decided that she'd better stay away.

Then she rang round the airlines to find a seat on a plane to Paris.

Chapter 3

Hannah arrived in Paris mid-evening on the Monday. The only flight she'd been able to get deposited her at Charles de Gaulle airport just before eight thirty and the shuttle bus then took her slowly into the city, dropping her off at the Opéra. The city was just as she remembered it: bustling, cosmopolitan, idiosyncratic, a curious mixture of purpose and laid-back living. Tired and encumbered with a suitcase and a bag, she opted for a taxi to take her on the final leg of her journey. Her father had given her his address a few years previously when, after a brief meet-up in London, there'd been a quick, impulsive show of affection and a voiced desire on both sides to stay in touch. It hadn't come to anything of course. She hoped he still lived at the same address.

She paid the taxi driver and stood on the pavement, looking up and down the street. It was now nearly ten thirty. The closed shops had their overnight lighting on, many of them with security grills in place, but there was a bar open further along the street and a mini-supermarket, both spilling light out onto the pavement. People still bustled to and fro though: people heading home; people going out to eat or maybe to a show; people catching up on food shopping. There was a security pad at the side of the double doors in front of her and another pad with an intercom at the top of it. She peered at the names by the buzzers on the intercom. There were six and, to her relief, her father's name was among them. But she froze suddenly: it was crazy to have come. What had she been thinking?

But it was too late to go back now. She pressed the buzzer for Dechansay and waited. She pressed again then held it and spoke into the microphone in the vain hope he'd hear her. She pushed her ear to the speaker to hear any response. None. He was probably out. On the off chance, she tried the door and, to her surprise, it opened. She grabbed her bags and went inside.

A deep archway led her through to a courtyard with blocks of apartments to left and right and a wall covered in some sort of vegetation ahead of her. Light shone from windows on either side, dimly illuminating the stone slabs below. A couple of low stone walls subdivided the outdoor space and an array of plant pots jostled for position. There were five visible doors but she had no idea which was her father's.

Then she became aware of the music. Piano music, jaunty and percussive. How could she not have noticed it before? It was coming from high up on the top floor of the building to her right where every window pumped out light. And as she peered across, she made out the shapes of two people standing by the furthest door, both smoking. She could see the gleam of light from their cigarettes as they drew on them.

Dragging her suitcase, Hannah made her way over. When the wheels of the case kept tipping on the uneven paving stones, she hefted it up and carried it. The shapes resolved into two men who both regarded her with frank curiosity.

'*Bonsoir messieurs*,' she said. 'I'm looking for Eric Dechansay. Can you tell me which is his apartment please?'

The two men both returned her greeting but looked faintly surprised. They glanced up at the top windows and one of them indicated the door behind them with a languid finger.

'Eric lives here,' he said. He looked down at her suitcase, across at his companion, then back at Hannah, and grinned. 'You're staying over?'

'Er yes, probably.'

'The old goat,' said the second man and they both laughed. 'You go through there.' He nodded towards the door again. 'And on up to the third floor. That's where it's all happening.' He gestured to the cigarette in his hand. 'We've been banished. That's the trouble with ex-smokers: they get so very precious about clean air.' Another look at her suitcase. 'But maybe you already know that.'

Both men laughed again. They'd clearly been drinking.

'He's having a party then?' she said.

'Yes. You didn't know?' She shook her head. 'Eric's parties are legendary. Go on in. I'm sure he'll be glad to see you.'

Hannah chose to ignore the innuendo and moved past them and in through the door. It was a utility space. She climbed the stairs, passed a closed door on the first floor labelled *Studio*, on and up to the third floor.

A wave of chatter, laughter and music engulfed her as she got to the top. The staircase brought her out by the door to a washroom. A woman emerged from it as she arrived, flashed her a smile and disappeared through an archway to a room beyond which looked like a kitchen.

Hannah dumped her bags in an alcove to the side and turned. The rest of the floor appeared to be one large space and it throbbed with people, some dressed up in partywear, many more in jeans, overalls or dungarees, looking as though they'd come straight from an art or craft studio. She hadn't allowed for this. Where was her father in all this mayhem and how on earth was she going to explain her arrival?

A man near the edge of the throng noticed her and came over. He was dark-skinned with a neat moustache and beard, his close-cropped hair just starting to show grey.

He flashed her a smile. 'Are you all right? You look a bit lost.'

'I'm looking for Eric.'

'Oh, Eric.' The man turned and looked back into the sea of people. 'He's in there somewhere.' He shrugged and turned back. 'There's food on the table over there if you can reach it. Help yourself. That's what it's there for. I'm Paul, by the way.'

'Hannah.'

'Sorry?' He turned an ear towards her. It wasn't easy to hear above the music and chatter.

'Hannah.'

He nodded with a look of mild surprise then offered to get her a drink. He made a move towards the kitchen but she stopped him.

'Thank you but I think I need to find Eric first.'

He shrugged with a disappointed smile. 'As you wish. I'll see you later.'

Hannah eased her way through the bodies towards what seemed the loudest, most animated part of the room and eventually emerged near a dining table spread with a range of finger food where people were idly helping themselves.

And she could see her father now too, his voice perfectly pitched to carry, telling one of his stories. He was standing at the edge of the dining area with a circle of rapt listeners, each with a glass in hand, hanging on his every word. Hannah held back as he finished his tale and his audience laughed raucously. It wasn't the sort of story you'd tell to a child. Then someone came and spoke to him and he turned away with a laughing remark and joined another group of people, holding court again.

Hannah abandoned any hope of speaking to him. A reunion here, like this, after who knew how long? An explanation of why she'd dropped everything and come? It was impossible in this noise with all these people looking on. There must be fifty or sixty of them. It would have to wait.

Feeling empty suddenly – the aeroplane food had been insubstantial and hours ago – she went to the table, grabbed a paper napkin and filled it with food. It was unlikely her father would even notice that she was here among all these people, especially while he was playing the genial host, but she'd keep out of his way for now and mingle.

The food was good and she ate as she began to ease her way around, pausing here and there, smiling and nodding at people. The conversations were as varied as the people making them: discussions about the poor quality of modern artists' pigments; the desperate efforts of a daughter to potty train a grandson; complaints that the government didn't do enough to support the arts. The food gone, she went to the kitchen which doubled as the bar, poured herself a glass of white wine and began to circulate again.

'...and I told her that I couldn't be expected to give away half my income just like that. What did she expect me to live on? I'm not made of money, and she was the one who chose to move out. I didn't want the baby anyway.'

'Exactly. She'll probably come crawling back, Roger. You stick to your guns.'

'I'm not sure I want her back.'

Hannah quickly moved on.

'...you've got an apartment, haven't you, Antoine? My neighbour's looking for one for her daughter."

'Sorry. I let it out a few days ago. To three blokes in fact. Didn't like the look of them honestly but they paid in advance and they're only short term. She could have it afterwards but it's not a great place for a young woman. Unless she's a mechanic?'

'She's studying dress design.'

Antoine laughed. 'Then no. It's over a garage, see. In fact I'm looking for someone to take it on. You don't know a budding mechanic who wants to run their own business do you?'

To Hannah's right, a woman in a paint-stained oversized shirt spoke intensely to a woman in an ankle-length floral dress.

'...I'm planning to organise a life class again, Adèle.'

'Good idea. There aren't enough.'

'But it's finding the models. Good ones are hard to come by, especially men.' The woman speaking, small and plump with a long grey plait down her back, suddenly noticed Hannah listening. 'Do you know any good male models?'

'Me? No, I'm afraid not,' said Hannah hastily. 'Sorry.'

'Shame. There must be some around.'

'Why don't you advertise?' suggested Adèle.

'But then you've no idea what you're getting. I suppose I could audition them though.'

The two women looked at each other and burst out laughing and Hannah eased quietly away.

She had now found the source of the piano music and homed in on it. With his back to the wall in a far corner, a man had set up an electric keyboard on a stand and was playing a ragtime tune with apparent ease, smiling, while a number of people danced nearby, showing more enthusiasm than timing.

Hannah went over. Piano music always drew her in, especially when it was played like this, with verve and joy. She started swaying along with the beat. The pianist flicked her a glance and grinned. She grinned back.

'*Salut*,' he said to her when the piece finished.

40

'*Salut.*'

'Come on, Gabriel.' A woman who'd been dancing came over and leaned over the keyboard. 'Play something else.'

'All right, all right.'

He waved her away, winked at Hannah and started playing a Rachmaninov prelude. Without the music. He made it look easy and Hannah knew it wasn't. He was good.

'Gabriel.' The woman was back. 'That's no good. You did that on purpose. Come *on*. Something we can dance to.'

He managed to bring the prelude to a satisfying stop and started playing a ragtime piece again. The small group of dancers began jigging and Hannah leaned against the wall and listened, sipping her wine, letting it wash over her. It had been a long day and she was tired; the music was therapeutic.

'No, no, I need a break,' Gabriel said when the piece ended. He waved the dancers away. 'Go and get yourselves some drinks.'

He turned to look at Hannah.

'You look like you need to sit down. Grab a chair.' He pointed to a folding chair beyond her. 'Come and talk to me. No-one talks to me; they just want me to play.'

Hannah grabbed the chair, put it near the keyboard stand and collapsed onto it gratefully.

'It's your fault for being so good,' she said.

Gabriel stroked the keys. 'This baby isn't so good though. Not like a real piano.'

'But more practical.'

'True. Getting a piano up here...' He glanced round with a shrug and a disconcertingly charming smile then stuck out a hand.

'Gabriel,' he said. 'Gabriel Berger.'

She transferred her glass to her left hand and shook his. 'Hannah.'

''annah? And when you speak I think I detect a little accent, yes?' he said. 'Are you perhaps...?'

'English. Well, half-English, half-French.'

'I see. You certainly speak French well.' He picked up a glass of red wine from a low table to his left and raised it to her before drinking. 'And you are a friend of Eric's?

She laughed and glanced around. 'Isn't everyone?'

Gabriel's smile lit up his face. Probably in his late thirties, he had expressive warm brown eyes and he studied her a moment before replying.

'It sometimes feels like that, yes. But I haven't seen you before. I know I would remember.' He paused. 'I live in the flat downstairs. In the evenings I usually play at restaurants or bars but...' He gestured towards the chattering crowd.

'You're a professional. I thought so. You're very good.'

'Thank you. I am, but for a friend I play for free.' He leaned forwards conspiratorially. 'And it makes sense to keep on his good side: he's my landlord too.'

'I see. How long have you lived here?'

'Only a few months. I got a job, a good job, playing at Au Bout de la Rue, the restaurant. Do you know it?' Hannah shook her head. 'Well, Eric was eating there when I started and told me about this vacant flat he had here. I was grateful. Apartments in Paris are not easy to find. Not in my price bracket anyway. It's small but it does.' He drank more wine. 'You should come to the restaurant one evening when I'm playing. I usually do a couple of nights in the week and always a Saturday. It's a good place. Do you live nearby?'

'No, I'm... only visiting. That is, I...'

Armed with drinks including another glass of red wine for Gabriel, the dancers had returned, interrupting Hannah and saving her from further explanation. They demanded more music and, despite feeble protestations, Gabriel seemed happy

42

to oblige. Hannah moved her chair and listened for a while then got up and returned to the kitchen. She drank a glass of water then grabbed more wine and began another tour of the room.

It was nearly one thirty when the first people started to leave and the party quickly began to break up. Eric was still chatting to people while a few women – why is it always the women? thought Hannah – began clearing empty dishes and the remains of food off the table and taking them through to the kitchen. Hannah automatically helped them.

It wasn't until there were just a handful of people left that Eric finally noticed Hannah. He froze, still as a ramrod, and stared at her. Now that he was no longer putting on his party persona she noticed how he'd aged since she'd seen him last. His hair was almost completely grey and his face, frowning with surprise, was heavily creased.

'Hannah?' Still he stared. 'Hannah? What the hell are you doing here?'

He didn't sound angry exactly but he wasn't welcoming either. The last of the party guests looked across then melted away, leaving only Eric, Hannah and one other woman who had come out of the kitchen at the sound of his voice.

'I came to see you,' said Hannah. 'I arrived a while ago but you were busy.' She gestured towards her suitcase and bag which still sat in the alcove.

'Eric, aren't you going to introduce us?' His companion was a striking, big-boned woman in a tight dress and high heels, probably a good twenty years his junior. Her amber hair fell in a cascade round her shoulders and down her back. She offered Hannah a friendly smile.

Eric cleared his throat. 'Jeanne, this is Hannah, my daughter. The one I told you about. You know, who restores old paintings. Hannah, this is Jeanne.' He didn't elaborate.

Jeanne came forwards and stuck out her hand, eyebrows

raised. 'I'm a friend,' she explained, 'and your father's occasional model too. It's nice to meet you.'

'Likewise.'

'Yes, yes, but I still don't understand what you're doing here,' grumbled Eric.

'Natalie rang me.'

'Natalie? *Natalie* rang you? Why?'

'Perhaps we should talk about it in the morning.'

Eric shook his head, exasperated. 'Have you never heard of the phone? Turning up here like a... like a... stray dog.'

'Really, Eric,' said Jeanne. 'That's not very hospitable.' She offered Hannah another smile. 'You must be exhausted. I'll go and make up the spare bed and put some towels out.'

'Thank you,' said Hannah. 'I'd appreciate that.'

Jeanne turned to Eric and kissed him on the cheek. 'Then I'll turn in, I think. You two need to talk.'

Eric still stared at Hannah, a perplexed expression on his face. He looked across at her luggage.

'You're planning to stay? Here?'

*

Daphne wasn't at work on the Monday. Something she'd eaten the previous day hadn't agreed with her and she'd spent most of the night up and down to the bathroom. The following morning, she called in sick, feeling weak and short of sleep. So it was that Nathan didn't hear about Hannah's mysterious phone call until the Tuesday and it quickly became obvious that Daphne had been waiting to fill him in all weekend.

She called him over as soon as he came in to work.

'I know you and Hannah are a bit at odds at the moment...' she began as he leant on her desk.

'What do you...?'

'But I thought you'd be interested to know about the call she had on Friday when you weren't here.'

'Why?' he demanded. 'Who was it from?'

'A woman. Hannah said it was her sister. The French one.'

'She never normally talks about her father's second family.'

'Well I'd taken the call so I suppose she felt she had to explain. The thing is, it was odd.'

'It would be. I didn't think they kept in touch. What was it about?'

'I don't know. They spoke in French but Hannah did sound cross and then the conversation kind of changed and she became... concerned. Or puzzled maybe. I couldn't understand a word of it but that's what her voice and expression suggested. Afterwards she pretended it was a normal chat, and when I said it didn't sound normal, she said "I'm not sure what it was really. It was kind of strange." Or something like that. Then she just passed it off.'

Nathan frowned. It sounded like typical Hannah: defensive, private and overly independent.

'Some sort of domestic dispute, I suppose,' he remarked dismissively.

Daphne looked at him indignantly. 'How can you have a domestic when you live in different worlds either side of the English Channel?'

Nathan couldn't answer that. 'She was going to stay with her sister this week, wasn't she?'

'Yes.'

He hesitated.

'Do you know her sister's surname?'

'I do.' Daphne looked at him triumphantly then glanced towards Timothy's office door which was closed. It sounded as if he was speaking on the phone to someone. Still she dropped her voice a little further. 'Her sister's listed as next of kin on our records so I know her address *and* her telephone number.'

Nathan leaned closer and offered an ingratiating smile.

'Would you be a dear and write her number down for me?'

'I shouldn't,' she said, reaching for a pen.

*

Eric was struggling to concentrate. The painting on the easel in front of him had hardly progressed all morning and it was Hannah's fault. Or perhaps he should blame Natalie, his lovable but wayward youngest daughter. According to Hannah, Natalie had rung her in Oxford and that was why she had turned up at his door the previous evening, unannounced and expecting to stay. It had been a late night, or rather an early morning, while they talked over a strong coffee in his case and a cup of tea in hers.

'You came because Natalie rang?' he'd said. 'But why?'

'I told you: she sounded worried. She said you'd had threatening letters.'

'Nonsense.'

'That's what she said your attitude was. So I worried too. What's going on?'

'Nothing. Nothing's going on. I didn't know you and Natalie were in touch.'

'We're not. But you have had letters?'

'How does she know?'

'She said she'd seen them. Where is she incidentally?'

'She doesn't live here. She lives in the Marais with her mother but she works in a restaurant a couple of streets away so she calls in now and then.'

'Au Bout de la Rue by any chance?'

'Yes, how do you know?'

'I spoke to the piano player earlier. He works there doesn't he?'

'Ah you mean Gabriel, "The Angel Downstairs".' Eric laughed. 'He hates it when I call him that.'

'So you haven't had any strange letters?'

'Look, my friends and I play games. Practical jokes if you like. They were just part of those, a bit of nonsense.'

'So why was Natalie so concerned? She must know about these jokes?'

'We didn't discuss it. I didn't know she'd seen them. She must have been snooping again. Which explains where my twenty francs went, the madam. Wait till I see her.'

Hannah was staring at him, frowning. She didn't believe him, he could tell. There was no reasoning with women, he thought, once they got a bee in their bonnet. He was rapidly losing his patience.

'The letters are my business and neither yours nor Natalie's. I will not have the two of you prying into my affairs.'

'God, no. After all, someone might think we were actually a family. Who are we to be concerned?'

'There is nothing, Hannah, repeat nothing, to be concerned about.'

'So can I see the letters?'

'I got rid of them.'

Hannah's eyes narrowed. Stubborn. Always was.

'This isn't the best time for you to visit,' he said.

'You're telling me to go?'

Of course he'd relented. He loved Hannah. She was bright and spunky and had a mind of her own, and she was the only one of his children – or his wives come to that – who understood his art and his need to create it. When he allowed her in, she was a ray of sunshine in his life, but he also

47

suspected that overexposure could burn him. Especially at the moment. He was confused enough without her probing mind needling at him, asking questions.

Now here he was on the Tuesday morning, trying to put the finishing touches to the portrait of Jeanne in the blue silk dress. He didn't need her to model for it any longer, he just needed to give it his full attention and he couldn't.

The tobacco tin preyed on his mind. It brought back unwelcome memories of his past and it had rattled him. Was it just another joke or was it a real warning? His stomach churned at the thought. And now he kept wondering where Hannah was and what she was doing. She'd been still and silent in her room when he'd grabbed a stale croissant and a coffee, found the letters and rehidden them, then come down to the studio. Jeanne had slipped out of the apartment soon after, off to a modelling job elsewhere.

His thoughts were distracted by the ringing of the phone. Florence jumped up to answer it.

'*Allô. L'atelier d'Eric Dechansay,*' she said carefully in her best telephone voice. She listened a moment then said '*Allô*' again. Suddenly she pulled the handset away from her ear and looked at it as if it were infected. She quickly put it down.

'Who was it?' said Eric.

'I don't know. He didn't speak. But I'm sure there was someone there. I could hear him breathing – sort of like he wanted me to hear him. It was creepy.'

Chapter 4

Eric had a *bonne*, a maid called Marie-Louise. No-one had told Hannah. Sitting eating a late breakfast at the dining table on the Tuesday morning, Marie-Louise had taken her by surprise, appearing on the top floor, already wearing an overall and ready to do battle in a pair of yellow rubber gloves. A small, dark-haired woman of maybe fifty with a wary smile, she had appeared less surprised to see Hannah. In fact, she hadn't looked surprised at all, which made Hannah wonder how many unexpected visitors – particularly women – her father regularly entertained at his breakfast table.

Hannah had been planning to attack the mess left over from the party of the night before herself but Marie-Louise insisted that it was her job; she had it covered and rejected any offer of help. She worked two mornings a week at Eric's apartment apparently, cleaning, changing linens and generally trying to maintain some kind of domestic order.

'But I don't clean the studio,' she'd said defensively. '*Monsieur Dechansay* won't let me. His assistants do that. Not that I could say how well they do it, mind you.'

'How many assistants does he have?'

'Two.' She'd sniffed and started work.

Hannah happily left Marie-Louise to the disorder and slipped down the stairs to go shopping instead. A quick survey of the cupboards and the fridge had shown that, other than

49

unappetising party leftovers, there was little fresh food in the house. Or any kind of food, come to that. Passing the door to the studio which stood ajar she'd paused for a moment but it was quiet inside. Presumably they were all at work. She passed on and returned to the apartment an hour and a half later with two bulging bags of food shopping which she slowly stowed away.

Thereafter, the day had dragged. Eric came upstairs briefly for lunch, expressed his dismay that she'd bought so much food and retreated to his studio again having successfully managed to avoid any meaningful conversation with her. She had then snooped around the flat, hoping to find the letters he'd received. If Natalie could find them, surely so could she?

But her search proved disappointing. The big bureau affair had looked promising and she did find some photographs of herself, her mum and her sister which she hadn't realised he'd kept. That was... surprising. And it did hold various other notes and letters but nothing like the ones Natalie had described. Had the girl been exaggerating after all? Did she like to be dramatic and attract attention? Hannah had no idea what her half-sister was like. But to go to the trouble of ringing someone she barely knew in another country? There had to be something behind it.

So perhaps Eric really had destroyed them, though she doubted that too. He'd been too quick, too glib when he'd said it, and there'd been a defensive look in his eye. So where then? His studio was too public a place to hide anything. His bedroom? Maybe but she couldn't go in there: it felt too personal. Being here, in her father's home, had only seemed to emphasise what strangers they were and it hurt. For all their distance and rare meetings, she'd thought she had a bond with him and just at the moment she barely felt it.

And now, with the clock showing half past five, she was again starting to question what she was doing here. If she could only pin Eric down and get him to talk, maybe the whole issue would resolve and she could go home with a clear conscience. Maybe there was no problem, just a young woman's overactive imagination. And why was she letting it bother her anyway? He wasn't. Nor did he want her there.

He'd said the right things last night: 'I'm sorry, I wasn't more welcoming but you turned up so unexpectedly. I was taken by surprise.' And: 'I've got a lot on my mind at the moment. I'm doing this painting and it could be good, you know?'

She did know. Artists could be very single-minded when they had a creative project that was going well, scared of losing the thrust of it.

But no, something was going on, she could sense it. Her father, usually genial, always quick to crack a joke or tease, never short of a story to tell, seemed lost for words. And touchy, too quick to lose his temper.

It seemed there was a side to him she hadn't seen before.

*

Back at the restoration studios in Oxford, Nathan was distracted, glancing occasionally at the scrap of paper with the phone number on it that Daphne had given him. Elizabeth, Hannah's sister, lived in Cheshire in the northwest of England. This much he knew. Also that she was a teacher and that, other than shared parentage, the two siblings had little in common. From the little he'd heard about her, he found it hard to imagine Hannah surviving a whole week in Elizabeth's company. Still, family was family.

But whether the siblings got on or didn't, it really wasn't his affair. Not now. Difficult as his relationship with Hannah had been in those early days, two years of working for the same company - and sometimes working on location together - had somehow made them into friends. Good friends. Then there'd been his desire to move their relationship up a notch. His mother would have called it courting. He'd decided he really liked Hannah. He was attracted to her, he couldn't deny it, and their tentative, cautious intimacy had suggested she felt the same way.

But it had been a spectacularly bad idea. It wasn't the arguing; they'd always argued and he rather liked it. She was smart and unexpected; it was stimulating. No, it was the business with Nick. Why had she been so secretive? If there was nothing to hide, why couldn't she tell him what was in Nick's letter? Better still, let him read it, put his mind at rest. And had Nick rung or had she rung him? Had she agreed to see this high-flying graphic designer with the pretentious handwriting? Part of him knew he should trust her – he'd never known her wilfully lie to him – but he'd been down this route before and still bore the scars. Even after more than two years, the memory of finding his fiancée cheating on him surfaced when he least wanted it and he wasn't going to go through all that again. At best, it was insensitive of Hannah; she knew what he'd been through. At worst, she was hiding something, a relationship she hadn't truly given up.

Their brief romance had died almost at birth.

But still the news of that call from France bothered him. It sounded odd. Something must have happened for Hannah's half-sister to ring like that. And he knew all too well how Hannah had a way of meddling. Sometimes she couldn't seem to leave things alone. Was it a financial problem? An illness? Eric beaten up by a jealous husband? Nathan had never met Hannah's father but he'd heard enough about the man to know he was something of a loose cannon. The possibilities circled in his mind all day but he kept pushing them away. Asking for

Elizabeth's phone number had been a rush of blood to the head, a hasty impulse not to be followed up. Hannah could look after herself.

Arriving home at the end of the afternoon, he screwed the paper up, threw it in the bin and went to make a mug of tea.

But barely two hours later he'd retrieved the number from the bin, picked up the phone and dialled. The ringing tone of Elizabeth's phone sounded, a hundred and thirty odd miles away and he mentally rehearsed various openings; they all sounded spurious. He was going to sound like a fool and was on the point of ringing off when Elizabeth answered, saying the number in smart, clipped tones, expectant and business-like.

'Hello,' he said cautiously. 'Is that Elizabeth?'

'Ye-es. Who is this please?'

'I'm Nathan. I work with Hannah. I wondered if I could have a word with her?'

'Nathan? Oh yes, I know. She has mentioned you. No, I'm sorry, she's not here.'

His heart sank. 'I thought she was coming to stay with you.'

'She was. Then she rang up on Sunday morning to say she'd come down with the flu or something and felt awful. She didn't want to pass it on and was going to rest up instead.' Elizabeth sounded unimpressed. 'I have to say, she didn't *sound* ill.'

'Sound ill?'

'Well…' She tutted impatiently. 'You know what I mean: no sniffles, croaky voice or anything. Anyway, was it important? She should be at home now, languishing on the couch I suppose. She seemed to think she was going to be prostrate all week. You could ring her there.'

'Yes, thank you. It was only something to do with a

painting we've both been working on. I'll ring her house.'

'Fine. Nice to speak,' she added briskly and closed the call.

Nathan paused, then rang Hannah's number. There was no answer and it finally cut through to the answering machine. He didn't bother to leave a message. Hannah's father lived in Paris. He was pretty damn sure that was where she'd gone.

*

Eric didn't come up from the studio until nearly seven. His assistants had knocked off at five as usual but he'd carried on, making the most of the light.

'You worked late tonight,' said Hannah.

Eric grunted and glanced round the top floor of the apartment. At least his daughter hadn't tidied up. But Hannah had never been the tidy, precise one; that had been Elizabeth. He wandered into the kitchen and Hannah followed him. He opened a cupboard. She must have bought half the supermarket. He pulled out a packet of biscuits, opened it and took one out.

'I wanted to crack on with the painting I'm doing,' he said. 'I think it's nearly finished.'

'I'd like to see it. Can I?'

'Of course. When it's finished.'

'But are you pleased with it?'

He looked at her in surprise, and waved the half-eaten biscuit. 'Yes. Good question. I think I am. Or will be.'

Hannah frowned. 'Why so surprised?'

'Virginie's first question was always: how much will it sell for?'

'And my mother?'

He paused, studying her face. 'Your mother didn't really

54

want me to paint. She wanted me to teach or do something else that was sensible, especially once Elizabeth was born.'

'But you were a painter when she met you.'

'Exactly. Never try to change people, Hannah. If change is needed, they have to do it themselves. They have to want to.'

He shrugged the subject away – it was too uncomfortable – took another biscuit and put the packet back in the cupboard.

'I've been looking out over the courtyard,' remarked Hannah. 'There doesn't seem much activity in the apartments on the other side.'

'There isn't. A big part of the block opposite belongs to a German businessman. He and his wife only use it occasionally. And the journalist who lives above Violette is a foreign correspondent for one of the newspapers. She's just gone away again somewhere.'

'Who's Violette?'

'The old lady in the ground floor flat opposite. Haven't you seen her? Always watching. Talks to her plants but she's harmless.'

'I think I did see her when I went out but she didn't speak. So tell me about Jeanne.'

'What about her? Like she told you: she's an artists' model. Very good, actually.'

'And she's your lover?'

Eric regarded her coolly. 'That sounds like an accusation.'

Hannah shook her head. 'I didn't mean it that way. I suppose I meant: is she special to you or...?' She stopped herself short.

He smiled. 'Dear Hannah, how very English you are sometimes. I'm guessing you want to ask if I have a host of women at my beck and call to warm my bed? Is that right?'

She coloured. 'No, it's not. Or perhaps it is. I don't want to say something wrong and feel a fool when I go for breakfast

55

and find another woman I don't know sitting at the table. I'd like to be prepared.'

Eric finished eating the second biscuit and paused before replying.

'If you find another woman sitting at my table, you have my permission to interrogate her. Except after a party. Then, you never know. I got up the one time to find a troupe of cheerleaders sleeping wherever they could find, all over the *salon*. The strange thing is, I didn't remember them being at the party at all and I'm sure I didn't invite them. They were with a visiting American baseball team apparently.'

Hannah grinned. 'You make these things up don't you?'

'Certainly not. Anyway, I'm going to grab a quick shower then I'm going out. I'll be eating out but you can sort yourself out can't you?'

'But we have to talk *Papa*.'

'No we don't. But I *do* need to go out.'

'When will you be back?'

Eric faced Hannah and took hold of her by both upper arms, shaking her gently.

'Hannah, stop it. Enough. You chose to come here; I don't know why. I did not invite you and there is nothing I want to talk about, repeat nothing. I'm happy to see you so have your holiday here if you want but don't pester me. I will not be cross-examined and if you keep doing that I'll ask you to leave.'

She looked shocked and he quickly turned and left.

Standing in the shower a few minutes later, Eric savoured the sensation of the hot water running down his face and body. It helped to clear his head, to calm him. He shouldn't have spoken to Hannah like that but she was too intrusive. Those big blue eyes of hers bored into him as if she were trying to read his mind. She really shouldn't go there. There was a lot she

56

didn't know and he was determined to keep it that way.

He slipped out of the apartment without seeing her again, opened the gate onto the street, looked once up and down, then set off for the metro station. There was someone he needed to see, someone from his past who might have the information Eric needed and, though he didn't relish the encounter, he didn't know who else to ask.

He found the nightclub, Le Rossignol, on a side street up in Montmartre. He'd heard on the grapevine that it was still there, the small but popular business Pascal Lechauve had started years before, when they were both young. Eric wasn't a nightclub man but, as far as he knew, the man still both ran it and lived above the club. They had been children together in the same village and, though in different years, had both gone to the same school. But, while Paris was the place they had both chosen to establish themselves, life had ultimately taken them in very different directions.

Eric pressed the buzzer outside and waited. There was no response. He tried again. A moment later the tiny intercom groaned wheezily.

'*Oui?*'

'*Bonsoir. C'est Eric Dechansay. J'ai besoin de te parler.*' I need to talk.

There was a nerve-chilling silence before Eric heard the lock on the door release. He opened it and went inside. It was a small, dark foyer with just one feeble light, high up on the wall to his left. Double doors to his right led to the dormant nightclub. Ahead of him was a flight of concrete stairs. He climbed them to a door which already stood ajar. Pascal stood back to let Eric in then went to stand by a drinks cabinet.

The apartment was equally gloomy. It was over-furnished and smelt of cigarette smoke. The floor was carpeted and felt sticky.

Pascal looked expectantly at Eric. 'What's your poison these days then? Wine? Whisky? Vodka? I'm out of brandy.'

'Red wine, thanks.'

'Take a seat.'

The chair Eric sat on was upholstered in a crimson velvet fabric. It too felt tacky as if too many drinks had been spilt on it and inadequately wiped off.

'It's been a long time,' said Pascal, lounging back on the nearby sofa. 'I hear life's been treating you pretty well though: exhibitions; wealthy patrons; some award or other. And you look well. A bit heavier of course. Like me.' He patted his generous paunch with a certain amount of pride.

'I'm doing OK. But you've got a good business here too I understand.'

Pascal shrugged and puffed up his lips dismissively. 'Yeah, not bad.' He took a swig of his vodka and regarded Eric speculatively. 'So, I'm guessing you don't want to buy a month's pass to the club, and, in case you weren't aware, I know nothing about painting. What exactly was it you wanted to talk about?'

'Gustave Daumier,' said Eric baldly. 'I want to know what you know about him.'

'I know what you know. We all went to the same school after all.' He paused and drank a little more vodka. 'You knew him pretty well, I thought. Better than me, they say.'

'Not so well,' Eric said quickly.

'No?'

'No. No better than anyone else.'

Pascal looked at him long and hard. 'Well what I do know is that he's not someone to mess with. But I imagine you already know that.'

'I thought he'd died in prison, somewhere down south.'

'You're out of touch, Eric. That was an old rumour. Of course Gustave has generated a lot of rumours over the years. He was in prison though, but I heard he was out. Maybe.'

'So where is he now?'

Pascal shrugged again and took another mouthful of vodka.

'Is he in Paris?' pressed Eric.

'I heard he might be. But I've heard rumours that he's in Bordeaux too. I haven't seen him personally if that's what you mean. If he is alive, I assume he's getting old like the rest of us. In fact he's a little older, isn't he? Must be pushing seventy now, don't you think? But we're none of us what we were.' Pascal almost smiled. 'We were adventurous in our youth though, eh? Of course we had to be.'

Adventurous. That was a euphemism if ever Eric had heard one.

'Do you ever go back?' demanded Pascal in a sudden change of tone.

'Back?'

'To Belédon-sur-Loire.'

Eric shook his head. 'Nothing to go back for.'

Pascal was silent a moment, taking great interest in examining the vodka in his glass.

'I hear Gustave had a son. Robert, I think his name is. Sounds like he's even more ruthless than Gustave was. *C'est son père tout craché, comme on dit.*' Chip off the old block, as they say.

'And is Robert in Paris?'

'I've no idea. Why are you so interested?'

'I'd heard rumours too. I wasn't sure if they were true.'

Pascal did smile this time, a sly, supercilious smile. He knew it was a lie.

'You know there were stories going round, years ago,

59

about things you might have got up to. But then you disappeared.'

'I worked in England for a while after the war.'

Pascal nodded slowly as if he already knew that.

Eric got to his feet and put the remains of the cheap, vinegary wine down on a nearby cupboard.

'Thanks for the drink,' he said. 'And for the information.' He paused. 'It was good to see you again.' Another lie.

Pascal grunted something non-committal and saw him to the door.

'Eric?' he said as he opened it.

'What?'

'If Gustave comes calling, don't cross him. Or his son. You were always too stubborn. Don't give them any excuse to play rough.' He raised his eyebrows and looked at Eric pointedly. 'If you haven't already, that is.'

Walking down the dingy staircase, Eric heard the door close softly behind him. What a slippery character Pascal was, all oil and innuendo. Going to see him had probably been a mistake. That man would probably sell his own mother for a quick profit if she were still alive. And the conversation certainly hadn't offered the reassurance he craved. His skin prickled with unease.

Once outside, looking up and down the street, he thought he saw a man waiting near the junction, standing still and furtively looking his way. He decided to head in the other direction. He'd find a different metro station, a different route home; he'd zig-zag streets, duck down alleyways if needs be, anything rather than be followed. He'd find a small place to eat somewhere out of the way.

There again, why bother? They knew where he lived.

*

It was eight-fifteen on the Tuesday night and Au Bout de la Rue was starting to get busy when Natalie saw Hannah walk in. Turning away from a table where she had been handing out menus, she saw the woman standing just inside the entrance, waiting to be offered a table. Years might have gone by but Natalie recognised her immediately, both from memory and from the photograph. It had to be Hannah. She remembered the bright clothes, the short, spiky hair and that challenging gaze. The woman was standing scanning the room, wearing loose, blue and purple satin trousers, a midnight blue top and a lilac jacket over. Big blue earrings dangled from her ears. Not pretty exactly but striking. Too striking: she drew attention and Natalie didn't like that.

Natalie had regretted ringing her almost as soon as she'd done it. Now she regretted it even more. She indicated to Joséphine that she'd attend to the newcomer, grabbed a menu and went over.

'*Bonsoir Madame*. Do you have a reservation?' she enquired loudly, then hissed, 'What the hell are you doing here?'

'I came to see you,' Hannah muttered. 'You are Natalie, aren't you? We need to talk.' She raised her voice and smiled. 'Sorry no reservation. Do you perhaps have a table for one?'

Natalie was tempted to say no but it wasn't true and the others would notice. It would only draw more attention.

'Let me see... yes, if you'd like to come this way?' She led Hannah to a small table against the far wall, roughly equidistant between the piano at the front and the cocktail bar at the rear where Baptiste did his magic. She handed her the menu. 'Can I get you a drink? A cocktail perhaps?' Jean-Luc always encouraged them to promote the cocktails – they were expensive.

'Not at the moment, thank you.'

61

As Natalie returned to the serving station, she saw Baptiste's eyes resting on her half-sister with barely disguised curiosity. Did he guess their relationship? She didn't want him asking questions. The leggy, handsome barman, a smart but enigmatic man originally from Martinique, had a way of acquiring information. She didn't want to be forced into talking about her father's other family. She didn't want to talk to Hannah either.

Edith took Hannah's order: a green salad followed by lamb cutlets with roast potatoes and just a carafe of water to drink. The restaurant was soon full. With a background babble of chatter and laughter, the waiting staff slipped into their usual frenetic routine, hurrying to and from the kitchen, carrying meals, clearing dishes, offering dessert menus. Gabriel was proving particularly popular that night and several people approached him to make requests. Natalie wondered how he could do that – play something dramatic and classical one minute, and a jazzy number the next, often without needing the music. He rarely seemed to refuse a request.

Then it was time for his break and, delivering meals to a nearby table, she saw him wander over to Hannah's table and stand talking to her for a couple of minutes. Why? Did he know her? How could he?

A few tables began to empty. Most of the remaining diners were still eating but Hannah wasn't. She'd long since finished and was dawdling her way through a glass of water. She already had the bill on the table so why didn't she pay up and go?

Hannah looked up at that moment and their eyes met. Natalie glanced round to check Jean-Luc wasn't watching and wandered casually over to stand by Hannah's table.

'We cannot talk here,' she whispered. 'It was crazy to come. What are you doing in Paris anyway?'

'You were the one who phoned me, remember?' Hannah hissed back. 'You worried me and I had holiday time owing, so I came.'

'I only wanted to find out what you knew. I didn't expect you to get on a plane. Why are you interfering?'

'I'm not. I just want to know what's going on.'

'Look, I'll get into trouble if I spend too long with you.' She hesitated, flicking another nervous glance towards the kitchen door. Jean-Luc still wasn't there. 'Do you know Gabriel?' she demanded. He was playing again, something quieter now, romantic.

'I met him on Monday when I arrived. My father was having a party.'

Natalie's eyes narrowed. 'You're staying at his apartment?'

'Yes.'

'He won't let me stay there.' Natalie realised one of her tables had finished eating. 'Look, I've got to go.'

'OK. Meet me tomorrow.' Hannah fixed her with her big, insistent eyes. They bored into her unflinchingly.

Natalie stared back. 'All right, all right. The Café Mandino on the Rue du Toit Rouge. Eleven o'clock in the morning.'

'I'll be there.'

A few minutes later, Natalie saw Hannah pay Joséphine, get her jacket and leave.

*

Gabriel became aware of someone at his shoulder.

'It got quite busy tonight.'

He looked round. It was Natalie.

'It did,' he replied.

'Lots of requests?'

63

'Quite a lot.'

The customers had all gone and he carried on collecting up his music from the top of the piano. When he'd first started, he'd kept it all tidy, pushing pieces back into his music case when he'd finished with them. At his interview, Jean-Luc had impressed on him that it was a sophisticated restaurant, that he wanted Gabriel to add to the atmosphere, not detract from it. Hence the velvet jacket and the bow tie. He'd been encouraged to play pleasing, gentle music.

But Gabriel was more used to playing in bars and downbeat music venues and, however hard he tried, 'sophisticated' didn't sit well with him. Slowly the music copies started to accumulate on the piano in the heat of the moment; his bow tie, feeling too tight, invariably ended up undone and dangling. And the music, prompted often by special requests, became increasingly funky. And the customers clearly liked it – they said so. Jean-Luc couldn't complain as they got repeat bookings and good word of mouth publicity. Gabriel and his music even reached the local press.

Now he bent over to retrieve the battered top hat which sat upside down on the floor by the side of the piano. There was a discreet sign inviting tips. Jean-Luc had encouraged it in the end; that way he didn't have to pay as much.

'They were an appreciative audience tonight,' Gabriel said with a grin as he pulled out a wad of notes.

There was an awkward silence.

'I gather you've met my half-sister,' Natalie said crisply.

'Your half-sister?'

She frowned. 'You went over to speak to her. Hannah.'

''annah? I didn't realise.' He nodded as the information began to make sense, then he smiled. 'I don't see a likeness.'

'There isn't any.'

64

Gabriel was amused and struggled not to show it. 'You don't like her?'

'Do you?'

He puffed out his lips, picking up the last of his music. 'I hardly know her.'

Natalie hung around him another minute or two expectantly, then wandered off. He thought she was a nice kid but a bit clingy.

Crossing the courtyard back to his ground-floor flat, Gabriel couldn't resist looking up to the windows of the apartment above where a couple of windows were lit up. Was Hannah staying there then? Their brief conversation at the party ran through his head again; she'd been very non-committal. Visiting, she'd said. So she was Eric's daughter and not a lady-friend. Interesting. He let himself into his flat, still thinking about her. He rather liked her: there was something about her. She was different, intriguing. But she could be a complication, nonetheless.

Chapter 5

Hannah woke early on the Wednesday morning and rolled over to glance at her watch on the bedside cabinet. It was barely six-thirty and she lay back, still listless from an indifferent night's sleep. The events of the last days began to parade across her mind like a series of flashbacks: her hasty decision to come to Paris; her father's surprise at seeing her turn up in the middle of his party; the uncomfortable evening at the restaurant the previous night.

She'd felt like a duck out of water, sitting alone in Au Bout de la Rue, waiting to speak to Natalie and trying to look nonchalant. It had only served to highlight just how much of an outsider she was. She might be able to speak French fluently, could even bluff her way through French mores and etiquette when pushed, but she was English more than French and caught somewhere between the two, always had been. Or perhaps she was being melodramatic and it was just the always discomfiting experience of eating alone in a restaurant. The music had been pretty special though and she smiled now at the thought. Gabriel was seriously versatile. An intriguing man. Melt-your-heart eyes too. She pushed the slightly disconcerting thought away.

Or maybe it had nothing to do with the restaurant or her cultural insecurities or even Natalie's cold shoulder; it was her father's behaviour that had her doubting herself. He had

66

returned home late the night before, had made a jovial remark about the dubbed American murder mystery she was watching on the television – 'Is there a butler? He's bound to have done it' - and said he hoped she'd made herself a nice meal. But he didn't give her a chance to say anything and had immediately retired to his room. One minute it seemed he was cracking jokes, the next he'd clam up and would be warning her off. She didn't know what to think.

Her thoughts naturally moved on to what he'd said about her mother: *...didn't really want me to paint. She wanted me to teach or do something else that was sensible.*

Hannah didn't know that. She had heard bits of altercations when she was small, occasional raised voices, quickly smothered. The arguments had been kept away from the children. Then her father had gone and her mother had never spoken of it afterwards.

Never try to change people, Hannah. If change is needed, they have to do it themselves. They have to want to.

You certainly can't change an artist, she thought. Her mother should have known that; she was a musician, a piano player. She couldn't have given up music - it was part of who she was – so why try to change Eric? But being here in her father's home, trying to navigate his wayward moods, threw a chink of light on the difficulties her mother must have faced. And he probably didn't sell much back in those early days; money must have been tight. Devoted to her father and gutted when he left, Hannah hadn't always been sympathetic to her mother and she felt a pang of remorse. Given the disaster areas which her own past romances had been, she was in no position to judge.

She sat up and threw her legs over the side of the bed. All this introspection was getting her nowhere. She went for a shower, got dressed and went upstairs for breakfast.

67

Eric was already sitting at the table. His plate was showered with croissant crumbs and he was cutting a peach into segments, juice dripping from his fingers. Hannah went to the kitchen, poured herself a glass of orange juice, cut a chunk of baguette and a lump of butter onto a plate and took them over to the table. Her father had eaten the peach and was just wiping his fingers on his napkin.

'*Bonjour Papa.*'

'*Bonjour chérie.* Sleep well?'

'Quite well, thanks. You?'

'Hm, yes. But I have been wondering if I'll still like my painting when I see it this morning.' He pulled a comical expression. 'I might hate it. Or perhaps the lady in the blue dress will have taken on a life of her own and simply wandered off in the night. You women can be tricky like that, you know. There'll just be her poor white rose left abandoned on the canvas, scuffed underfoot and starting to lose its petals.'

He winked and drank the last mouthful of his coffee. He reached out a hand to put on top of hers, left it there for the blink of an eye, and was quickly up and carrying his dishes through to the kitchen. A moment later he'd gone downstairs.

Hannah ate her breakfast alone and in silence. There was a pattern forming here.

Natalie wasn't at the Café Mandino when Hannah arrived but she was early so she found an empty table on the pavement terrace outside, ordered a tea and waited. It was five past eleven when Natalie eventually strolled slowly up, her expression signalling loudly that she was there under protest. She gave her half-sister a long look then slumped down onto the spare seat and regarded the tea-bag cast aside on the saucer of Hannah's cup, lip curling.

'Tea? At this time in the morning?'

'I don't drink coffee.'

68

Natalie raised her eyebrows but said nothing. She ordered a *café crème* from the waitress and sat back, eyeing Hannah accusingly.

'You've got a nerve coming to the restaurant like that last night. What the hell did you think you were doing?'

'Having a meal. My father had gone out and I wanted to see you.'

'You could have got me into trouble. And that place is a gossip factory. Baptiste doesn't miss a thing. They'll start to talk if they realise who you are.' She stopped speaking suddenly and looked hunted.

'What?' said Hannah.

'What do you mean, what?'

'You know what I mean: you've just thought of something. What is it?'

'I told Gabriel that you were my half-sister. I assumed you'd already told him.'

'I had no reason to. I can't see that it matters anyway.'

Natalie's *café crème* arrived and Hannah ordered another cup of tea. When the waitress had gone she leaned forward onto the table and fixed Natalie with a look.

'So tell me about these letters you found.'

Natalie was stirring a sugar cube into her coffee and avoided eye contact.

'I told you: they were kind of threatening. Just notes really. A couple of sentences each, that's all.'

'But they bothered you enough to make you ring me.'

'Only for information. I was curious. I don't suppose they mean anything.'

'*Papa* insists they don't. He claims they're part of a game he plays with his friends.'

'You talked to him about it? I suppose you told him I'd found them. Thanks a bunch. Now he'll be cross with me for snooping.'

'Well you were, weren't you? And taking money?'

'I didn't.' Natalie was all righteous indignation. Hannah raised her eyebrows and kept her eyes fixed on her sister's. 'OK, yes, I might have. But only a couple of ten-franc notes.'

'He noticed. I assume he lets you have a key.'

'No. There's always one under one of the flower pots outside.'

Hannah's tea arrived and she dropped the fresh tea bag in the new cup of hot water and left it to steep.

'I can't find the notes,' she said. 'Where were they?'

'In the *secrétaire à abattant* among a bunch of other letters and photos.' She glared at Hannah. 'There were two of them. I put them back where I found them.'

'I looked there. He must have moved them.'

Hannah extracted the teabag from her cup and fell silent, musing on any significance that might have and where he might have put them. They must be in his bedroom.

'So you told him I'd rung you?' Natalie complained.

'Of course. I had to explain why I came.'

'And why did you come?'

'I was concerned. I thought I might be able to help.'

'I don't see how.' Natalie took a long draught of her coffee. 'I don't suppose there's anything to do. It'll be nothing. My father,' she added, with a note of pride, 'is a typical artist. He's rather eccentric and so are a lot of his friends.'

'Granted. I've met some of them. Come on, tell me about these notes. What did they say exactly?'

'I can't remember now.'

'Try.'

Natalie sighed heavily. 'One of them said something about him being watched and not being able to run away from his

70

past. It said he owed this guy, whoever he was, something like that.'

'There was no name on them?'

'Of course not. The second one referred to the past as well in some way. And it said: *don't go anywhere*. I just thought they were creepy.'

'They are. Have you noticed any strangers hanging around his apartment?'

'No.'

'I suppose you're not there that often.'

'No, I live in the Marais.' Natalie knocked back the last of her coffee and pushed the cup and saucer away. 'They were probably nothing, a joke, like he said.' She paused. 'When are you going back to England?'

'I don't know.'

Natalie regarded her balefully. 'Gabriel's got a girlfriend, you know.'

'And you're telling me this because?'

'Because you seem to be making a point of getting friendly with him.'

Hannah shook her head. 'Not at all. I told you: I met him by chance. And I like piano music. Do you?'

Natalie shrugged.

'What's she like?' said Hannah.

'Who?'

'His girlfriend.'

'I don't know.' Natalie got to her feet. 'I have to go.' She leaned forward over the table in a menacing way. 'Don't go playing the hero, 'annah. It's nothing to do with you. Go home and if there's anything that needs sorting out, we'll do it ourselves. We don't need you.'

She left before Hannah had a chance to respond. Hannah fingered the two bills for the drinks which had been pushed under the glass ash tray. She'd be paying for Natalie's coffee too then.

Nathan had been to Paris only once before, on a school trip. His French had been rudimentary, the itinerary seemed to have been designed to cover the most boring aspects of the city – to a bunch of thirteen-year-old boys at any rate – and he'd bought a crêpe oozing seafood in a creamy sauce from a street vendor which had disagreed with him in a very unpleasant way. He'd spent the last full day of his short trip in the bathroom as it violently removed itself from his system. It wasn't an auspicious memory.

His French was still basic and, whilst he knew Paris was supposed to be beautiful, he remained to be convinced. From where he now stood, it looked like every other big city: frenetic, noisy and grimy. He'd arrived at Roissy Charles de Gaulle airport at ten-thirty that morning, had spent an age waiting for his luggage and negotiating passport control, and had now been deposited by the shuttle bus somewhere in the centre of the city. It was twelve fifteen. He glanced round. The easiest thing to do was to grab a taxi, state the name of the hotel he'd booked into and be dropped at the door but, needless to say, there were no taxis in sight. Besides, it was almost certainly too early to check in.

He unfolded the Paris map he'd acquired at the airport and studied it. Maps he understood so he could do this. Apparently he was on Rue Scribe which meant he was on the wrong side of the river but there was a metro station marked not far away. He folded up the map, picked up his suitcase, and set off purposefully.

Fifteen minutes later, emerging onto the street from the

Saint-Placide metro, he consulted the map again, somehow managed to negotiate buying a ham sandwich and a bottle of water from a *boulangerie* nearby and headed for the Jardin de Luxembourg. He found a bench to sit on to eat his sandwich and kill some time. It was sunny and pleasantly warm and he yawned. He'd had an early start that morning and he was looking forward to getting into his hotel room and crashing out for a bit.

Only then would he try to locate Hannah and her father.

*

In the studio, Eric put what he hoped were going to be the final touches to the lady in the blue dress. You could never be quite certain when a painting was finished. He put it on one side to dry but kept it close at hand, propped up, so he could look at it now and then, sidelong, in case anything struck him about it: something odd; something wrong. A tutor had suggested the trick to him when he'd been a young, raw art student, the same guy who'd advised turning the picture upside down. *You'll be amazed what you can learn about colour and balance when you look at the image in a different way.* Wise words. That had been at the Beaux-Arts de Paris, a lifetime ago. He pushed the thought away. Too many other, darker, memories came hot on its heels.

The phone rang and he looked across. Mark had got up to answer it, said a few words in English then put his hand over the mouthpiece.

'It's a Sean Borovski, an American. He says he spoke to you last week about a commission he wants to make. He'd like to arrange to see you in person to discuss it further.'

He handed the phone over and Eric exchanged some pleasantries then fixed up an appointment for the following morning. He was relieved, firstly that it wasn't another silent call and, secondly, that this would be a significant commission. Commissions were definite money, unlike the speculative pictures on show at galleries and exhibitions which were as likely not to sell as to find a buyer. Artistic merit and inspiration had little to do with it; some of the best paintings never found a buyer. He had a storeroom full of them to prove it.

He wandered over to Mark's work station and examined the canvas currently on his easel. The young man was showing promise. Though only paid a basic wage, in return for helping with menial tasks around the studio Eric offered tuition and guidance as well as overseeing Mark's occasional input on Eric's paintings. Mark didn't have a lot of time for his own work but he was starting to develop a style of his own. He was currently working on a view of the Seine and Eric discussed it with him, pointing out a couple of weak passages and making suggestions. Florence flicked them a glance now and then. Still very new, she hadn't progressed beyond simple tasks yet and was preparing a canvas for him.

'Can I disturb you?'

Their heads all lifted as one and turned. Hannah had come down from the apartment above and was standing just inside the door to the studio, looking expectant.

'Yes,' said Eric, taken aback. 'Yes, yes, of course. Hannah come and meet Mark. He's from England too.' Eric switched to English and turned to Mark. 'Kent, isn't it?'

'Yes.'

'Hannah is my daughter from my first marriage. Lives in Oxford now and restores old paintings for a living.' He leaned towards the young man conspiratorially. 'Very clever.'

'I'm sure she is.' Mark stuck out a paint-smeared hand. 'Nice to meet you.'

'Likewise,' said Hannah and they shook hands.

'And this is Florence,' Eric said in French. 'She's our beginner. Working her way through the gears, so to speak.'

'*Enchantée*,' said Florence. Her hands were covered in dust from sanding down the gesso on the canvas and she kept them to herself and smiled thinly.

Eric put his arm round Hannah's shoulders and shepherded her towards his side of the studio. He didn't want her getting involved in a conversation with them.

'To what do we owe the honour?' he joked. 'Not looking for work surely? Though I could find you some if you're keen. Just don't tell me I'm mixing my paints the wrong way and they'll all crack up and fall off the canvases in a few years' time.'

'Actually I was hoping you'd show me "the lady in the blue dress". But I can see her.' Hannah left him and went to stand a couple of metres from where he'd propped the painting up. She stared, silent. He waited, almost holding his breath. Her opinion mattered more to him than he dared admit. In the end he couldn't wait any longer.

'Well?'

'It's wonderful,' she said and when she turned to look at him, her eyes were shining. It was genuine. Not that she'd have scrupled to tell him if she thought it was bad. Not Hannah.

'Well, that's a relief. My career has not been a complete waste of time then. I'll be sure to tell Jeanne that my daughter approves.'

Hannah laughed then turned back to the painting. 'The way you've caught the light on the dress. And that rose. And she has such a wistful expression. It's quite haunting.' She fixed Eric with a chastening gaze. 'You won't do anything else to it, will you?'

'Now you mention it, I do think there's something

missing, don't you? I'm wondering about adding an animal, just by her skirts here.' He walked closer to the picture and gestured to the bottom of the canvas. Hannah was staring at him, open-mouthed. 'Perhaps a monkey, giving a little tug on her petticoats? What do you think?'

She opened her mouth to speak and Eric winked and smiled and she threw back her head, then shook it, grinning.

'Now go,' he said with a wave of his hand, 'and let me do some work.'

'Are you coming up for lunch?'

Eric shook his head. 'I'll have a sandwich down here today. Florence has already been out to get them.'

'Oh, OK.'

He spent the rest of the afternoon thinking through the commission for the American, jotting down notes and sketching out ideas to put before the man the next morning. By the time his two assistants left at five o'clock, it felt like it had been a satisfactory day.

He'd just taken off the big old shirt he wore for painting and thrown it over the back of his chair when the phone rang again. His first thought was Sean, wanting to change the appointment. He picked it up.

'*Allô,* Eric Dechansay.'

'So you do sometimes answer the phone yourself,' said a gruff, scratchy voice in French. 'I did wonder.'

Eric felt his throat constrict. He couldn't quite breathe. 'Who is this?'

'You know who it is. A ghost from your past.' The man laughed. 'You play the innocent very well but I think it's time we stopped playing games, don't you? You have something of mine and I want it. A simple cash donation will do nicely. I include some interest – you've benefited from it long enough. Let's say six hundred thousand francs.'

76

'What? I don't have that kind of money. And I ...'

'Just shut up and listen. You owe me and you do have the money. I've been making some enquiries about you. What about that nice little apartment you've got in Antibes?'

'But that's...'

'I said shut it. I'll give you twenty-four hours to get the money together then I'll be in touch with a time and a place to drop it off. I want small denomination notes, Eric. And don't get any stupid ideas about going to the police. We both know that your cupboard has skeletons in it. You don't want them rattling in front of the police do you? And remember, I know where you live. Such a nice studio. I also guess you'd struggle to paint with a broken hand. They never really heal the same, you know. No more pretty pictures.'

The phone suddenly went dead and Eric stared at it, hypnotised. Was he in some kind of nightmare? This couldn't be happening, could it, except that the last words still echoed in his ears. Then he looked up to see Hannah standing by the door again, watching him. It was unnerving the way she crept around like that.

'Who was that?' she demanded.

'No-one.'

Her eyebrows hit her hair-line.

'I mean no-one you'd know. Wrong number.' His mouth was on automatic pilot; his head was all over the place.

'It wasn't a wrong number. You said you didn't have that kind of money. What was it about?'

'It was just some crank trying to sell me something. Something expensive.' He forced a laugh. 'Some wonder gadget that would revolutionise my kitchen. As if. I mean, you've seen my kitchen. I don't do cooking. Coffee's a stretch.'

'This isn't a joke, *Papa*. Please tell me what's going on.'

'When will you stop pestering me and accept what I'm saying?' he said savagely. 'For God's sake. I don't need your interference, Hannah. And I don't need you here.'

He turned away.

'I dare because I found these,' she was saying. 'I know you're lying. What happened to you in the past? What's making you so scared?'

He turned back. She was holding a small book, an old book with hand-painted botanical illustrations in it, the book he'd hidden the notes in and left in his bedroom. And there they were, cradled in the pages where she had flipped it open.

'You've been in my bedroom. Is there no privacy in my own home?'

'I did go in, yes. I saw the pile of books on your bedside table. Remember how we both used to look at books together when I was little? You helped me learn to read. I remember this book. You loved it and I did too. Probably because you did. I saw it there and picked it up to look through.'

He shook his head and closed his eyes. When he opened them again she was still staring at him, a frown puckering her forehead.

'You should go, Hannah. Go back to England. None of this concerns you.'

'Of course not. I'm not really part of the family, *your* family, am I? I don't count.'

Her voice resonated with anger and hurt. She thought she was being rejected. Again. Even after all these years, she had never got over the pain of him leaving and coming back to France. It was all he could do not to go to her and hug her, to tell her that he was sorry, that he really wanted her to stay. But in all honesty he didn't. He had no idea how this was going to play out because he struggled to grasp exactly what was going on. It would be better for everyone if she went home.

'Fine,' she repeated when he said nothing. 'I'll go. There's clearly nothing for me here.' She paused. 'But I'll go tomorrow, if that's all right. It's too late to arrange a flight tonight now.'

'Of course.'

The doorbell rang and they both jumped, looked at each other then turned their heads to stare at the doorway to the stairs as if someone might appear there. After all, the front door wasn't locked – he'd planned to maybe do it after his assistants left but hadn't got round to it. But only a stranger wouldn't have tried the door. Eric crossed to the window and peered down to the courtyard below. Whoever was there was standing too close to the door to be seen.

'I'll go down,' he muttered. 'You stay here.'

Heart pounding, Eric went down the stairs, paused a moment behind the door, then pulled it open.

The man standing outside wore pale denim jeans, a navy-blue sweater and glasses. He was on the tall side with dark hair just starting to grey at the temples and he had a frustrated, distracted air.

'*Monsieur Dechansay?*' he said.

'*Oui. Qu'est-ce que vous voulez?*' Eric demanded abruptly. What do you want?

'*Je… er… je travaille avec Hannah.*' The man pulled a pained expression. 'Do you think we could speak English sir?'

Hannah had ignored Eric's instructions and appeared now at his side. She peered at the newcomer.

'Nathan?' she exclaimed. 'What the hell are you doing here?'

Chapter 6

Nathan looked round the restaurant and liked what he saw. It was small and had a friendly, intimate atmosphere with red and white checked tablecloths and a nightlight candle glowing in a squat glass jar on each table. On shelves behind the bar stood a selection of French wines with attractive labels and on the wall nearby, two framed certificates proclaimed the establishment twice an award winner in a gastronomic competition he had never heard of. It was evidently an independent family-run business but, unlike many such places, it had menus in both English and French so he knew what he was ordering. It wasn't far from his hotel either and he liked that too.

But the atmosphere at their table was thick with resentment. Sitting opposite him, Hannah's blue eyes, darker than ever, glittered with suppressed anger and she'd said virtually nothing since meeting him at the restaurant. They had ordered food and the waiter had just put a carafe of red wine on the table with two glasses.

Nathan waited for him to be out of earshot. 'Look, I know me turning up like this is weird.'

'You do? Wonderful.' She spoke slowly; she might have been speaking to a child except that sarcasm dripped from every word. 'Then perhaps you'd like to explain why. And don't give me that nonsense you told my father about a job in

80

Rennes finishing sooner than expected and having a couple of days to kill.'

'No, well... still I thought it was quite imaginative. He was very charming about it.'

'Forget my father's charm. Explain what you're doing here.'

'Look, I came to make sure that you were all right. I'd heard...'

'Well excuse me if I find that hard to believe. The last time we ate at a restaurant like this, you couldn't wait to see the back of me. You made that graphically clear. And frankly, as I said at the time, I'm glad we had it out then and didn't spend any longer on the farce that was our short-lived and excruciating romance.'

Her voice had risen making other diners turn to look.

Nathan leaned forward onto the table.

'You didn't exactly hold back that night either,' he hissed. 'Remember? You hit well above your weight believe me. But whatever's happened between us, it doesn't mean I'm going to stand by and see you get into trouble.' He stabbed an angry index finger towards her. 'You attract trouble like a magnet attracts pins.'

Hannah leaned forward too till they were spitting distance apart.

'You're here to protect me from myself? Well isn't that big of you. But A...' She held up one index finger under his nose and counted it off. '...I am not in any trouble, and B...' She tapped her middle finger. 'I don't see what qualifies you to come to my rescue. Trying to play the hero again, I suppose. Well you're not needed so you can go.'

'I wish. But what about your father?'

'What about him?'

She straightened up defensively and Nathan was sure he'd

read the situation correctly. He sat back but kept his voice down.

'You had a phone call from your half-sister, here in Paris, right? That's not happened before, has it? A half-sister you barely admit to in fact. Then you drop everything and come batting across the channel like there's a fire burning here and you're the only one who can put it out. It doesn't take a mastermind to work out that maybe your father needs help.'

'Daphne told you.' The anger flashing in Hannah's eyes had started to subside; resignation was setting in.

'Uhuh. Who else? She thought it sounded odd. She said you sounded concerned but then joked it off. She's too smart to be fooled like that. And too caring. It rang alarm bells for me too. I thought here we go again. Fools rush in and all that.'

Hannah glared at him, brow furrowed. He poured wine into both their glasses, lifted his and drank a mouthful, nodded his approval and set the glass down.

'So no,' he said, 'there was no job in Rennes. In point of fact I'm officially off sick. I took a leaf out of your book and claimed the flu. It worked with Elizabeth so I thought why not? Although, it didn't really because she clearly thought you were shamming.'

'You spoke to Elizabeth?'

'How do you think I worked out that you'd come here?'

'You shouldn't have done that.' She sighed. 'I didn't think Elizabeth would buy it. Not really. But what could she say?'

'So now that we're both here – and God knows why – tell me what it's all about. Why did your half-sister ring? What is her name anyway?'

'Natalie.' Hannah ran her finger round the base of the wine glass, back and forth then raised her eyes to his face. 'I'll tell you if you promise not to interfere.'

'What were you planning to do?'

'I haven't planned anything.'

'Fine. Then we can both promise not to interfere,' he said drily. 'Maybe you're overthinking it anyway.'

'Maybe. I'd like to think so.' She drank some wine. 'But no, Natalie has never called me before. I hardly know her and she didn't make much sense anyway.'

She gave him a brief resumé of the phone call plus the subsequent conversation with her sister.

'I was beginning to think she'd made the whole thing up, like a stunt to get attention, but I found the notes myself this afternoon, stuffed inside an old book in Dad's bedroom. There was a third one which must have arrived since Natalie saw them. It said: *A little bit of proof that I am the person you think I am. I'll ring soon and tell you what I want. Be ready.* I think that was it. I'd just come down to challenge him about them when I heard him answer the phone and it was clearly someone threatening him. He looked so scared.'

'What did he say?'

'Something like: "I haven't got that sort of money". Then a couple of times he tried to speak but wasn't allowed to. I've never seen him turn so pale. But when I challenged him about it, he said it was a wrong number, then pretended it was someone selling something. I can't get any sense out of him. Now he wants me to leave which just makes me more concerned. I don't know what it's about and I don't know what to do.'

Their food arrived and they didn't speak for several minutes as they began to eat. Nathan paused to pick up his wine.

'So your dad wants you out of his apartment,' he said.

'Yes.'

'Perhaps he's right. Perhaps you should go home, let him sort whatever it is out by himself. If there is anything. What do you think you could do anyway?'

She stared at him a moment, frowning, then carried on eating as if the food on her plate was the only thing in the world that interested her.

'I'm just saying. He clearly feels more threatened with you there.' Nathan shrugged. 'And you might be putting yourself in danger by staying.'

Hannah's eyes narrowed. She put down her knife and fork. 'So this is the whole point of you coming here: to tell me I should go home? Really helpful. I'm supposed to leave him to it while I swan off back to England, let him get murdered in his bed maybe, while I wash my hands of the whole thing?'

'You're being melodramatic.'

'You didn't see his face when he was on that call.'

Nathan took another mouthful of wine and nodded thoughtfully. 'OK, I get your point but it sounds like extortion to me. And your dad wants you out of harm's way which makes perfect sense too.'

Hannah sat back and picked up her wine glass. She looked around the restaurant casually, not meeting his eye. 'What do you think of your hotel?'

'It's all right. It's clean. The bed's comfortable enough. I'll let you know when I've seen their breakfast.' His eyebrows lifted in surprise. 'You're thinking of moving into my hotel?'

'Maybe. You'll be leaving anyway.'

He chose to ignore that. 'It doesn't seem busy; I guess they might have a room. But moving two blocks away isn't getting you out of harm's way. You don't know anything about your father's world or the people around him. Who can you trust?'

'But these letters are coming from outside. From someone in his past.'

'Possibly. Or possibly it's someone who's feeding him a line. Either way, it doesn't mean there isn't someone else close

84

to him that's involved. What about this restaurant where Natalie works? You said she didn't want them asking questions. Why? What about your father's neighbours? There was an odd woman peering at me from behind a load of pot plants when I entered the courtyard. And one guy actually came out - the one from the flat below - asking who I was looking for. Gabriel, is that his name? Kind of suspicious I thought.'

'He was just being helpful.'

'Nosey more like. He looked like he was keeping track of who came and went. There was something about him I didn't like.' He shook his head, lips pursed.

'Nonsense. Gabriel's a piano player. Brilliant. I've heard him. My father was having a party the night I arrived and Gabriel was playing.'

'What kind of party?'

'The kind of party where people eat and drink and have fun, what do you think?'

'And who was there?'

'Everyone. I have no idea.'

'Exactly. You don't know anything about any of these people and yet you expect to sort out which crazy and potentially dangerous idiot is sending him these letters.'

'I suppose you count my dad as someone I don't know as well?'

'No. Well yes. All you seem to know about him is that he lives on the edge. Your words as I remember.'

'Only because he doesn't fit into a neat box. So maybe he doesn't file his tax return on time and tends to know all the movers and shakers who get things done. So what? It doesn't make him a criminal.'

'I never said he was. Don't overreact.'

'Well, I'm worried,' she blurted out, then dropped her

voice when she saw people turning again. 'Wouldn't you be too? I have to stay. I think he might be in over his head this time and I'd only worry myself sick back home.'

'And what are you going to do?'

'I don't know.' Hannah took another sip of wine. 'Maybe just being here and talking some sense to him will help. He can be impulsive.'

'So that's where you get it from. Look Hannah, Natalie's here. You can't do more than her.'

Hannah made a derisive noise. 'Right. You haven't met her. She'll be a big help.'

Nathan put his glass down and gave a wry smile. 'That's probably what she thinks about you.'

Hannah scowled at him and they started eating again.

*

Eric sat at a table near the cocktail bar at the rear of Au Bout de la Rue. He'd tried to ring Natalie earlier in the evening and he'd ended up speaking to Virginie instead.

'What do you want with her?' his ex-wife had demanded.

'Only to talk.'

'You never seemed that interested in talking to her when she was growing up. Or me, come to that.'

There'd been a long, meaningful pause. It always came back to Virginie, sooner or later. Eric would be the first to admit he hadn't made a good husband, at least not the kind she had wanted, but she hadn't been as pure as the driven snow either. And she'd expected it to be glamorous, married to a well-known artist; she'd expected him to be rich and their life to be a succession of parties and trips to the Riviera where she would mix with the beautiful people while he toiled away at his easel in a chic, bohemian way. Needless to say, it hadn't

86

been like that and she'd soon tired of the reality.

'She's out,' she said now, managing to sound both disinterested and accusing at the same time. 'She's working this evening.'

'I'll catch up with her later then.'

So he'd rung up and booked a table at the restaurant and was now sitting drinking a Negroni, courtesy of Baptiste's skilled hands, and wishing he hadn't come. This wasn't the place to have a meaningful conversation with his youngest daughter and he felt on edge. He'd ordered *steak frites* and that was a mistake; he wasn't hungry. That last phone call gnawed at him. It might have been Gustave's voice but it had been so gruff and coarse. Though after decades of cigarette smoking, who knew? Perhaps it was someone else entirely: Gustave had always been good at getting others to do his dirty work and he wouldn't be working this blackmail alone. Of course there was his son, Robert, but the voice wasn't young enough to have been his. Or was it all a bad joke? No, he had to accept the reality: the tobacco tin meant Gustave. And Gustave had no sense of humour.

Baptiste came over to his table, asking him how he was, how the painting was going. He had a new assistant, didn't he? What was she like? It occurred to Eric that he had been so gregarious over the years that too many people knew altogether too much about him. Though not his early life. He had joked about it sometimes – the trials and tribulations of a starving young artist – when interviewed by art journalists, but he'd never given anything away. And he smiled at Baptiste now and said all the right things again but was relieved when the man drifted back to his bar.

He sipped his cocktail and glanced towards the piano. Gabriel played well, no question. When he'd mentioned his need for accommodation, Eric had had no hesitation in offering him the flat below him. The previous tenant had just moved on and it had worked out well. Gabriel paid his rent on time and he was a genial, obliging kind of bloke, good to have around. A musician of course so he was a bit odd, but that didn't bother Eric; he was used to odd people.

Natalie brought his meal over. 'Can I get you anything else?'

He shook his head. 'I need to talk to you, Nat.'

She glanced round. 'Not now.'

'When I leave then – you get my jacket and show me out.'

He ate what he could of his meal, paid and got up to go. Natalie did as she was told and met him with his jacket by the door. He persuaded her to step outside with him.

'You said something about having some holidays due,' he said.

'Yes. Next week. Why?'

'I've changed my mind about the money. I think it would be good for you to get away for a while. Have a break. Why don't you go down to the apartment in Antibes?' He stopped short, remembering that Gustave knew about that place. 'No, I forgot it's being decorated. What about going back to England with Hannah? I could ask her. You could get to know each other properly. That'd be good, wouldn't it?'

'You've got to be joking. Why would I do that? I don't like her much and I know she doesn't like me.'

'Nonsense, I'm sure she does.' Her expression spoke volumes. 'OK then, what about that place in the Loire valley we went to a few years ago? It was beautiful and peaceful. A good place to relax.'

'Langeais?'

'Yes. Find somewhere to stay there. I'll give you the money to cover it.'

'Why?'

'You asked for money.'

'But you said no.'

'Well I've changed my mind.'

Natalie nodded. 'OK,' she said slowly. 'And Hannah's going home?'

'Yes which means I'll have some peace for a while without the two of you, thank God.'

She grinned. 'All right. I'll send you a postcard.'

He panicked then. 'No, no, don't do that. I hate postcards – they just make you wish you weren't working.'

'But you like working.'

He grunted. 'Have you mentioned those notes to anyone else apart from Hannah?'

'No.'

'Good. I was going to tell you: I found out this afternoon that it was a joke: an old friend who thought he was being funny. You know what my friends are like. Anyway, you can forget about them.'

'Really? A bit twisted, isn't he? Still, good.'

'I'll get you some cash and drop it off at your apartment tomorrow. Lunch-time. You will be there?'

She nodded and went back inside and he left. He'd be able to think more clearly when the girls were gone. If only he'd had a son. It had never bothered him before but right now he thought a son might have been useful – a big guy with bulging muscles and a short temper preferably.

*

Natalie and her mother lived on the third floor of an apartment block on the other side of the river from the Latin Quarter. 'The right side,' as her mother used to say, 'in every sense of the word.' The building itself was unprepossessing but the apartment was light and nicely decorated. It had a good living-cum-dining space and its two bedrooms were separated by a shower room which at least allowed a small amount of privacy. Not enough as far as Natalie was concerned, but some.

Virginie was in bed when her daughter got home from work on the Wednesday night and she was clearing up her breakfast things when Natalie wandered into the kitchen the following morning. There was a tiny breakfast bar and Natalie, wearing a thin satin wrap over her nightie, slid onto one of the two stools.

'Is there any coffee going?'

Virginie eyed her up. 'Heavy night?'

'Just didn't sleep that well.'

'Oh? Why not?'

'*I* don't know, do I? I just didn't.'

In fact, she had been restless. The conversation with her father had been running repeatedly through her head and she'd been trying to come to a decision about her holiday. But confiding in her mother wasn't a good idea. Experience had taught her that. Virginie either trivialised any concerns or made a drama out of them; there was no middle ground. Natalie watched her mother put more coffee on to brew. They had a new filter machine and loading it was still a novelty.

'Your father rang here last night, asking for you,' Virginie said, pressing the on switch and turning to look accusingly at her daughter as if she personally was at fault for the call. 'When I told him you weren't here, he said he'd speak to you later.'

'He came to the restaurant.' Natalie spoke without thinking and inwardly groaned. Now there'd be an inquisition. 'It was quite busy,' she added quickly. 'Lots of tourists – Belgians, Germans and Americans last night.'

'What did he want?'

90

'*Papa?*' She shrugged. 'He wanted to give me some money for my holiday next week.'

'Really? Unusually generous of him. Got a guilty conscience has he?'

'I've no idea. It was too noisy to talk much anyway.' Natalie nodded her head towards the coffee-maker. 'You haven't put much water in that machine.'

'I'm not having any more now. I've got things to do.'

'Such as?'

'I've been meaning to tell you: Léo has asked me away for a few days. He's got a job down in Biarritz – some consultation or other. Anyway he suggested I come along. It's been really quiet at the shop these last couple of weeks so I thought the girls could manage without me.'

'When will you be back?'

'Monday I think.'

The machine dripped its last few drops of coffee into the jug and Virginie waited a couple of minutes then switched it off. She picked up the jug, poured its contents into a cup and handed it to her daughter then leaned against the units again.

Natalie regarded her mother speculatively. 'Is it serious with Léo then?'

'Maybe. Anyway, I'm going to pack then I've got an appointment to have my hair done. Will you be here this afternoon before I go?'

'Probably.'

Virginie flicked a cloth round the worktop, then bustled out, looking purposeful and animated. Natalie reflected that it was only her mother's imminent trip that had saved her from further interrogation. Was Léo likely to last the course? She doubted it. Her mother had been through a string of manfriends since her divorce; they never lasted.

She sat slowly drinking her coffee. Her father's behaviour

was a bit strange, even for him. Why did he suddenly want her to go away? Was it something to do with the notes? But he'd said they were a trick, a joke. Maybe a group of his friends had made a bet on how much they could make him sweat. Men, she'd discovered, could bet on the most absurd things. She regretted ringing Hannah now but at least her sister was going home. That was a relief.

Her thoughts turned to the money her father had promised her. She wasn't keen on going to the Loire valley. Why there? It was so far from everything, well from Paris anyway. And out with a friend the other night, she'd met a guy who'd asked for her phone number and he'd actually rung up the previous afternoon to ask her out. How often did that happen? She had arranged to see him at lunch-time on the Friday and, if they hit it off, it would be a real pain to go away right after. Timing was everything. He might have moved on by the time she came back and it didn't look like Gabriel was interested in her. With some extra money she could at least have a good time. No, she wouldn't go away. Her father need never know.

Decision made, she went to shower and dress.

Chapter 7

Eric had already gone down to the studio when Hannah went up to breakfast on the Thursday morning and it was barely eight o'clock. She didn't linger either and fifteen minutes later she was back in her room, packing her things up, a cup of tea cooling on the side. As she packed, she wondered yet again if she were doing the right thing but there was no way she could leave yet. To Nathan it might seem a simple decision but not to her. To him, the fact that her father had abandoned her and Elizabeth as children meant that she owed him no particular loyalty. He'd made that point to her in the restaurant last night. But it wasn't that simple. Families never were.

By the end of the meal, they'd called a truce. Maybe it was weariness, their arguments all burnt out, but Nathan had insisted on staying on in Paris too. He wanted to explore the city, he'd said, and then regaled her with an amusing account of his only other trip to the city and said it deserved to be given a second chance.

'But definitely no crêpes this time, with or without seafood.'

She'd laughed, relieved at the change in atmosphere. 'Fine. Do the sights. It is a beautiful city, trust me.'

'And what will you do?'

'Maybe visit some old haunts. I love Paris. I'll let the place work its magic on me.'

By twenty to nine she'd heaved her bags downstairs to the utility area at the bottom then climbed the stairs back to Eric's studio. He was sitting at his work table with a slew of drawings spread out in front of him and he was alone: his assistants didn't arrive till nearer nine. She walked across to stand and look over his shoulder.

He turned his head and smiled. 'Morning, sleepy-head.'

'I get the feeling you're avoiding me.'

'Of course not. I do work, you know. I've got an American coming to see me this morning about a commission. I'm preparing for him.'

'Then I hope it goes well.'

He turned on his stool fully to face her, taking hold of both her hands.

'Don't take it personally, Hannah. I've got things to do. For instance, I'll be working all today and I'm going to a Private View tonight. You'd be better off going home. I can't entertain you at the moment.'

'I don't want to be entertained. This is all about the phone call and the letters, we both know that.'

'I told you: the letters were jokes. And the phone call too was a hoax. You were right – it had nothing to do with trying to sell me something. And it threw me, I must admit. It had me quite worried there to start with. But a friend of mine has admitted to it now. I spoke to him last night.'

'What's his name?'

'You don't know him.' Eric pouted at her. 'You think I'd lie to you?'

'You did before. You promised me once that you'd be back but you never came. You just left.'

The words were out of her mouth before she'd had time to think and now they were there, hanging in the air between them.

Eric squeezed her hands. 'I know. Will you never forgive me for that?'

'You've never said you were sorry.'

There was a taut silence. 'This is different,' he said coldly. 'I want you to trust me.'

'*Trust* you? I want to.'

'Then do. When's your flight?'

Hannah pulled her hands out of his and moved away to the nearby window. Like all the windows, it looked out to the apartments in the facing block and down to the courtyard below.

'I'm staying in Paris,' she said, with her back to him. 'At a hotel. Now I'm here I'm going to finish my holiday.'

'I see.'

She came back and handed him a piece of paper with the details of the hotel on it. After the meal the previous evening, she had called there and booked a room.

'If you want to contact me, this is where I'll be. I've packed and put my bags near the door at the bottom. Is it all right if I leave them there for a couple of hours till I can get into my room?'

'Of course.' Her father frowned then suddenly stood up and put his arms round her. 'You have a good time. I wish I could spend some time with you, I do really. Maybe next time you come, we could do Paris together, properly.'

For a moment, an intense ache seemed to grip Hannah from deep within. It felt like it was growing, paralysing everything inside her, trying to stop her breathing. Still pressed against her father's chest, she swallowed hard, then pulled abruptly away. She reached up and briefly kissed his cheek.

'I'd like that,' she said.

Letting herself out into the courtyard a few minutes later, she saw Gabriel at the door to his flat. Dressed in a big sloppy

95

tee shirt and denim jeans, he was holding a cup of coffee and yawning. He smiled when he saw her and waved and she wandered over to speak to him.

'*Bonjour*,' she said. 'You look like you've only just got up.'

'I have. Don't judge me: I work late.' He self-consciously rubbed the stubble on his cheeks. 'Sorry, I haven't got round to shaving yet. Can I offer you coffee?'

'Thanks but I don't drink it.'

His forehead puckered. 'For health reasons or...'

'I don't like it.'

'You can't possibly be half-French.'

'I sometimes wonder myself.'

He grinned. It was infectious. And those melting brown eyes danced a little when he smiled.

'I don't know how long you're staying but I was hoping I could play you some more music sometime? Not on the electric keyboard – on a proper piano. I'm getting one later on today. We could have a drink one evening maybe?'

Hannah hesitated but couldn't think of any good reason not to. It was too tempting.

'I'll be in Paris for a few more days but I'm moving today. I'll be staying at a hotel on the Rue Berthollet.'

'Oh? Well, that's wonderful. It's not far. I'm free this evening if you are?' He raised his eyebrows and offered a quizzical smile. 'I've written something I'd like to play for someone, to try it out. You can tell me what you think.'

'I'm not sure my opinion's worth canvassing. But all right. What time?'

'Say seven thirty? Do you like pasta? I could knock us up a bit of supper too.'

'I love pasta. I'll see you then. Thanks.'

She smiled and the date was made. Nathan's pejorative remarks about the piano player taunted her but she laughed them off. After all, he hardly knew the man. In fact, she was going to enjoy telling him that she had a date.

*

Nathan had offered to give Hannah a hand with her bags and install her at his hotel. He'd suggested they drop the bags off then have lunch at a little brasserie he'd noticed not far away and they arranged to meet at twelve o'clock at Eric's. But when he arrived, maybe five minutes early, he found Hannah in the courtyard with Gabriel, another man and an upright piano. A van had been parked on the road outside and the two men appeared to be trying to manhandle the piano all the way from the roadside to Gabriel's apartment. Progress was slow. In fact, having got it to the far side of the arch, they now weren't moving at all and Hannah was laughing.

As Nathan approached, Gabriel was talking animatedly and waving his arms about and Hannah was laughing again. Annoyingly, Nathan's French wasn't good enough to understand what he was saying. Hannah turned and hailed him.

'Your timing's good,' she said in English. 'The guys are trying to get this piano into Gabriel's apartment. Can you give them a hand? These stone slabs are so uneven, it's got to be lifted. You've met Gabriel, haven't you? And this is Jean-Pierre.'

'Hi,' said Nathan.

Gabriel nodded and Jean-Pierre took the cigarette out of his mouth and raised one arm in the classic strongman pose.

'We do not have enough muscle,' he said in stilted English, grinning.

'OK, so what do you want me to do?' said Nathan.

97

Jean-Pierre suggested he join him at the rear while Gabriel took the front and somehow they made slow, jolting progress across the courtyard, paused to negotiate the doorway to the apartment, and, panting, got it inside. With some more directions from Gabriel in both English and French, they bundled it into position against the far wall.

Nathan glanced round. It was a tiny place, untidy and cluttered, and now the piano dominated it. Jean-Pierre and Gabriel both shook his hand and thanked him and a few minutes later he'd grabbed Hannah's bags from Eric's ground floor and they were on their way to the hotel.

'A piano player who doesn't have a piano,' Nathan remarked acidly as they walked.

'He's got a keyboard. Anyway, he's got one now. Apparently Jean-Pierre knew someone who was getting rid of it.'

'Handy. You've met him before then?'

'Not really. He was at my father's party the night I arrived. I remember seeing him, that's all.'

'It sounded like half Paris was there.'

She didn't respond and they marched along in silence. Hannah checked in, they stowed her bags in her room, then went out for lunch. It was a warm day with a fitful sun and they found a table on the *terrasse* of the brasserie. Only a handful of tables were occupied. The waiter hovered so they chose quickly and ordered. Hannah looked restless.

'How long do you expect to stay at the hotel?' Nathan asked casually.

'I haven't thought.'

'Could prove expensive.'

'I'll manage.'

The waiter reappeared with their drinks: a beer for Nathan and a sparkling water for Hannah. An awkward silence fell.

'How's your mother?' said Hannah.

'Fine, thank you. We spoke Monday as usual.'

'Good.'

The silence returned.

'What does Jean-Pierre do?' said Nathan.

'He runs a bar apparently. Gabriel has played there a few times. He plays at Natalie's restaurant too.'

'Gets about, doesn't he?'

Another strained silence fell until the waiter brought their food. Nathan had ordered a burger and fries and ate as if he'd been starved for days. Hannah had chosen a chicken salad and he watched her fastidiously pick out the olives, putting them on one side.

'You never told me you didn't like olives,' he remarked.

'It's never come up.'

'But you eat olive oil.'

'That's different.'

When they'd both finished, Hannah took the last slice of baguette out of the basket on the table, tore a piece off it and put it in her mouth. She crumpled up her paper napkin and dropped it on the plate. Nathan's was neatly folded. They both looked, noted the fact but didn't comment.

Nathan sat back, cradling his glass of beer.

'So if you don't have any plans, why don't you show me some of the sights of Paris?'

'Haven't you seen most of them?'

'I told you, I spent most of that trip in the bathroom. I remember visiting the Louvre and Notre Dame before the dodgy pancake. I missed out on Sacré Coeur and Montmartre and I've always wanted to visit the Musée D'Orsay.'

'Then you should. It's very good. I've only been once, soon after it opened. The old railway station makes a fascinating backdrop. And Sacré Coeur's worth visiting for the view alone.'

'So?' He leaned forward, putting his elbows on the table. 'Where do you go when you want to be in quintessential Paris?'

'Me?' She chewed another piece of the bread while she thought. 'A walk by the river maybe. Or a meal down one of the back streets in a tiny restaurant where the chef comes out from the kitchen to ask whether you've enjoyed your meal. That's my idea of the real Paris. Or wandering into one of the little squares where all the local old people come out and sit on benches in the evening sunshine to put the world to rights.'

He sat back. 'Sounds good. Let's do it. So long as I get to see some sights too. I brought a camera; I want pictures.'

'Look, Nathan, I am not your tour guide. You shouldn't even be here. Make a miraculous recovery from your flu and go back to work. I'm sure you're right: I'm overthinking the whole thing with my father. I'll just potter about a bit then come home.'

He looked at her hard and long. 'You don't mean that. Don't lie to me.'

'I'm not.' She glared at him. 'I don't know what I think. I want to believe him but I'm not sure so I'm going to hang around for a couple of days. Just to see. If nothing else happens, I'll go home.' She hesitated, glancing away. 'I would like to know more about my father's past though. He's never talked about it and he certainly won't now, but he has a friend who runs a gallery and they've known each other a long time. I thought I might go and see him this afternoon, have a chat, find out a bit about what my father did when he returned to France.'

'Why?'

'Why not? I'd like to know.'

'What kind of man is this gallery guy? Another of your dad's dubious friends?'

'He seemed nice enough. It's a good gallery.'

'That's no recommendation. I'm coming too.'

'No. You'll make it seem like a thing.'

'A thing?'

'Important. Significant in some way. I want to chat to him informally, not with you heavy-breathing down his neck. You are not invited. Go and see the sights. Visit Sacré Coeur. Go for a cruise on the river.'

Nathan regarded her a moment then turned to attract the attention of the waiter.

'*L'addition s'il vous plait*,' he said with a strong English accent. The bill, please. 'See,' he told Hannah, 'I'm getting the hang of this now. I'll be fluent in a couple of days.' He paused. 'OK, you go and see your dad's friend. I'm going to the Musée d'Orsay.'

'There'll be an awful queue now. Mornings are better.'

'That's my problem. Let's meet for an aperitif before we have dinner and you can tell me what you've found out from this "friend".'

'I can't tonight. I'm seeing someone.'

'What someone? How many people do you know in Paris?'

'What the hell business is it of yours? Honestly Nathan, you're the limit. Get off my back.'

'It's Gabriel, isn't it?'

She pressed her lips together hard, glaring at him.

'Yes. So? I knew you'd be pleased. He's offered to play me some music.'

'I'll bet he has. Some music? Oh come on.'

Her voice rose. 'And who are you, my mother? I'm not sixteen and...'

She cut off as the waiter came over, glanced between the two of them and put the bill down on the table. They both silently produced the cash to pay their respective share and the waiter withdrew, casting them a final look.

Hannah dropped her voice. 'Don't you dare start telling me who I can and cannot see, Nathan. You don't have that right.' She stood up, grabbing her bag from the back of the chair and pulling it onto her shoulder. 'Remember, I didn't ask you to come here.'

Nathan watched her walk away. He'd mishandled it again. Of course the woman was impulsive and stubborn and infuriating and a host of other toxic characteristics. But she was Hannah too: big-hearted, loyal, passionate, smart and with the loveliest eyes he'd ever seen, even when she was cross. He sighed. He had created this situation. The debacle of their last date back in Oxford regularly played across his mind. In retrospect, he recognised that he'd said things he shouldn't have. He'd allowed fear and jealousy to get the better of him and he'd been wrong. That was becoming increasingly clear to him. And he knew he should apologise but somehow the opportunity to do so and pick up the relationship they'd had before that row felt like a boat that had already sailed.

And now she was dating bloody Gabriel.

*

Hubert Blois ran his art gallery in a side street off the Boulevard Saint-Germain, a double-fronted shop on two floors where he displayed a range of modern work at prices only the well-heeled would be likely to pay. Hannah had met him twice before. The first time had been during her spell working at the Louvre. She had met up with her father for lunch, a strained encounter not long after seeing him with Natalie, neither of them apparently certain whether to mention it or not. They had arranged to meet at the corner of the Boulevard and he'd insisted on calling into the gallery on their way to the restaurant. Hubert showed some of her father's work and had recently sold a couple and now needed replacements. The second time she had been on a visit to Paris with a friend – the daughter of a wealthy man who had given his beloved offspring a generous amount of money for her birthday - and the friend wanted to buy herself a painting. Hubert had recognised Hannah and in consequence had offered a good deal on something her friend loved. But it was a long time ago now and she wondered if he would still remember.

He was with a customer when she entered and a young woman assistant came over instead, asking if she could help.

'I'd like to look around if I may,' said Hannah, and the woman smiled an acknowledgment and retreated.

Hannah slowly circled the exhibits. Her father still had work there and she studied each in turn, looking for changes in his style or palette but mostly simply enjoying the vibrancy of them. His colours were often vivid and even his more sombre works always had a flash of colour in them. He had a weakness for flowers, simple unassuming ones, nothing showy, and often incorporated them into his work in a small, understated way. And his paintings had such immediacy and clarity. She found herself wondering how his work could be so eloquent and yet the man himself be so obscure, so fenced off behind his larger-than-life persona. Not for the first time, she wondered if she really knew him at all.

''annah. It is 'annah, isn't it? Eric's daughter?'

Hubert had come up beside her. His dealings with the other customer were finished and his assistant was even now taking a painting off the wall to be wrapped. Hannah turned as he spoke and smiled and he reached out to take her hand and lift the back of it to his lips. He kept hold of it and put his other hand over the top.

'I am so glad to see you again. Eric tells me you have become a wonderful art restorer, much in demand.'

'He said that?'

Hubert puffed out his lips with a look of surprise. 'Yes, of course. I don't see him so often of course – only when I sell his paintings. Then he's keen to see me.' He laughed. 'You will have a drink with me, yes? Come into my office.' He relinquished her hand and, without waiting for a reply, turned to lead the way.

His office was large and plush, though a morass of untidy paperwork was spread across his desk. Hubert waved her to one of the leather armchairs in front of it and went across to a cabinet by the wall on which stood a tray with an array of bottles on it. This, she assumed, is where he brought his wealthy but undecided clients, to smooth talk them into a purchase.

'A glass of wine?' he offered her now. 'This is a rather fine burgundy.' He rested an index finger on the cork of a bottle already half empty. 'Or I have a delicious Vin Santo here if you'd like something sweet? Or a cognac perhaps?'

'A small glass of the burgundy, please.'

He poured them both a glass – a generous measure – handed one to her and sat down in the armchair opposite. He raised his glass in tribute and sipped the wine.

'Your French is as impeccable as ever,' he said, 'but to what do I owe the honour of this visit? Are you on holiday, or working in Paris again?'

'Just a short holiday. I don't get here as often as I'd like.'

'No, of course. But once the channel tunnel is open it'll be so much easier won't it? Hopefully you'll be able to pop over and see us frequently. I might even visit London a little more. But you're not in London I think?'

'No. These days I'm based in Oxford but my work takes me all over. *Santé*.' She raised her glass and took a drink, nodding her approval. He smiled with satisfaction.

'So… a holiday. And yet I sense this is more than a casual visit.'

She shrugged the remark away with one shoulder. 'I do like the opportunity to see my father's paintings without him breathing down my neck. I don't often get the chance.' It was true as far as it went.

'And…?'

She smiled ruefully.

'It is true that I hoped to have a chat with you.'

Hubert frowned. 'Eric is not ill, I hope?'

'No, not at all. It's just that… *Monsieur Blois*, even after all this time, I don't know much about my father's life. You know that I am one of two daughters he had from his first marriage?'

'I believe he said as much. And please call me Hubert.'

'Thank you. When he left England to return to France, I didn't see much of him for a long time. I still don't.' She managed a weak smile. 'An occasional visit. It's not easy when we are so far apart.'

'*Naturellement*.'

'And *Papa* is… reluctant to ever talk about himself. I'd like to fill in some of the blanks, get to know him, what his life was like afterwards, do you see? I think you've known him a long time?'

He nodded slowly, then smiled, reminiscing. 'I have. I remember when I first met him. My father ran our gallery then. It wasn't here you understand but it was good. Your father turned up one day with three paintings I think, wrapped in a grubby piece of sacking, tucked under his arm.' Hubert shook his head. 'He had a shock of untidy hair and a smudge of blue paint on one cheek and he was cocky, full of what a great painter he was. My father wasn't impressed. He was on the point of asking him to leave, but Eric unwrapped his paintings and...' He whistled softly. '...they were good. Better than good. My father said he'd take them though Eric drove a hard bargain. He wanted a higher return than we usually give on them. We have our expenses too, you know. Anyway they argued for ages and I watched and listened and we became friends after that. I liked his style. There was no false modesty about him: he knew he was good and he wanted it recognised. But he never boasted about anything except his work and he was always good company.'

'Can you remember what year that was?'

Again Hubert puffed out his lips, shaking his head gently side to side.

'I'm not sure. Maybe sixty-two, sixty-three? I think he hadn't been back in Paris long then. It was only later, when I got to know him better that he told me he had lived in England for a while. Of course, his work spoke for itself and before long he was selling well and making a steady living. He was quickly making a name for himself.'

She grinned. 'And partying, I imagine. He has always liked a good gathering, somewhere to tell his stories.'

'Oh yes, Eric always liked an audience. He married again of course but he did his share of the social scene in those early days. He mixed and mingled. You can meet useful people that way too.'

'Do you remember anyone in particular he mixed with? Special friends? What were these people like?'

Hubert's brow furrowed. 'I'm not sure what you're asking, 'annah. He mixed with all sorts of people: the well-to-

106

do - they sometimes like to invite artists, you know; makes them look avant-garde themselves. And then there were other artists of course and dealers, models and even, yes...' The frown was replaced with a wry smile. '...one time he was commissioned by a monastery to paint an image of the Holy Mother and Child. He spent some time with them I believe. They made their own wine, you understand? They got on well, he told me. I'd like to have been a fly on the wall.'

Hannah smiled again but felt a pang of regret. 'He never told me about any of this. Hubert, did he...' She tried again. 'Did he ever get into trouble?'

'Trouble?' The frown returned. 'Well a prank here, a prank there. A practical joke, that kind of thing. He is a terrible joker, you must know that. There was one time, he got the framer to frame one of his canvases the wrong way round. He'd painted something loosely on the back, something horribly banal, and the chap who'd commissioned it nearly had a fit when he saw it. The real painting was on the other side.'

'What happened?'

'Eric only let it run a short time. It was awkward to start with but the man saw the funny side of it. Eventually.'

'So nothing serious? I mean no major row or falling out?'

His eyes narrowed. 'There is something in particular bothering you, isn't there? I think you should be having this conversation with your father.'

'He won't talk to me about it.'

'Even so... I don't recall anything serious.' He paused, then leaned forward and spoke in a softer voice. 'I did have the impression that maybe something hung over him from before, from his childhood perhaps. He would never talk about his school days or his family. Though, truthfully, he is not alone in that. Many people do not speak of the past, what with the war and, well, families can be tricky, *hein*?' He waved an energetic, admonishing index finger at her. 'But if you want specific information, 'annah, you must ask him. And if he will not talk, perhaps it is something you should not know.'

Hannah nodded thoughtfully and sipped at the wine.

'Did he ever talk about his time in England?' she asked.

'No, not really.' Hubert regarded her kindly. 'He keeps all the personal things deep down, *chérie*. Men do this, you must know that. It doesn't mean he doesn't care.'

She managed a smile.

Leaving some twenty minutes later, she reflected that the meeting had been interesting but hadn't moved her any further forwards. Was Hubert telling the truth? Had there been no scandal, no suspicious behaviour of any kind? No-one with a grudge? Perhaps he genuinely didn't know. Perhaps there was, something from way back, from before Eric travelled to England. She remembered asking him once why he'd come to England and left his home country behind. He said he'd wanted to broaden his horizons as well as improve his English. English was such an international language in business, he said.

The letters might have been a joke. But the expression on her father's face when he'd received that phone call was still etched into her mind. No real friend would make a joke like that. Maybe Hubert was right: *Perhaps it is something you should not know*.

*

Eric spent the day arguing with himself. He didn't have the money that was being demanded of him hanging around the apartment – who kept that kind of ready cash? – and he would certainly struggle to raise it at short notice. Yes, he had property and he had savings but neither gave him easy access to money. And he had worked hard for it all, over many, many

108

years. He didn't want to hand it over to Gustave of all people. Any of it. The whole thing stuck in his throat.

But there would be more phone calls, he knew, and more threats. Unless of course he could talk Gustave round. Eric prided himself on being able to charm people, to cajole them and win them over, but Gustave? Eric couldn't pretend that he wasn't scared. The Gustave he knew of old was dangerous to be around, and the threat of physical violence chilled him. He didn't consider himself a brave man. That was why he was in this mess: he had always tended to run away from problems rather than confront them.

In an effort to quell the chattering voices in his head, he tried to focus on his work. The meeting with Sean Borovski had gone reasonably well. The American and his wife, Marianne, had visited Paris many times together and he wanted a painting of the place to give to his wife as a birthday present. But he wanted something personal, not a stereotyped image of the Eiffel Tower or Notre Dame, the kind of picture he could have bought in any number of galleries across Paris. On the phone he had mentioned some of their favourite haunts and Eric's sketched up ideas had given them a starting point for discussion. By the end of it they had fixed on a view of a café in a small square on the left bank, shaded by plane trees and with a fountain at the square's centre. It was somewhere that had memories for them and that Eric also knew well. Sean supplied a few photographs of his wife and himself and asked Eric to slip their faces into the picture in a small, subtle way. 'Marianne would love that.' It wasn't something Eric normally did but he felt the need to please today; he wanted concord. He also needed money. He quoted a considerable fee; the man agreed, paid a deposit and went away happy.

The afternoon dragged. He jumped at every noise and began to notice Florence watching him, her eyes darting away whenever he glanced in her direction. His distraction was clearly too obvious and he tried to hide it. He wandered across and talked to her about the mediums she was mixing for him, explaining the different properties of them and when they should be used on a painting. He was sure he'd told her before but she didn't seem to remember much. His heart wasn't in it anyway, his thoughts returning inexorably to Gustave and the next call, trying to decide what to do.

It was twenty-past five in the afternoon when the call finally came and the assistants hadn't long gone. Did Gustave know that? Was he watching the place even now?

'*Allô, oui?*' Eric said into the phone.

'Have you got it?'

'No.'

'You're kidding me, right?'

'No, I told you: I don't have that kind of money. Gustave, is that you? Can't we talk about this, man to man?'

The caller laughed unpleasantly. 'There's nothing to talk about. And you don't get to say no, Eric. A "no" means there'll be consequences. And you won't like them, trust me. I'll give you one more chance to reconsider.'

'There's nothing to consider. I haven't got the kind of money you're talking about and in any case I don't owe you…'

'I'll ring again tomorrow.'

The phone went dead. Eric stared at it as if it might suddenly speak again, tell him it was all a joke, a laugh. It couldn't be for real, surely? It would be Laurent, saying, 'Come on, Eric, I got you going there, didn't I? Paid you back for all those tricks you've played on me.'

But the phone remained stubbornly silent. He was kidding himself.

Chapter 8

Gabriel didn't do romance. A long time ago there had been a childhood sweetheart - a girl who had gone to the same school. He'd adored her and thought it was going to be a forever love affair. Then at nineteen she had gone off with the local football star who'd secured a trial with one of the top-flight teams. Gabriel had to admit that the guy did have a touch of glamour about him. He didn't. He had been an indifferent pupil, his mind frequently wandering, his head full of tunes. Sport, other than for a bit of light-hearted fun, passed him by and, though he was a talented musician, he lacked concentration and self-discipline. His piano teacher had wanted him to become a concert pianist; it didn't interest him. He'd become an itinerant musician instead, finding work where he could. Sometimes he had done things he didn't like and, yes, he had made some bad choices over the years. But who hadn't? You did what you could with what was thrown at you, that was his philosophy. Whatever got you through.

Of course there had been other women in his life, albeit briefly, but nothing serious. Disappointment had made him wary; life had taught him to keep moving. But, as he cut an onion ready for the promised pasta meal with Hannah, he couldn't deny that he was looking forward to spending the evening with her. She was different to many of the women he'd met. She was vivacious and smart and had a head for music –

not a combination he'd come across before. And then there were those blue eyes: penetrating, challenging and not a little mesmerising. There was a hint of excitement about her, of intrigue and adventure. Of course it wasn't ideal that she was Eric's daughter but that was just the way the cards had been dealt.

It was twenty-five past seven when Gabriel heard steps on the stones of the courtyard. He had left his front door open, waiting for her, and heard Violette Février's strident voice hailing the visitor. He flicked one last glance round the small flat, decided it was as tidy as he could make it, and crossed to the doorway. *Madame Février* was standing by the line of pot plants which marked one of the boundaries of her little garden, peering over them in the gathering gloom.

'*Bonsoir Madame,*' Hannah was saying as she moved closer to Violette's domain. 'It's me, Eric Dechansay's daughter. We spoke this morning if you remember.'

'Yes, I thought it was you. But I thought you'd left.'

'Well I have really. I'm staying somewhere else now but I'm back to visit. You've got a lovely garden, *Madame*. It must take a lot of care to keep it so nice.'

The woman smiled vaguely and fondled the glossy leaves of a large evergreen plant. Gabriel had no idea what it was; he'd never grown a plant in his life. Violette turned to another pot and bent over, prodding at the compost round its base as if Hannah had never been there.

He watched Hannah leave and come towards him. He liked that she'd taken the trouble to speak to Violette. He'd noticed many people treat the old woman as if she were foolish or senile; they'd ignore her, perhaps thinking she threatened them in some way. But she was harmless. Just another outsider, someone who didn't quite fit in, left stranded while the world

112

careered on by. Violette glanced up and he raised a hand in greeting. She stared at him and withdrew inside.

Then Hannah was upon him and smiling when she saw him waiting for her.

'You can't sneak in here without being seen, can you?' she said.

'Certainly not. But I think she's lonely. She's got a daughter, she told me, but they're not on speaking terms. Her plants are her life. Come in.'

'Sorry, I'm early. It's pathological I'm afraid.'

'No problem. I'm as ready as I'll ever be.'

She thrust a small box at him. 'I was taught always to bring something for my host. They're chocolates. I hope you're not allergic.'

'Definitely not. Thank you.'

She walked past him and into his home. There wasn't much of it, just one bedroom and a shower room and a tiny kitchen at the rear. The front door led straight into the living room. Hannah walked across to the piano, surveyed it then turned to face him.

'It looks at home. It must be good to have a proper piano here.'

'It is. Though all the movement sent the tuning out, as you can imagine. I think I've got it something like now, but it might slip again. Bear that in mind when I play for you.'

'It'll be fine. I'm looking forward to hearing your new piece.'

'Let's have a drink first. Quell my nerves.'

'You get nervous? It doesn't show.'

'I do when it's something I've written. The fear of rejection, you know.'

She laughed and already he was pleased. She was peeling off her jacket and he took it and hung it up behind the door.

'I have a chilled Chardonnay and some *crème de cassis*,' he said. 'Would you like a Kir?'

'Thank you, yes.'

She sat down on the edge of one of his two battered armchairs and watched him walk to the little kitchen at the rear. When he returned carrying the two glasses she was still sitting on the edge of the seat and it occurred to him that she was a little nervous herself. He handed her a glass and raised his own.

'*Santé.*'

She reciprocated and he sat down to face her on a low stool nearby.

'So... you're staying in Paris. I'm glad.' He paused and looked at her quizzically. 'Natalie told me that you're her half-sister. Why didn't you tell me that at the party?'

'I didn't know you. I didn't think it mattered.'

'I was glad to know you weren't Eric's girlfriend.'

'I thought Jeanne was his girlfriend? Or does he have more than one?'

Gabriel shrugged. 'I just thought...' He grinned ruefully. 'I don't know. I don't pry.' He took a sip of Kir. 'So why have you moved out?'

'He's busy with a commission and I felt in the way. But I didn't want to leave yet. I have some holiday time and I like Paris.'

'Me too. Obviously.'

'Are you from here?'

'No, no. I grew up in Fondettes.' To her blank expression he added, 'it's a suburb of Tours. You know Tours?'

'I know where it is.'

'But I've moved around a lot. And you? What do you do for a living?'

'I'm a conservator of paintings. I grew up in a village not far from Cheltenham – you wouldn't know it. I trained in

114

London. Since then I've moved around too. Now I'm based in Oxford but I get sent all over the place to work on people's paintings.'

'You've inherited the artistic genes from Eric then. And you like to travel?'

'I like not to be pinned down.'

He grinned. 'Me too. So Eric fell in love with an English girl but couldn't stay away from France?'

She nodded. 'I guess.'

'How old were you when he left?'

'He came and went for a while. I was eight or nine when he moved out completely.'

'It's difficult, isn't it. My father disappeared when I was ten. Just upped and off. I've no idea where he went.'

'And your mother never heard from him again?'

He shook his head. 'In the end she married someone else. I had a step-father.' He pulled a face.

'Not good?'

'I left soon after.'

She settled further back in the chair.

'Have your travels taken you to England at all?'

'Once. It put my schoolboy English to the test. I played piano in a bar in London then in Kent for a few weeks. It was good.'

'But not good enough to stay?'

He shrugged again, smiling. 'I missed French food. No, seriously, I did miss home. Anyway, let me play this piece for you. You can tell me what you think.'

He took one last drink, put the glass down and went to sit at the piano where the music was already on the rest.

'Will we disturb your father, do you think?' he said, turning round.

'No, he's probably up on the top floor. And he's going to a Private View somewhere later if he hasn't already gone. Knowing him, he'll be there a while.'

'Good.' Gabriel turned back to the piano and put a hand to pat the top of it. 'Here we go girl.'

He was nervous. Nerves rarely bothered him when playing other people's music – a little tightness before he started perhaps, the usual boost of adrenaline at a performance - but this was different and he particularly wanted Hannah to approve of it; he'd been thinking about her when he wrote it.

He took a slow breath, rested his fingers for a moment on the keys, then started. It began gently, lyrically, then developed, speeding up and becoming punchy with a pronounced dance rhythm before settling again into something softer. After a few minutes it finished with a sudden return to the dance theme and ended with a loud, dramatic chord. He left his fingers there for a moment then straightened up.

There was silence.

'*Formidable*,' exclaimed Hannah and clapped.

He spun round on the piano stool to look at her, frowning. 'You mean that?'

'Of course or I wouldn't have said it. I loved it. It was so many things rolled into one: emotional and fun and lively. But it didn't sound finished. I thought there was going to be more.'

'No, I think you're right. There does need to be more. I'm just not sure what it is yet.'

'Tell me,' she asked with a grin, 'do you always speak to your piano?'

'Certainly. It would be rude not to.' He hesitated. 'I should get on and cook our meal but there's not much left to do. Don't expect anything too special, will you?'

A small round wooden table stood between the sitting room and the kitchen and he had laid it with cutlery and

116

napkins and wine glasses. He served spaghetti with a Bolognese sauce and a green salad on the side, offering a fruity red wine to go with it.

'What's this commission your father's working on?' he asked as they ate.

'I don't know anything about it. He doesn't talk about his work when it's in progress.'

'He's very sociable though, isn't he, your father? Gets on with people. I didn't expect it to be honest. I think of artists as being more... retiring.'

Hannah grinned. 'What, stuck away in an attic, not speaking to anyone and only eating when the masterpiece is finished?'

'Something like that.'

'No, he's definitely not like that.'

'He must have had an interesting life.'

'I suppose so.'

'I'm sorry. Of course you haven't seen much of it - being in different countries, I mean. Does he not talk about it, his life's experiences?'

'Yes and no. He's a great raconteur. But they're just anecdotes; I never know how much is true. I think he exaggerates.'

'Still, he has been successful. I mean he should be; he's very good, I understand. I'm afraid I don't know much about art.'

Hannah rested a watchful gaze on him.

'So what have you been doing? Between Kent in England and here, where were you?'

'Here and there. I travelled south for a while, spent a bit of time round Avignon. The jazz festival there is really good. Have you been?'

'Not yet. Did you stay in Nice too? I like Nice.'

117

'Only briefly. So many of those places down there are almost too beautiful, don't you think? I didn't fit in. In any case, I'm really not good at staying anywhere too long.'

They ate the remainder of their pasta in silence. He'd found out what he wanted to know: that Hannah didn't know much about her father's past. He was glad: he didn't want her involved.

He offered fruit or ice-cream for dessert but Hannah said she'd had enough.

'It was delicious though. Thank you. What I would like is for you to play the piano again. Would you?'

'Of course. But have some more wine.' He poured some into each of their glasses. 'It'll make me sound better. What would you like to hear?'

She smiled. 'Didn't I hear you play Débussy's *Clair de Lune* the other night at the restaurant? My mother used to play that and I loved it.'

'Your word is my command.'

He took a mouthful of wine, then sat at the piano and played again, this time without music. When he glanced round a few minutes later, Hannah's eyes were closed and, though she was smiling, there were tears on her cheeks.

'It is lovely,' he admitted when he'd finished. 'The risk with playing all the time is that you begin not to notice any more. It's good to have someone remind you how beautiful some pieces are.'

Hannah was impatiently brushing her cheeks. He left the piano stool and came to kneel in front of her and put a hand up to her cheek.

'Are you all right?'

'I'm fine. I'm sorry for the tears. It brings back such memories of my mother. She died a couple of years ago and I still miss her. Crazy, isn't it? We used to argue all the time.'

'That's not crazy. It's normal. Just because you argue with someone, it doesn't mean you don't love them too. Perhaps the arguments are fiercer because you do love them.'

She smiled ruefully. 'I guess. It just upsets me that I didn't appreciate her enough when she was here.'

Gabriel found himself leaning towards her and the next minute he was kissing her softly on the lips.

'Don't be upset,' he murmured and kissed her again, putting one hand round the back of her head this time, the other to her waist. After a moment's hesitation, she responded and it became something much stronger, probing, more needy on both sides.

Suddenly Hannah wrenched herself away, leaning back and putting the back of her fingers to her lips.

'I'm sorry,' he said, sitting back on his heels. 'I didn't mean to offend. I – just - well, I so wanted to do that.'

'No, it's OK. There's no need to apologise. It's just... Gabriel, I'm not sure I want to get involved right now. Life's complicated enough.' She glanced at her watch, then finished the last mouthful of wine. 'And I think I should be going.'

She looked round for her bag, found it down the side of the chair and got to her feet.

Gabriel stood too. 'I could make you coffee. Honestly, I'm not looking to make anything complicated.'

'I don't drink coffee, remember?' She smiled and was already turning to go. 'And I do need to get back now.' She pulled her jacket off the hook by the door and Gabriel quickly stepped forward and held it while she shrugged it on.

'Shall I walk you back?'

'No. I'll be fine, thank you. It's not late.'

'Can I see you again?'

She hesitated. 'I'm not sure how long I'm going to be here.'

'You can't leave yet. I need you around so I can finish composing my piece.'

'Why do you need me for that?'

'Inspiration.' He'd used this sort of line before but he wasn't sure he'd ever meant it as much as he did now. 'Though I suppose if I had to I could make another visit to England.'

She grinned. 'And brave the food?'

'Exactly. So that might be difficult. Look, which hotel are you staying at?'

She told him and he grabbed a notepad and wrote the name down.

'But Gabriel...'

'No, don't say anything.' He scribbled some numbers on another sheet and tore it off to give to her. 'My phone number – if you decide you're going to be around and would like to meet up. Promise me you'll think about it. We could go somewhere, do anything you like.'

'OK. Thank you. For the meal and especially for the music. It was good. I mean it.'

Kissing him lightly on the cheek, she left.

Gabriel closed the door behind her and leaned against it. He hadn't expected to like her so much and he did want to see her again. And whatever was stopping her, he thought he could win her round – there was clearly a mutual attraction. But there again, perhaps it would be better if he didn't. It hurt to even think it but maybe it would be better for everyone if she just went back to England.

*

Eric had arranged with Jeanne that they would go to the Private View together and once out on the street he hailed a taxi. It was a relief to be out of the apartment and distracted. He'd looked around suspiciously on leaving, but there had been nothing out of the ordinary, no-one lying in wait for him. The evenings were getting lighter, there were more people out and about and everyone seemed intent on their own mission for the evening; no-one cast him even a second glance. He asked the taxi to call at Jeanne's place in Bercy and they went on together, crossing the river to the Marais where Colette's studio was.

'I thought you'd bring 'annah with you,' Jeanne said as she got in.

'She's gone to stay in a hotel. A friend from England turned up and is staying there.'

'That's no reason why she couldn't come. I rather liked her. I was hoping to see her again.'

There was an implied reprimand and he didn't reply. This seemed to have happened a lot lately: barbed comments but nothing you could put your finger on. But there was no way he was going to start explaining the situation to Jeanne and certainly not in the back of a taxi. They lapsed into silence.

He'd known Colette for years. She was a small, stocky woman, her short hair now greying, with a direct manner and a surprisingly girlish giggle. He liked to support her. In any case, it was just what he needed: a crowd of people chattering and laughing and Jeanne's soft company. He'd done too much brooding lately. He wanted to put the uncomfortable parting with Hannah out of his mind and he was determined to forget Gustave too. If Eric stood up to him, the man would find someone else to persecute, someone easier. After all, they did go way back and that must count for something. As he had done for years, Eric drew a veil over what had happened in that previous life. He'd almost convinced himself that it had never happened.

Colette's pictures were proving popular. She and two other artists had studios at an old printing works and the

121

exhibition was being held in the large communal space at its centre. She produced images which fitted well in the history of the surroundings, water-based paints and dyes mixed with collage, often using magazine or newsprint. Some of her pictures had a poster-like quality themselves. They were topical and modern and had been framed appropriately in simple white-coated mouldings. Eric hadn't seen many red dots indicating 'sold' placed on them yet, but by Parisian standards the evening was still young and people were still arriving.

Jeanne squeezed his arm. 'I've seen Evie and Jacques over there. I'll just go and have a word.' She eased through the crowd and was gone.

Eric got another glass of red wine and circulated again.

'Eric, *chéri*.'

A woman of middle years wearing a skin-tight dress and with a feather boa round her shoulders draped herself across him in an affectionate embrace, carefully holding her wine glass aloft. He got a feather in his mouth and spat it out. She pulled away but still kept one hand latched onto his shoulder.

'How are you darling? You look tired. You've been doing too much, haven't you?'

'You always tell me that, Annabelle, and I always say the same thing: no. And if I were a workaholic, I wouldn't be here, enjoying your delightful company, would I?'

She squeezed him playfully and laughed, then glanced round the room.

'You're still with Jeanne then?' She pouted. 'No room for anyone else?'

'If there ever is, you'll be the first to know, Annabelle.'

She laughed again, gave him a playful tap and drifted away. Wild horses, he thought.

The red dots proliferated; it was going well. Eric got talking to a dealer. Dealers often infiltrated these events, looking for new talent, checking out the interest for an artist's work. Some were straightforward business people, some rather more dubious. They circulated and listened, asked questions and sometimes left their business card. Eric knew this woman quite well: she'd been around the scene for a while.

'How's your work going?' she asked him. He assumed it was politeness: she mostly dealt in more avant-garde work than he produced.

'Pretty well, thank you.'

'Oh? Good.' She regarded him archly. 'I'd heard you'd been trying to offload some paintings at bargain prices to raise cash. I was a bit shocked. Things not been going so well lately, Eric?'

'No-o. Where did you hear that?'

She shrugged. 'I'm not sure to be honest. On the wind, I suppose. A suggestion that some people regard your work as being a bit passé. Not that I'd say such a thing of course. But these things do go around.'

'Well the wind is wrong. I have my usual outlets. Usual prices. Nothing different. I'm selling, taking commissions. All is fine.'

'I'm glad to hear it.'

They both moved on but the conversation had unsettled him. He finished the second glass of wine and grabbed another and did another slow turn of the exhibition but the event had lost its appeal. Eventually he sought out Jeanne. She was still with her friends. There were four of them in fact, one of whom he noticed was a smart-dressed man he hadn't seen before, a handsome guy with olive skin. Whoever he was, he was paying Jeanne close attention and they were locked in an apparently intense conversation. Eric managed to catch her attention and get her on one side.

'I'm thinking of going,' he said. 'What about you? I thought perhaps you'd like to come back with me tonight? Now Hannah's gone, we'll have the place to ourselves.'

'Oh Eric darling, I'm not ready to leave yet. I've been talking and haven't even seen all the exhibits yet. If you want to go, I'll make my own way home. Do you mind terribly?'

He swallowed his disappointment. 'No, if that's what you want.'

She frowned. 'Is there something the matter?'

'No, no.'

He noticed her friends looking their way curiously. He shuffled a step or two further away and she came with him.

'Are you not feeling well?' she asked, looking concerned. 'Only it's not like you to…'

'I'm fine. Absolutely fine.' He glanced towards the handsome man who was still looking Jeanne's way altogether too proprietorially. 'I've just had enough, that's all. And I thought you might have too.'

'Well no, I haven't.'

'You'll be all right to get home?' He couldn't resist another glance towards that man.

'Of course.' She leaned over and gave him a peck on the cheek and, after a parting word with Colette, he left.

He found a taxi to take him home but barely registered their route. Normally he enjoyed watching his city as it hit a different gear for the evening: the lights, especially the way the big landmarks were illuminated against the sky; the people walking and talking; the frenetic traffic and hooting of horns; even the way the taxi would impatiently weave in and out of the endless queues.

124

But his mind was now on Jeanne. Of course there were others in her life, he knew that. There were no questions asked and no ties and it had been fine to start with, but increasingly he found he didn't want to play the field. He was getting too old for that. What he wanted now was stability and comfort. But why would Jeanne want to be with him when there were so many better fish in the sea? She was beautiful and still young. She'd just been indulging him, being kind. It was a sobering thought. Had she been hoping to go to the exhibition with that olive-skinned man all along? Were they already an item? He had never felt his age quite as much as he did that night.

It was nearly eleven o'clock when he paid the taxi driver off and let himself into the courtyard. Violette's lights were on and he saw her silhouette appear in the doorway of her flat. He called out a greeting and she silently withdrew. He'd forgotten to leave his outside light on again but the light coming from Gabriel's apartment was enough for him to see his way. He plodded to his front door, groping in his pocket for the key then looked round sharply, he wasn't sure why. There was no-one there. But as he put his key to the lock, the door swung back a few centimetres into darkness. This time it hadn't even been closed properly.

He pushed it gingerly right back, heart pounding, and peered inside, but it was too dark to see. A flick of the switch by the door and light filled the entrance hall. It was empty. Breathing a little more easily, he climbed the stairs but the studio door was wide open too and when he switched the light on he had to gasp for air. It was a scene of devastation: tables overturned, paint and mediums thrown on the floor, brushes broken in two and tossed down, paper torn into shreds and scattered like confetti everywhere. His easel had been knocked down and the hinges smashed; it looked like a skeleton whose joints have all been dislocated. Thank God there had been no canvas on it. But thinking of canvas made Eric pick his way quickly across the debris to the racks below the stairs.

He hadn't even reached them when he could already see that his fears were realised. His completed paintings, left to dry or to be stored, had been pulled out of the racking and dumped on the floor. Someone had taken a knife to them, cutting a cross in the middle of each. Eric swallowed hard. The luminous painting he had recently finished of Jeanne in the blue dress, his best in a while, was there on the top, slashed. He felt sick.

A little message from Gustave.

Chapter 9

Hannah was already at one of the small tables in the hotel breakfast room when Nathan made his way down. It was a well-lit but intimate space in the cellars of the building, its gothic stone arches like a rib-cage supporting the ceiling. She had a basket of breads and pastries on the table beside her plate as well as a large cup of hot water with a tea bag dangling in it and was in the process of buttering one half of a crusty roll when he walked in.

Her table was only set for one but Nathan walked across to join her and stood behind the chair opposite.

'You won't mind if I join you?' he enquired.

She looked up at him, raising her eyebrows. 'Be my guest.'

She finished spreading the butter and opened a tiny jar of jam. The young waitress emerged from a doorway beyond the further arch and, when she saw where Nathan was sitting, took a place setting from a nearby table and bustled up to lay it out in front of him.

'*Bonjour Monsieur. Thé ou café ce matin?*' she said. Tea or coffee this morning?

'*Café s'il vous plait. Avec lait chaud.*' He offered her a winning smile and she beamed back at him and left for the kitchen.

He looked at Hannah. 'See, I even remembered to ask for hot milk. I'm getting the hang of this French thing. I told you I would.'

'So you are. If anyone needs tea or coffee in an emergency, you're definitely their man.'

'Don't make fun of people who are making an effort.'

'I'm not making fun of the effort.'

'What then?'

'It doesn't matter.'

The waitress returned with a large steaming cup of coffee, a small jug of hot milk and another little wicker basket containing two bread rolls, a croissant and a brioche. A saucer on the table contained a few miniature packets of butter and another jar of jam. He took some butter and picked up the jam.

'*Fraise*,' he read and frowned. 'That's strawberry, isn't it?'

'Yes. You can have this one if you prefer.' Hannah offered the jar she'd opened but not yet started. 'It's blackcurrant.'

'Strawberry's fine, thanks.'

He poured some milk into his coffee and picked up the croissant, pulling a piece off it.

'I'm quite relieved to see you here this morning.' He popped the chunk of croissant in his mouth.

'Relieved? Why?'

He swallowed. 'You had a date with a strange man. At a place where strange things have been going on.' He pulled off another piece of croissant. 'How did it go?'

'Very well, thank you. And the strange things haven't been going on at his place.' She removed the teabag from her cup. 'He played me a piece he's recently composed. It was very good. He really is a brilliant pianist. He's wasted playing in restaurants and bars.'

'Is that all he does?'

'Meaning?'

'Meaning, does he play anywhere else or do anything else? It can't be an easy way to earn a living.'

'He seems to have modest needs. Perhaps he prefers to be happy in his work rather than wealthy.'

'Perhaps. You didn't answer the question: does he do anything else?'

'I didn't answer because I don't know. I didn't ask and I really don't care.'

She'd finished the bread roll and took a mouthful of tea. He noticed she was drinking it black, the French way.

'Nothing unexpected then?' he pressed. 'About the evening?'

'What a strange question. I'm not sure what I expected. Anyway, how was the Musée d'Orsay?'

'You were right: long queue. Worth it though.'

'And last night?'

'I went to Au Bout de la Rue. Gabriel's restaurant, except that he wasn't there of course.'

'Why there?'

'Why not? I was curious to see your half-sister. And the place. The sort of people she was talking about. It's quite upmarket, isn't it? It's certainly expensive.'

'It is rather. Good food though.'

He broke a bread roll in two and spread it with butter and jam. Hannah got up and took an apple from the fruit bowl on the side and bit into it.

'So tell me about the chap at the gallery you went to see yesterday,' said Nathan. 'What did you find out from him?'

'Not a lot. He's known my father since soon after he came back to France but he doesn't know of any feuds or rows. Nothing that would fuel the sort of hate mail my father seems to be getting. He did say that he'd sometimes felt that there was something from way back, perhaps an issue with family, but he didn't know for sure. He said Dad was good at being the life and soul of a party but didn't give much of himself away.' She snorted. 'That's certainly true.'

'Did your father ever mention any problems with his family to you?'

'No. He told me his own father died young but he wouldn't talk about it.' She sighed. 'Anyway, it doesn't look like there's anything I can do. I'm wasting my time here. It probably is just someone with a sick sense of humour.'

'You want to go home?'

'I don't know.' She looked to be fighting an internal battle. He wondered if it had anything to do with Gabriel. 'Maybe I'll stay a little longer, enjoy Paris since I'm here.' She paused. 'Were you still planning to stay?'

'Sure, a day or two. With the weekend coming up there's no rush for me to get back.'

'OK then. We could visit Sacré Coeur and Montmartre today if you like.'

'Sounds good, yes.' He hesitated. 'Are you OK, Hannah?'

'I'm fine. Why?'

'Oh nothing.'

The woman from reception appeared in the doorway, holding a piece of paper.

'Is there a Hannah Dechansay here?' she asked in French.

'Yes, that's me,' said Hannah. 'What is it?'

'There's a woman on the phone who wants to speak to you.' She glanced at the paper. 'A Jeanne Duval.'

Hannah abandoned the apple and quickly went back with the woman to reception. She returned barely five minutes later and, still standing, picked up her tea cup and downed the remains of her tea. She grabbed her handbag.

'Jeanne is a friend of my father's. She said he wasn't himself at the Private View last night and she was worried about him so she's just called round to see him.' She paused, swallowed. 'His studio's been trashed, Nathan. I have to go.'

He dumped his coffee cup back on the saucer and got up. 'I'll come too.'

*

Hannah stood just inside the doorway and surveyed the studio in dismay. The image of disarray and destruction was shocking. She felt tears prick her eyes. Nathan came to stand beside her and swore softly.

'It's terrible, isn't it?' Jeanne murmured in French. She had opened the door to them and she seemed overwhelmed all over again as she looked back at the room. 'I couldn't believe it when I saw it. How much hatred does someone have to do something like this? And to a man who never hurts anyone?'

Nathan looked at Hannah who translated for him.

'Where is *Monsieur Dechansay*?' said Nathan.

''e is up the stairs.' Jeanne made an effort to speak in English and pointed. ''e is in a shock, I think. When I arrive, 'e tries to…' She waved a hand towards the mess. There was a black bin bag already half full, standing in the middle of the room.

'…clear it up,' suggested Hannah.

'Yes. But I tell him to go up the stairs. I try to clear it and Marie-Louise comes soon. The *assistants* too, they can 'elp. *D'habitude,* all they do is argue.'

'We can help too,' said Hannah.

'I think it would be better if you go up to your father.' Jeanne had slipped back into French. 'Make sure he is all right.

He wouldn't talk to me at all. Too shocked, I think, but he needs someone there.'

Hannah nodded and translated again for Nathan.

'I'll stay down here and help,' he said. 'You go.'

Hannah nodded and made her way upstairs, unconvinced that she was the right person to do this; her relationship with her father at the moment was brittle at best. But apparently Jeanne had tried ringing Natalie and had got no answer – 'Doesn't surprise me; she's a madam, that one' – before finding Hannah's scribbled note with her contact details. She'd insisted Eric would want family with him at a time like this. So Hannah was it.

When she reached the top floor, her father was sitting at the table with a cup of black coffee in front of him, staring into space.

'*Bonjour Papa,*' she said.

He looked up and she walked slowly over and sat down in the chair to his left. The coffee looked untouched.

'I am so sorry for what's happened,' she ventured. 'I can't quite believe it.'

He studied her face then looked down. 'No. Neither can I.'

'Have you been able to salvage anything?'

He shook his head. 'Not much. A few tubes of paint. Some unused canvas. Bits.'

'How did they get in?'

'Mm?' He looked up again and shrugged. His eyes looked as though they were fixed on images from far away, the past maybe. 'I don't know. The door wasn't forced.'

'Someone who found the key then.'

'Or who can pick a lock.'

'Do you know anyone like that?'

He didn't answer.

132

'You shouldn't leave a key outside,' she said on a sigh.

'I keep moving it. You think it's my fault?'

'Of course not. I just... That coffee looks cold. Shall I make you another? I could do with some tea.'

He nodded, looking disinterested, and she took the cup and saucer back to the kitchen, refilled his filter coffee machine with coffee grounds and put the kettle on. A few minutes later she went back to join him, carrying a tray with his coffee things, a cup of tea for herself and a basket of breakfast pastries. She knew he loved brioches.

'Help yourself to a pastry, *Papa*. I bet you haven't eaten this morning.'

'I'm not hungry.'

'Even so.' She paused, taking a sip of tea. 'When did you find the mess?'

'Last night. I got home from the Private View and it was just there, like that. Everywhere. I couldn't touch it to start with. I just couldn't. I kept staring at it, thinking I was having a bad dream. It all felt polluted. Soiled. All my things.' He put a hand up to rub his forehead then fixed her with hurt eyes. 'Did you see the painting of Jeanne? The blue dress?'

'No. Was that damaged too?'

Another unconscious shake of the head. 'Destroyed.'

'My God,' Hannah murmured under her breath.

She picked up a brioche. Perhaps if he saw her eating, he would too. She bit into it.

'Mmm, these are good,' she murmured. He didn't seem to register. '*Papa*, you must eat. You'll make yourself ill. Please. Drink some coffee at least.'

He picked up the cup and took a sip then offered her a weak smile and a nod.

'Thank you, Hannah. Thank you for coming.'

'Please tell me who it is that's doing this to you.'

133

He took a deep breath and let it out slowly.

'Please?'

'Someone who wants money from me. More money than I could possibly raise without a lot of time and difficulty.' He took another mouthful of coffee. It seemed to be helping. 'And, even if I could, there is no end to it, is there? Blackmailers. They always come back for more.'

'So you must go to the police.'

'No.' His eyes became more alert suddenly; they flashed a warning at her. 'No, I'm not going to involve the police.'

'Why not? They're the ones best placed to...'

'Because I'm not. These people are clever at keeping under the radar. It'll just make it worse for me. I think I'll grit it out. They'll lose interest in the end.' He paused then fixed her with another look. 'I don't want you to do anything. Don't say anything to anyone. I don't want you involved.'

'But I am involved aren't I? I'm your daughter.'

Still he looked into her eyes, speaking slowly and carefully. 'It would be better for me if you weren't here.'

She frowned. 'You obviously know who it is.'

'I have suspicions.'

'But how can they blackmail you? What with?'

'I don't want to talk about it, Hannah. It's better if you don't know.' He paused and spoke slowly, deliberately. 'That's all I'm going to say on the matter and I insist you won't tell anyone else. Promise me?'

'I can't just...'

'Promise me.'

She lifted her hands in a show of defeat. 'OK yes I promise.'

He drank the rest of his coffee and got to his feet.

'I'm going to see what else can be salvaged from the wreckage down there. And I need to figure out what to tell

Mark and Florence when they turn up for work. It's too late to stop them now.'

'I'll come down and help.'

*

'What the hell?' Mark said, automatically exclaiming in English when he saw the devastation.

'I know,' Eric heard Nathan say. 'We've been trying to clear it up but I don't think we've made much impression yet.' He stuck out a hand. 'Hi, I'm Nathan, a friend of Hannah's. I didn't realise Eric had an Englishman working here.'

'Mark.' They shook hands. 'What happened?'

Eric quickly came over.

'A burglar,' he said in English. 'Couldn't find what he wanted I imagine, so he decided to show his anger by destroying my property instead. Probably wanted money or jewellery... or maybe drugs. Yes, I imagine only a drug addict would be desperate enough to do this.' He surveyed the room gloomily.

Mark took a few steps over the debris towards the cupboard where he kept his things but stopped short.

'My stuff too,' he said wanly. He turned. 'Is it the same upstairs?'

'What? No, no. He must have been disturbed or just gave up. Come to think of it I had left a bit of cash out. Perhaps it was enough.'

'The door didn't look damaged. Did they find the key?'

'I suppose so. I haven't looked yet to see if it's there.'

'Have you called the police?'

'There's no point. They'll just come and take a look, get in the way and ask a lot of stupid questions. They won't do anything.'

135

There was a moment's hesitation but Mark simply nodded and Eric thought he'd got away with it and when Florence arrived a couple of minutes later, he told her the same story. He put them to work, helping sort through the wreckage looking for viable materials to save, putting into rubbish bags all the unusable items. There was paint, dry pigments and a variety of mediums and oils ground into the wooden floor but it was impossible to clean it up until the space had been sorted and cleared.

Jeanne had had to leave – she had a modelling assignment on the other side of the city – but Hannah and Nathan worked alongside the two assistants while Eric kept being called upon to make decisions about whether something could be saved. He was on the point of smashing up the stretchers on one of the torn canvases when Hannah stopped him.

'But these could be repaired,' she insisted.

'No. Look at it. He's cut right through the middle, the bastard.'

He put the end stretcher to the floor and with his foot, savagely broke it away from the rest and the torn canvas ripped with it.

'Please *Papa*, don't. I could do something with them.'

He threw the bits of wood and canvas in the rubbish bag nearby.

'I can't keep them,' he almost shouted. 'They're ruined for me, don't you see? Ruined, whatever clever things you think you can do. I don't want them here.'

He picked up another but his hands were shaking with emotion and he had to put it down again.

'If you're sure you want them gone, I'll do it,' she said quickly. 'You go and make yourself another coffee. Have a break. Anything we aren't sure about we'll put on one side till you come down again.'

'Maybe you're right. I didn't sleep much last night.'

He trudged up the stairs.

Despite his misgivings, part of him was glad Hannah was there. There were no histrionics such as Virginie would have produced, nor the foolishness Natalie so often came out with. Hannah was purposeful and business-like. Nathan too. Though it might have been better if he hadn't told her about the blackmail. Eric had another coffee and fell asleep in the chair. It was a good couple of hours before he returned to the studio.

Over a long day they managed to salvage a few things but there was a great deal of rubbish. Nathan had examined the easel and decided it could be repaired with new hinges, some screws and a screwdriver and, with Eric's agreement, he set about doing it. Tainted or not, Eric knew he had to work or he'd go mad. As for most of his art materials, he'd have to restock. Most of them could be bought locally or easily ordered in and he had enough money in his current account for that. He rang a locksmith and had a new lock fitted on the front door. The spare key had indeed disappeared but he'd have had a new lock either way – anything to keep the bastards out.

By the end of the afternoon the studio was cleared and as clean as they could make it and the two assistants were ready to go.

'I'll pay to replace your things,' Eric told them before they departed. 'Write out a list of what's gone and I'll make it good.'

'Thank you, sir,' said Mark. He looked expectantly at Florence. 'We're grateful, especially in the circumstances.' He gave her another look. 'Aren't we Florence?'

'Yes, yes, thank you,' she said, and glared back at Mark. 'I was going to thank him,' she added peevishly.

That just left Hannah and Nathan still in the studio. Walking back to where they stood near the bottom of the stairs, he could hear them arguing too.

'I've told you before,' Hannah was saying. 'I can't leave him to cope with all this alone.'

'Fine, I'll stay,' said Nathan. 'You go back to the hotel. I'll keep an eye on him.'

She laughed.

'Well thanks for that vote of confidence,' he grumbled.

'Oh Nathan, really? Look, I appreciate the offer but how can you keep an eye on him when you struggle to understand what's being said? These guys, whoever they are, aren't going to offer you a translation to make it easy for you.'

'I'll manage.'

'No.'

'No,' Eric agreed, coming up behind them. 'Neither of you is staying. I don't remember inviting you. Thank you for all you've done but please go now. I need to start writing some lists and planning and I need peace.'

'But suppose they...?'

'No, Hannah, that's my final word. Go.'

There was a brief, tense silence while they both looked at him, sizing up his resistance.

'OK, come on.' Nathan was already moving towards the door. 'Let's go and brush up, then find something to eat. I'm starving.'

'All right. Look, I won't be a moment. I've left my things upstairs.'

Eric wandered off to look at the paint they'd managed to salvage and the next minute they'd gone. The apartment felt very empty and very quiet. He walked slowly round it, trying to absorb this new situation. He stroked a finger along the top of a newly cleaned and upright table, examined the repaired studio easel and nodded approvingly at Nathan's handiwork, and stood looking out of the window down to the courtyard.

138

For the first time since he'd lived there, he considered the possibility of moving. Perhaps it was time to review his life, to make changes. As long as he could paint he'd be all right; he didn't have to do it here. He didn't even need the prestige he'd had before or his name in art magazines. It had been fun but it didn't matter. So long as he could paint, he could do it anywhere, just make enough to live on.

He was still lost in these thoughts when he heard the studio phone ring and slowly walked across to it.

'*Oui, allo?*'

'Did you get my little message, Eric?'

'I got it. Gustave? Look...'

'You see how easily a life can be destroyed. All the things you take for granted can go in a moment, just like that.' A snap of fingers echoed in Eric's ear. 'Perhaps you liked the stories I've had circulated about you too? I was just showing you how easy it is to spread rumour and gossip. They could get a whole lot worse, trust me. Be sensible.'

'I can't pay the money you're asking for. And I know you think I owe you but I don't. I didn't take it, Gustave. I never...'

'I'm not interested in your excuses and lies, Eric. Of course you took it. And now you don't have a choice. I want money. From you.'

'You're not listening to me, Gustave: I can't pay you.' Eric took a deep breath. 'And I won't.'

Gustave laughed and the phone went dead.

*

Natalie swivelled on her stool and glanced round the room. This nightclub her friends had suggested was a bit of a dive. They'd said they'd heard the cocktails were cheap and the music was good, but everything about the place looked tawdry.

139

She suspected that the three of them could only afford all these drinks because inferior bootleg alcohol was being flogged as if it were the real thing. And being diluted. Not that that had stopped her drinking it. She was already well on her way to getting smashed and that suited her just fine. The guy who'd rung her up to ask her out to lunch today had stood her up. The world was full of bastards, she'd decided. So she'd decided to have a good time anyway, but she did wish she was doing it somewhere with a bit more class. That was the trouble with working at Au Bout de la Rue: it gave you a taste of smart life; it made you want more. Not likely on her pay.

Her thoughts inevitably turned to Gabriel. Now that guy had class – an indefinable something about him – though he clearly didn't have a bean; it was foolish to moon over him. Even so, she did like him. As if thoughts of the restaurant had conjured him up, she caught sight of Baptiste over the far side of the room. In fact she could have sworn he was looking straight at her. She did a double-take but now the sea of people on the dance floor were obscuring her view. She must have been mistaken. Baptiste didn't do dives like this. Did he? She didn't know much about him except he wasn't one for mixing with the waitresses. He was an aloof kind of guy, deep.

Natalie and her friends had another drink and got up to dance. It was a classic rock track by Johnny Halliday and they were all pretty well-oiled now and not too steady, giggling when they lost their balance or bumped into someone else. A man shuffled over and started dancing opposite Natalie, forcing her to make eye contact, insinuating himself. He was dark and thick set with a weight-lifter's arms. He wasn't her type and she didn't like the way he was looking at her so she moved away, said something in the ear of one of her friends and went to the cloakroom, checking behind to see he didn't follow her. It was a relief when she came out to see no sign of him. Even so, creeps like that left her wary and uncomfortable. She managed to persuade her friends to leave a short time later.

By the time she got back to the flat she had already sobered up a little. She made herself a cup of coffee and enjoyed having the place to herself for once. There was none of that nonsense with her mother suddenly appearing from her bedroom, asking questions and offering opinions.

She sat in her favourite armchair and reflected on the evening. She was doing something wrong; these weren't the places to meet the good guys. Again she thought of Gabriel. He hadn't shown any signs of having a girlfriend and if Hannah was on the way back to England, the coast was clear. Natalie knew where he worked and she knew where he lived. It was up to her to do something about it.

Chapter 10

Hannah checked in on her father first thing on the Saturday morning. He met her at the door, beaming. His sombre mood of the day before appeared to have all but evaporated.

'So, have you heard from him again, this blackmailer?' she pressed, barely waiting to exchange a greeting.

Eric hesitated for the blink of an eye.

'Do you know, I have.'

'And?'

'And I told him I wouldn't, *couldn't* pay.'

'So what did he say?'

'Of course he was taken aback. A bit quiet you might say. Bullies aren't used to anyone standing up to them.' He gave a shrug with one of his isn't-life-a-funny-thing smiles. 'Anyway, I think that it'll all blow over now.' He waved a dismissive hand. 'It's something and nothing. A silly grudge.'

'So why won't you talk about it?'

'Because it doesn't deserve the time. I've got things to do, lists to make, orders to put in. In fact I'd *like* to get on.' He ushered her away.

Back at the hotel, Nathan was waiting for her news.

'How is he this morning?'

'Fine. Worse than fine: ebullient. As if the chaos of his studio was just a blip, a minor inconvenience.'

Nathan nodded slowly, staring at her. 'There's something you're not telling me.'

'What do you mean?'

'I could tell last night. You were holding something back and the pressure was killing you. Tell me. I might be able to help.'

She scoffed. 'You won't.'

'Then there clearly is something. Don't be so pig-headed and independent. Spill it. Stop pretending you can sort this out by yourself.'

'And what? I can't but you will: the hero, riding in on a white charger to rescue us all?'

He looked at her balefully.

She sighed. 'OK. Yes, there is something, but I promised Dad I wouldn't tell anyone.'

'I get it.' He mimed zipping his lips.

'He finally admitted to being blackmailed yesterday. Said he had his suspicions who it was but he wouldn't tell me. Refused to say anything else about it in fact. Now he's saying he's had another call but told them he wouldn't pay and thinks he's called their bluff, and that's the end of it.'

'He really thinks that?'

'I have no idea what he thinks. It's always a performance, an I'm-a-conjuror-and-I-can-pull-a-rabbit-out-of-a-hat kind of act. He makes me want to scream. Look, let's go sightseeing before I go mad. We can't do anything useful here anyway.'

They took the metro to Sacré-Coeur and afterwards explored Montmartre and the Place du Tertre, the now traditional hangout of artists, and jostled with all the other tourists to see the latest artworks displayed on easels, in racks and propped up against trees. A few of the artists worked on site, finishing a painting while a gathering looked on or touted for sales of instant portraits. Hannah and Nathan paused to see a man draw a charcoal portrait of a young girl while her mother stood watching.

'Why don't you have your portrait done?' Nathan muttered to Hannah.

'No chance. Have one yourself if you're so keen.'

'Me? Nah, yours would be way more decorative.'

She turned, frowning, but he was engrossed watching the charcoal being traced rapidly across the paper.

'Look at that,' he murmured. 'He's good.'

They lunched at a bistrot, then went on one of the boat trips on the Seine. While the recorded commentary explained what they could see on each bank in a succession of languages, Hannah was free to let her thoughts wander. Her eyes saw the soaring gothic arches of Notre-Dame as they sailed past but she barely registered them.

It was Gabriel, not her father, who preoccupied her thoughts at this moment. The evening with him still lingered in her mind: good food, wonderful music, an easy-going, casual kind of date. But then there had been that kiss. She supposed she'd been naïve but it seemed to have come from nowhere, and yet what had surprised her most was the strength of her own response. She liked Gabriel, she couldn't deny it, but this was hardly the time to have a fling with the man. And she didn't do flings anyway. She'd always thought they were like sponge cake: nice when you were indulging in it but ultimately unsatisfying and leaving you wanting more.

But she would like to see him again and his attention was flattering. Her morale could do with a boost right now. She stared out sightlessly as the boat drifted along while the arguments for and against getting involved with this man she hardly knew circled in her head.

'Where shall we eat tonight? That place last night wasn't very good.' Nathan looked at her more closely. 'Hannah? Are you there?'

'Mm?'

The boat had long since turned and they were already nearing the end of the tour. Hannah forced herself to focus on what he was saying. He was peering into her face with one of his tolerant expressions.

'Tonight?' he said. 'Any idea where we should eat? Or maybe you were planning to go to Au Bout de La Rue again?'

Hannah shook her head. 'Natalie's got some holiday. Dad said she's gone away.'

'You don't get on with her anyway. I wasn't thinking of Natalie. I thought you'd want to see your boyfriend again, hear his magical piano playing.'

'He is not my boyfriend and I had no such thing in mind.'

'Of course, he'd give you a private performance any time you wanted.'

The boat had docked and they stopped talking while they got in the queue and shuffled their way to disembark.

'Look,' she said as they made terra firma, 'will you stop with the innuendo? I have no plans to see Gabriel and it's none of your damn business, even if I did.'

'No, you're right. I mean, why would you want a friend to look out for you? It's not as though you've ever got into trouble before, is it? And you do know so much about the man.' He paused and looked her straight in the eye. 'Don't you?'

'What have you ever known about the girls you date before you dated them? Do you have a tick list or something which they have to fill in before you offer them a drink? No, don't tell me, you probably do. How on earth did I manage to avoid it?' She turned away. 'I can't believe we're having this conversation. Let's go and get a drink.'

*

145

Nathan didn't mention Gabriel again. Like an obstinate teenager, Hannah would be more likely to see him the more he warned her off. They stopped at a cafe just off the Champs-Elysées and wandered back along the broad, tree-lined avenue, trailing through the crowds filling the pavements, marvelling at the noisy streams of traffic in both directions, the constant cacophony of car horns blaring. They paused to look in windows, saw the tomb of the unknown soldier, then climbed to the top of the Arc de Triomphe and enjoyed the views across the city.

Hannah was a good guide and Nathan had finally started to understand the attraction of Paris. He was enjoying himself. The elephant in the room was Eric. Neither of them spoke of him but he was still there and Nathan thought of him often. What was it that stopped him from talking? Something that made him nervous of the police? It had to be. Something dark from his past, something he daren't let see the light of day.

When they called in at Eric's studio early on the Saturday evening, the room had already started to look like a place of work again. Eric had been out to buy fresh art materials and had set himself up in his usual space with sheets of cartridge paper already covered in drawings strewn across the table. He was his usual irrepressible self.

'Look. I'm back in the saddle. Can't keep a good man down, as they say. Where are you two off to?'

'We're going for a meal,' said Nathan. 'But we're not sure where yet. Do you want to come, sir?'

'Please don't call me sir. Makes me feel like your, what's the word...' He raised a triumphant finger and grinned. '...headmaster. Eric is my name. And no, I will not come, thank you. I have things to do.'

'Have you had any more calls?' asked Hannah.

146

'No, no. All is quiet.' He smiled and winked. 'You see. I told you.'

They left him to it. What else could they do?

They called again on the Sunday morning and since peace still appeared to reign they went out again. It was a warm, sunny morning and they idled along beside the river, pausing to check out the *bouquinistes* – the sellers of second-hand and antiquarian books – whose lock-up stalls gave the left bank a jaunty yet sophisticated air. As well as books, there were prints and posters, postcards and tourist souvenirs. Further on, they drank tea and coffee at a riverside café and watched the boats pass by.

Later they stopped for lunch at a bar which did sandwiches and sat at a table on the terrace outside. It wasn't until they'd nearly finished eating and were sitting with their glasses of beer that Hannah finally referred to the elephant again.

'So, no word since Friday. Maybe it actually is over?' She didn't look at him but ran a finger through the condensation on the side of her glass.

'Was that a question? If so, I have no idea, but I doubt it.'

Hannah took a sip of beer, put the glass down again and cast a languid glance round the terrace as if it had been a casual remark and had no significance. He began to wonder if she was going to follow it up when she turned and looked directly at him.

'Does it ever work like that, do you suppose, that the target stands up to the threats, doesn't hand over money and whoever's making them just slithers back under a stone again?'

'I suppose it might. If the blackmailer thinks their target will be easy and then finds out he's not. Maybe they just move on to someone else who will be.'

'Do you think that's what's happening here?'

'I don't know. Do you?'

Hannah shook her head and drank another pull of beer.

'You're not going to go home yet are you?' said Nathan.

'No, not yet.' She hesitated. 'But you go.' She hesitated, tracing the condensation again. 'Thanks for your help with Dad's studio.'

'What will you do if something else happens?'

'Help him pick up the pieces, I suppose.' She shrugged. 'He talks well but he's bluffing. He's scared. I'm sure of it.'

'I think so too.' Nathan knocked back the last of his beer and set the empty glass down purposefully. 'Why are you doing this, Hannah? He's made it clear he doesn't want you here.'

'Don't start that again.'

'But why put yourself through this?'

'Because.' She frowned but wouldn't look at him.

'Because what?'

She lifted her head and glared at him. 'Because he's my father, OK? Because in between all the tall stories and the dubious friends and the dodgy goings-on, he's not a bad man. I know he isn't. Sometimes, when he lets the act drop, just sometimes I get a glimpse of the real man. And he's my father again, the man who took me to the fairground as a kid and who sat reading books with me.'

He saw her eyes fill and neither of them spoke again for several minutes. Hannah finished her beer.

'Well, I think I'll stay on a bit longer.' Nathan pulled the wallet out of his pocket. 'I've only missed three days of work so far. I'll ring Daphne tomorrow. I think this is going to be a serious bout of flu. I had two weeks off with it once.'

He tossed some money on the bill on the table. Hannah did the same. 'Could we visit the Père Lachaise cemetery this afternoon?' he said. 'I was reading about it. Jim Morrison's buried there.'

'Lots of famous people are. Yes, if you want. You can get a map at the entrance which tells you where they are. But first I need to go back to the hotel. I'd like to have a shower and put something cooler on.'

'Sure. I'll do the same.'

But when they got back to the hotel, there was a message waiting for Hannah at reception.

'A man phoned earlier, hoping to speak to you,' the receptionist said. 'When I said you weren't here, he left a message.'

'What?' she said anxiously.

The young man handed her a folded piece of paper and she turned away to open it and her expression brightened.

'It's all right, it's from Gabriel,' she said. 'He's asked me to meet him later if I'm free. For tea. Somewhere I won't have been before.' She grinned.

'I see.' Nathan walked away from her to the lift and pressed the call button.

Hannah joined him, pushing the note in a pocket.

'You don't mind do you? I'm intrigued.'

'Of course, you must go.'

'I'm sorry about the cemetery but it's not difficult to find. There's a metro station called Père Lachaise. It's right on the corner of it.'

'Fine. Whatever,' he said shortly. 'I'm not that bothered.'

Once back in his room, Nathan threw his sweater and a bag with a book and a couple of souvenirs on the bed then, in a fit of temper, kicked the wicker rubbish basket. It fell over and rolled across the room. Luckily, it had been emptied that morning. He sat down heavily on the edge of the bed.

'Bloody Gabriel,' he said venomously.

*

Gabriel's message had been cryptic:

Would you like to share afternoon tea with me this afternoon? Somewhere you'll never have been, I'd bet on it. Come to the tea rooms Chez Béatrice at four. They're off the Rue Mouffetard. Ask any of the shopkeepers near the junction with the Rue Ortolan. I'll be waiting. Please come. Gabriel.

Tea rooms? Gabriel? How unexpected. That was one of the things she liked about him: he was surprising, unpredictable. He didn't fit in a neat box any more than her father did. And he made her feel special too, really wanted. So she decided to go in spite of her reservations, in spite of Nathan's warnings (or perhaps because of them), just to see him again, the temptation too strong.

She found a *tabac* and went in to ask about Chez Béatrice. Yes, the woman behind the counter knew Béatrice, smiled oddly as she said it, and gave Hannah directions.

The place was certainly off the beaten track. A narrow archway from a side street further up the Rue Mouffetard gave access to a longish courtyard. There were more shops here – tiny independent, niche shops selling hats, antique maps and map books, and hand-made stationery embossed with flower designs. And there was a shop selling glove and string puppets and, in the window, a string puppet of a clown had been automated to dance and then wave at the window. Hannah paused to watch it, enchanted.

The tea rooms were at the far end. There was a wide window and a glazed door with the name above it but, from the outside, it looked like the front room of someone's house. Outside an array of potted geraniums surrounded a bigger pot housing a rosemary bush and an even larger one accommodating a small olive tree.

150

Hannah pushed the door open and went in. Gabriel was already there, sitting at a table at the back. He immediately came to greet her, leaning in to kiss her on both cheeks.

'I'm so glad you came. Come, take a seat.'

'This is a well-hidden secret, isn't it?'

She sat in the chair opposite his, slung her handbag over the back of it and looked round. Bigger inside than it looked from the square, it did appear to occupy the ground floor of someone's home. The tables were laid with lace tablecloths and blue and white striped china cups and saucers, and most of them were occupied. An assortment of delicious-looking pâtisseries were on display in two glass-fronted cabinets and the walls were crammed with framed photographs: stills from theatre productions and music hall girls, and posters advertising theatre productions. And right at the back on the farther side, stood an old upright piano.

'What do you think?' said Gabriel, watching her face.

'I think it's amazing. How did you find it?'

He puffed out his lips, dismissively. 'Oh, you know, in my line of work I meet all sorts of people. I get to know about these things.'

She grinned. 'I'm sure you do. And I suppose you bring all your lady friends here?'

He looked offended. 'Certainly not. I've kept it to myself until now. But you said you only drank tea. I thought you'd like it.'

'I love it.'

'Then tell me what you want to order. I was waiting – hoping – to see you before I ordered.'

According to the menu on the table, a wide range of teas was on offer: black, green and herbal. Hannah chose a Ceylon tea, Gabriel said he'd have the same and they both picked out a patisserie from one of the cabinets. Béatrice herself took the

151

order. She was sixty if she was a day but her carefully coiffed hair was an implausible strawberry blonde and her make-up generously applied. Something in her bearing and her expressive, exaggerated movements suggested that she too had been on the stage. Hannah suspected that if she looked hard enough, she'd find Béatrice's photograph on the wall too.

Their hostess put her arm round Gabriel's shoulder and gave him an affectionate hug.

'Our Gabriel,' she said, to Hannah. 'Such a talented boy.'

'Not so much of a boy,' he remarked drily.

'From where I stand, you are, *chéri*,' she laughed. 'Have you heard him play, *Mam'selle*? Wonderful.'

'Yes, he is.'

'We'll get a tune out of you before you go.' She tapped Gabriel playfully on the shoulder, offered a coquettish smile and left.

Gabriel grinned as he watched her walk away then turned back to Hannah.

'I didn't think you'd come.'

'The proposition was too intriguing.'

'And does it live up to expectations?'

'Definitely.' Hannah paused. 'You seem to know Béatrice very well.'

He shrugged. 'Not really. She's like that with all her regulars. Treats us like her children, her protégés.'

'She's an actress, right? Or a dancer?'

'Both. Some time you should give her the chance to tell you about her heady days on the stage. Some of her stories...' He raised his eyebrows suggestively. 'They might make you blush.'

Another waitress, wearing a small lace-edged apron, brought their pot of tea on a tray with two plates bearing their pâtisseries.

152

Gabriel waited till she'd gone then sat forward again.

'So tell me what you've been doing.'

'Some sight-seeing. Nathan – you remember: he helped with the piano? – hasn't seen much of Paris before. We've been doing all the usual places.'

'And who is he exactly?'

'He's someone I work with.' Gabriel was looking at her sceptically. 'He'd finished a job in Rennes earlier than expected and decided to take a few days' holiday and come on to Paris.'

'Lucky you were here to show him round then.'

'I think he wanted to take advantage. As you know, his French isn't great.'

Gabriel picked up his pastry and examined it before biting into it. 'Mm. Good.'

Hannah did the same and chewed for a minute before pausing.

'Gabriel, you see people coming and going in your courtyard, don't you?'

'Sometimes. When I'm not playing.'

'I wondered if you'd seen anyone on Thursday night, I mean, after I left, going to my father's place?'

'Thursday?' Gabriel put his pastry down and picked up the teapot. His brow puckered. 'No.' He poured tea into each of the blue and white striped cups. 'But of course there was some problem in his studio that night, wasn't there?'

'How did you know?'

'I bumped into Florence on Friday and she mentioned a break-in but she was a bit vague. Have you any idea who it was? Was anything stolen?'

'No. Florence shouldn't have said anything.'

'Why not? If there was a burglary...'

'It was nothing much. My father doesn't want to make a fuss about it. I just thought you might have heard something.'

'No. I went back to the piano after you'd gone. I was working on that composition of mine.'

'Of course.'

The conversation faltered as they finished their pastries and started on the tea. Gabriel put his cup down and sat back. Hannah became aware of him watching her.

'Have you forgotten what I look like?' she said eventually.

'I just like to watch you. Is that bad?'

'It's uncomfortable.'

'Then I'm sorry and I won't do it.' He looked pointedly away, angling his head awkwardly to look at the wall to his left as if studying the photograph there. 'Your sister is having some days off I gather. She wasn't in the restaurant last night. My God, this is killing my neck.'

Hannah laughed.

'I give in. You can look at me.'

He turned back, grinning. 'What a relief.'

'Natalie had some holiday owing. She's gone away.'

'Oh? Where?'

'I don't know.'

'I suppose, like most sisters, you don't always get on.'

'I couldn't say; I hardly know her.'

'Very diplomatic.' He smiled and drank some more tea. 'And what about this Nathan chap. Do you get on with him? He looks very serious.'

'He's not always serious.' She frowned. 'You seem very fixated on Nathan.'

'I'm assessing the competition.'

'He isn't. Look, if you must know, we did date a couple of times. It didn't work out. He really isn't competition.'

'Good.'

154

They finished drinking their tea just as Béatrice came over and asked Gabriel to play the piano.

'Everyone is waiting for you.'

'I was just waiting to be asked.' He grinned and got up, picking up his music case which had been propped up against the table. 'Would you help me, 'annah, by turning the music?'

'If you want.' She followed him to the piano.

He stroked the top of it. '*Bonsoir chérie.* You remember me, don't you? Gabriel. How are you?'

He sat down on the stool in front of it and riffled through the music in his case as Hannah stood waiting. He pulled out a folded sheet, put it on the music rest and glanced sideways at her. It was an arrangement of *Anything Goes* by Cole Porter and Hannah followed the music keenly, scared of missing the page turn. She was dimly aware of Béatrice swaying to the music behind them and when he finished he got an enthusiastic round of applause from everyone in the room.

'You don't really need me to turn the pages, do you?' Hannah muttered. 'You can do it yourself. I've seen you do it at the restaurant. You probably know this music off by heart anyway.'

He flicked her a smile. 'But then I wouldn't have the pleasure of having you by me,' he murmured back. It was a long piano stool and he patted the space beside him. 'Sit with me while I play.'

He played another couple of pieces and he finished with the one he'd recently written himself. He had extended it and now the ending felt more resolved. He held the final chord and when he finally lifted his hands he got another round of applause. He turned to Hannah.

'Better?'

'Yes. It's wonderful.'

They left soon after with Gabriel promising Béatrice that

of course he would return soon, lifting her hand and kissing the back of it.

They walked down the street, apparently with no aim, looking in the windows of shops, pointing out trees coming into leaf or already in blossom. Gabriel reached for her hand and Hannah let him take it. She felt like a teenager, smitten, nervous, excited. Foolish. They just kept walking, weaving the streets.

'We're nearly at the river, aren't we?' she said eventually, looking round. 'Yes, there's Notre Dame. We should turn round.'

'Does it matter? We can take a metro back. But before we do that I need to get a few things and there's a supermarket over there. Will you come back for dinner tonight? If you tell me what you'd like to eat, I'll buy it and cook it for you.'

Hannah hesitated. She eased her hand out of his grip and rammed both her hands in the pockets of her cotton trousers.

'Don't you think we're going too fast?'

'Fast? How can that be? We've just been drinking tea.' He looked confused. 'You aren't here for long. We don't have time to waste.'

'No, you're right. But that's part of the problem. It's pressure. I think maybe another time, Gabriel. I should get back now and I'd like to check in on my father, maybe take him out for dinner later.'

'I see.' He looked disappointed but managed a weak smile. 'I understand.'

'I had a great afternoon. Thank you for introducing me to Béatrice.'

'But I will see you again before you leave, won't I?'

'I'm not leaving yet.'

He leaned in and softly kissed her and they parted.

Hannah strolled slowly down the street, vaguely heading

for the next metro station, her head full of contradictory thoughts. She felt like she was on a carousel, doomed to keep going round and round. She liked Gabriel, but it wouldn't work. It had all been too hasty, too impulsive. But she did like him. She kept walking and, wrapped up in her own thoughts, hadn't noticed the man who was following her.

She turned down a narrow, one-way street which cut through to where she thought the metro station was and glanced at her watch: six twenty-five. She'd spent nearly two and a half hours with Gabriel and it felt like barely an hour. But she'd no sooner let her arm fall than she felt a hand press hard against her mouth and another arm came from the other side and across her waist, pinning her left arm down. She started to struggle but whoever was holding her was too strong and she became aware of a car crawling up the street behind them.

'We want to talk to you,' the man growled in her ear. 'Your daddy needs a bit of encouragement it seems. You'll persuade him, I'm sure.'

Hannah squirmed and kicked but it just made him hold her more tightly. Then somehow she managed to get her mouth open enough to bite the palm of his hand and draw blood. As he pulled it away, swearing, she twisted in his grip, elbowing him hard in the midriff. He gasped and loosened his hold round her waist just as the car drew to a stop nearby. Turning, she brought her knee up hard into his groin.

As he doubled up in pain, she began to run, faster than she'd ever run in her life before, and heard a shout behind her and a car door slamming. In a minute they'd be after her and she kept running till she reached the junction with the main road, then turned wildly. She'd been right about the metro station – it was on the corner – and she ran down the steps, weaving in and out of the people coming up, colliding with a

157

man and shouting an apology before half-tumbling, half-running down them again.

She shot a look back up the steps but no-one seemed to be on her tail yet. She reached in her bag for her pass, thanking her lucky stars that she'd thought to buy one to last the week, and threw herself at the nearest barrier. It didn't matter which train she got or where she went, she just needed to get away. The passageway to the platform was crammed with people and she was forced to slow down and mingle. Waiting on the platform, she kept looking back to the entrance and, when the train arrived, pushed her way on board then stood behind a group of young Americans. One of the men was tall and broad and she kept behind him while the train pulled out. Glancing up at the map on the train wall, it was a relief to see that she was heading south.

Half an hour and another train later, she was on the road to the hotel and running again as though her life depended on it. She paused at the entrance to the hotel, panting, and looked round; there was no sign of anyone following her. She stopped at the reception desk for her key, barked the room number at the receptionist, and took the stairs up to the second floor two at a time.

When Nathan opened his door she had never been so pleased to see anyone in her life and almost fell into the room.

'What the hell?'

'Shut the door,' she gasped and sat down heavily on the side of the bed, leaning forward over her knees. 'We need to change hotels. Whatever's going on, it isn't over yet.'

Chapter 11

Eric was in the *salon* on the top floor when he heard the doorbell ring. He'd locked the front door. He had got into the way of doing that now, and the bell rang for a second time as he walked across to the glazed door to the balcony and opened it far enough to look down to the courtyard. It was Hannah and Nathan. He emitted a sigh of relief and went down to open the door.

'No, we just need to find a different hotel,' Hannah was saying as they walked in.

'We've been through this already. No, *we* don't. *You* need to go home. *I'll* change hotel, just in case. But they won't be interested in me.'

'I've told you I'm not going anywhere.' She produced a wry grin. 'Anyway, with the damage I inflicted on that man's privates, I doubt he's going to be coming near me any time soon.'

'It's not a laughing matter, Hannah. Has it not occurred to you that it's simply going to make him more determined to get his own back on you next time?'

'There won't be a next time: I'll be looking out for him. And are you suggesting I shouldn't have done it? I suppose I should have been more lady-like and let him drag me off. Is that what you're saying?'

Eric was beginning to think he was invisible.

'What man?' he demanded. 'And what do you mean, drag you off? Will the two of you stop bickering and tell me what's going on?'

'Sorry *Papa*. Can we go upstairs? We need to talk.'

'We certainly do,' added Nathan. 'This has got beyond a joke.'

Eric installed them in the *salon* while he went in search of three glasses and a bottle of cognac. He had a feeling he was going to need a stiff drink. He put it all on a tray and took it over to the coffee table. He poured them each a generous measure, handed the glasses out and sat down opposite Hannah and Nathan who were sitting side by side on one of the sofas, as far apart as they could, like fractious adolescents. Their bickering had now subsided into a strained silence.

'Someone tried to abduct Hannah,' Nathan said abruptly. 'About an hour ago. She managed to escape, thank God, but it seems that whatever you told her or you might like to think, the people persecuting you haven't given up yet. The man told her...'

'Can I tell this?' said Hannah. 'After all, I was the one who was there.'

Nathan waved an impatient hand and stopped speaking.

'He told me you needed encouragement,' she said to her father. 'He said he was sure that I would encourage you.'

'I think it's time we went to the police,' said Nathan.

'No,' Eric snapped. 'No police.'

'With due respect, Eric, it's not all about you now, is it? Hannah is the one they tried to snatch.'

'Did you see the man?' Eric leaned forward towards Hannah urgently. 'Did you see what he looked like?'

'Not really. He wasn't that big, but he was stocky and strong.' She gave an involuntary shiver then screwed her face up and closed her eyes. 'He had dark hair and eyes – I'm not sure about the eyes - and he smelt. Oh and he had a tattoo on the back of his hand.'

'What of?' demanded Nathan.

She opened her eyes. 'I don't know. I didn't take my time looking at him; I was too keen to be out of there.'

'Of course.' Eric felt a chill run down his spine. He forced a taut smile towards his daughter. 'You must have been terrified.'

'Do you recognise him?' she said.

'No,' he lied and drank some cognac. 'Just a strong arm, I imagine, trying to frighten you.'

Hannah scoffed. 'He was successful then. There was a man in a car too. I didn't see him at all.'

'I'm sure your reaction will make them think twice.'

'Think twice?' exploded Nathan. 'Yes, they'll think of a different way of grabbing her next time. They're clearly not planning to back off. Look, Eric, this has to stop.' He turned to Hannah. 'And you're playing with fire, fraternising with that piano player. It can't be a coincidence that he invited you across Paris this afternoon and that's when they jumped you.'

'He has nothing to do with it. If I'd agreed to have dinner with him tonight as he'd asked I'd still have been with him now and not walking back by myself.'

'No, you'd probably have been walking straight into a trap laid by him. And you wouldn't have got away at all.'

'You're talking nonsense.'

'*Eh, eh, ça suffit*,' bellowed Eric. 'Enough. I don't believe Gabriel is involved in this. I know him. But you're right, Nathan. It does have to stop.' He took a deep breath, let it out slowly and spoke more calmly. 'I'll see if I can come to some arrangement with them next time they phone.'

'Suppose they don't phone?' challenged Nathan.

161

'I'll sort something out.' Eric leaned forward to pick up the cognac bottle, offered it to the others who refused and topped up his own glass. He drank an ample mouthful, savouring its comforting warmth in his mouth and throat. 'There are people in this city who know where people like this can be found.'

'No, you mustn't put yourself in danger,' said Hannah.

Eric took another drink, put the glass down and turned to face Hannah, pulling his shoulders back. 'Hannah, I want you to go back to England. Please stop trying to force a situation here. You are the problem now. You must go.'

'Exactly,' said Nathan triumphantly. 'They're using you to get to Eric. What have I been saying?'

Hannah frowned, looking at first one, then the other. She fixed on her father's face.

'So I'm the problem?' She looked for all the world as if he'd slapped her. 'It's nothing to do with someone from your past, I suppose, some dodgy escapade you were mixed up in, which you refuse to admit to or talk about. No, of course, I'm the problem. So I shall go. And then you'll have to look for someone else to blame.' She got to her feet. 'If I can just use your phone, I'll ring the airline now.'

Eric stared, shocked at the bitterness in her voice.

'Yes... yes, of course, use the phone. You know where it is.' He watched her stalk off, comforting himself that this was the right thing to do. He turned back to Nathan. 'You can go too Nathan. I'll be fine.'

Nathan's eyes narrowed. 'Are you sure about that?'

'I'm sure. Please. Go and tell her to book two tickets.'

Eric wasn't sure at all. But this was his affair to sort out and if Nathan stayed, he was pretty sure Hannah would stay too and he couldn't bear to think of her being caught up in it. If he alienated her for it, so be it; it was in her own best

162

interests. He had created this problem all those years ago and now he was paying for it. Hannah's description of the man attacking her sounded like Gustave as he was all those years ago. It had to be his son, Robert. Eric knew he'd been naïve to think it would all go away and to think Pascal had been exaggerating. *Son père tout craché,* he'd said.

If Robert really was a chip off the old block, this wasn't going to be pretty.

*

Gabriel was peeling a potato in his tiny kitchen that evening when he heard the phone ring. He put the knife and potato down on the chopping board, wiped his hands on the tea towel and went through to answer it.

'*Oui?*'

He listened, his expression slowly darkening.

'But she got away?' he said. 'Was she hurt?'

Again he listened.

'No, no, look,' he protested, 'this is getting out of control. I didn't sign up for this. She's nothing to do with this. You didn't tell me... What?'

Gabriel could feel his free hand clenching and unclenching as he listened.

'I'm not involved. Don't put that on me. I'm only involved because you made me be involved. But that doesn't make it right. Information, that's all you said you wanted. You said there'd be no violence.'

He listened again.

'All right. All *right*. But she's probably been scared off now anyway.'

He closed the call and replaced the phone on its stand. He hoped Hannah was all right. He liked her, more, much more,

163

than he'd expected and, though he'd dearly like to see her again, there was no doubt now that it would be better if she went away.

*

The first flight Hannah could book was a late-night flight on the Monday evening. Nathan insisted on making his own booking but they ended up with tickets for the same flight anyway which meant they had a whole day to occupy, or as Nathan insisted on describing it: a whole day in which to stop Hannah from being dragged into a car and kidnapped.

After leaving Eric's apartment – a difficult, terse parting – they'd had a meal at a busy, tourist-filled restaurant, not far from the hotel. Nathan had insisted they should stay where it was busy. He'd kept trying to make small talk but Hannah wasn't in the mood and when they got back to the hotel – carefully, constantly checking who was around – they both retreated to their own rooms.

When she got down to breakfast the next morning, Nathan was already there. He was sitting reading a copy of *The Times* newspaper, a cup of coffee going cold on the table in front of him and the crumbs of a croissant left behind on a plate.

She slipped into the seat opposite and stared at the front of the newspaper.

'That paper's two days old,' she remarked.

He flipped the newspaper down and looked at her over the top of it.

'I know. But at least I understand it and it was the only English paper they had.' He folded the newspaper up completely and put it on the floor by his chair. 'I went down to the kiosk at the end of the street. I wanted to see if anyone was watching the place or if someone would follow me.'

164

The waitress appeared with a basket of bread and pastries and put it beside Hannah, took her order for tea and left.

'And...?' prompted Hannah.

'And there didn't seem to be anyone.'

'Good.'

She took a bread roll from the basket, split and buttered it, then picked up a jar of raspberry jam from the selection on the table.

'I've been thinking about that attempted snatch,' she said as she spread the jam on one half of the roll.

'What about it?'

'It felt professional. I mean these are serious crooks. It doesn't feel like a simple personal vendetta. And there was something about the man who tried to grab me, something I feel I should remember but I can't. It's driving me mad.'

'If they're professional crooks, the police will know them. It'll make it easier to track them down. We should tell them.'

'But my father doesn't want us to.'

Nathan leaned forward. 'But that was before you got dragged into it.'

'Because I insisted on getting involved. That was my choice, not his.'

'Yes, and how has he treated you for it? He's looking after himself, Hannah. He's not thinking about you.' He sat back and fixed her with a look of frustration. 'I know he's your father but I still don't understand why you're so supportive of him. He keeps you at arm's length all the time. Why jeopardise your own safety for him?'

'You don't like him, do you?'

'I do actually. But I don't like the way he treats you. And I don't like this whole scenario. I don't like that he won't go to the police.'

'There's no proof is there? Of anything. They couldn't do anything if he did go.'

'That's not why he isn't going. He's scared.'

'I told *you* that.'

'Yes, but what exactly is he scared of? Or who?'

Hannah finished her bread roll and didn't reply. Nathan hailed the waitress and asked for another cup of coffee. They both lapsed into silence and Hannah picked up her teacup. She could still feel the weight of accusation in the air between them.

'Families are complicated,' she murmured and drank some tea.

The waitress brought Nathan his second coffee and Hannah waited until she'd gone.

'Yes, my father frustrates me. Yes, he annoys me. Yes, I wish he cared more. But I suppose he's done the best he can. It's the way he is. I mean, you want your parents to like you, don't you? You want them to be proud of you, you can't stop yourself. You think of them as some kind of ideal beings. And then you reach an age when you realise that they aren't perfect, any more than you are. They're just muddling through.'

'I suppose so. But it's no reason for you to sacrifice yourself for them. Or beat yourself up because you think you've failed in some way. Eric's battles aren't your battles, Hannah.'

She silently regarded him for a moment then finished her tea.

'I suppose I'd better do some packing,' she said.

*

Eric had arranged for a delivery of two new tables and chairs for Mark and Florence to work at, as well as a fresh batch of

166

canvas, papers, brushes and paints. The few things he'd bought at the weekend wouldn't go far. He wanted them all to get back to work as quickly as possible, wanted to draw a line under the events of this past week and retrieve some kind of normality. He had been promised that the deliveries would arrive on Monday morning by special carrier. The cupboards which housed the two assistants' personal work and materials were still usable; only their contents had been ruined and though Mark was still grumbling about his lost materials and work, Florence appeared remarkably sanguine. She even joked about it which only made Mark grumpier and set off another argument.

In the end, the two deliveries arrived within a half hour of each other and the two assistants were quickly occupied, positioning the furniture, sorting out goods and stowing them away. There were still some materials needed and Eric asked Mark to make a list and ring the suppliers to order them in.

'I could give Florence the list and she could go and collect them,' said Mark. 'Or I could go.'

'Yes, maybe... No. Get them delivered. There's something you wanted to work on, isn't there? Let's just get down to work.' Eric didn't like the idea of either of them going out; he didn't know who might be loitering outside. He'd waited till they'd arrived to unlock the front door that morning and he'd locked it again after them.

The studio settled into relative peace and Eric picked up where he'd left off on the Saturday, working on the commission for the American, still playing with the composition on paper, trying out ideas, honing them. It was early afternoon when Virginie turned up at the studio and the peace was broken.

Eric's ex-wife was tall and leggy. She had been a fashion model when he'd first met her, most of her work coming from

167

catalogue shoots and advertisements, and, though she was still attractive and statuesque, these days her waist was a little thicker, her hair more carefully coiffed to disguise her age. Naturally impatient and demanding, she knocked at the door downstairs and when no-one immediately opened it, shouted to get their attention. Florence looked across at Eric who nodded and she quickly ran down the stairs to let her in.

Virginie strutted into the studio ahead of Florence, stopped and looked round. Eric guessed she was looking for Jeanne. They had met a couple of times and it hadn't gone well. Neither woman backed off from a verbal fight. Now, satisfied that Jeanne wasn't there, Virginie looked across at Eric.

'I need to speak to you,' she said.

'Certainly.'

'Somewhere more private.' She cast a dismissive glance towards the assistants. 'Upstairs?'

Without bothering to wait for a reply, she returned to the stairs and went up. He followed behind. What was it this time? Money probably. It usually was. Despite the years since their divorce and her generous personal settlement, despite Natalie being now grown-up and self-supporting – in theory – Virginie still assumed he had some responsibility to provide for her.

Virginie paused when she got to the top floor and cast a long look round.

'Can I get you a coffee?' Eric offered as he came up behind her.

'No thank you.' She was wearing high heels as usual which gave her a small height advantage. She looked down her nose at him. 'I've come about Natalie. Is she here?'

'No. Why would she be here?'

'Because she comes to you whenever she gets fed up or wants money. I know she complains about me to you, Eric. But

168

if she's moved in here for the weekend without telling me, there's going to be trouble.'

Eric frowned. 'She hasn't. She's gone away for a few days. Didn't she tell you?'

'Tell me what?'

'She wanted a holiday and I gave her a small contribution to her expenses. She was going to Langeais in the Loire valley. You remember we went there once?'

'She told me you'd given her some money for her holidays but she didn't mention the Loire valley. When was this?'

'Wednesday evening. Did she mention going anywhere else?'

'No, nowhere. I've been away for the weekend and when I got back to the apartment just before lunch, the door wasn't locked. When I looked in her room, her things are still all there.'

'All of them? She'll only have taken a few things. It's getting warm now. And she might have bought new, you know, with the money I gave her.'

'But her handbag is still there and her purse was left out on the side. There was a half-eaten brioche in the kitchen too and a cup of cold coffee, half drunk.'

Eric hesitated. He didn't feel good about this. 'Her mind does flit about; she can be forgetful,' he said slowly. 'And she does have more than one handbag. Or she's bought a new one. You know what she's like about buying things. Was there money in the purse?'

'No. No bank card either.'

'There you are then.'

'Is there something you're not telling me, Eric?'

'No, of course not. You're always looking for drama in everything. I'm sure she'll be in touch or just turn up. She's probably met someone and is enjoying herself too much to

169

think. You know how she is: head in the clouds most of the time.' He offered his most winning smile. 'But you've been away too? Did you have a good time?'

'Ye-es,' she said slowly, her indignation and concern slowly fading. 'Very good. I never get bored in Léo's company.'

She couldn't resist the inevitable dig but at least she seemed mollified and a few minutes later she'd gone.

Eric tried to settle back to work but his mind wouldn't focus. Normally, he wouldn't have worried unduly about Natalie: she could be absent-minded and easily distracted. Not locking the apartment door – he could imagine her doing that. He could see her buying a new bag and purse for a trip too. But these weren't normal times and the phone call, when it came at half past six, came as no great surprise. He had just gone upstairs to the apartment and he answered it with a leaden feeling in his heart.

It was the same familiar voice.

'You really have been stupid, haven't you? You were always going to have to pay. Why did you make me do it?'

Eric opened his mouth to speak but found it was too dry. He ran his tongue over his lips and tried again.

'Do what?'

'Oh come on, Eric. We both know. She seems like a nice girl. You really should look after her better. I'll be in touch. Of course, the price will go up now. You should have paid before. And, remember that young girl who worked for you last year? Such a shame what happened to her. You don't want Natalie to be found like that, do you? So don't go to the police, Eric. Because I'll know. And you won't see her alive again.'

'If you dare touch one hair of her head...' Eric shouted into the receiver.

But the phone had gone dead and Eric stared at it, numbed.

170

This was a nightmare, unreal. He began to pace up and down, up and down and Edvard Munch's painting *The Scream* came into his mind. He wanted to scream too, to shout, to vent his desperation and impotence but couldn't seem to articulate anything.

He had no idea what to do but knew he ought to do something. Anything. He'd have to find some money, perhaps see what he could sell quickly. He could do that, couldn't he? He'd find a way to get his money out of those fancy locked-in accounts, some of it at least, and take a hit on whatever the penalty might be.

He was so shocked, he struggled to think clearly. He'd never thought it would come to this. Even the attempt on Hannah hadn't convinced him. He'd thought it was a stunt, a scare tactic and that was how she'd managed to get away: they'd never really meant to take her in the first place. But now Natalie... He'd been fooling himself all along.

It occurred to him that he needed help and he didn't know who to turn to. He wanted to talk it through with someone. Jeanne wouldn't do; she seemed too involved with that other man now, too distant. He had friends of course, artist friends, drinking friends, but no-one he dared trust with this kind of information. They might talk and if word got back to the kidnappers... No, he needed someone reliable, discreet, clear-headed.

Then he thought of Nathan. He hardly knew the man but he trusted him. Something about the way he behaved with Hannah, about the way he held himself and addressed people, they all gave him confidence. Plus the man wasn't emotionally involved; he could be objective, rational. And if Hannah came back too, so be it. He didn't want her involved but she was at no risk now; they'd taken Natalie instead. Maybe they'd intended to all along.

171

He glanced at the clock and went to the phone. Hannah and Nathan should be at the airport by now. He could stop them before they boarded their flight.

Chapter 12

Nathan woke to a strange bedroom. He could sense it even before his eyes were open and he was fully conscious. It wasn't the hotel room he'd not long left. There was something about the feel of the sheets on the bed, the smell in the room – that still, dead smell of a room not often used – and the quality of the light. It was a thin, sharp brightness, searing his eyelids from the left. He rolled away from it onto his right side and stretched out an arm, hit something and blinked his eyes open. It was the wall. The single bed was pushed up against it.

He took a moment to orientate himself before it all came back: he was in the smallest of Eric's two spare bedrooms, normally a dumping ground for whatever didn't fit in anywhere else and it had one tiny window, high up on the wall. He rolled onto his back again and eased himself up on his elbows, scanning the room. Boxes, a couple of old suitcases and a battered case that looked like it might house a musical instrument had been pushed to the far wall. And Nathan's bags were on the floor too, some of their contents deposited nearby on any available surface. There was just enough floor space to get to the bed. Though, given how tired he'd been last night when they'd finally settled, he thought he could have slept on the floor somewhere if necessary. It was Tuesday, wasn't it? He glanced at his watch – ten past six – and he lay back down, staring at the ceiling.

The previous evening still felt unreal, like something out of a movie. They had been at Charles de Gaulle airport, drinking yet another coffee to pass the time before their flight, when he'd heard his name on the loudspeaker system. The appeal had been made in French then English and it had taken him a moment to register that it really meant him. No-one had ever paged him before. Hannah, lifting her head with a frown from the book she was reading, was quicker on the uptake.

'That's you,' she said. 'Go on. There can't be another Nathan Bright here.'

Half an hour and a phone call to Eric later and they were in a taxi, heading back into central Paris.

Eric had welcomed them to the apartment as if he hadn't seen them for years, embracing them, offering drinks, offering food.

'Have you eaten? I've still got most of the stuff you bought last week, Hannah. I haven't eaten much of it. Please, help yourselves. Whatever you want.'

He was over-energised, talking too fast, slipping back into French, then apologising to Nathan for it. Eric was nothing if not a good host. It was one of the things Nathan liked about him. He insisted they ate then made themselves comfortable before he'd talk. On the phone he'd told Nathan that he had an emergency and he needed the man's help. He'd refused to be more explicit, apologised for the inconvenience, and said he'd make sure they weren't out of pocket over their flights but could they come back to see him. Straight away. He didn't want to talk over the phone.

It was after ten by the time they'd finally eaten, cleared away, and were all installed on the two sofas in his *salon*. Eric had got the cognac out again.

'So what's happened?' Hannah said, never one to waste time on preamble. 'They've been in touch again, haven't they?

174

Why did you ask for Nathan? *Papa*, will you please tell us what's going on?'

'Yes.'

Eric still hesitated, as though, having bottled it up for so long, now he had them in front of him, he couldn't quite bring himself to talk about it. He took a deep breath and then it all came out in a rush.

'It's Natalie. I suppose it's... The thing is... Well, she... she's been kidnapped.'

'What?' exclaimed Hannah. 'When? How? I thought she'd gone away on holiday. Did they follow her?'

'I don't know. I don't know.' Eric's voice was rapidly rising. 'He doesn't chat with you and tell you bedtime stories. He states bare facts and puts the phone down.'

'Was it the same man as before?' asked Nathan.

'Yes, yes,' Eric said impatiently.

'And what did he say exactly?'

'He said I'd been stupid, that I'd made him do it. I should have paid him like he asked. Then he said Natalie was a nice girl and I should look after her better.' Eric's voice caught and he paused a moment and swallowed. 'He said something about the young girl who worked for me last year, that I didn't want Natalie found...' Again he swallowed. '...found in the street like she was.'

'What girl was that?' said Nathan.

'Angélique. The *assistante* I employed before Florence. She was mugged not long before Christmas. The police called me to identify her. She'd been viciously stabbed. I thought it was just a random, opportunistic attack.'

'It might have been,' said Nathan. 'He might be using it to frighten you. Don't let him spook you. You need to keep a clear head.'

'Yes, yes, of course you're right.'

'Did he ask for money again?' said Hannah.

'He said the price would go up now. He said he'd be in touch.'

'Are you sure he genuinely has Natalie?' asked Nathan.

'I think so. Virginie – Natalie's mother – called this morning. She'd got back from a weekend away to find the apartment door unlocked and Natalie's personal belongings still in the flat. The girl hadn't said anything to her about going away. It looks as though she stayed in Paris after all.'

Eric took a mouthful of cognac then stood up with the glass still in his hand and paced about restlessly.

'I told Virginie it was typical of the way Natalie behaves and I tried to persuade myself it was true but, after that phone call...' He paused to take a pull of brandy. 'I think I'll ring Mark and Florence first thing in the morning and tell them to take some days off. We'll make it an early Easter break. I can't cope with them in the studio while this is going on.'

'I don't think that's a good idea,' said Nathan. 'You should do everything you usually do. Really. Don't let them see that you're frightened. People like this rely on fear to get their way, to control you.'

'You think?' said Eric. 'You may be right. I'll try and carry on as normal.'

'You seem to be an expert all of a sudden,' Hannah remarked to Nathan. 'How do you know what these people are like?'

'I read.' He glared at her. 'Don't you?'

She glared back, then turned to her father. '*Papa*, you have to go to the police now. It's gone too far.'

'I can't. He said he'd know if I did that and I'd never see her alive again. They're obviously watching us.'

There was silence for a minute while the significance of this sank in. Hannah met Nathan's gaze.

'So what will you do?' said Nathan.

'I'll pay them. What else can I do?'

'Will you be able to?' asked Hannah.

'I don't know until he comes up with a figure. It won't be easy but I'll have to. Somehow.'

'Shouldn't you tell Virginie now?'

'What's the point? She hasn't got any money and she'll only worry. Anyway, you don't know her: she'd fuss and get in the way when what I need to do is think. She'd probably talk too and that's the last thing we need.'

They hadn't said much after that. Some long silences, a few desultory remarks, an attempt to sound positive about the situation though none of them felt it. Before retiring to bed, Nathan reiterated his opinion that Eric should carry on as normally as possible and Hannah told him to get some sleep.

'It'll all sort out,' she'd said reassuringly, offering an unconvincing smile. 'I'm sure it will.'

Now, with too much going on in his head and unable to settle, Nathan sat up on the side of the bed. He'd kill for a cup of coffee. Would he disturb anyone if he went to the kitchen and made one? He shrugged on a tee-shirt and padded upstairs. He looked at the filter machine but searched for instant coffee instead and found some at the back of a cupboard. He'd just filled the kettle and put it to boil when Hannah joined him, the tie of her cotton dressing gown loosely knotted round her waist.

'I thought I heard you come up.'

'I wanted a coffee. Couldn't sleep?'

She shook her head. 'You?'

'Some.'

He added more water to the kettle and set it to boil again. Hannah leaned against the cupboards.

'This is serious, Nathan.'

177

'It is. Have you had any brainwaves about what we should do?'

'None. I can't get what happened to me out of my head. I feel responsible. If they'd taken me, Natalie would have been safe.'

'That's ridiculous. You can't think that it was your fault. You fought back; it was the natural thing to do. And whichever of you had been taken, your father's problem would have been the same.'

She frowned. 'I want to go to the police.'

'I do too but I don't think we can go behind your father's back. If anything happened to Natalie because we did...'

'We'd never forgive ourselves,' she finished for him. She paused. 'And he'd never forgive me. You notice it was you he asked for at the airport, not me?'

'He was panicking. He wanted a man because men fight. Not that I'm much help in that department: I've never been one for brawling. But he also wanted someone not involved, I imagine.' She was looking at him doubtfully. 'It was practical not personal, Hannah.'

The kettle boiled. Nathan poured water onto a teabag in one of Eric's large breakfast cups and onto a spoonful of instant coffee in another. Hannah produced a carton of long-life milk from the fridge for his coffee but took her tea black. She looked round and listened for a moment. There was no sign of Eric. He'd probably stayed up late, drunk too much cognac and was still out for the count.

'The thing is,' she murmured, cradling the cup, 'that even if he does everything they say, there's no guarantee that Natalie will be released alive.'

Her eyes looked even bigger than usual, searching his, anxious, pleading. She wanted him to tell her that she was wrong, but she wasn't and she wouldn't have believed him if

178

he'd told her otherwise.

'I do read too,' she said, when he didn't reply.

*

She wasn't sure how long she'd been there. They had blindfolded her and tied her hands behind her back so she couldn't take it off. There was nothing in the room to give any indication. There was no window as far as she could tell, just a single feeble electric light hanging from the ceiling. A small amount of light seeped in around the blindfold which was a scrap of fabric folded over and tied behind her head. But the light was off now. Was it night-time?

It was a small room, she knew that. When they took her there, they'd pushed her in through the door then, after three or four steps, pushed her down onto some kind of camp bed which she'd later found out stood against a wall.

'What's this all about?' she'd demanded for the umpteenth time.

'Your daddy owes us money,' the man had finally said and laughed. 'And you're going to make him pay up.'

As soon as he'd gone, turning the key in the lock, she'd got up and cautiously moved round the room, trying to figure out what was there. It was difficult without the use of her hands and she stubbed both her toes and her nose but found nothing much. Just the bed and a table or maybe it was a desk. The place had an unpleasant smell too that she couldn't quite place and preferred not to try. Sometime later they'd brought a mug of hot coffee and a chunk of baguette made up into a cheese sandwich. For the time it took her to consume them, the man had released her hands. This time it was a different guy; she could tell from his voice. He was kinder, less brutal. When she asked for the toilet, he took her arm and led her out of the room, round a corner and a few more steps, then into another room, shutting the door behind her. She'd pushed the blindfold up. It was a filthy bathroom. When she'd finished, taking her time and washing her hands and face afterwards – though there was only one grubby towel to use – she banged on the door.

'Put the blindfold back,' the guy said when he opened it and roughly did it himself. The glimpse she got suggested he was about the same age as she was and skinny, with a mulish, nervy look.

'What's the point?' she protested but he said nothing and took her back, then tied her hands behind her back again.

'Tell me why you're doing this,' she begged him, but he wouldn't explain.

'You do as you're told and you won't come to any harm.'

She wanted to believe him but as the hours ticked by, she wasn't so sure. More coffee, another dry cheese sandwich, more getting sore and stiff stuck in this hole of a room.

'Why can't I have my hands free? I can't go anywhere.' she'd demanded the last time the man had attended her, rubbing her wrists. It was the skinny one again. 'My arms hurt and I can't sleep.'

'You'll try and escape.'

'I can't, can I?'

A long pause.

'S'pose not. But I've got to keep you tied up.'

'Says who?'

He didn't reply and he tied her up and locked her in again. She'd tried to get comfortable on the bed but it wasn't easy and she kept having to move. Sleep was fitful.

Now, she guessed it might be morning again. Probably not even twenty-four hours since the two bastards had pushed their way in while she was having breakfast. 'Always use the spy hole before you open the door,' her mother regularly preached.

180

She wished she'd paid more attention. But, hell, it was usually a neighbour or a delivery man; thugs with knives coming to abduct you had never been discussed.

How long was it going to be? Who on earth were these people to her father anyway? Those notes. She'd been right all along. There hadn't been anything funny about them. This was no joke.

*

'I think we should do some asking around,' Nathan said to Hannah when they finally sat down to a proper breakfast. 'Natalie probably isn't being held too far away. She'll be in Paris somewhere. There must be some leads we can get to find her. Of course it would help if Eric told us what he knows about them.'

Eric, unusually terse and monosyllabic, had already gone down to the studio having barely swallowed more than a strong coffee and a couple of bites of a brioche.

'To find her?' said Hannah. 'It's a big city, Nathan.'

'What's with the negativity? Aren't you the one who's always rushing in where angels fear to tread?'

'Well yes, OK, maybe. But this is Natalie we're talking about. Asking around might put her at risk.'

He fixed her with a look. 'And you said you didn't think paying the money would necessarily guarantee her life. How do you suggest we save her if we don't do something constructive to find out where she is?'

'But how are we going to do that?'

'You're good at getting people to talk. You could start with your father.'

She shook her head. 'He won't tell me anything. And if I push it, he'll guess what we're doing and lose it. He'll think we're jeopardising Natalie, just by talking about looking for her. And he might be right.'

'I know. But we're damned if we do and damned if we don't. It's a gamble. Will they release her if Eric pays the money, if he *can* pay what they ask? Maybe, maybe not. If they thought they could get more out of him at a later date, they'd probably release her. But if they ask so much money that he's cleaned out, that's not likely to happen. They sound like complete thugs. That mention of the murdered studio assistant chilled me to the bone.'

'You said he was just using that tragic attack to put pressure on my father.'

'I said he might be. I was trying to keep your father calm. How did the blackmailer know that the girl worked here? It was months ago.'

'It was probably in the newspaper.'

'Hm. In the small print at the bottom of a short piece maybe. Let's say his knowledge is too close for comfort.'

'Oh God.' She shuddered. 'I wonder when they'll ring again.'

'Who knows. They're trying to crank up the tension and pressure. They might wait which would at least give us more time to find out where she is. You really need to push your father for more information, Hannah. He's the key to this. He obviously knows something about these people.'

'OK, OK, I'll try, but he keeps stonewalling me.'

'You need to catch him at the right moment. Ply him with cognac or something. In the meantime, we'll find out what we can. Carefully. You can be charming when you want to be.'

'Thank you so much.'

'You're welcome. Charm some information out of people. Flash those eyes around. I can make myself out to be a bit slow or eccentric. I'm English. They'll expect it and think I'm harmless. We can do this. Sitting around fretting isn't going to get us anywhere.'

He fixed her with what he hoped was a positive look. She needed to come on board with this.

'All right,' she said slowly. 'But treading very carefully. We're playing with dynamite here and I can't pretend I'm not scared.'

'Of course you're scared. Only a fool wouldn't be. I'm scared too.'

'Where do you suggest we start?'

'I think we start with the people closest. Anyone we can get to talk, preferably alone. Get people to let their guard down. They might know something they don't realise they know. Apparently trivial pieces of information might give us a lead. But be careful with Gabriel.'

'You hardly know the man and you've already judged him.'

'I just want you to be cautious. Don't give too much away to him.'

'OK, OK. And what do we do if, by some chance, we manage to find out where she is? These men aren't going to hand her over just because we ask nicely.'

'Let's cross that bridge when we come to it.' Nathan sighed. 'First I need to make a phone call.'

'Daphne?'

He nodded.

*

'Nathan?'

Daphne's tone suggested she'd been expecting him to call but she said the name softly, as if trying not to be heard.

'I see you recognised the voice. And I was trying to sound

all French and sexy. How disappointing.'

'Is that what you were doing?'

'I'm hurt.'

'And why French? Is there some significance to that?'

'No, not at all.'

'Is Hannah having a good holiday?'

'How would I know?'

'I thought you might have heard from her.'

'You know Hannah and me: we're not big on sharing information.'

'Oh I know that,' she said drily. 'Do you want to speak to Timothy? He's in the office and not on the phone. I could put you through.'

'No, no, probably better not to disturb him. You can pass the message on.'

'You're not coming back yet then.' It was a statement. She'd been expecting that too.

'Not just yet. I'm sorry I fudged things before, claiming illness but the truth is there's an issue in the family – quite serious really - and it's not resolved yet.'

'I'm sorry. Timothy will be too. Do you have any idea when it will be resolved?'

'It's kind of up in the air at the moment. We're working on it.'

'We?'

'Me and, er, other family and friends. Tell Timothy I'll be back and will explain as soon as we get it sorted, I promise.'

'Good.' She hesitated. 'Whose family exactly?'

Daphne missed nothing. He laughed.

'You are a tease.'

'Nathan?'

'Yes?'

'Be careful, whatever it is you two are up to.'

He closed the call and exhaled slowly. He kept trying to sound positive for Hannah's sake. He wanted her to go along with his plan but he knew there were dangers involved. He just hoped he was right.

Chapter 13

Start with the people closest. Anyone we can get to talk, preferably alone.

It sounded simple enough but Hannah had serious misgivings. Suppose it all went wrong and these people mentioned, however innocently, that questions were being asked? Careless gossip could cost Natalie her life.

Not that Hannah knew her half-sister very well. A couple of weeks ago, she'd have told anyone who cared to listen that the woman meant nothing to her. There was the blood link of course but, with no significant contact for all these years, did that really count for anything? And there was too much baggage: heartache that her father had abandoned his English family when she'd wanted him so much; resentment that he'd started a new life and a new family in France, then jealousy that he'd spent more time with his youngest daughter than he'd ever spent with her and Elizabeth. Elizabeth had never seemed to care but Hannah did. Natalie had had a father to play with after school, to ask for help with homework, to take her out on trips; Hannah had felt that loss keenly while trying to pretend she was fine. There had been days, she still remembered, when she had ached for him.

At her age she supposed she should have grown out of it but she recognised that those feelings were still there, just pushed a little deeper down inside her. She'd spent too many wakeful hours the night before thrashing it over in her mind, soul-searching, and not liking what she saw. For years, she'd been blaming Natalie – when she'd allowed herself to think about it at all. But it wasn't Natalie's fault. The girl was simply caught in the middle of the disarray that was Eric's domestic arrangements, the same as she was. Hannah had started to feel some sympathy for her half-sister and the girl certainly didn't deserve to be kidnapped and held for ransom. She must be terrified.

If they were going to do something constructive about it she needed to focus. After ringing Daphne, Nathan had now gone out for a walk. He said he wanted to scout out if anyone was watching and maybe talk to the independent shopkeepers nearby. They tended to notice things, he said, knew locals, spotted strangers.

'Won't that look pointed?' she'd suggested.

'I'll be casual. I'll buy something here and there.'

'And make discreet, probing conversation with your schoolboy French?'

'Don't patronise me.'

'I'm not. I'm just saying that what you'll learn could be limited.'

'If I try they'll feel sorry for me. Most of them will have a little English too. It's worth trying.'

'Yes, all right. But if you're going out, you can get more food in.'

She gave him a list and when he'd gone, went down to the studio. Her father appeared engrossed in his work on the commission. Both assistants were at their respective work tables and looked up as she poked her head round the door. Mark nodded; Florence caught her eye and smiled faintly. Any kind of casual, private chat was out of the question and Hannah wandered on down and out into the courtyard.

187

There was no sign of Gabriel: his door was closed and she couldn't hear the piano. She was a little disappointed but not surprised. Still in bed no doubt.

It was a beautiful spring day and she moved out into the sunshine. Bees were buzzing round the rosemary in Violette's pot garden and Violette herself was there, bending over, lovingly poking and prodding at her plants. But she'd heard Hannah's soft footfall and quickly straightened up, looking round.

'*Bonjour Madame Février*,' Hannah called across. 'How are you today?'

'*Bonjour Mademoiselle.*' Violette looked at Hannah guardedly. 'I'm not so bad, thank you. The sunshine helps my arthritis a little.'

The old lady seemed disposed to talk this morning so Hannah crossed to the edge of her garden. 'Yes, it is a lovely morning.'

'How is your father?' said Violette. 'I haven't seen him much lately.'

'He's fine. Working as usual.'

She grunted. 'Men are always working aren't they?' Violette looked down and round as if suddenly distracted and bent over to pinch out the growing tip on a stem of one of the geraniums. She straightened up again and fixed Hannah with a sudden accusing gaze.

'You're back then? I thought you were staying somewhere nearby?'

'Just for a few days. I do love Paris, especially in the springtime.'

Violette pursed up her lips as if the idea was a novel one, then looked at Hannah sidelong. 'Perhaps you'd like a coffee?'

'I'm afraid I don't drink coffee but I'd love some tea if you have any? Or a glass of water?'

188

The woman looked surprised then pleased. She almost smiled.

'I can make tea. Come and have a seat.'

She waved Hannah into her little garden and to one of the wrought-iron folding chairs which sat either side of a small, round table. She bustled inside and Hannah sat. The metal table was inlaid with colourful patterned tiles, some of which were cracked, and a couple of flies crawled over them where grains of sugar had been spilt. Hannah heard Violette moving around inside, occasionally talking to herself, but she suspected the old lady's distracted demeanour masked a keen mind. Those eyes of hers looked shrewd enough; she didn't miss much. She might have some useful information to share if only she could be persuaded to part with it.

She returned bearing a tray with two cups and saucers on it, moving stiffly and rocking from one leg to the other. Hannah jumped up to take the tray from her and placed it on the table.

'*Merci Mademoiselle.*'

'Hannah. Call me Hannah,' she said in French.

Violette nodded and eased herself down into the chair opposite then waved an impatient finger at the cup of hot water with a tea bag dangling in it.

'I forgot to bring milk.'

'It's fine. I don't need it.' Hannah grinned. 'I am half-French.'

Violette almost smiled again and picked up her cup of black coffee.

'My father keeps odd hours doesn't he?' said Hannah, removing the tea bag from her cup. 'I hope he doesn't disturb you too much with his parties and visitors.'

Violette shrugged.

'It's nice to be out in the fresh air,' Hannah remarked, casting about for something to kick start the conversation. 'I

189

daren't speak up there in the studio. It's so silent. I don't know how my father's assistants cope. Still, maybe they're not the talkative kind. I don't really know them.'

'Mark can talk when he gets an opportunity,' Violette said drily. 'That's the English one. Sometimes he stops and chats. He drinks tea too but he takes milk and his accent's too strong; I don't always understand what he's saying.'

'Does he live far from here?'

'Near the Porte D'Orléans, in a basement apartment. It's damp, he says, but he can't afford anything better yet.'

'What about Florence? Does she stop and chat too?'

'Pfff,' Violetta shrugged dismissively. 'She's always in a hurry, that girl.' She leaned forward conspiratorially. 'She only started here after that other one got killed. Did you hear about that?'

Hannah nodded. 'Terrible thing.'

'Yes. And this one won't stay. She has a young man sometimes waits for her. Only time she ever looks happy.'

Violette straightened up. A sparrow had flown in and was pecking about on the ground. She levered herself out of the chair and tottered back into the apartment, emerging a moment later with some bread which she crumbed and threw on to the paving stones. She looked round then upwards. The sparrow had flown away as soon as she'd moved.

'I was late today, wasn't I?' she said to the air around her, then sat down again. 'Sometimes they come to the table to eat. But they probably won't while you're here. They don't know you.'

Hannah smiled and glanced round. 'It's nice and private here, isn't it? Do you get many strangers coming in?'

'We get people looking for the studio sometimes. But not often.' She paused. 'There was a man here before Christmas mind you. I had a cold and was inside, keeping warm, but I saw

190

him come into the courtyard, nosing around, odd-like.' She wrinkled up her nose. 'I didn't like the look of him. We should lock that gate but that keypad thing and buzzer is broken. The whole mechanism needs replacing but no-one else seems to care. In any case your father likes people to be able to come and go,' she added bitterly. 'He says it helps his work. Perhaps you could speak to him about it?'

'I will. What did this man do, the one before Christmas?' prompted Hannah.

'Him? Nothing. He saw me watching at the window and left.'

'But he was definitely a stranger?'

'I only saw him for a moment. I couldn't tell you anything about him.'

She began to look hunted and Hannah let it drop. She drank some tea, replaced the cup and waited a couple of minutes before speaking again, trying to sound casual.

'I thought I saw someone coming here last Thursday when I was leaving. I'd been visiting Gabriel if you remember? There was a man outside and he was behaving oddly too. Did you see anyone?'

Violette frowned. 'No. Was that late?'

'Maybe half ten, eleven o'clock.'

'I was probably watching the television. I don't sit and watch for people,' she added defensively. 'I just sometimes notice.' Violette eyed her up. 'Someone came to cause trouble, didn't they? Mark said.' She paused again then fixed Hannah with a defiant gaze. 'But I don't get involved in other people's business. I don't know anything about it.'

She stood up suddenly and was now murmuring to a bird that had landed in the olive tree.

Hannah finished her tea and left. If Violette had seen someone, she clearly wasn't prepared to say.

Eric had slept little the night before. Long after Nathan and Hannah had gone to bed, he had stayed up, fretting over his finances, poring over the paperwork he held for them, trying to figure out how he could raise money for Gustave.

He'd tried to be sensible over the years. He knew what it was like to be poor, to live hand to mouth and, although when he'd first started to earn good money it had been tempting to spend it wildly, he had always made sure to keep a little back. As time went on, he had sought out financial advice and had bought his first property – 'there's always a good return on property', his adviser had said – and, when more money was available, he had put money into shares and bonds too. But the financial crises of recent years had wiped a lot of money off his accounts and his income always fluctuated anyway. From what he could see, the sums didn't look good.

As soon as Nathan and Hannah had gone out that morning, Eric had gone back up to the apartment and phoned his financial adviser to get more accurate and up-to-date information. The man he'd used for years, plodding but reliable, had retired and had been replaced by a young guy with a breezy, irritatingly cocky manner.

'I need to raise some money quickly,' Eric started by saying. 'I need to know how much I can get access to.'

There was the sound of a sharp intake of breath.

'It's never good to take money out without notice, *Monsieur Dechansay.*'

'I know that and I wouldn't be asking if it weren't important,' he responded impatiently. 'It's not your advice I'm after here; I just need to know the figures.'

'Well...' There was a long pause while the man looked into it. This chap was heavily into computers. Eric had trusted the previous man more with his paper files and folders. 'Let me see,' the guy muttered, 'some of your money can't be released until the end of the investment term.'

'Can't we do anything about that?' Eric said sharply.

'I'm afraid not. And you'll be paying a penalty to release a sizeable amount of the rest. It's the price you pay for higher interest rates, *Monsieur*.' After another pause he quoted a figure. 'That would be about the best you could do at short notice,' he said.

'I don't think that'll be enough. Could I raise a mortgage on the house in Antibes?'

'A mortgage? *Monsieur Dechansay*, that would be very expensive, given your age. And that's assuming anyone would do it. Lenders have become very wary of late. I'd have to look into it but it would take a while to organise. Your financial situation would be scrutinised and there'd have to be a valuation on the property. These people don't move quickly.'

'I don't have time to do all that.'

The call ended and Eric felt hedged in. Time was not on his side. Gustave, he knew only too well, was not a patient man.

*

Hannah had been back in the apartment half an hour when Nathan returned, carrying two bags crammed with food.

'Do we really need all this?' he demanded as he dumped the bags on the worktop in the kitchen.

'With three of us to feed and you eating every meal like it might be your last? Yes, we do.' She started to empty one of the bags, pulling out tomatoes, green salad and then a packet of chocolate chip cookies. 'And I see you added to my list too.'

He shrugged, pulling bread, butter, ham and cheese out of

193

the other bag. 'Sometimes you need stuff to graze on. There are custard creams in there somewhere too. And crisps, three different flavours.'

'Fine. Did you learn anything from the shopkeepers?'

'Yes and no. The woman who runs the *tabac* said she'd seen two men hanging around over the last few days but never at the same time. They'd both been in to buy cigarettes.'

'Taking it in turns then. Did she describe them?'

'One in his thirties, she guessed; the other maybe a bit younger. One was broad-shouldered, heavy, with short stubby hair and a tattoo on the back of his hand. Exactly. The man who tried to grab you. The other was slighter and more quietly spoken. She hasn't seen either of them in the last couple of days. They're not from round here, she said.'

'They aren't here so much because they've got Natalie now. Did she get suspicious about why you were asking?'

'I told her I was staying locally and someone had said there were a lot of pickpockets about. I wondered if she'd heard the same.'

'You knew how to say pickpocket?' said Hannah, incredulous.

'Of course: *voleur à la tire*. I brought my old pocket dictionary with me.' He pulled it out of his pocket and waved it at her before emptying the last of the shopping from his bag onto the counter. 'What have you been doing?'

'Talking to Violette. She claims she didn't see or hear anything on Friday night but I think she might have. Either way, she's not saying. She's either scared or doesn't want to get involved. She did see someone in the courtyard before Christmas but said she couldn't describe him. Mark often chats with her apparently. Florence less so but she's got a boyfriend she often meets after work who apparently lights up her life.'

She paused. 'And Florence only came to work here after that other girl was killed.'

'So she might be a plant and the boyfriend might be one of the guys hanging around, you think? It's possible. What do we know about her?'

'Nothing.'

'Mark might know something. I'll try and speak to him later.'

'Suppose he's a plant?'

'Mark?' Nathan scoffed. 'He's a serious artist. I talked to him when we were clearing the studio. Anyway, he's English.'

'Oh, for goodness' sake.' She shook her head and began putting the food away.

*

'So I guess there's been some development then?' Mark looked at Nathan expectantly.

'Development? I'm sorry, what do you mean?'

Florence had left early, apparently pleading a dentist's appointment, and Eric was at his work table at the other end of the studio, working on his commission. Unsurprisingly he appeared to be struggling to concentrate and kept staring into mid-air.

'I mean,' said Mark, eyebrows raised, but dropping his voice, 'that there's something going on. You and Hannah are back here. I thought Hannah had left. I'm not a fool, Nathan. Something's going on. Thieves don't usually break into places like this. What's here for them? And so much vandalism. I'm guessing Eric has some unhappy friends. He's upset somebody. And now Hannah's back and you're here too. What's it all about?'

Nathan grinned. 'Nothing sinister. Work's quiet so we

decided to extend our holiday and Eric's let us stay over.'

'If you say so.'

'Why? Would you expect Eric to upset someone?'

Mark pulled a face, glancing across at his employer. 'No. He's a stickler for his work but he's not a bad sort. Pays on time. Expects you to work but he's fair if you do. Good teacher too.'

'And you're doing a watercolour? Is that your preferred medium?'

'Eric encouraged me. He said it's a good way to get ideas down quickly, to work out the colour balance and areas that need detail before moving on and developing a bigger picture.'

'I see.' The sound of piano music drifted up to them through the windows from the courtyard. 'I imagine that music might be distracting sometimes.'

Mark shrugged. 'It doesn't bother me, to be honest. You get used to it.'

'Do you know Gabriel?'

'Just to exchange the time of day with. Why?'

'I just wondered. He seems to live a removed kind of life. I don't think I'd like it.'

'I suppose that's musicians for you – they live in their own world. I've no idea what he gets up to. Sorry I need to concentrate here.'

Mark had been mixing colours in one of the reservoirs of a large compartmentalised ceramic palette. Now he loaded a brush with water and, using broad strokes, began to wet the stretched paper on his board, starting at the top and slowly covering the sky area of his drawing, carefully avoiding a couple of building shapes loosely sketched in on the horizon.

Nathan watched for a moment then wandered off to glance over Florence's work-table. She had been preparing a canvas with gesso for Eric and it had been left to dry. There was little that seemed personal to her lying around on the table, nothing that offered any insight into the woman. There was a sketch pad – an essential accoutrement for any artist – but the drawings in it were little more than doodles. There appeared to be no particular planning or development of her ideas in it. It looked completely haphazard, like something a bored schoolchild might do in the margins of an exercise book.

He returned to Mark who had finished the wash and was now perched on his stool, studying the preparatory drawing he'd made, waiting for it to soak in.

'Doesn't Florence do much art work of her own?' Nathan enquired.

Mark shook his head. 'Not really. You see Eric needs assistants to do the more mundane jobs and leave him free to paint. But assistants – that is most studio assistants – have aspirations of their own. They work for a basic wage but also get taught by the accomplished artist. I guess you know this since you're an art restorer? Anyway, I've been here longer and I'm more advanced. I've learnt a lot. Florence is the newcomer. By the time I'm ready to move on, maybe start my own studio, she'll take over as senior assistant and he'll take on someone new. Except...' He hesitated. '...well, I'm not sure Florence is in it for the long haul.'

'What makes you say that?'

'Just an impression. She's not that committed. I'm not sure why she's here. She spends more of her time mooning over some chap she's keen on.'

'Who's that?'

'I don't know. She doesn't like to talk about him. Her father wouldn't approve, she says.' Mark leaned down to look at the damp paper from the side to see if the water still looked glossy on the surface or if it had sunk in. 'Nearly.' He straightened up. 'You sound suspicious. Do you think her boyfriend might be involved in some way with this vandalism and stuff?'

'I've no idea. What do you think?'

'It had crossed my mind. He sounds a bit of a jerk and never has any money. Sorry, I think I need to crack on and get the colour on.'

He dipped his brush in the mixed colours, a soft but vibrant blue, and began to wash it on the damp paper starting at the top. It sank in and feathered pleasingly and Nathan left him to it.

He glanced at Florence's table again as he headed for the stairs. Could small, defensive Florence really be caught up with a brutish gang of kidnappers? Perhaps if she was completely smitten with one of them. Maybe they should try following her when she met this boyfriend of hers? But it would be hard to do without being seen and that could be disastrous.

Frankly, Nathan found the scenario unlikely. If someone was in with the kidnappers, it was more likely to be Gabriel – he was sly and smooth and calculating. It would be good to know more about that man.

Chapter 14

How long was Eric going to have to wait for Gustave to 'be in touch' again? Time was dragging painfully. He dreaded the next call but badly wanted to get it over with too, just so he could plan, or negotiate, do something. Anything.

Hannah and Nathan cooked a meal for them all on the Tuesday evening – a surprisingly good beef casserole with roast potatoes and green beans – and Eric opened a bottle of wine and he and Nathan discussed varnishes at length, their clarity and their longevity, as if it were the only thing that preoccupied them. In fact they all talked about anything and everything except the kidnapping. When the first bottle of wine was finished, Eric opened a second; he needed it.

He'd intended to discuss the situation with them, to explain how tricky his finances were and how difficult it would be to pay a big ransom, but he struggled to articulate it. He had come up with a plan, an outrageous idea really, and he didn't think it would work and was terrified of what that might mean.

In his head, he kept going back in time to a dark, hungry night and a nerve-stretching creep towards the silhouette of a large, elegant house. It was an image which he'd carried with him for decades, but he'd always managed to put it away from him, tidily boxed and locked away in a folder labelled *Don't go there*. Now the image had broken out and seemed to lurk incessantly at the corners of his mind. Even the wine wasn't helping and all three of them were like cats walking on hot coals. When the phone rang just before eleven, Hannah physically jumped.

Eric had kept the handset beside him all evening. He grabbed it but his mouth was suddenly like sandpaper and he ran a dry tongue ineffectually over his lips before answering.

'*Âllo, oui?*'

'So Eric, after...'

'I haven't got it.'

'You don't know what I want yet.'

Eric launched himself to his feet and began to pace about. 'It doesn't matter. It would take me weeks to get together any significant money.' His voice rose. 'Months maybe, do you hear? You can't keep my daughter shut up for that length of time.'

'I can do what I want, Eric. I'm the one calling the shots, remember. And I want eight hundred thousand francs now and it'll keep going up if you keep stalling.'

Eric stopped pacing abruptly. 'I want to speak to Natalie. How do I know you've got her? Let me speak to her.'

He heard the phone being put down and odd noises from further away. It was a couple of minutes later when the phone was picked up again.

'*Papa*? Is that you?'

'Natalie *chérie*. Are you all right? Have they hurt you?'

'No, I'm OK. It's horrible here though *Papa*. They...'

'Right,' Gustave said abruptly into the receiver. 'Now you know we have her and she's fine. So it's time to pay up. I want eight hundred thousand in small denominations.'

'Look, I told you that I didn't take the stuff and it's true. It's true, Gustave. It's still there for all I know. In fact it's bound to be. I hid it well, then ran. When the news broke about the break-in, nothing was said about finding the loot, just that

200

a load of treasures had been stolen. But I can tell you where I hid it and you can get it and sell it. You'll make far more money than you can get from me, especially selling at today's prices. I've looked at every way I can to raise money and I just can't do it. It's the truth. But I'll tell you where the stuff is. It's so long ago, everyone will have forgotten about it now so it'd be easy to sell.'

'It'd have to be. Because if we get caught, you're going down too Eric. And you know what for.'

Eric didn't reply. Gustave had gone quiet and all he could hear were a couple of muffled voices talking hurriedly in the background. He glanced at his two companions. Hannah was translating what she'd heard him say to Nathan.

Suddenly Gustave was talking in his ear again.

'There's no way we're going to follow some wild goose chase, Eric. You're probably leading us into a trap. I can't believe the stuff will still be there after all this time, but hey, if that really is what you did with it, I'm prepared to consider it. But you can go and find it yourself and when you've got it, we'll arrange a drop. You go and collect it, then we'll have something to talk about.'

'But that'll take time. It's been so long. Can't you release Natalie? I'll find it, I promise Gustave, and you can have it all.'

'Natalie stays with me. I don't trust you as far as I could throw you, Eric, and you've got nothing to bargain with. I'll give you till Friday. You either get the money together or you get the loot. And when you think of double-crossing me or going to the police, just remember the body of that girl in the street.'

'Don't hurt Natalie. Please. If you touch her I'll...'

He heard the phone go dead and stood, staring into space.

'What?' he heard Hannah say. 'What did you hide, *Papa*?'

He shook his head. 'This isn't a good time to explain. It's

201

nothing. I... Look, it's getting late and I need time to think. I'm going to bed. I'll sleep on it. I think you should get some rest too.'

'What?' Hannah exploded. 'You can't just leave it at that.'

But he put the phone back on its base unit, ignoring her growing indignation and walked away and down the stairs to his bedroom, shutting the door firmly behind him.

*

Hannah wanted to go after him but Nathan stopped her.

'Let him go. He's shocked and upset and needs to sort it out in his own mind.'

'But he's not been frank with us. Something clearly happened, years ago now, and he's not saying what it was. He was talking about something he'd hidden.'

'I know. But he must have a reason.'

'It was illegal, that's the reason.'

'Almost certainly. At the risk of sounding like I'm saying "I told you so", I did keep questioning how legitimate your father was.'

She rolled her eyes. 'Thanks. I thought you said you liked him.'

'I do.'

'Anyway, he is legitimate. He's a legitimate artist. He works and he pays his staff and he pays his bills. He's talking about something that happened years ago.'

'Exactly. And you don't keep something bottled up for decades and then spill it easily. Let him sort his head out. Look, there's still some wine left. Shall we finish it? Let's just try and unwind.'

'No, thanks.' She flapped an impatient hand. 'I'm going to bed too. I need to think. I'll see you in the morning.'

A short time later, she heard Nathan use the bathroom and go to his room then the apartment sank into silent slumber. Hannah didn't. She sat up in bed and all the conflicting thoughts circling in her head refused to let her settle. On the contrary she wilfully worried at them, sure that something useful would materialise if she pushed and chewed at them long enough. It didn't; she just became more frustrated. At heart she knew she was fighting the idea that her father had done something so illegal, so awful, that it had come back to haunt him and create this dilemma. It couldn't be true. But clearly it was.

In the end, she tried to quell her agitation by reading but failed to concentrate. She attempted a crossword; the clues seemed meaningless.

It was near one in the morning when she heard a door opening and got off the bed to creep to her own door. She opened it a crack, just in time to see her father's heels disappearing up the stairs. For a moment she stood there, motionless, then grabbed her cotton wrap and followed him.

She found him in the kitchen where, ever the tidy one, Nathan had replaced the half-emptied wine bottle and the dirty glasses. Eric had taken a fresh glass out of the wall cupboard and was pouring wine into it. Hannah cleared her throat and he turned, surprise and then discomfort etched on his face.

'Hannah.' He forced a smile. 'Couldn't you sleep either?' He glanced at the bottle and seemed to fight some internal battle. 'Care to join me in a glass of wine?'

'Sure. Why not?'

She'd replied in English, she wasn't sure why. Distancing herself from him perhaps.

Eric poured out the remaining wine evenly between two glasses and offered her one.

'Thank you,' she said crisply, again in English. 'Shall we sit?'

She led the way through to the *salon,* took a seat on one of the sofas and watched her father sit on the one opposite. He cradled his wine glass and stared into its burgundy depths.

'Cheers,' she said, raising her glass.

He did the same then there was silence, and it lingered, a stick in the throat kind of silence, prickly and tight. Hannah sat back, still holding her wine, sipping it now and then, and waited. She was cross, upset, confused; she didn't dare let herself speak. Eric broke the silence instead.

'You've changed,' he said. He spoke in English too.

'I've changed? *I've* changed. In what way, might I ask?'

'You're harder. You used to be more forgiving.'

Years of frustration bubbled up inside her, took hold and began to spew out.

'You think I'm being hard on you, is that it? Expecting you to talk and explain what's going on – that's unreasonable is it? Do you know how it makes me feel, knowing that you're lying to me and keeping things from me?' She sat forward and held up a hand with her finger and thumb indicating a distance a couple of centimetres apart. She felt tears threaten and swallowed them back. 'I'm here though, aren't I? Not because you asked me but because I was concerned. And what thanks do I get for that concern? Jokes and tall stories and brush offs. And now silence. If I used to be more forgiving, it's because I was desperate, desperate to have your attention, whatever it took. Maybe I'm finally wising up and realising that I was wasting my time. It never mattered what I did, I never had your attention. You didn't care about me, about any of us. I don't know why you went to England in the first place when you couldn't wait to get back to France and start again.'

'You did have my attention.'

'It didn't show.'

'I thought I was doing the right thing. Your mother and I... well, you know how it was. We weren't right for each other. It was a mistake. We couldn't live together. So when I decided to leave I thought it would be easier for you and Elizabeth if you weren't so attached to me.'

'You thought you were making it easier? Really? Are you sure it wasn't just easier for you? I adored you. Didn't you notice? You never explained. A brief parting – you said you'd write – and you'd gone. You never did write, not to Elizabeth and not to me. It was years before you made contact and even then it was minimal. And you're still doing it. Is all this silence now supposed to make it easier for me again? Well I've got news for you: it doesn't. It makes me feel rubbish, still not worth your attention or your trust.'

Eric stared at her and his face crumpled. He shook his head slowly.

'I'm sorry, Hannah, really, I am. But you don't understand. It's complicated.'

'No, I don't understand – because you've never taken the trouble to explain.'

'Explain what? What do you want to know?'

'You know what. Why we're in this mess. Who Gustave is. Why this is happening to you. What you're hiding.'

Eric finished his wine in one long gulp and sat forward, putting the glass down. He stayed there, staring down at the floor, flicked a glance up at Hannah then looked down again. Eventually he started speaking in a slow, low voice, as if he'd gone to confession.

'I was fourteen when the war started. To you it's a history lesson; to me, it could have been yesterday. We lived in a small village, Béledon-sur-Loire, a couple of hours from Paris: me, my kid sister and my parents. My father was a teacher at the local school – I think I told you that once – just a basic history teacher and Mum stayed at home, looking after us, keeping a few chickens, growing vegetables. They were good people. Mum was artistic. She could draw beautifully but her family didn't have the money to train her. It wasn't easy for women back then to have a career anyway.' He paused. 'You know about the war, how France was occupied?'

It was a statement; he knew she did.

'Of course.'

'It was a shock to hear that the Nazis had marched into Paris, huge, but we didn't do too badly to start with. The Germans were taking everything but it was easier living in the country. There were patrols that came through but they didn't bother with us. We muddled along, listened to the radio, just carried on. Then things got harder, food and fuel were in short supply. My father hooked up with the resistance though I didn't realise to start with. And even when we found out, he wouldn't talk about it; he didn't want us involved. But we found out in the end that he was going somewhere to write and print pamphlets: anti-Nazi propaganda, calls for resistance.

'I was showing some talent in art and my mother wanted me to pursue it. My dad had reservations but she pushed and in 1943, when I was eighteen, I got a place to study at the École des Beaux-Arts in Paris. My father thought it was crazy to go up to Paris but Mum said that the art school was still running and life had to go on. She overruled him. It was true that somehow we'd all settled into a strange, adapted life, just taking each day as it came, managing. Mum said I'd be fine. I'd be a student, after all, that they wouldn't be interested in me and I had to get my education.'

Eric paused again and rubbed a hand across his forehead.

'Paris was a strange place. There was a spurious normality about it but the Nazis were everywhere. They loved the

206

nightlife and filled all the theatres for the shows. But day to day life was tough. You were watched and questioned if you did anything out of line and food was a problem. I went back home now and then, hitching lifts – there wasn't a lot of food there either but more than in the city. Then one time, my father had gone. Apparently his resistance cell had been noticed and a couple of them had been taken away and shot. He left but wouldn't tell Mum where he was going – if he even knew. He said he was heading south, that was all. My mother said she and Sophie were all right and I should carry on at school.

'The next time I came home – it was January forty-four – I bumped into a boy I'd been to school with. Not a boy any more, no more than I was, and never someone I was friends with. He was broad and strong and tricky, always getting into trouble. But he'd never picked on me and our world had become so skewed, so unreal I suppose, that it was still good to see a familiar face, to catch up on the old times before the nightmare started. Anyway, he seemed to have mellowed a little.'

Eric laughed hollowly. 'How wrong can you be? He was just playing nicely with me to get me on board for his scheme.'

He fell silent and put both hands up, holding his head between them as if there was too much in it and he had to hold it in. Hannah waited. She had never heard him talk like this before and was scared to stop the flow. In the end, she couldn't help herself.

'What scheme?'

He swallowed. 'Money, Hannah. He wanted money, said that everything we needed we could get if we only had the money. He was plausible. He stressed how hard it had been for my mother, that she pretended it was OK for my sake but she struggled, how much better I could make it for her. There was food around, black market food, if you only had the means to pay for it. And he knew how to get some money: burglary. He made it sound so simple. There was a big house on the fringe of the village. Everyone locally called it the *château*. The people there didn't mix much with the rest of us; they weren't even there a lot of the time. And they'd gone away now, he said, gone south to somewhere safer. There was just a couple of staff – a husband and wife – left behind to take care of the place. It would be easy, he said. The couple lived in a cottage separate from the house. And the owners were so wealthy, they'd never miss a few things gone missing. Nonsense stuff, he told me. Glamorous knick-knacks that we could sell.'

Eric looked up, meeting Hannah's gaze. 'Of course I knew we shouldn't but my mother looked so thin. I think she kept giving all the food to my sister. I wanted to help. I was desperate to do something. Do you see that?'

'Of course I do,' murmured Hannah. 'I had no idea.'

'So we made a plan, or rather he did, and we sneaked over there after dark one night with an empty sack. There wasn't a big moon, just a crescent which offered a bit of light but not enough to show us up. We tied cloths round our faces just in case. Gustave had brought a crowbar and a flashlight and I took a big screwdriver, just so we could force a window maybe.

'As it turned out, it was easy to get in. The house was quite run down when you saw it up close and the windows were old and didn't fit. Inside it was like the people had just walked out. They must have left in a hurry because so much was still there, just abandoned. There was no money, which Gustave was disappointed about, but there were lots of nice things. We took anything that was portable and looked valuable. There were a couple of beautiful carriage clocks, watches, some fancy figurines that we wrapped up in pillow cases and a jewellery box, studded with stones. There was jewellery too, stunning pieces. I was amazed they hadn't taken it all with them but I suppose you can't take everything if you're on the run.

'There were some great paintings too. I'd have loved to study them but of course there was no time. And bookshelves full of wonderful old books. Anyway, we'd got some stuff and I said we had enough and let's go. Gustave wanted to find more but we'd got nearly a bag full already and I wanted to be out of there.'

He fell silent again, looking down, rubbing his forehead.

'Something happened,' said Hannah.

'Yes,' he said on a sigh. 'The caretaker must have heard something or noticed Gustave's flashlight. We heard a noise, like the telephone clicking and then he was there with us suddenly, switching on lights and shouting. It all happened so quickly. So much shouting. He said he'd rung the police and they'd be there any moment. Gustave had pulled his face cover down from his face and the bloke said he knew who he was and we wouldn't get away with it. The next thing, Gustave had thumped him over the head with the crowbar and the man was on the floor, bleeding. He looked bad and I went to help him but Gustave pulled me away and said we'd got to go. Now, straight away. He pushed me towards the window and I climbed out but it was a couple of minutes later before he scrambled out too carrying our bag of loot. Once outside, he pushed the bag on me. He said they'd probably come looking for him. The police knew him, he said, so he'd go away for a while, then he'd be back and we'd split it up. He patted me on the face and said he knew he could trust me. "Good boy Eric", he called me, "with the innocent face. No-one will suspect you." Then he'd gone.'

'And he left you with the bag?'

'Yes. I didn't know what to do. I couldn't go back to check on the caretaker: I was scared of being caught. And I didn't want to take the stuff home because I didn't want my mum being involved. I ran. The house had a few outbuildings and I dodged from one to the next, trying to keep out of sight. Then it occurred to me that maybe I could hide the bag for a while. There was a derelict building, an old stable block I think. The stable hand used to live with the horses back when it was built and there was an area like some living quarters and an old bread oven in the wall. I pushed the bag in it, right to the back and shoved some twigs and stones in front of it. The door was hanging from one hinge but I managed to get it to close. Then I was gone, sneaking back to my mum's. I left for Paris again the next day.'

'And you never went back for the bag?'

Eric shook his head. 'Before I left for Paris, Mum told me there was uproar in the village. There'd been a break-in at the *château* and the caretaker had been killed, hit several times over the head. I was shocked, horrified. Gustave must have finished him off while I was outside. It made me feel sick to think of it. I couldn't believe I'd been so stupid as to let him talk me into it because I knew he was a thug and I didn't want anything to do with him or any of it ever again. Fortunately he had left the village. I didn't go home for a while after that and when I did I heard talk that he'd gone to a cousin's place in Lyon and was working down there. A few months later the word was that he'd been put in prison. There'd been more robbery and more violence.'

Eric got up suddenly and walked up and down.

'I've tried for years to put it behind me. I'd forget it all if I could but my mind won't let me. I sometimes see that man lying on the floor in my dreams. I'm an accomplice to a murder Hannah. That's why I haven't said anything. That's why I can't go to the police.'

Hannah said nothing, letting all this new information slowly sink in.

210

'And you didn't see Gustave again?' she said, at length.

'No, thank God. We heard my father had been killed, shot by the Germans. My mother died later that year from pneumonia – she was too weak to fight it – and my sister went to live with an aunt. There was nothing for me back home so with the Allies slowly winning back France and movement possible, I decided to make a fresh start and managed to get on a boat over to England. I wanted new memories, clean ones.'

Hannah frowned. 'I wish you'd told me.' She paused. 'It sounds like a spur of the moment thing, that you never meant to stay.'

'I didn't know what I intended to do. I told you I came to England to get experience, learn the language and that was true. I didn't expect to fall in love.'

Hannah hesitated, scared to ask but then had to. '*Were* you in love?'

'With your mother?' He smiled sadly. 'Of course. But you can love someone and still not be able to live with them. We didn't have enough in common. With each year it became clear that we wanted different things out of life, a different way *of* life. Anyway, after I returned to France I heard that Gustave had died in prison. I can't say I grieved. I got on with my work and hoped one day I would forget completely. I felt like I'd been given a second chance and I wasn't going to blow it. I worked hard.'

'And then Gustave turned up, leaving notes and making phone calls. Not dead after all.'

'Exactly. I didn't believe it to start with. It wasn't all lies, Hannah. I persuaded myself they were bad jokes. But he always looked for an easy way to get money and he thinks I owe him; he thinks I cheated him. I suspect he's been in and out of prison. I imagine he saw a report somewhere of an

211

exhibition of my work and came to look for me, thought his number had come up.'

There was a sound by the open door at the top of the stairs and they both looked round.

'And now you've suggested he go and retrieve the stolen goods himself.' It was Nathan. 'Except he won't go and insists you go yourself. Forgive me for eavesdropping. I woke up and thought I could hear voices so I came to investigate.'

'That's right,' exclaimed Hannah, turning to look at her father. 'You did say something about promising to find it.' She looked back at Nathan. 'How long have you been there? What did you hear?'

'The story of the heist that wasn't. I didn't want to barge in so I waited on the stairs.' He walked over to join them.

'You're right: he thinks it's a trick,' said Eric. 'But the stuff might still be there. Unless someone's knocked the old stable block down of course.'

'Or renovated it,' added Hannah.

'Or that.'

'But if the sack and its contents had been found, surely it would have been big news? You'd have heard,' said Hannah.

'I've never paid a lot of attention to the news.'

Nathan came over to sit beside Hannah. 'Suggesting the loot as a ransom was a huge gamble.'

'I didn't know what else to suggest. I had to offer something.'

'OK then. We should go and look,' said Nathan. 'That could be the answer.'

*

Natalie heard the key turn in the door and a second later it opened.

'I've brought you some food,' said a man's voice.

It was the gentler one again. She heard him cross the room then felt his hands behind her back, untying the rope round her wrists.

'It's morning, isn't it? What day is it? I get confused, sitting in the dark like this.'

'It's Wednesday. Seven o'clock.'

'I hope it's not another cheese sandwich,' she grumbled, rubbing at the skin on her wrists.

'It's ham and I put some tomato in too. I'll get you a hamburger and fries later. There's a place I've seen on the next road.'

'Good. I'd like that.'

She snatched at the cloth round her eyes, pulling it down. Every time she'd been to the toilet since that first visit, she'd been told to put the blindfold back on before she came out but she'd had enough of their rules and constraints.

'That's better,' she said, blinking. 'I can't stand that any more.'

She took the opportunity to look at him properly. He was clean-shaven with razor-cut hair, pale and spotty. His eyes were wide now with dismay.

'You've got to stop pulling the blindfold down. You're going to get me into trouble. You're not supposed to see me.'

'I'm fed up with it and I want to see what I'm eating.' She picked up the chunk of baguette and pulled it apart a little to check what was inside.

Another man appeared in the doorway, stocky and forbidding. He glared at them.

'What's going on? You should have closed this, Patrice. And why isn't she blindfolded?'

She recognised his voice. This was the man who had first brought her here, rough and heavy-handed.

213

'It slipped,' said Patrice. 'Sorry Robert.'

The man swore then shrugged. 'Never mind. It won't make any difference in the end.'

'Who are you?' demanded Natalie. 'What's going on?'

Robert walked across and bent over her, his face a few centimetres from her own. His breath was stale and acrid. She guessed he'd been drinking heavily the night before.

'Your father's being stupid, that's what's going on. He's not keen to give us what he owes us. But he will.'

He ran his fingers down her cheek then cradled her chin, pursed his lips up and considered her. A moment later he'd slipped his fingers down till he was gripping her neck so tightly she could hardly breathe.

'We're going to find out just how much he loves his darling daughter, aren't we?' he sneered, and released his hold.

Natalie immediately raised a hand to slap him but he caught her arm and held it, laughing, then walked back to the door where he turned.

'OK, take the blindfold off and leave the rope off but just make sure you lock her in when she's finished,' he said and left, shutting the door behind him.

Natalie rubbed at her neck where she could still feel the pressure of his fingers. She looked up at the young man who was now fumbling at the knot on the back of her neck.

'Why won't it make any difference in the end?' she demanded. 'What's he going to do? You've got to protect me from him, Patrice. He scares me.'

Patrice pulled the cloth away from her neck, looking uncomfortable. 'You just do as you're told.'

'Why does my father owe you money?'

'I... I'm not sure. Something from years ago.'

'How much money?'

'You ask too many questions. A lot, that's all I know.'

214

'But he's not that wealthy. If he can't pay it, what will happen to me?'

Patrice hesitated. 'He'll pay. We just want what he owes us,' he added, as if he'd learnt it by rote.

'But I haven't done anything to you,' she pleaded. 'I'm not responsible for whatever you think he did.'

Patrice's frown deepened.

'Just eat.' He pointed at her plate and turned away.

Chapter 15

It was nearly nine o'clock on the Wednesday morning when Nathan finally went to the kitchen to get his breakfast. The late-night conversation between the three of them had dragged on for more than an hour after he'd joined them and he'd taken ages to get back to sleep afterwards. Inevitably he'd overslept. Eric had probably been at work for a good half hour or more already and, to judge from the number of plates in the kitchen, Hannah had already breakfasted too. He felt the kettle; it was still warm. She'd been and gone.

The discussion from the night before still circled in his head. Eric had looked shocked when he'd gatecrashed their conversation and suggested they do their own search for the spoils of the robbery.

'But I don't know if I can find them now,' he'd protested.

'What choice have you got? You clearly assumed Gustave would be able to.'

'I was only going to give him directions. I rather hoped he'd take the bait. But I suppose I could still find them.'

'Shouldn't we try to find Natalie before going on a treasure hunt?' interposed Hannah.

'Find her?' said Eric. 'How can we find her? We've got no idea where she is. And even if we did, how would that help? They aren't going to hand her over and I'm not going to do anything to put Natalie in jeopardy. In any case, it would take too long and if I don't come up with something for Gustave soon, he might...' Eric left the thought unfinished. He waved an impatient hand, brushing the suggestion away. 'No, Nathan's right. But if someone's going to go looking for those old stables, it's going to be me. It's my problem.'

'You shouldn't go alone,' said Hannah. 'They might follow you.'

'True.' Eric nodded thoughtfully. 'I suppose I could ask Gabriel to come with me. I don't think he usually works Wednesdays. He's young and strong. I bumped into him yesterday and he was most sympathetic about my bungled burglary. Florence had told him about it apparently. I despair of that girl.'

'And what did you tell him?' demanded Nathan.

'Nothing.' Eric shrugged. 'I may have said something about old ghosts from my past being a bit heavy-handed. Don't look at me like that Nathan. I like the man. I trust him. He promised he wouldn't mention it to anyone.'

'Really Eric, that wasn't wise. Someone has been feeding Gustave information about us. Someone on the inside, someone close to you.'

'Why do you say that?'

'Because the man who tried to abduct Hannah knew she was your daughter. He couldn't have known that from just following her so someone must have told him. And the only people who knew are the ones who come here. It could be anyone who's visited and heard or guessed that Hannah was your daughter but it's most likely to be someone close to you. Perhaps one of your assistants even. Or Jeanne.'

Nathan flicked a quick look at Hannah. 'And what do you really know about Gabriel? When I talked to him he was very hazy about his background. He evades questions like a politician.'

'If you questioned him like an inquisitor, I'm not surprised he was evasive,' said Hannah.

'I agree with Hannah,' said Eric. 'Gabriel's OK. Private, yes, but I know him. I know all of them. I can't believe any of the people around me are capable of that.'

'Nathan does have a point though,' Hannah conceded. 'This Gustave guy does seem to know too much. You're too trusting.'

Nathan tutted impatiently. 'The point I'm trying to make is that it should be me that comes with you.'

'I don't want to involve you,' said Eric.

'But I already am involved. We should go at night, in the dark, or you might be seen. Let's go tomorrow night.' He glanced at his watch. 'That is, tonight. You said the village – what's it called: Béledon-sur-Loire? – is a couple of hours away by car. Say we set off from here around ten, maybe ten-thirty? You have got a car, I suppose, Eric?'

'Yes,' said Eric doubtfully. 'It's in a private *parking* a block away.'

'I'm coming too,' said Hannah.

'No,' Eric and Nathan said together. 'You're not.'

She rolled her eyes.

Now, cutting a huge chunk of baguette with the bread knife then splitting it in half, Nathan wondered where Hannah had got to. Why did she have to be such a loose cannon? In the two years he'd known her, he'd never felt quite so distanced from her as he did now - even when they'd first met and that hadn't gone well. But it felt worse now because they had been close for a while and that made this distance hurt. It was like a great divide, a chasm between them. You could see but you couldn't touch. You talked but weren't sure you could be heard or if the other was even listening.

It was his fault, he knew. If he wanted to win Hannah back,

it was up to him to do it. But given the way she seemed to be smitten by Gabriel, that looked next to impossible. He'd already lost her.

Nathan made himself a cup of coffee and took the bread and the coffee over to the table. Of course if Gabriel proved to be a rat, she might need comforting. No, that wouldn't work either. Hannah wasn't the kind of woman to lean on you when she hurt; she'd lick her wounds in private, keep everyone at a distance and pretend everything was all right.

He sighed, spreading jam on the bread. He couldn't wish for that anyway. Everyone would suffer if Gabriel proved to be a traitor. Even so, if there was something suspicious to find out about this mysterious piano player, now was the time to do it. The idea grew in his head. It wasn't about what you knew, it was who, and Jean-Pierre might know. Gabriel had played at his bar – they seemed to be good friends – and Jean-Pierre looked like an approachable sort of chap.

As soon as Nathan had finished his breakfast, he'd thought he'd go and ask.

*

Hannah had gone down the road to the newsagents but buying a newspaper was just an excuse to get out of the apartment, to move and to think. Her brain hurt, still reeling from the night's revelations. So her father had apparently been a burglar and an accessory to murder. It was shocking and she struggled to process it but, in his defence, he and his family had been starving and his own father had been shot by the Nazis. She couldn't imagine how difficult life must have been for them during the occupation. But why didn't he tell her all this years ago, not wait until he was pushed into a corner and had it prised out of him like a winkle out of a shell? And at the back of it

219

all, she couldn't help but wonder what else was buried beneath that gregarious, larger-than-life personality, what other events he might have carefully omitted to mention.

She opened one of the gates and let herself out into the street. It was dry but overcast with a light breeze. She looked up and down, checked to see if anyone was watching, then wandered up the road to the newsagent's, took a couple of issues from the rack of newspapers outside and went in to pay.

When she got back to the courtyard, Gabriel's door was open. He'd laid a cloth on the little table in his yard and clipped it on in two places against the breeze. As she walked past he appeared from his flat, carrying a glass of orange juice in one hand and a plate with a croissant on it in the other. He stopped short when he saw her, smiled broadly and called a greeting and she went over to speak.

'A late breakfast?' she remarked.

'Yes. Join me? Orange juice? Croissant? I've got some chocolate brioches too. Your father loves them. Perhaps it runs in the family?'

'No, it doesn't. But I'll have a glass of orange juice, thanks. I can only stay a moment.'

He went back inside and emerged with another glass of juice and waved her towards the second chair. He glanced at the newspapers in her hand.

'So you're back here, with Eric,' he remarked casually. 'I thought I'd seen you. And your colleague too.'

'That's right.'

He appeared to be waiting for a further explanation but she didn't give one.

'Were you working at the restaurant last night?' she asked. 'Was it busy?'

'Yes. It usually is these days. A good crowd.' He took a bite of croissant, watching her. 'You seem preoccupied.

220

Problems?'

She forced a smile. 'Not at all.'

'When I saw your father yesterday he said something about old ghosts from his past. He seemed to be implying that they were responsible for the break-in and all the vandalism. I was shocked to be honest. It's hard to believe anyone could hold a grudge against a man like Eric – he's so genial. How is he bearing up?'

'Oh, he's OK, thank you. You know what he's like.'

'Never lets the world get him down?'

'Not in public anyway.' Already she thought she'd said too much but at the same time she blamed Nathan for poisoning her mind against this man. 'Have you thought of publishing your new composition?' she asked brightly. 'Have you ever done that with a piece of your own?'

'I approached a publisher years ago, when I was very young and optimistic. They weren't interested. There are too many wannabe composers out there, I guess.'

'You should try again. You're very talented.'

'Thank you, but I think you're biased. At least I hope so.'

Hannah refused to make eye contact and drank some orange juice.

'So has your father figured out how he annoyed these ghosts from his past?' Gabriel persisted. 'Has he worked out who it is?'

'Why do you ask?'

'I like your father. I worry for him.'

She smiled again in spite of herself. 'He's not always genial you know. It's not a huge stretch to see that he might have annoyed someone. He can be quite difficult – artistic temperament and all that.'

Gabriel grinned. 'Even so. It seems like an extreme reaction.' He finished the croissant. 'Have you heard from

221

Natalie? Is she having a good time?'

Hannah hesitated, a second too long. 'She's only been gone a few days. I wouldn't expect her to call yet. In fact, from what I've seen of her, if she's having a good time, we'd be the last ones to hear.'

Gabriel's eyes narrowed. 'Really? I'm surprised. She seems quite the outgoing type to me, always talking to the other staff at the restaurant. Likes to tell us what she's been up to. Are you sure she's all right? There couldn't have been an accident or anything?'

Hannah laughed awkwardly. 'No, I shouldn't think so. And I haven't found her that chatty to be honest.'

'Perhaps because she doesn't know you very well. She's very close to her father though.'

'Is she?'

'Of course. Just as you are,' he added. 'So I'd have thought she'd have rung. She pretends to be very independent but she seems a bit lost sometimes.' He hesitated. 'The thing is, Hannah: I saw a man watching her the other day.'

'You did? When was that?'

Gabriel frowned and pulled a face. 'I'm not sure which day it was now but there were three or four of us all arrived at the restaurant just before opening for the evening and there was this guy on the other side of the road, staring across at her. I was going to say something but with all the chatter the moment passed and I forgot. It's just now with you saying you haven't heard from her that it reminded me.'

'Was he kind of stocky, broad-shouldered with dark hair?'

'Erm, yes. Yes I think he was. Why, do you know him?'

Hannah didn't reply. She'd spoken on impulse, out of turn.

'Look Hannah...' He reached across and put his hand on hers. '...there's clearly something going on and I'd like to help. Please let me. Who was that man?'

She looked into his eyes and saw an expression of such sincerity and concern that the temptation to talk to him was overwhelming. The next thing she knew she was telling Gabriel about the kidnap, how some thugs wanted money and were prepared to go to extreme lengths to get it. It was such a relief to talk.

Still, she felt a moment's panic.

'But look, you mustn't say anything to anyone,' she said firmly. 'They've threatened to kill her if the police get involved and I believe them. They're brutes.'

'Of course not. I won't say a word. But poor Natalie. And poor you, you must be worried to death.' He squeezed her hand gently before letting her go and reaching for his juice. 'Will your father pay them? Can he pay?'

'It's complicated.'

She hesitated again but what was the point in prevaricating? Her father had already taken Gabriel into his confidence, had even been ready to take him on the expedition that night.

'The thing is: my father was involved in something years ago: a robbery, when he was very young. It was the plan of this man who's trying to extort money from him. They were disturbed and left without the stuff they'd taken. Eric hid it and the other guy ran away. Now this man blames my father for taking the loot for himself and living off the profits. It's not true. He didn't. It's still there... or it might be. So if we can get it and hand it over, the kidnappers will let Natalie go. At least I hope so.'

'You don't believe them?'

'How can you believe someone who kidnaps innocent people?'

'Point taken.' He put his glass down. 'But you shouldn't be involved in this. Let me help.'

223

'No, it's fine. Nathan's going to go.'

'Ah yes, Nathan.' Gabriel's expression darkened. 'So when are you going to do this?'

He was asking too many questions and she felt another wave of panic, stronger now. Suppose Nathan was right, after all? Why had she felt the need to say so much?

'I'm not sure what they've got planned exactly, Gabriel. Look, I've got to go. My father will be worrying about me.'

'Of course. I understand. But you will let me know how it goes, won't you?'

She got up and he immediately stood too, reaching for her hand again. He leaned forward and kissed her on the lips: a brief, sweet kiss, tender and gentle and a moment later she'd moved away, back towards her father's front door with a sick feeling in the pit of her stomach, wondering if she'd just made a fatal error.

She didn't notice Nathan on the balcony above, looking down on them, watching.

*

Gabriel sat down again, watched Hannah go in the door of her father's apartment, and restlessly got up and went inside. He immediately made for the piano and played Beethoven's *Für Elise*, leaning into the emotion of the piece, pouring himself into it, feeling at one with the wistful nature of the music.

Deceiving Hannah was getting harder all the time. He liked her. He was wary of admitting it to himself but he thought he loved her. Certainly he badly wanted her in his life. He imagined waking up beside her every morning, perhaps watching her sleeping, the only time he thought she'd be still and not challenging both herself and everyone else around her. The thought pleased him and made him smile.

224

But this double-life he was leading was killing him and if she found out, he knew it would be over. Hannah, he was sure, wouldn't tolerate lies and deception. It wasn't his fault; he'd been put under a lot of pressure; he'd not been given a choice.

He finished the piece and reluctantly walked across the room to pick up the phone.

*

Jean-Pierre's bar, Nathan had found out, was to the south, on the fringes of the fourteenth *arrondissement*, a twenty-minute walk away, Mark had told him. More, if he dawdled. Mark had met the guy a couple of times, he said, and had once visited his bar. He said Jean-Pierre seemed like a straightforward kind of bloke.

If Nathan had had any doubts about checking out Gabriel, the little scene he'd just observed down in the courtyard had dismissed them completely. Hannah had returned to the apartment with a strange look on her face, at once exhilarated and uneasy and when she saw Nathan it became almost furtive. She was carrying two newspapers and had thrust one at him.

'I saw this *Telegraph*,' she said, 'and thought you might like it. They only had one left.'

Nathan took it and glanced at the date. 'One day late. That's remarkably good. Thank you.' He'd fixed her with a look. 'Everything OK out there?'

She hesitated. Why? Did she know he'd been watching her? She couldn't have; she hadn't looked up. He was tempted to ask her outright what the two of them had been talking about but stopped himself just in time. She wouldn't say and their fragile relationship might shatter completely. Perhaps it was better not to know.

The walk did him good. They had been living in a strange

bubble these last couple of days and he took his time, looking in shop windows as he passed and glancing around, soaking up the atmosphere of the city and trying to get perspective. Even so he couldn't quite get Hannah's furtive expression out of his head.

Mark's directions had been good but the bar, when he found it, was closed. Nathan glanced down the alley alongside it and saw double doors opened wide back and someone sweeping the place out, getting rid of the grime and smells of the night before. He strolled down the alley and found it was Jean-Pierre himself. He tried to remember what he'd practised saying. He was determined to make the effort and hopefully encourage the man to be forthcoming.

'*Salut,*' he said. '*Je m'appelle Nathan.* Er, *je suis l'ami de Hannah. Vous vous souvenez de moi?*' Do you remember me?

The man stopped brushing and stared at him, frowning, then suddenly smiled and nodded.

'*Ah oui. Salut Nathan.*' He'd thrust out a hand to shake Nathan's hand then spouted a long sentence which the Englishman didn't understand at all. Too many words and too fast.

'I'm sorry,' he said. 'Too fast. I don't understand. Er, *je ne comprends pas.*'

'I remember, you do not speak a lot of French I think?'

'I'm sorry, I don't. My French is slow and basic but I am working on it.' He smiled sheepishly. 'I'm relieved your English is so good.' He looked round and waved a hand to indicate the brush and the mop and the bucket he could see inside. 'So you do everything here including the cleaning?'

'Yes, I run the bar. I clean. I do everything. There is a little help but...' He shrugged, puffing out his cheeks. '...I can't afford to pay for much. It is a small place.' He brightened up

226

and put the brush to one side. 'Come in Nathan. You will have a coffee with me?'

'Thank you, yes.'

'Good. I like an excuse to stop. Espresso is good, yes?'

'Fine.'

Jean-Pierre led the way to the bar and got busy with the coffee machine at the far end of the counter. Nathan slid onto one of the bar stools and his host came back a few minutes later with two double espressos and a glass of water for each of them. He picked up a packet of cigarettes from behind the bar, offered them to Nathan who refused, and lit one up for himself, drawing on it and blowing out a thin column of smoke.

'So what has brought you here?' he said.

'Hannah told me you'd invited us to come sometime.'

'I did. I remember. But I expected you to come in the evening: you and Eric's charming daughter.'

'I was passing.'

Jean-Pierre nodded, looking unconvinced. 'How is 'annah?'

'She's OK, thank you.'

'I hope you are both there next time Eric has a party.'

'I'd like that too but we'll have to leave soon to go back to work.'

'Ah yes, you work together.'

'Restoring paintings.'

Jean-Pierre nodded, looking barely interested. Nathan paused, unsure how to lead this conversation. Jean-Pierre was only an occasional visitor to Eric's, it seemed. It was most unlikely he was the informer but he didn't want to take chances. This needed to be kept casual. He flicked a glance towards the piano which stood against the wall.

'Does Gabriel often play piano here?'

'Gabriel? Yes, he plays but not so often.' He shrugged.

'More before he found the job at Au Bout de la Rue. The customers like him.'

Nathan sipped at the espresso and replaced the cup on the saucer. 'Mm, good coffee. Tell me, Jean-Pierre, how well do you know him?'

'Gabriel?' Again the typical Gallic shrug suggesting he either didn't know or didn't care. 'A little. He is a brilliant player of the piano, no?'

'Yes.'

'He is perhaps... obsessed with it. But that isn't what you want to know.' Jean-Pierre looked at him shrewdly. 'You know, I have a woman who works here – her name is Lisette – and I like her very much. I live alone. I am divorced. But one day, I think perhaps I would like Lisette to live with me. I cannot tell her this yet, you understand, but I hope. And if a man comes into the bar and... *comment ça se dit en anglais...?*' How is it said in English? He rolled his eyes at Nathan and stroked his hair back suggestively.

'Flirts with her?' suggested Nathan. 'Pays her a lot of attention?'

'Yes, exactly. Then I become very... protective. I want to know who this man is, what he does. *Enfin tout.* Everything.'

'I see.'

'Good. And I think that you and 'annah work together but you are also good friends?'

'We are. We've been working at the same place for two years now.'

Jean-Pierre raised his eyebrows. 'But you also want to be more than friends I think.' He waved an index finger at Nathan. 'I saw you watch 'annah with Gabriel when we moved that piano. You don't like to see her with him, am I right? He is competition, yes?'

Nathan smiled ruefully. 'I see that you've found me out,

Jean-Pierre. I admit it. I'd like to know whatever you know about him.'

'Then I shall tell you, my friend.' He nodded. 'I understand. I shall tell you.'

Chapter 16

Eric drove an old Peugeot. It had been a good car and had served him well but he wasn't fond of driving. He had learnt how to drive back when he was young, when it had seemed exciting and had been useful. But for many years now he had lived in the city and a car was neither necessary nor desirable. He walked; he got the metro; occasionally he caught a bus. He only kept the car for trips into the countryside or holidays. Increasingly, he rarely used it.

But here he was wending his way out of Paris at ten-twenty in the evening, in the dark. And, sweet Jesus, the roads were so busy these days and everyone seemed in such a hurry to get somewhere. Eric was happy to go slowly; he wasn't sure he wanted to get there at all.

It was hard to believe he was doing this. For years after the break-in he'd had nightmares about it, seeing that man lying on the floor, bleeding. He'd sworn he'd never go back near that house again as long as he lived. And now this. And he couldn't chicken out; Nathan was sitting in the back and Hannah – they hadn't been able to stop her coming – was sitting beside Eric in the front. They had all pored over the map together prior to leaving. While Eric knew where the village was in theory, he hadn't been there in years. New roads had been built, many had changed their classification and he remembered little of the route anyway. Or perhaps he'd purposely forgotten.

They were driving along in silence, peering at every road sign with Hannah occasionally offering advice at a junction, whether wanted or not. The whole project was absurd when you stopped to think about it. It was like some comic caper from an old black and white movie, except there was nothing funny about the situation, only their attempts to resolve it.

They must have been nearly half way there by the time Hannah broke the silence, half-turning to look at Nathan as she spoke.

'What do we do if the thugs turn up, looking for the stuff themselves?' she said.

Eric glanced in the rear-view mirror. Nathan was staring at Hannah but didn't reply. Eventually Eric did.

'They won't. Gustave won't risk going there. I knew it was a long shot, suggesting it to him. From what I've heard, he's never been back to the village. He's too scared to.'

'But the only person who saw him that night is dead,' said Hannah. 'What's the risk?'

'It's a small village,' said Eric. 'The man died and Gustave disappeared. I'm sure most of them guessed it wasn't a coincidence, given his reputation. There won't be many of those people alive now but the story will have circulated and been passed on. That's what villages are like. If he doesn't have to be there, he won't come.'

He hoped he was right. The three of them were no match for Gustave and his son and whoever else might be around: those men were ruthless. He wished Hannah had stayed at home. And then there was the other question: what would he do if the goods weren't there?

'What makes you think the thugs will turn up?' asked Nathan, leaning forward to speak into Hannah's ear.

231

She didn't move but hesitated for the briefest second. 'They might follow us. They've been keeping an eye on us, haven't they. Have you been watching to see if anyone's driving behind us?'

'I've looked,' he said, sitting back.

They lapsed into silence again.

It was well after midnight when they reached Béledon-sur-Loire. It was a small village, a little to the north of Orléans, though not as small as it had been when Eric was a boy. The years had brought some small-scale development, mostly on the flat land to the east and south of the settlement. But the big house they'd all called the *château* was built on higher ground to the west and no amount of staring at a map would help them find the exact spot. Eric had hoped it would be easy once they were close but nothing quite tallied with his memory. He kept looking for familiar features in the landscape but it was hard to see in the dark. Luckily there was a three-quarter moon, and though cloudy, the sky cleared enough at times to pick odd things out.

There was the little shrine to Our Lady on the side of the road where someone had recently put fresh flowers, and the ruined windmill up on the ridge where they'd played as children. And here was the cemetery. It had grown considerably since Eric was a child. He wondered if he'd still be able to find his mother's grave there.

Then he came to the turn off and recognised it immediately, a single-track, tree-lined road on the right which led up the low hill to the chateau. It looked to have been resurfaced not long ago. His heart sank. There was the proof that the house had indeed been modernised by some new owner, the outbuildings all refurbished, sold off or knocked down. There would be no hope of finding the all-important treasure.

'This is it,' he said and turned slowly, reluctantly, into the lane.

Nathan leaned forward again. 'We shouldn't get too close.'

'The house is a long way up and there's a place to pull off before you get there. Or at least there used to be.'

They all sat, tense and silent, as the car chugged up the winding road. There was still a pull-off. The entrance to a path through the woods offered some rough ground beside the road and Eric nestled the car in as tight as he could under the overhanging branches.

'You used to be able to use this path through the wood to get to the house and its grounds,' he said.

'Then let's try,' said Hannah.

'Are the grounds fenced off?' asked Nathan.

'There used to be stone walls and a lot of them had fallen down. But what it's like now...' His voice trailed off.

'Do you think it's the same people who own the house. Or maybe their relatives?' said Hannah.

'I've no idea.'

Eric had brought a torch and they needed it as they picked their way through the woods, over tree roots and around fallen branches. A little over ten minutes' walking brought them out onto more level ground and the house stood over to their left. Eric stopped short. It felt surreal to see it again, silhouetted against a gently moonlit sky, the way it had been that awful night.

He was frozen to the spot.

'Where now?' hissed Hannah. 'I can't see any lights on at the house. And the walls still look in a bad way. See, there's a tumble of stones there where that part is crumbling. *Papa*, which way?'

'*Quoi?*' He forced himself out of his stupor. '*Par ici.*' He

233

headed to the right, circling the perimeter of the estate and they followed him, treading as quietly as they could. After a few minutes he paused again. 'Here's the service gateway. There used to be an actual gate here. I think the stables are over there.' He pointed then glanced left, heard nothing, and set off again. Once upon a time there had been greenhouses and a kitchen garden but it was hard to make out anything now - it was all so overgrown. Eric felt a spark of hope kindling in his belly, the first he'd felt in days. There had been no major overhaul of the estate. Perhaps this was going to work after all.

By the time they reached the stables clouds had spread over the sky, killing the moonlight, and Eric flashed his torch at them. They had fallen into serious disrepair. Weeds infested the building and a sapling was growing out of the end where the horses had been kept, breaking its way through the stone wall and dislodging the roof tiles, leaving the interior open to the sky. Eric heard a noise and froze again, looking round nervously. But Nathan had already picked his way through the empty doorway at the intact end of the stables and Hannah had followed him. Seeing no-one around, Eric followed after too, moving cautiously to the doorway. The door had long since gone and he peered inside, pointing the torch.

'Hannah, get out,' Nathan was saying. 'This place could fall down at any moment.'

'Just get on with it,' she said.

Nathan shook his head and turned to look at Eric. 'If you're not coming in, can I have the torch?'

'Yes, here. The oven was somewhere over there.' Eric pointed.

Nathan shone the light in that direction. Weeds covered the walls inside too but after a couple of minutes he found what looked like the outline of a small door. Hannah immediately moved past him, feeling her way round the edge of it, pulling tendrils and leaves off, looking for the catch.

'Got it,' she murmured and tried to turn it. 'It won't move.'

'Here.' Nathan elbowed her out of the way. 'Take the torch and I'll try.' He pulled more weed off then tried the handle again, grunting with the effort. 'It's starting to give. There. Yes, we're in.'

He pulled the door open and it dropped a little on its one hinge but held firm. Eric could hardly breathe as Nathan ferreted inside the filthy old oven and then there it was: he'd pulled out the sack and with it all the dust of the dead leaves and rubbish Eric had piled in with it. Neither Nathan nor Hannah could move for coughing.

'*Mon Dieu,*' murmured Eric, stunned. 'It's still there. I didn't think it possible.'

Nathan brought the slowly disintegrating bag out into the fresh air and put it on the ground. Hannah shone the torch on it as he opened up the top.

'It looks like it's all still here,' she said, carefully foraging inside.

Something rustled away to their left and this time they all straightened up and turned to look. But there was only the haunting call of a tawny owl somewhere towards the house. The clouds parted and moonlight suddenly flooded the grounds.

'We should go,' muttered Nathan. 'Now. We can check the contents again.'

He carefully gathered up the sack in his arms and they moved stealthily back the way they'd come, looking round now and then to check they weren't being followed. All they heard was another call from the owl and the sound of a car engine being started somewhere back towards the village. Nathan walked even faster and the others hurried to keep up.

'I feel really bad about taking this stuff,' Hannah murmured to Nathan, managing to get alongside him.

'What choice do we have?' Nathan muttered back.

Eric, trailing behind them, heard. He couldn't agree more, but just at this moment he didn't care.

Back at the car, Nathan paused and pointed at the ground next to where they'd parked. There were clear tracks of another vehicle which had been parked next to their own.

'Those weren't there when we left,' he said.

They all looked slowly round, then at each other.

*

Hannah cleared everything off Eric's dining table and Nathan took the items out of the sack, spacing them out on the table top, and they all stood back and regarded the spoils of their shady expedition. It was nearly three o'clock in the morning but no-one suggested going to bed. Hannah felt like her eyes were on stalks but still the spoils of Eric's juvenile burglary transfixed her.

There were two carriage clocks, one of them in a stunning dark blue enamel and ormolu with vivid pale blue Roman numerals. And two jewellery boxes, one enamelled and gilded, the other studded with precious stones and inlaid with mother of pearl. And there were four watches too, both men's and women's, all gold-cased, and a couple of beautiful figurines. Four silver goblets with an intricate design chased into their surfaces stood next to an elegant silver pitcher with the same design. The silver was all seventeenth century, inscribed and dated, a present or a presentation set for someone. And then there was the jewellery itself: rings, bracelets, necklaces and earrings, most of them gold, decorated with sapphires, emeralds, rubies and diamonds. Even after all this time, packed away in their hiding place, they all still had a lustre and mesmeric charm, glinting in the artificial light. It was the kind of treasure trove most people only dreamt of.

'So,' said Hannah, breaking the silence. 'We've got it then.'

'Mm,' said Nathan.

'It all looks in good condition.'

'Mm.'

'It must be worth a fortune.' She turned to look at her father. He was staring at the assembled hoard, silent, his expression hard to read. 'What did that man say to you? He'd ring again at the end of the week?'

Eric nodded but didn't look at her. 'He said he'd give me till Friday.' He paused. 'I think we should put it all away again now, maybe in a box or something. I think I've got one.'

'We should take photographs of it,' said Nathan.

'Why?' said Eric.

'I just think we should. We need a record of everything we're doing. Just in case.'

Hannah frowned. 'You think we might be double-crossed?'

'By Gustave? Why would you think that?' Nathan said scathingly. He continued to stare at her. 'You talked to Gabriel today, didn't you?'

'Ye-es. So?'

'Did you tell him we were going to Béledon-sur-Loire tonight?'

'No.' She hesitated. 'Well, yes and no. I mentioned broadly what we were doing. Dad had already told him about the issue with ghosts from his past so I didn't see any harm. And I didn't tell him any details and I didn't say where we were going, just that we were going to retrieve something.'

Nathan sighed and threw his head back. 'Great.' He

walked away and threw himself down on one of the sofas. 'And you don't see a link between that and the car parked next to ours in the woods?'

Hannah followed him and stood glaring down at him.

'You're obsessed with Gabriel.'

'And you're not?' he retaliated.

'If he's in with Gustave and it was Gustave who followed us to the village, why didn't they just take the goods from us when we'd got them, huh? It doesn't make sense.'

'Because Gustave wants *me* to hand them over,' Eric interposed quietly. 'It's personal for him. I've known it all along but I tried not to believe it. He wants me to feel scared and he wants me to grovel to him with all this...' He waved an expansive hand at the table. '...because I welched on the deal. He thinks I've had a cushy life at his expense. His problems have nothing to do with the fact that he's a thief and a murderer of course. No, he wants me to suffer and feel small. I bet they followed us to check that we were really going to get it.'

He looked drained suddenly and slumped down onto the other sofa.

'Maybe you're right,' said Hannah slowly, 'but that doesn't mean that Gabriel is involved, does it?' She looked back at Nathan. 'They could simply have followed us, like I said.'

'Certainly there's a reason why Gabriel might be involved,' said Nathan bluntly. 'One he's carefully neglected to tell you, I imagine. He's a criminal too. He has a record and he's been in prison.'

'What? No, come on. Now you're going too far. You're making that up.'

Nathan got to his feet again, making her step back. They stood face to face, glaring at each other while Eric looked from one to the other, frowning.

238

'What's this all about?' he said. 'Nathan?'

'I am not making it up,' said Nathan as if Eric hadn't spoken. 'How dare you even think I'd do that? I went to see Jean-Pierre earlier, or rather yesterday, and he told me. He's known Gabriel a while.'

Hannah's expression clouded and she turned away, walked to the table then turned again, completely unaware of what she was doing.

'But...' She shook her head. 'I can't believe it. What did he do?'

'He was in with a gang of burglars apparently. He used to play piano at society functions. It was a good way to get information about what people had and where they were or, more importantly, when they weren't there. He's adept at ingratiating himself with people, getting them to let their guard down. He's an informant, Hannah, and he was sent down for it. He has history in this kind of thing.'

'Gabriel?' said Eric. 'I'm shocked.'

Hannah came back and sat down heavily next to her father.

'How could he?' she said. 'He used me.'

Eric reached out his hand and put it on top of hers.

'We all make mistakes with people, Hannah,' he said softly, squeezing her hand. 'We want to think the best of them. Sometimes they let us down. He fooled me too.'

She shook her head, bewildered. A minute later she was on her feet again.

'I'm going to bed,' she announced and stalked off.

But she couldn't sleep and didn't bother to try. She propped herself up on pillows and sat there, playing over the last few days with Gabriel, wondering how she could have been so naive. It wasn't as though it was the first time a man she'd liked had proved to be a rat but this time she'd thought they'd had something special, that Gabriel was different. At

239

her age she should have known better.

She ran her hand through her hair, making it stick up wildly. How could she have been so stupid? Indignation and anger bubbled up inside her and she was tempted to go down and confront him right now, bang on his door and force him to get up, to admit what he'd been doing and explain himself. But she couldn't until this was all over and Natalie was safe. He'd only deny it. Better that he didn't realise they were aware of his charade.

She eventually drifted into an uneasy sleep where a softly played piano sounded sweetly, hauntingly. It was beautiful to start with, then started to get louder, and louder. Then tormented. And suddenly it stopped completely. And it wasn't Gabriel who was playing: it was her mother sitting on the piano stool, staring straight ahead of her, tears running down her cheeks.

Hannah woke with a start. The light was still on and she stared around, trying to place herself. Reality crowded back in on her and she reached for a paperback and sat up reading, searching for a more comfortable place for her thoughts.

*

Alone in the little bedroom next door, Nathan struggled to settle too. He had gone to bed soon after Hannah but it was more than an hour before his overactive mind allowed him to drift into a fitful sleep. By eight o'clock, he was up again and in the kitchen, glad to be moving. There was no sign of either Eric or Hannah. On the whole he was glad.

He took his breakfast to the table but barely noticed what he was eating. He knew he'd been right to look into Gabriel's past but thought he'd handled it badly with Hannah. He'd never seen her look quite so shocked. But how could she have allowed herself to be hoodwinked by the man? It was obvious to anyone with half a brain that Gabriel was too smooth, too slippery.

And, for all that he'd suggested it, Nathan was far from convinced they'd done the right thing last night. Being in possession of all those stolen goods made his skin crawl. Eric insisted that now all they could do was wait for Gustave to ring but Nathan could see so many ways in which this might not end well.

Eric appeared as he was finishing his coffee. He greeted Nathan, said something about how well the previous evening had gone all things considered, sounded implausibly cheerful about it, and walked into the kitchen. The man should have been on the stage. But there was still no sign of Hannah; she was probably avoiding him. Not that she had anyone to blame but herself. A few minutes later, he went out.

Violette was up and talking to her plants again and Gabriel's apartment was shut up and quiet. Nathan opened the gate and went out onto the street, taking his lugubrious thoughts with him.

*

When Hannah finally came to she was twisted over on one side and the paperback she'd been reading had fallen and lay closed on the bed beside her.

She picked up her watch from the bedside table and checked the time. It was already ten past nine but she was reluctant to move. The strange events of the night before and the broken, ghosted sleep seemed to have settled into her bones and muscles and she felt unutterably weary.

She sank back into the pillows, snatches of something she'd been dreaming about drifting through her thoughts, an

241

intangible nonsense that she tried to put away from her.

But the formless shadow refused to be dismissed and she found herself trying to recall it instead, to give it some shape, and slowly it came back. She'd been on the side street with that odious, smelly man grabbing her from behind. Why was she still dwelling on that? She'd relived it over and over and there was nothing new to be gleaned from it. She screwed up her face, trying to fasten on what was bothering her. That smell that had hung around him – not the sweat, the other one – that's what it was. It was familiar but what was it? It was there, somewhere at the back of her mind, but she couldn't get a handle on it. She closed her eyes and forced herself to relive the moment again, to feel his unpleasant arms around her, to smell his hot breath against her cheek.

'Oil,' she exclaimed, eyes popping open as she sat up in the bed. 'He smelt of oil, that's what it was. A smell that gets stuck in your nose and you can't shift it. Was it oil paint? Or stand oil, or maybe linseed oil from an art studio? Perhaps Natalie is being kept at another artist's studio. That would make sense. Someone Dad knows.'

Except that she couldn't see the disgusting man who'd accosted her as an artist or as one of her father's friends. And it didn't fit anyway because it wasn't the right oil. No, it was... She smiled as it came to her. It was the smell of an automotive garage, one of those greasy places where you took your car to be serviced and tried not to touch anything in case you ended up with black oily fingers.

Wide awake now she flung herself out of bed, her mind in overdrive, trying to create something useful out of this information. She knew that there was a link somewhere in her head to something someone had said, and it might just be the link they needed. She grabbed clothes and toiletries and walked to the bathroom, still chewing it over and would have talked it through if there had been anyone around to talk to, but there wasn't. The doors to the bedrooms of both the men stood open, the beds abandoned and unmade.

It wasn't until she'd showered and dressed and was sitting eating her breakfast with a large cup of tea beside her that she remembered who it was that had mentioned a garage since she'd been in Paris and she almost choked on her bread. Then she heard distant sounds of people talking down in the studio and went to the top of the stairs and stood listening. She could hear Nathan's voice. It sounded like he'd just come back from somewhere and now he was coming up the stairs.

'I know where Natalie is,' she announced as he came into sight.

Chapter 17

'Where?' demanded Nathan.

'I don't know *where* exactly,' said Hannah. 'Not yet, that is. But she's at a garage. Or rather, she's in a flat above a garage.'

Nathan's brow furrowed and he wrinkled up his nose in disbelief.

'What? How do you know this? And what do you mean by "a garage"? As in a house garage or a petrol station or...'

'No, no, a garage where they service and repair cars.'

'But there must be hundreds of them round Paris. How does that help?'

'Because I know how we can find out.' She laughed. 'Isn't it crazy? I knew all along but I didn't realise I knew until now. I need to speak to my father. I can remember the man's name but I don't know where he lives.'

She made a move to pass him and go down the stairs but he grabbed her arm.

'Whoa. Just slow down. First explain to me what this great revelation is.'

'But we need to get on and find her.'

'What we need to do is be careful and plan. Tell me how you know all this.'

'Look, when I arrived, my father was having a party. I told you, remember? OK, so there must have been at least fifty people in here and I hung around and chatted a bit but mostly I stayed on the periphery. I was a gate-crasher. But I listened and I overheard all sorts of conversations, like you do.

'And there was a woman asking a man if he knew of any apartments to let and he said no. But then he turned to the man behind him – I'm sure he called him Antoine – and said didn't he have an apartment somewhere to let? And Antoine said he had but he'd let it out a few days ago. To three blokes who'd already paid in advance. Just a short let. He said it was over a garage but the garage isn't being used at the moment. He was looking for someone to take it on.

'And the thing is Nathan, I've remembered the smell I got from that man who tried to grab me: it was oil. Car oil. Like from a garage. OK, don't look at me like that. I know it sounds a bit tenuous. But it's got to be the same people; it's too much of a coincidence. Three men? Recently let? So now I need to ask Dad where Antoine's flat is and we can track them down.'

He kept hold of her arm, not letting her down the stairs.

'Be careful who's listening,' he said. 'The walls have ears. And don't mention any of this to Gabriel.'

She shook his hand off angrily. 'What do you take me for?'

Nathan watched her run down the stairs. Hannah did sometimes get carried away but in the past her instincts had been good. It was a promising lead. And knowing where Natalie was would be a major breakthrough, but knowing what to do about it, that was another matter.

*

Antoine Fabron ran a small studio and workshop in the tenth arrondissement near the Gare de l'Est, two metro trains from where Eric lived. He was a stained-glass artist, making

245

decorative pieces and door and window installations as well as occasional larger-scale commissions. That's what Eric had told Hannah when she'd gone down to the studio and asked about him, moving in close to her father and speaking softly.

'Can we trust him?' she'd said. She glanced across to Mark and Florence. 'And keep your voice down.'

Eric frowned. 'Can we trust Antoine?' he muttered. 'Of course we can. I've known him for more than twenty years.'

'That's no reason. You've known Gustave a lot longer than that and he's a crook.'

Eric shrugged dismissively. 'But he always was, Hannah. Antoine's OK. He's a brilliant artist. People underestimate what's involved in producing art glass you know. It takes a lot of planning and a keen eye. And patience.'

Hannah smiled indulgently. Antoine's talent as an artist clearly made him unimpeachable in her father's eyes.

'But why do you need to see Antoine?' Eric added.

She dropped her voice still further, leaning forward to murmur in her father's ear.

'It's a long story but he might have a lead to where Natalie is being held.'

'Antoine? But he...'

'He owns a flat which he lets out. It's over a garage. Just trust me on this. Do you know where this flat is?'

'Me? No.'

'Then I need to speak to Antoine.'

'Hannah, I don't want you doing anything rash.'

'I won't.'

Ten minutes later she'd slipped out of the apartment while Nathan was in the bathroom. He'd wanted to come along but she was determined to do this alone. She was the one who'd messed up with Gabriel and she needed to make amends.

Antoine's workshop was one of six in an old converted

fire station. The place was subdivided with partitioning but each unit was open at the top and a mixture of sounds, voices and music filled the air. A sign on the wall at the entrance displayed a map and who was currently using each of the units. Hannah studied it and made for the workshop at the rear on the right. The door was open and Antoine, a big, broad-shouldered man encased in a huge navy apron, was bending over a table, meticulously marking out a shape on a piece of blue sheet glass while a radio played softly in the background. She waited until he'd finished and had straightened up before speaking.

'*Monsieur Fabron*? Could I talk to you for a few minutes?'

Antoine looked round.

'I'm afraid I've got a waiting list for commissions,' he said. 'But there's a display of my ready-made work in the shop at the end of the hall if you'd like to take a look.'

'I'm sorry, I've not come about your work. I'm Hannah. I'm Eric Dechansay's daughter. I saw you at his party last week. Perhaps you remember me?'

Antoine's eyes widened. 'Eric's daughter? I remember you, yes, but I didn't realise you were his daughter.' He nodded, looking her up and down. 'He never told us he had another beautiful daughter, though you're just what I might have expected. He's a rascal, that man. What a dark horse. Coffee?' He pointed to a jug of filter coffee sitting on a hot plate.

'No thanks. I won't keep you long. I just want a quick chat.'

'No problem. Please, have a seat.'

He perched on a high wooden stool and Hannah saw a battered pine chair by the wall, and sat on it. Antoine regarded her quizzically.

'I understand you have a flat which you let out,' she said.

247

He shook his head.

'I can't help you there. It's already let out and there are others queueing for it.'

'No, I don't want to rent it. I want to know who you've let it to.'

His eyes narrowed. 'Why?'

She hesitated. 'I can't say why but it is important that I find out. It's important to my father.'

He didn't immediately respond, studying her face. 'Is this one of Eric's practical jokes? Because, you know, I don't go in for that. Some of the others love that stuff but I don't.'

'It's not a joke. I promise.' She fixed her gaze on him with as earnest an expression as she could muster. 'It's serious, and it's urgent or I wouldn't ask. I thought I overheard you tell someone that three men had taken it. Is that right?'

He pursed up his lips and nodded slowly. 'OK, yes. The lease was signed by a young guy, in his twenties I'd guess. Patrice Dubois his name is. He didn't say much and the rent was paid in advance by an older man, maybe his father.' He paused. 'I didn't like the look of the older guy if I'm honest, none of them in fact, but I need the money and the place isn't much. He said they wouldn't want it beyond the end of this month.'

'And there were only three of them?'

'Yes. Why?'

'What does the flat consist of?'

'It's a good size. It's got three bedrooms, a living area and kitchen, and a bathroom. But it's a dump and it's over a garage, see. It belonged to an uncle who left it to me when he died last year. He used to rent both the flat and the garage to the mechanic who ran the place, but he moved out a couple of years ago. I should probably try and sell it. I don't know what I'd get for it though.'

'Can you tell me where it is exactly?'

His eyes narrowed again. 'You're not going to cause me any trouble, are you, 'annah? 'Cause I really don't need any trouble.'

'I am not going to cause you any trouble,' she said firmly and sincerely hoped she was right.

Walking back through the gates into Eric's courtyard nearly an hour later, Hannah saw Gabriel sitting out on his terrace, a coffee on the table beside him. He stood up as she drew near and smiled a greeting.

'I was hoping to see you,' he said.

'And here I am.'

'I'm glad. Have an orange juice? Or a cup of tea? You see it's breakfast time again.' He waved a hand towards an empty plate. 'I have more croissants and brioches inside if you'd like.'

'No, I'm fine thanks. Maybe a tea though.'

'Coming up.'

She installed herself in the spare chair while Gabriel disappeared inside. She'd decided to play along with Gabriel's little game but she wasn't going to get stung this time. She thought her disenchantment and sense of betrayal would give her all the protection she needed against those bewitching brown eyes.

He returned with a tray.

'I thought you might change your mind,' he said, putting it on the table. It held a cup of hot water with a teabag dangling in it and a plate with two croissants and two brioches on it.

'You think I'm fickle then?' she said in English as he removed the cup and saucer and placed it beside her.

He looked at her blankly. 'Fickle?'

'Sorry,' she said and changed to French. '*Capricieuse.*'

'I can't believe that you are,' he said warmly. 'Not for a moment.'

'I think perhaps you don't know me very well.'

'I'd like to.'

She smiled enigmatically and extracted the tea bag from the cup.

Gabriel glanced round the courtyard. Violette had gone indoors but still he dropped his voice.

'Tell me about Natalie. Is there any news? How did it go last night?'

'I'm too embarrassed to say.'

'Don't be.' He leaned forward in his chair and put out a hand to take hers. 'You can tell me.'

She shook her head. 'You'll think I'm so gullible.'

'Why?'

'It was all a ridiculous joke. You probably know that my father is terrible for silly jokes? He has this ongoing game with some of his friends: they play practical jokes on each other. It's become ridiculous, like a competition to see who can be the most shocking. I can't believe it at their age. Anyway, one of them took my father in and it took me in too. I didn't go last night but he did and he said it was a wild goose chase. He didn't tell me the details, but what a horrible thing to do.'

'So your father told you it was just another of their jokes?'

'Yes.'

'That doesn't really make sense. Did you believe him?'

'Yes. Why? Shouldn't I have? Do you know something I don't?'

'No... no, of course not. That's good,' he stammered, pulling away from her. 'I mean really, it's good news.'

Hannah picked up her cup of tea.

'So you think Natalie's all right?' he pressed.

'She's on holiday. *Papa* says she hardly ever writes or phones. Not unless she wants something, usually money.' Hannah laughed. 'No news is good news apparently. But it's kind of you to worry about her.'

Gabriel nodded, looking preoccupied.

'Are you going to stay until after the weekend? Please say you are. I'm off tomorrow night and we could go out for dinner – somewhere I'm not playing and no-one knows us.'

'That sounds wonderful, Gabriel and I'd love to but I can't tomorrow. I'm sorry.' She sighed. 'I think my father is planning one of his parties again.'

'When?'

'I'm not sure exactly. This weekend probably so I'm going to be busy. He thinks it'll be a send-off for us. More likely it's an excuse for him to get his friends in and drink too much.'

'So you are leaving?'

'I have to. I need to work, Gabriel.'

Barely ten minutes later, she'd finished her tea and got up to leave. Gabriel stood up too taking hold of both of her hands, looking straight into her face.

'Hannah, are you absolutely sure your father's telling you the truth about Natalie?'

'Yes. Why are you behaving so oddly?' She frowned. 'Are you sure you're not hiding something from me?'

'Of course not. I just wondered.' He moved to encircle her with his arms and kissed her softly on the lips. She didn't stop him. 'I just don't want to see you get hurt.'

'That's an odd thing to say. But I'm glad if that means you don't plan to hurt me.'

''annah, darling, I couldn't hurt you. Truly I couldn't.' He hesitated. 'And I don't want you to leave. We could make it, you and I. Don't you think? We're birds of a feather, restless, always looking for the next adventure. Why don't we go on this voyage together?'

'And what would we live on?'

'We'd manage. I make a living. You have many talents;

251

you'd find work. Do you want to be stuck in a rut for the rest of your life, working for people who don't appreciate you? The same routines, day in, day out? I can't see it, can you?'

Their eyes locked and she found herself transfixed by him again. She wanted to believe in his honesty so much it was like a physical pain. Her flippancy deserted her.

'Do you mean it?' she asked.

'Of course I mean it.'

'I'd have to think about it.' She pulled a hand free and gently pushed him away. 'Sorry, I must go.'

'Promise you will think about it.'

'I will.' She nodded, still looking at him as she moved away.

Going back up to the apartment, her thoughts were more confused than ever.

*

Every hour felt like a day, waiting on the next call. Eric did what he always did when times were hard: he immersed himself in his work. It was a godsend, a way to slip into another place for a while, somewhere free from the anxiety and fear which gnawed at him.

Sitting round the dinner table on the Thursday night, Hannah told him about her meeting with Antoine and explained why she was convinced that his flat was where Natalie was being held.

'But it's the wrong name on the lease,' protested Eric. 'I don't know a Patrice whatever his name was.'

'But Gustave wouldn't put his own name on the lease, would he?' said Nathan. 'It'll be a made-up name. Antoine probably didn't check it with a driving licence or anything.'

'Nathan's been to look at the street the flat is on,' Hannah

252

persisted. 'Just to check it out.'

'You what?' Eric turned angry eyes on Nathan. 'Suppose they saw you? What do you think they might do to Natalie? That was irresponsible.'

'They didn't see me.'

'How can you be so sure? It's not worth the risk.'

'Then how will we plan a way to get her out?' said Hannah. 'Tell me that.'

'We don't. We wait for the phone call.'

There was a protracted silence. Eric became aware of Hannah and Nathan exchanging looks.

'What?' he demanded. 'What is going on with you two?'

'Suppose they don't keep their word?' said Hannah. 'Suppose they don't let Natalie go whatever you give them?'

'We've got the hoard from the robbery,' snapped Eric. 'It's what Gustave asked for. I'll give it to him and he'll release her. If we do as we're told, it'll work out. I am not prepared to risk making him angry playing silly games, do you hear?'

They finished eating in silence. Again he saw Nathan and Hannah exchange a look. They'd done little but argue since they'd arrived in Paris but he sensed them ganging up on him now and he resented it. And Hannah had a way of poking at things and not stopping till she got the reaction she wanted.

'Don't you think it's time you told Virginie what's happening?' she ventured now.

'No. She can't help and she could cause a lot of problems. She'd go rushing in. Never thinks before she does something.'

'But she'll never forgive you if...' Hannah stopped abruptly.

'If it all goes wrong?' Eric snorted, tossing his napkin onto the table. 'She'll never forgive me anyway. The whole thing will be my fault as far as she's concerned and, God forgive me, this time she's right. But there's nothing she can do unless her

253

latest boyfriend is an obliging millionaire, which I doubt. She keeps looking for one but hasn't managed it yet. In any case, it won't go wrong and that's that. I do not intend to explain my past to everyone.'

He thumped his hands down flat on the table either side of his plate and levered himself to his feet.

'So I don't want to hear any more about your fancy theories and plans. You will not jeopardise Natalie by doing anything you think is clever. Springing her from her captives is not an option. This isn't a movie and you are not the cavalry. Just stay out of it, do you hear?'

He got up and stormed back downstairs to his studio.

*

No longer trussed up like a chicken, Natalie spent a lot of her waking hours by the door of the little bedroom to which she was confined, listening. Most of the time she couldn't hear much. The men's voices droned on in the sitting room which was round a corner from the short passageway leading to the bedrooms and it was hard to pick out the words. Only when one or other of them got heated could she hear clearly, though they did argue a lot. Robert, the man who'd put her in this hole in the first place, was the fieriest of them all while Patrice was quieter and only occasionally raised his voice, usually in retaliation for something Robert had said. As time passed she realised they didn't get on. The older man – Gustave, who apparently was Robert's father – sounded tough and hard but kept yelling at them both to calm down. 'I've got it worked out. Just stop bickering, the two of you.'

She was trying to keep track of the days but increasingly they melded together, a homogeneous mass of time, tedious and slow and boring. She'd asked Patrice if she could have something to read, a magazine maybe. In the end he'd brought her a couple of books.

'I found these on a shelf with some other books in the sitting room,' he said. 'They're old.' He shrugged and dumped them down on the little table beside the bed.

Natalie picked them up. They were dusty and the paper was yellowing. One was a thriller and the other some sort of historical romance. She pulled a face and dropped them again.

'Hey, just read the damn things,' Patrice said. 'This isn't a hotel and I'm not your bloody servant.'

'Sorry, Patrice,' she said quickly. 'Thank you for getting them. I mean it. I do.'

She couldn't afford to alienate the only half-decent human being she had any contact with. Robert scared her. He didn't bother with her much but when he did, he was abusive and threatening. Violence never felt far away and she was frightened of him. She needed Patrice on her side.

Now raised voices had her pressed up against the door again, listening. She figured it might be Thursday evening which would make it her fourth night in this dump. It sounded like Robert was venting again.

'What makes you think he'll pay up, *Papa*? This has been such a waste of time. You thought you were being cute with him but you've given him too much slack. He might take off, have you thought of that? We should move in on him, check he hasn't done a runner.'

'No, he won't go anywhere and leave her here.' That grumble was Gustave. What he said next wasn't clear.

'Why did you give him so long, Gustave?' Patrice said. Natalie struggled to hear him. There was a pause. When Gustave spoke again, he sounded closer. He'd got up, probably making his way to the kitchen. One of other of them was always eating or drinking.

255

'Because it makes him worry. It makes him scared. By the time I ring again, he'll be desperate to get this sorted and there'll be no more nonsense. I want him to regret double-crossing me. He's so smug.'

'What's our little mole saying?' said Robert, who seemed to have got up and followed his father.

'Apparently it all looks the same as normal. Eric's still working and it's impossible to find out anything.'

'See,' said Robert vehemently. 'I told you. He doesn't sound scared. Let's just get rid of the girl and go and take him for whatever he's got.' He laughed unpleasantly. 'I'll do it.'

'Not yet,' said Gustave. 'He's a faker. He sounded bloody scared on the phone. And I don't want to stick my neck out going to his place again. It might be a trap.'

'You think he's gone to the police?'

'I don't know. I'm not taking any chances. We'll see what he says tomorrow. We still need the girl for now. Our insurance.'

'She knows too much,' grumbled Robert.

'Yes. I've been thinking about that. When we've got what we want, then you can get rid of her. But do it quietly and make sure it won't lead back to us.'

Robert said something obscene and laughed again.

'O my God,' breathed Natalie, still pressed up against the door, and crumpled to the floor.

256

Chapter 18

Friday. Today was the day Gustave would call with his instructions. It was the first thing Nathan thought when he woke up that morning, a little after seven. Given the restlessness of his sleep, he suspected it had never left his mind all night. It certainly made it impossible to wallow dreamily in his bed and a couple of minutes later he was up and in the shower. He was dressed and upstairs making coffee when Hannah appeared in the kitchen too, looking heavy-eyed and sombre. They exchanged a brief greeting and went about getting their respective breakfasts without another word. A heavy pall of silence seemed to have fallen on them since Eric's admonition of the night before. Even at the table, they barely made eye contact.

'Have you seen my father?' Hannah finally asked. She was rotating her empty teacup back and forth on its saucer by the handle. They had both already finished eating; neither of them seemed to have much appetite that morning.

'No. He'd gone down to the studio by the time I got up.'

She nodded, stopped scraping the cup to and fro and agitatedly pushed a hand back through her hair. The next moment she was up and marching towards the kitchen, and returned a few minutes later with another cup of tea.

'Try and relax, will you?' said Nathan, and immediately wished he hadn't.

'Relax? Really? Are you relaxed?'

He hesitated. 'No. No, of course I'm not, but getting uptight isn't going to help anything.'

'Well, granted, and if you've got a smart way to feel good about what's happening, do share it. I'm all ears.'

Nathan sighed and said nothing. A moment later he made himself another coffee and again they sat in tense silence, drinking then staring at their cups. Now it was Nathan who realised he was drumming a restive middle finger on the table. He became aware of Hannah watching it.

'I have such a bad feeling about this,' she blurted out, then glanced towards the stairs and dropped her voice. 'I don't trust this cheap crook Gustave to keep his side of the bargain.'

'Neither do I.' He shrugged. 'But without your father's agreement, what can we do? And until he gets the phone call, we don't know how it's going to play out anyway.'

'No. But I've been thinking about the hand-off and our options. There are three men, right?'

'Ye-es. So?'

'So if one or possibly two of them go to the drop to get the loot, there'll only be one or two left behind with Natalie. Better odds, don't you think?'

'You mean: time an assault on the garage flat for the same time as the hand-off, whenever that is?'

'Yes.'

'Your father is convinced it'll be Gustave himself who goes.' Nathan frowned, still thinking it through. 'Your theory's fair as far as it goes. Except we still can't be certain that that flat is where Natalie is. And if only Gustave goes to the drop as Eric expects, two men guarding Natalie is still a big problem. They probably have weapons and aren't afraid to use them. We don't. Either way they're thugs. Plus we don't have experience at this kind of thing and, I hate to point out the obvious, but you are a woman.'

'Thank you for noticing. Even so, I'm not completely incapable.'

'I know, but in what could turn out to be an ugly fight...?' He raised his eyebrows and shook his head.

'Weren't you the one who suggested rescuing Natalie in the first place?'

'Yes. But I've been thinking about it since and I don't like the odds.'

'I don't like the odds of Natalie coming out of this alive either,' said Hannah darkly.

'We could still tell the police.'

She blew out a long breath of air, looking agonised. 'I wish, but behind my father's back? In any case, without his involvement, what do you think the chances are of them taking us seriously? Two Brits with no evidence? And he doesn't want the police to know what he did.'

'He should tell them then, own up to it.' He felt like adding, 'like a man,' and thought better of it.

'I agree.' She gave him a warning look 'But that's his decision, isn't it? Tell me again what this garage is like.'

'OK. There's a door to the street with the number on it which Antoine gave you. I assume there are steps behind it up to the flat and almost certainly another door. Next to that is a big up and over metal door which I assume opens onto the garage workshop. I suppose there might be access from the workshop to the flat. I didn't dare try either the personal door or the metal one. And there's a gated archway beyond the personal door. I watched from the end of the street for a bit but there was no obvious activity.'

Hannah grunted thoughtfully. 'I bought a large-scale map of Paris yesterday. It's interesting.'

She got up and was gone, slipping down the stairs to her

259

bedroom. A minute later she was back and moving things to one side of the table so she could spread the map out. They leaned over it, side by side.

She placed an index finger down on the map. 'You see, it looks like there's an L-shape of units at the back of the building you were describing. They suggest work buildings to me, maybe offices or industrial units, and that looks like a small private car park serving them.'

'So there might be a way in from there?'

'It's possible, isn't it, if we can access it? It's hard to tell from this but maybe that archway leads round to the back too? Perhaps we should go and look.' She folded the map up and sat down.

Nathan went back to his seat and retrieved his coffee. 'I'll go this morning.'

'Why you?'

'Because we can't both go – we'd look too obvious. And you're far more noticeable than me, trust me, especially in a place like that. And yes, I'll be careful not to attract attention.'

For once, she didn't argue and Nathan drank a mouthful of coffee.

'You spoke to Gabriel yesterday,' he remarked casually.

'Yes.' Hannah frowned. 'You were watching me.'

'No. I'm here with nothing to do, waiting around, so I look out of the windows a lot. What am I supposed to do? I happened to see you in the courtyard.' She said nothing. 'How did it go?'

'I'm amazed you didn't ask me before.'

'I hoped you might say.'

She frowned, reached for her cup of tea and immediately put it down again. He supposed it had gone cold; his coffee was.

'The thing is, Hannah, we...' he began.

'Look, I didn't give us away, if that's what you want to know. I told him that my father and his friends have a strange idea of playing practical jokes on each other, that he'd told me that the break-in and the supposed kidnap were all a prank. I said that the trip the other night was a wild goose chase.'

'And he bought that?'

'He was surprised. Too surprised. I said, why, did he know more about it than he was telling me? He insisted he didn't but I'm sure he did. You can be happy that he is what you said he was.'

'I'm not happy about it.' He hesitated. 'Are you all right?'

'Of course. I'm fine.' She paused as if weighing up her words. 'He was still all concern and attentiveness. He wants me to stay in Paris. Or wherever – somewhere in France I assume. To stay with him anyway, wherever he goes next. He thinks we're suited: restless, wanting new adventures. He may be right about that. And then there's our shared pleasure in music.'

'But he's...' Nathan began but Hannah fixed big warning eyes on him and he stopped short. 'What did you say?'

'I said I'd think about it.'

Hannah picked up her plate and the remains of her tea and marched off to the kitchen with them.

Nathan stayed at the table and pushed the coffee away. He'd wanted to try to talk to her, properly talk about his mistake, his regret, his feelings. He'd been working himself up to it for the last couple of days but she'd cut him short and the truth was he had no idea what to say. Now, less than ever.

*

Several phone calls came through to the studio that day. Each time, Eric answered quickly, expecting Gustave; each time he

261

was disappointed. Mark and Florence kept looking up, evincing surprise and curiosity at his unwonted determination to answer every call himself. But it wasn't until six o'clock when Eric was back up in the apartment that the long-awaited call from Gustave finally came through. He'd put the handset on the dining table and was walking up and down when it rang and he almost ran in his hurry to get back to it.

'Let it ring a couple of times,' Hannah said quickly. 'Don't let him see how anxious you are.'

'And ask to speak to Natalie again,' Nathan added.

Eric flicked his gaze from one to the other, took a deep breath and pressed the answer button.

'*Oui allô?*'

The pause came the other end and Eric, all thoughts of pretending to be calm rapidly disappearing, was about to speak again when Gustave's voice grumbled in his ear.

'The Père Lachaise cemetery opens at eight thirty in the morning. Be there as soon as they open, division thirty, with the goods. You have got them I suppose?'

'Yes.'

'Come alone. If you tell the police, she's dead.'

'I want to speak to her.'

'You already have. She's fine.'

The line went dead. Eric stared at the handset then walked slowly across the room to put it back on its stand. He turned to face Hannah and Nathan.

'Tomorrow morning,' he said. 'Eight thirty. Père Lachaise, division thirty. I've got a map of the place somewhere.'

He felt dazed and wandered over to the *secrétaire* and began poking around in the cupboard at the bottom.

'I thought he'd pick somewhere quiet and out of the way,' said Nathan.

'Paris is relatively quiet first thing in the morning,' said Hannah. 'It's the evening when it's jumping with people. And a cemetery is probably as quiet as anywhere could be at that time. Plus, I know the Père Lachaise. It's huge and full of trees and tall monuments; you can slip out of sight quickly there. I suspect he's picked an area that the tourists don't all flock to.'

'You're right.' Eric had found the map, unfolded it and was staring at it as if it might make sense of what was going on. 'It's not one of the tourist hotspots. It should be relatively quiet.' He meticulously refolded the map but kept hold of it. 'I've got a leather bag that will hold all that stuff, no problem. It's old and scuffed and looks like a regular work bag so shouldn't draw much attention. I'll get it out now and put everything in it ready.'

'Are you sure you should go alone?' said Nathan. 'I could...'

'No,' Eric said sharply. 'He said I had to. And you..' He felt a sudden fondness for this obliging but rather precise Englishman and smiled kindly. '...would stand out a mile. I'll be fine. And while I'm packing this stuff away, you two decide where we should eat tonight. I don't wish to be rude, Hannah, but your cooking is only marginally better than mine. I feel the need to dine out.'

*

Hannah couldn't face sitting in a restaurant, making small talk, pretending everything was all right when it wasn't. She knew how her father would be: talking too much, trying too hard, behaving like he had everything under control. She had her own personal demons to sort out anyway and that wasn't going to happen clustered around a small table in a busy, cacophonous restaurant. She needed to be alone.

She waited until they were about to leave, then broke it to Nathan and her father.

'I'm sorry, I've got a headache. I'm going to stay in this evening, maybe have an early night.'

Nathan looked concerned. 'Will you be all right here alone?'

'Of course. No-one's going to come here tonight, are they? They're getting what they want.'

'That wasn't what I meant.'

'I'm fine. I need to be quiet, that's all.'

Eric smiled knowingly at Hannah. 'A night on the sofa will make you feel better,' he said, with the air of one who was used to women's troubles. 'A hot drink. Perhaps some aspirin?' He slapped Nathan on the back. 'Come on, young man. Let's go and see what delights Paris has for us tonight.'

Hannah watched them go with mixed feelings. She wanted the time alone but she worried about them. Oddly she worried about Nathan more than Eric. Was he ready for her father's brand of evening out? Would Eric think going on from the restaurant to a friend's place or even a nightclub inappropriate in the circumstances? She doubted it. And Nathan didn't speak that much French, not enough to get out of an awkward situation. Still, he'd invited himself into this mess and she supposed he could look after himself.

She made herself a sandwich and a cup of tea and switched the television on. Eric's television was small and old; he rarely watched it. She found a game show and left it on for the background noise and distraction but her thoughts wandered all the same.

How was Natalie doing? Had they treated her well? Hannah's brief acquaintance with her sister gave her no clue as to how she would cope mentally with what was going on. Was she even still alive? The thought chilled her. Yet again, she was convinced they were doing this all wrong. They were out of their depth. If only her father could be persuaded to go to the police and admit what he'd done and ask for their help. But then what might Gustave do to Natalie?

She was lost in these thoughts, going round and round in circles, when the front doorbell rang. It was locked, she knew; she had locked it herself. She went over to the window and looked down but the angle was too tight. If there was someone still there, she couldn't see them. All she could see were the lights in Violette's front room.

The knock came again. Her certainty that Gustave and his cronies wouldn't bother her that night disappeared instantly. She slipped quietly down the stairs into the studio, listened again, and carried on down to stand behind the door, barely breathing. There had been no further ringing. Perhaps whoever it was had gone.

'Hannah? Are you there?'

The murmured voice the other side of the door made her jump.

'Hannah, it's me, Gabriel,' he said in French. 'I need to talk to you. It's important.'

She was rooted to the spot, confused, conflicted. Maybe it was a trick – after all, he wasn't what he pretended to be. Still she struggled to see him as the enemy and her curiosity taunted her. What did he have to say now? She turned the key, opening the door a crack and peering out.

'Can I come in?' he whispered.

She stuck her head out just enough to glance up and down the courtyard. He appeared to be alone so she pulled the door back to let him through, quickly closing it behind him.

'What is it?' she demanded brusquely.

'I've been thinking. A lot.' He hesitated and glanced at the staircase. 'You are alone, aren't you? I thought I saw the others go out. Only I haven't been completely frank with you. Can we go upstairs and talk properly?'

Again she paused, then wordlessly led the way up to the apartment.

'Do you want a drink?' She tried to sound offhand. 'Wine? Cognac?'

'Cognac, thanks.'

She took her time at Eric's drinks cabinet, getting two glasses out and pouring a generous measure into each. When she turned back Gabriel was sitting on one of the sofas. She handed him his drink and sat opposite him, took a sip of brandy and leaned back, studiously indifferent.

Gabriel took a long pull of brandy and stayed sitting forward, leaning on his knees. He looked at her, then looked down at the wooden floor.

'I've...' He took another pull at his drink. 'I've got a prison record, 'annah. I used to be involved with some crooks.' He flicked a glance up at her to see her reaction.

Hannah forced a laugh. 'Really? Just a small thing you forgot to tell me, was it? Did it not occur to you to mention it before asking me to live with you?'

'I... well, yes, I suppose so. I was scared you'd lose interest in me.'

'It doesn't matter. I already knew.'

'What? How?'

'Someone told me.'

He frowned. 'But who...' His eyes lit up and he nodded. 'Jean-Pierre.'

'Yes. He told Nathan – though only because Nathan asked.'

'Your friend is very careful to look out for you, I think.'

'Because he was suspicious. And he was right, wasn't he?'

'It's true: I haven't always been completely honest, *chérie*,

266

but when I talk about how I feel for you, all that is true. Every word.'

'Don't call me your *chérie*. You hardly know me. And I certainly don't know you.' She took another sip of brandy, determined not to get drawn into this conversation. 'So you were in prison,' she added coldly. 'Why tell me now?'

'Because I still hear things. That's how I got involved before, you see. Piano players – we hear things. People tell you or you overhear something. It used to be useful to some thieves I met. I wasn't making much money back then and they recruited me, so to speak. I was young and foolish and I genuinely thought it was harmless: only rich people losing a few trinkets; no-one getting hurt. Well, that's what I told myself anyway.' He shrugged. 'I chose not to think about it.'

'And now you're doing it again?'

'No, absolutely not. I've changed. I have.' His voice had risen and he was almost on his feet. He subsided. 'But I still hear things. I know a few people...' He rocked his head side to side. '...people who live on the edge of the law shall we say, and know what's going down.'

Hannah shook her head with a wry smile. 'What, at Au Bout de la Rue? I find that hard to believe.'

'I do work at other places too, not so smart. Lunchtimes or on my nights off. I play here and there to earn a few extra francs when I can.' He paused and took another long pull of brandy. 'The thing is, 'annah, the kidnapping of Natalie isn't a joke, is it? There's talk.'

'How? What sort of talk?'

'Someone always knows. A word here, a word there. Cheap gossip among people who don't even know who your father is and care less. What I'm trying to say is, I'd like to help.' He made a point of looking at her then, forcing her to meet his gaze. 'Please let me help.'

267

Hannah looked into his brown eyes and felt the usual pull. She forced herself to look away.

'Tell me what's happening,' he pressed. 'I want to help. I want to make it up to you. Surely I can do something?'

Hannah got up and slowly circled the sofas, round and round. She thought of their ambitious and probably foolhardy plan to find and free Natalie while Gustave was with her father. She thought of Nathan saying how just the two of them wouldn't be able to cope with the other two thugs which made it too risky. But if they had another man on their side, wouldn't that make it feasible? It was a gamble: Gabriel's whole romance scenario could be a trick, an ongoing part of his act. He could be lying through his teeth. Or not. Eventually, she walked back to stand in front of him.

'There might be something you could do,' she heard herself say.

*

Only Eric would consider dining out in a restaurant the evening before a meeting with his daughter's kidnapper, Nathan thought. The man's ability to carry on his life in the face of the chaos around him was impressive. Every now and then the façade crumbled, allowing the briefest glimpses of his emotion and distress but they were quickly covered up and the jaunty manner would return. Nathan almost envied him.

Going out through the courtyard gates, Eric informed Nathan that he didn't think much of the restaurant he and Hannah had suggested; he knew somewhere much better, a small place off the beaten track where they did the most wonderful *boeuf bourguignon* using an old family recipe. Nathan didn't care much where they went. He was more preoccupied with why Hannah hadn't come with them. Was

268

she really feeling bad or did she have an assignation? He dismissed that idea. She wasn't one to dissemble, not to him anyway.

Or maybe she was.

He tried to put the thought away from him while he idly perused the menu and ordered, but immediately it returned. Even the arrival of their food did nothing to dispel it.

She had withdrawn into herself these last weeks, he had to admit. And since meeting Gabriel she had been restive and distracted. Maybe she would hide something from him if she thought he'd disapprove, especially after the debacle of their last date.

'Not eating as heartily as usual, I'd say,' said Eric in his lightly accented English. He pointed an accusing knife at Nathan's plate where the cutlery had already been placed, the remaining food abandoned. 'I don't think you've heard more than one word I've said all evening.'

'I'm sorry, Eric. I'm a bit preoccupied.'

'Clearly. I don't suppose it would have anything to do with an attractive young woman with large blue eyes, would it?'

Nathan didn't know what to say. Hannah's father was the last person he could confide in.

'Believe me, Nathan, you'll not find a better woman anywhere than Hannah. Of course, she is my daughter so I am biased, but that doesn't stop it being true. She's not easy though, is she? Headstrong, is that the right word?'

Nathan smiled ruefully. 'It is. One of many I could think of.'

Eric laughed, laid his cutlery down and picked up his glass of Bordeaux, a rich velvety red wine. He drank a mouthful and fixed his gaze back on Nathan. 'You like her, that's obvious. More than like, I suspect. Have you told her?'

'It's complicated, sir, I mean, Eric.'

'What's complicated about it? You tell the girl you love her and you make her feel special. If you're lucky she'll feel the same way. If not you have to move on. Do you think she likes you?'

'Yes. Maybe. She did.' He sighed. 'The thing is I pushed her away a few weeks ago. I was jealous and said some stupid things. Now I think it's too late to get back to where we were.'

Eric nodded sagely. 'I see. Yes, I see. Tricky. But if you explain that to her the way you have to me...' He raised his eyebrows and shrugged. '...and she likes you a lot.'

'That's the problem: I don't know any more.'

'She's not easy to read, is she? Elizabeth now, she was as transparent as glass. Hannah never was. She runs deep, as they say. And Natalie, well she...' He stopped suddenly as if he'd only just remembered the situation and emotion got the better of him. It quickly passed. 'I think Hannah likes you. A lot. You should apologise to her, say you made a mistake and ask her if she'll have you back.'

'But she's met someone else.'

'Oh well, in that case...'

Eric puffed out his cheeks dismissively and resumed eating while Nathan reflected on how futile the conversation had been. A few minutes later Eric finished eating, drained the wine in his glass and picked up the bottle, topping up Nathan's glass before filling his own.

'If you're referring to Gabriel,' he said, as if the conversation had never paused, 'that is difficult. He's a very charismatic man – to a woman, I think.' He paused theatrically. 'I can see your problem.'

Nathan winced.

Chapter 19

Hannah was sitting watching the television when Eric and Nathan got back.

'You're still up then,' said Eric comfortably as the two men came up the stairs and into the sitting room. 'Aspirin work, did they?'

'I didn't need aspirin, thanks.'

'I thought you wanted an early night?' said Nathan.

'I changed my mind.'

'Woman's prerogative.' Eric winked at Nathan then looked back at Hannah. He cleared his throat. 'But I think I'll get off to bed early tonight. I'll need a clear head in the morning.'

Hannah watched him go and looked back at Nathan.

'What was that all about? He never goes to bed early.'

'It's not that early. It's nearly eleven.'

'It's early for him.'

Nathan shrugged and moved towards the kitchen.

'I'm going to make some tea,' he said over his shoulder. 'Do you want one?'

'Er yes.'

She followed him into the kitchen and leaned against the cupboards as he began filling the kettle.

'How did it go?'

'What?'

'The evening.'

'Fine. Eric chose a different restaurant to the one we came up with but it was fine.' He switched the kettle on and put a teabag in each of two cups. Eric didn't possess a teapot. 'How was your evening?'

'Fine.'

Neither of them spoke again until the tea was made and they were back in the *salon*, sitting on separate sofas.

'I was hoping to get a chance to speak to you,' she began. 'The thing is, I had a visit this evening. From Gabriel.'

Nathan scoffed and shook his head. 'Of course you did. I knew there was something up when you didn't come with us.'

'I didn't know he was coming,' she protested. 'He just turned up. He wants to help, Nathan. It seems he knew about Natalie being grabbed because he'd heard gossip about it.'

'Oh come on, pull the other one.'

'Will you listen? He hears things at the bars and places he plays at. He just does. And he confessed to me that he'd been in prison and explained how he'd got involved – with no prompting from me. He just came out with it. He admitted he'd been stupid but he insists he's clean now.'

'Well he would, wouldn't he?'

'Are you going to listen to me or just sit there making snide remarks?'

'Hannah, you're so taken in by this guy. Just listen to yourself. You're blind to what's going on and you're usually so smart. So he admits to knowing about Natalie and you don't think that's surprising? Just gossip? Please. Can't you see past his pretty music and charming smile?'

'Don't patronise me, Nathan. Yes, I admit I fell for the guy and it's possible he's just giving me a line but don't you see how he might be useful?' She glanced towards the stairs but there was no sound of her father. Still she dropped her voice.

272

'You said yourself that we should try to get Natalie out because we can't trust Gustave to let her live. We need someone else to help us and Gabriel could do that.'

'And if he's being paid by them?'

'I don't think he is.'

'Why don't I find that reassuring? Don't tell me, you've already filled him in on our plan? How perfect for them. Now he can warn Gustave and his merry men that we're coming.'

'No. Just listen, will you? I wanted to speak to you first. I said there might be something he could do to help but nothing definite yet. You didn't think we could do it alone, the two of us, but with another man? Yes, it's a gamble, Nathan, but it's a gamble if we don't rescue Natalie as well. At least consider it. If he is working for Gustave, why would he come and offer help? My father has already agreed to hand over the loot from the robbery. There's nothing for them to gain.'

'Unless he came to be sure that the exchange will take place and we haven't told the police.'

Hannah frowned and blew out her lips. 'I suppose that is possible.'

They both drank their tea and fell silent.

'OK, compromise,' Nathan said eventually. 'Eric's rendezvous is for eight thirty. Suppose we sleep on it and get up early, say six o'clock, to see what we think then? If we decide to go ahead we can finalise how we'll set about rescuing Natalie, then tell Gabriel just before we go. If he's that keen to help, he'll cope with being woken up but he won't have much time to warn them.'

'All right,' Hannah said slowly. 'But we can't tell my father.'

*

'*Oui?*' Gabriel, wearing a tee-shirt and night shorts, peered blearily round his front door. '*Tiens*, Nathan. It is very early, isn't it?'

He spoke in his hesitant and heavily-accented English, then glanced over Nathan's shoulder as if checking to see if he was alone.

'It's not that early. It's just after seven,' said Nathan. 'I'd like to talk. Can I come in?'

Gabriel's expression suggested surprise but he stepped back to let Nathan in anyway, then closed the door.

'Coffee?' he offered and scratched his head.

Nathan glanced at his watch. 'Sure, thanks.'

Gabriel disappeared through a door at the rear of the room and Nathan could hear sounds of cups being got out and water running. He looked round the living space of the small apartment. It looked little changed from his one and only previous visit. The newly acquired piano was dust-free and gleaming while the rest of the room was cluttered and shabby. There were piles of music and even a pile of books. Nathan stepped nearer and fingered a few of them. There were a couple of biographies of famous musicians and composers as well as a travel guide to the Caribbean and a couple of fiction titles – thrillers to judge from the covers. So Gabriel actually read? He was mildly surprised. In fact Nathan wasn't sure what he expected to see. Signs of dubious wealth perhaps.

Gabriel returned with two small cups of strong black coffee and handed one to Nathan. He still looked half asleep.

'Do you want milk?' he grunted.

'No, this is fine, thanks.'

Gabriel waved his free hand to the two mismatched easy chairs. 'Please, sit.'

There was a strained silence. After being awake half the night, Nathan had come to the conclusion that rescuing Natalie was something they should attempt, provided they had help. But Gabriel? Really? Unfortunately Nathan couldn't think of anyone else to ask and, after much deliberation, he thought it was worth trying. Over a very early breakfast he and Hannah had discussed - and argued – at length over how they would set about it and then he had insisted that he was the one who would speak to Gabriel.

'Because I'm not emotionally involved,' he'd said and, after another brief argument, it was settled.

Of course he was emotionally involved; it was just that, unlike Hannah, Nathan's emotions towards Gabriel weren't good ones. Fortunately there'd been no hassle with Eric. Hannah's father hadn't heard any of their discussion and he'd already gone to make the rendezvous by the time Nathan left the apartment, determined not to be late.

Now Nathan looked at Gabriel warily.

'I understand you know about Natalie's kidnap.'

'D'une façon.'

'Pardon?'

Gabriel shrugged. 'I think you say: in a way?'

'I see. But you know where she's being kept I suppose.'

'No. All I hear is gossip. Nothing definite.'

Nathan was having cold feet. 'I don't know if I can trust you.'

'You can trust me. I promise.'

'Promises are cheap.'

Gabriel opened his mouth to reply but closed it again and swallowed some coffee. Again they sat in silence. Nathan drank too. He sighed.

'I understand you offered help. I can't pretend I do trust you but it looks like we have to. We're scared that the people holding Natalie won't release her just because they've got the goods they asked for.'

'Why wouldn't they?'

'Because she knows them all. Because she's a witness. Perhaps just because it's less trouble. Anyway, we want to try to get her out.'

'You are going to rescue her?' Gabriel looked stunned.

'Yes. You have a problem with that?'

Gabriel pulled a face and slowly shook his head.

'Good. Eric is going to meet the ringleader of the kidnappers at eight thirty to pay them off. That will be the time we move in to get Natalie out. There should only be two others left behind which makes the odds better.'

'Do they have guns?' demanded Gabriel.

'I don't think so but I don't know. Do you?'

'Have a gun? Me? No. Have you?'

'Of course not. Are you still prepared to help?'

Gabriel grimaced but nodded. 'Yes. But Hannah mustn't go. It'll be dangerous.'

'She insists on going and at the end of the day it's her decision. I couldn't stop her if I tried. No-one could.'

'You mean me. You think I could not.'

Nathan didn't comment. You can try, he thought. I'd like to see that.

'And Eric, he goes alone to this meeting?' said Gabriel. 'Is this safe? Where is it?'

'The Père Lachaise cemetery. I don't know how safe he'll be but he and this man were friends once.'

'A strange kind of friendship, I think. So where do we go? Is there a distance between the two places? You know where Natalie is, I suppose?'

'You ask too many questions. We need to get going. We'll explain on the way.' Nathan drank the remainder of his coffee in one long draught and stood up. 'You've got ten minutes to get dressed. I'll wait for you.'

'No. I'll come to Eric's door in ten minutes. I'll be ready.'

'I'm going to stay here, Gabriel, till you're done. Then you can't warn anyone.'

Gabriel faced him, unblinking. 'If you do not trust me, you should not be taking me with you. I will come to your door or I won't come.'

Nathan met his gaze then silently turned away. Gabriel followed him to the door.

'I know you don't like me, Nathan and I realise that you want 'annah for yourself. But I believe it's me she wants. We have a connection. You'll have to accept it.'

'I'm not going to discuss Hannah with you. You hardly know her.'

'And you do? It is not necessary to have time with someone to know her. And a long time is not always enough.'

Nathan leaned forward, speaking slowly and emphatically.

'You can boast how much better you know her than I do if you want. They're just empty words. But if you let us down, if you betray her trust, you will be sorry. I promise you that.'

Gabriel stared at him, expressionless, and wordlessly opened the door, and Nathan walked back to Eric's apartment. He wished he could have left it even later to include Gabriel but he needed the man awake and with all reflexes functioning. This could turn out to be very unpleasant.

*

With the stolen goods stowed discreetly away inside the worn leather bag, Eric left the apartment at five to seven and made for the Censier-Daubenton metro station. If he headed north and west he could pick up the Gallieni line at Opéra and only change once on his way to the cemetery. The bag hadn't

277

seemed heavy when he'd first packed it but it certainly felt heavy now.

The underground platform was still fairly quiet and he had time to look around and check who was there. No-one seemed to be following him. When the next train rumbled into the station, he quickly got on board and managed to find a seat near the door. There was enough time and to spare but he was anxious, scared of missing his connection, of doing anything wrong.

As the train moved off, shaking and clattering along, he wondered what lay in wait for him. It had been decades since he'd last seen Gustave yet that terrible night in the war was still impressed on his mind. What Gustave had done still shocked him to the core. The war and the occupation had been a nightmare and everyone had found their own way of surviving, some good, some bad – none of them had been quite the same people by the end of it as they were at the beginning. But to kill an innocent man like that, all for a bag of trinkets...

He got off the train at Opera, moving with the crowd up and across to the Gallieni line and caught a train heading east. It was getting busier now and he stood in the vestibule between the doors, pressed between two Asian women talking animatedly in a language he couldn't name and a French woman who turned to glare at him because his bag was sticking in her back. He barely noticed. Doubts coursed through him. He should have told the police; he should have confessed years ago to what he and Gustave had done; he should have told them about the kidnapping. But it was too late now to change anything. If this all went wrong, he alone would be responsible for whatever happened to Natalie. The carriage felt airless suddenly; he couldn't seem to breathe.

The train finally rattled into the Père Lachaise metro station and Eric gulped in the fresh air as he climbed the last steps of the stairway and out into the street. He caught his breath then moved on.

The cemetery gates were still closed and Eric stood around, trying to look nonchalant. Of course he was early. Too early. When the gates were finally opened he moved slowly, reluctant to draw attention to himself. He had brought his map with him but had virtually committed to memory the plan of the area he needed. Division thirty was to the south of the cemetery, off the Avenue des Acacias. A maintenance truck passed him and a few minutes later, further along one of the walkways, he saw a man pushing a cart with a bucket and some tools – more staff but very few visitors. He felt ludicrously conspicuous but no-one seemed interested in him or in his heavy bag.

He arrived at the rendezvous and shuffled along the path, looking around. He hadn't been here in years and he'd forgotten the serenity of the place. Set up here on the side of a hill and planted with hundreds of mature trees, it was easy to forget that he was still in the heart of the city. It felt wrong to be here, disrespectful, doing something so sordid among all these silent graves. A woman passed him carrying an arrangement of flowers in a pot. They exchanged a nod and he watched her turn off onto a narrower path that led to the tombs behind the main route. He realised he had wandered. Was he still in the right place? There was no sign of Gustave. Or perhaps the whole rendezvous was a set-up, a way to torment him. What devious tricks was Gustave up to now?

'So you came,' said a voice behind him. 'It's been a long time, hasn't it?'

Eric spun round. Gustave had appeared nearby on a narrow footworn track which wound between a tree and a tall, old tomb, its wrought iron gates covered in rust. How long had he been there? They stood and stared at each other. Gustave had changed. There were shadows of the youth he had once been but the slim waist had long since gone and a heavy neck now masked the lines of his jaw. His hair was thin and grizzled and a pronounced scar ran from one corner of his mouth down onto his chin.

'It's been a lifetime,' said Eric. 'The world is a different place since we last met.'

'Don't fool yourself: nothing much changes.'

Gustave looked up and down the path, then raised a hand and gestured a peremptory index finger for Eric to follow him. He walked back up the track and stopped suddenly, turning. The branches of a tree hung around their heads and an assortment of tombs and monuments crowded around them.

'You didn't need to hide,' said Eric. 'I'm alone, just like you said.'

'I know. I've been watching you.'

'You can let my daughter go now. She's done you no harm.'

Gustave produced an ugly smile.

'Not like that other daughter of yours.' He snorted. 'Robert couldn't stand up straight for hours after she shoved her knee in his groin. He hasn't forgotten either. Still, he shouldn't have let her get the drop on him, should he?'

He looked at the bag Eric was holding.

'You got it all then? I believe that's mine.' He stretched out a hand and Eric passed him the bag. Gustave opened the top and looked inside, using his other hand to feel the contents and bring a couple of items into view. He grunted and closed it again.

'It's all there, Gustave, everything we took. I told you I didn't take it. I didn't want it, not after what happened.'

'I told you to take it home and we'd share it out later. I was relying on you. You knew how much I needed the money.'

'We all did. Money meant choices, it meant not going hungry and cold. But that's no excuse for killing. That made you as bad as the Nazis.'

'Listen to you, all self-righteous. You don't know the half of what I've been through, just trying to make ends meet. And I didn't go there intending to kill that man. Sometimes you have no choice. He shouldn't have called the police. He'd have identified us. It was his fault.'

'It was his home, his job. He had a right to defend it. I didn't sign up for killing.'

'If you were so pious, why didn't you go to the police and hand yourself in then, *hein*? It was because I killed him that you were able to get on with your life and not be slung behind bars. There was no-one to identify you. Don't pretend you're better than I am.'

'I didn't want to be executed for something I didn't do. I didn't kill him. And you just left me to face it. You disappeared.'

'I wasn't going to hang around. Someone would have fingered me. Whereas you?' Gustave poked Eric's chest with his finger. 'No-one was going to think nice boy Eric was involved. But when I came back you'd gone too. Rumour had it you'd gone abroad. I really thought you'd had the guts to hock the stuff.'

Eric shook his head. 'We shouldn't have done it.'

Gustave scoffed. 'Easy for you to say. You always had talents, Eric, talents I didn't possess. If it wasn't your drawing, it was that mouth of yours, telling stories, making people laugh and listen, charming your way through. And you've done very well for yourself. You don't know what it is to struggle, to worry where the next meal's coming from.'

'I've had my share of struggles. I've worked hard for what I've got. Stop wallowing in self-pity and do some honest work for once in your life. Take that stuff and be damned. I just want my daughter back. Now. I've fulfilled my share of the bargain.' Eric's self-control snapped and with both hands he grabbed Gustave by the collar of his jacket, pulling tight and shaking him. 'Where is she? You give her back to me.'

Gustave started coughing and tried to fend him off. 'Hey, hey, she's not here,' he rasped. 'And if I don't get back to the others in the next half-hour, they've got instructions to get rid of her.' He coughed again. 'Permanently. So I suggest you let me go.'

Eric reluctantly loosed his grip and Gustave swallowed and smoothed his collar down.

'That's a nasty temper you've got there, Eric. Remember, I just want what's mine.' He raised the bag. 'I'll take this little baby home and check it out. I need to know I've got the right stuff. It was all the real thing, I remember – worth a lot of money.' He waved a hand. 'You go. I'm not having you following me.'

'What about Natalie?'

'I'll be in touch. Go.'

Eric met Gustave's gaze and stood, leaden, but he had no choice. He reluctantly retraced his steps and headed back to the metro.

Chapter 20

Hannah reflected that of all the foolish things she had done in her life – and there had been many – this was by far the dumbest. She, Nathan and Gabriel were on the metro, heading to rescue Natalie. Or they were walking straight into a trap.

Up in Eric's apartment before leaving, Nathan had briefly described to Gabriel the nature of the place where Natalie was being held and Hannah had pointed out the garage on the map.

'How do you know that's where she is?'

'That doesn't concern you,' snapped Nathan. 'There's a run of offices at the back and a private car park. I managed to get a look at the flat from by the offices. It looks like there's a half-glazed door onto a balcony at the back with a fire escape down to the car park. When we get there, I'll take the front door and you go round the back. You can smash the glass if the balcony door's locked.'

'Divide and conquer,' Hannah said. 'We'll take them by surprise.'

Gabriel looked from Hannah to Nathan and back again.

'This does not sound like a good plan,' he said.

'You have a better one?' challenged Nathan.

Gabriel pursed up his lips and shook his head. 'I think only...'

'We're not asking you to think,' said Nathan.

'Look, don't argue.' Hannah flicked a look between them.

'Please. We're supposed to be doing this together. If we fall out we hand the advantage over to those thugs.'

'Yes, of course, you are right.' Gabriel offered her one of his charming smiles. 'We will do this.'

Standing in the underground train now, holding tightly to the rail above her head as they careered round a bend, Hannah thought Gabriel had good reason to doubt their plan. The venture felt a great deal less sensible in the doing than it had in the safety of Eric's apartment.

The road the garage stood on was a good ten minutes from the metro station and they walked there in silence. The whole street looked run-down. From where they stood a newsagent's, a greengrocer's and a *boulangerie* nestled together at the nearest end on the right and the baker was standing outside, smoking a cigarette. He eyed them up on their arrival, then quickly lost interest, tossed his cigarette butt into the road and went back inside. Beyond the shops was a large semi-industrial laundry business and then the garage, with its metal up and over door firmly closed. There were two small windows above the metal door, presumably to the flat.

The left-hand side of the road was mainly occupied by offices and businesses, some of which had showrooms to the street. Hannah saw bathroom and plumbing equipment in one and, beyond, what looked like a display of photocopiers. There were a couple of pedestrians out on the street but mostly it felt like an unloved, forgotten backwater.

'Wait, look,' hissed Hannah, quickly turning and feigning interest in the newsagent's window. She slipped into the shop's recessed entrance, pulling Nathan in too and caught Gabriel's eye. The shop door was open and Gabriel obligingly slipped inside.

'What?' said Nathan.

'That guy at the other end of the street. I'm sure he's the

one who tried to grab me. Don't let him see you looking.'

Nathan, still staring in the window, edged back onto the pavement a step and glanced along the street.

'It's all clear,' he muttered a couple of minutes later. 'It is the right place. I saw him disappear in through that personal door.'

'He didn't see you?'

'No, he was carrying something in some paper bags. Food probably. He looked preoccupied. Where's Gabriel? Let's get closer. I'll go ahead. Keep into the side of the pavement. They won't have an angle to see us if we do that.'

They walked casually along, glancing in windows, turning occasionally to make pretence of a remark but saying little. Gabriel said nothing and kept glancing around furtively.

'Just act natural,' Hannah murmured to him.

He rolled his eyes at her with the suggestion of a grin.

When they reached the garage, Nathan paused and gently tried the door. It was locked and he swore.

'I didn't expect that. Stupid of me. I thought they'd only lock the door of the flat itself.' He tried it again then pushed at it with his shoulder. 'No, it'll give them too much warning if I try to break it down. We'll all have to go in at the back. We've got a better chance there.'

He slipped through the gate at the side and Hannah followed him down the alley. Presumably the people in the offices didn't work Saturdays for there were no cars in the car park. They edged to the bottom of the fire escape, a narrow, turning metal staircase. Arranged haphazardly around the bottom of it were a few dried-out plant pots with the stalks of dead flowers in them. They could see similar pots up on the balcony.

'Where's Gabriel?' Nathan whispered urgently, looking round.

There was no sign of him and Hannah felt her insides lurch. She turned, desperately searching for him. She was the one who'd insisted he should be brought along, she who had fallen for his excuses and his stories. Had he got cold feet and gone or was he about to betray them?

She darted along the alleyway and back onto the street. The personal door at the side of the garage was now open but Gabriel was nowhere to be seen. He must have had a key all along. She peered into the gloom beyond the doorway and took a step inside but her eyes struggled to adjust to the darkness. Then a hand came across her mouth from behind, strangling any noise she might make.

'Quiet,' Gabriel murmured in French. 'It's me. I picked the lock.' He released his hand. 'Is Nathan ready?'

'Yes. I didn't know you could pick locks.'

'There are a lot of things you don't know about me. Is it still clear out there?'

'Yes.'

'*Alors*, go and tell Nathan that I've got in. First, check your watch.'

She turned back to the doorway and tilted her watch to the light. 'OK.'

'In three minutes I shall go in at the top. He should go in at the same time. And Hannah?'

'What?'

He put a hand up to her cheek. 'Pass the message on and then go. Please. I don't want you hurt.' His eyes silently pleaded with her.

She pulled her gaze away and slipped back to the rear of the block to give Nathan the message.

'He's in?' he hissed. 'How the hell did he do that?'

'He picked the lock.'

'That's what he told you anyway.'

286

'Nathan, listen.'

They heard a woman cry out from the flat above and they both looked up.

'I don't know,' the woman shouted. 'Let me go, will you?'

Then they heard a slap and the shouting stopped.

'That's Natalie,' whispered Hannah. 'It was very clear so the balcony door must be open. We've got to get up there Nathan.'

She started up the metal stairs and Nathan quickly followed. Both wearing soft-soled shoes, they made little noise. Hannah paused just before the top and Nathan edged in beside her. The balcony door was ajar and Natalie's voice could be heard again, quieter now, as well as two different men's voices. Hannah checked her watch, waited a few seconds then nodded at Nathan.

The next minute they were thrusting the door back and were inside.

Afterwards, Hannah would find it hard to remember exactly the order in which everything happened. She recalled seeing Natalie pushed down on the sofa while Robert, the brute who had grabbed her on the street was leaning over her sister, gripping one arm savagely and twisting it. Natalie was begging him to leave her alone. She remembered seeing the younger man too who seemed to be trying to calm the situation down. But what she recalled most clearly was the look of shock on the faces of the two men as she and Nathan entered and, a second later, Gabriel burst in through the other door.

Nathan launched himself at Robert with a force Hannah had never seen him use before, pulling him off Natalie and punching him. The man retaliated violently, knocking Nathan back over the sofa and forcing him to scramble to get to his feet again before the next assault. Their fist-fight continued in a fury of blows while the younger man went for Gabriel who parried and with one left hook, knocked the guy to the floor. In the chaos, Hannah ducked between and around them to grab Natalie who had rolled off the sofa and was cowering, trying to get out of the way. Hannah dragged her towards the front door, careless of her complaints and bruises, desperate to get her away and to safety.

They were near the door and Hannah was helping Natalie scramble to her feet when more men came piling through it. In a matter of moments they'd taken hold of the kidnappers, pinning their arms behind their backs and cuffing them. The police, it seemed, had arrived. But how? No-one had rung them. Hannah was stunned. Had they been followed? But how could they have?

Then she saw Nathan on the floor with blood all over his face. His glasses had fallen off and he wasn't moving. Immediately she abandoned Natalie and went over to kneel beside him, putting a hand to his neck to check his pulse. His heart was still beating.

'Thank God,' she murmured.

His eyes opened and he peered at her blearily.

'You're alive,' she said stupidly. 'Are you all right? You're bleeding.'

She pulled a clean paper tissue out of her pocket and dabbed at the cut by his mouth. His nose seemed to have stopped bleeding but one eye was already starting to puff up and his jaw looked livid with developing bruises.

'Ow,' he said.

'Don't be a baby. Can you move?'

'I don't know. Probably. I've lost my glasses.'

She glanced round then reached over. 'They're here. Amazingly they don't seem to be broken.'

He took them off her and put them on. 'That's better. Except my nose hurts.' He struggled to lean up on one elbow and felt it gingerly. 'Well at least I can still move but... ow, everything hurts.'

'Have you broken anything?'

'I'll let you know.' He looked round the room. 'Where did the police come from?'

'I've no idea, but I'm glad they did.'

'Well whatever, Hannah Dechansay, we did it.' He managed something approaching a smile, then winced. 'Your father was wrong: we were the cavalry.'

She grinned back. 'We were, weren't we? You were amazing.'

'Thank you. I'm glad you noticed. Are you all right?'

'I'm fine.'

'How's Natalie?'

Hannah looked across. Natalie was already sitting perkily on a chair, chatting happily to one of the policemen, putting a hand up to tidy her hair.

'It looks like she's taken it all in her stride,' Hannah remarked drily. 'She certainly looks better than you do.'

The officer in charge came over to check they were all right and introduce himself.

'I was so glad to see you,' Hannah said in French, 'but how did you know to come here?'

He pointed to Gabriel. 'We got a phone call. We'd been expecting one but it ended up being very last minute or we'd have been here sooner.'

Hannah's face puckered into a frown. 'Gabriel rang you? I don't understand. And what about Gustave, the ringleader of these animals? Has he got away?'

'He's being picked up even as we speak. We were following him. We had a couple of *agents* at the cemetery to watch what went on and we had some people following you too.' Another officer was trying to call him away. He nodded and looked back at Hannah. 'You are 'annah Dechansay? Before you go, you and your friend need to answer some questions. One of my officers will be with you in a minute.'

'Of course.'

'We have also taken your father in for questioning.' He moved away, firing commands at his junior officers.

Nathan managed to ease himself up into a sitting position, frowning, flexing his legs and hands, testing them out.

'What was all that about?'

Hannah translated for him.

'Good God, what's been going on here?' He flicked a glance towards Gabriel. 'He's got some explaining to do,' he added grimly.

She turned. Gabriel was now sitting on the sofa looking woebegone, watching her. Their eyes met.

'Are you all right?' she called over.

He didn't speak for a minute, eyes locked on hers, then he held up his left hand.

'No, I'm not. Just look at it. It's already going blue. No black. I've probably broken something. I don't know what I was thinking, throwing punches. I'm a piano player. I can't play the piano with a broken hand. Suppose it doesn't mend properly?'

'You'd better go to the hospital,' she said, 'and have it checked out.'

He grunted and nodded, still watching her. His usually warm and magnetic eyes had an accusing look and she tore her gaze away.

*

In the end Nathan went with Gabriel to the hospital. He wasn't keen but Hannah urged him to go and when the police

290

suggested it too, even offering to take them both, he finally agreed. His body did feel battered. The two men barely spoke in the back of the car and were quickly separated at the hospital. After a long wait and then a thorough examination, Nathan was allowed to leave. He had no idea where Gabriel was and didn't bother to find out. What he wanted was to soak his aches and pains in a long, hot bath. Too sore to contemplate using the underground, he caught a taxi and was deposited on the pavement outside Eric's home. It was already nearly half past three in the afternoon.

He walked stiffly into the courtyard, knocked on Eric's front door and waited. Two minutes. Three minutes.

The door opened and Hannah stood there, looking pale.

'You're all right then? I was so worried.' She stepped back to let him in but glanced out into the courtyard before closing the door. 'Is Gabriel back too?'

'I don't know where he is. He was waiting in a different place, then disappeared. He might be back or still there; I've no idea.'

'I've been looking out every few minutes, waiting to see you arrive, but I haven't seen him yet.'

Waiting to see me, thought Nathan, or Gabriel? He didn't dare ask.

'Any news of your father?' he asked instead.

'No, not yet. Before I left the officer said we'd need to go into the station to make formal statements. Tomorrow or the next day. So tell me, what did they say? Are you OK?'

'Just bruises. They did a couple of X-rays. Nothing's broken. It just feels like it.'

'You look awful. Can I help you?'

'No, I can manage, thanks.' He dragged himself up the three flights of stairs to the living quarters and eased himself down on one of the sofas with a grunt. He felt weary to his bones and couldn't yet face the effort of going for a bath.

'Have you eaten?' Hannah said. 'Can I get you something?'

'I had a very dry sandwich and a plastic beaker of coffee from the foyer kiosk. I'd like a cup of tea please.'

Hannah went off to the kitchen. He very much wanted to talk to her and this was his opportunity, while they were still alone. Who knew when he'd get another chance, and he had to do it before she gave her answer to Gabriel.

But the peace and quiet of the apartment enveloped him, the sofa was soft and comfortable, and his aches had subsided a little. His eyes felt incredibly heavy and he rested his head back, forgetting the tea. Yes, that was nice.

A moment later he was asleep.

*

'I *am* being quiet, Hannah. Don't fuss.'

The sound of Eric's voice brought Nathan to.

'Ah, you see, he was awake anyway,' said Eric loudly. 'How are you, Nathan? I've been hearing about your exploits from the police. And from Hannah. You do look a bit beaten up, young man.'

Nathan frowned, trying to get a bearing on his surroundings. In his head, he'd been on a boat with Hannah on the Broads in the east of England, feeling the breeze against his cheeks, listening to the slap of the water against the hull. They'd been on a trip together in the sunshine, planning a pub lunch together. The reality, when he looked round, was a disappointment.

Hannah came into his line of vision.

'I made you tea,' she said, 'but it went cold. You've been

292

out for a couple of hours at least. I'll make some more.'

Nathan sat up a little straighter and grimaced. 'A couple of hours? Really?' He looked at Eric. 'So you're back. How did you get on at the police station?'

'Fine, fine. I had a lot of explaining to do as you can imagine but I think we came to an understanding.'

'Meaning?'

'Meaning that they understood what I tried to do and what a difficult position I was in. It seems they knew about the little arrangement I had with Gustave. They knew about Natalie too so they understood that I was trying to keep her safe.'

'How did they know all this?'

'Gabriel. He's a dark horse, isn't he? Anyway he was just arriving home when I did. I told him to come over and we can all have a chat, catch up. That'll be him now. I left the door unlocked.'

'So they didn't arrest you as such?' Nathan peered at his watch; it slowly came into focus. 'You were there a long time.'

'No, no arrest. I answered a lot of questions and made a statement. Apparently the fact that the property didn't leave the site till I needed the kidnap ransom helped and they knew I wasn't the one who killed that poor man. They were listening at the cemetery. Imagine. They had a couple of guys there, dressed as gardeners, hiding out of sight. I think I saw one of them on my way in. Clever, eh? Anyway, I am not to go anywhere.'

Eric said this last phrase slowly and emphatically then smiled. 'Not that I had any plans to, as I told them. I've got a commission half-painted. It's for a birthday present so I've got a deadline. Ah, there you are, Gabriel. Come in, come in. Hannah, we'll definitely need that coffee now. Or perhaps something stronger?'

'Not yet, *Papa*. Let's celebrate later.'

'You're right, you're right. But we should definitely have a party soon, I think. We all deserve that.'

Typical Eric, Nathan thought. Under investigation by the police with possible charges to answer and he plans a party. He looked across at Gabriel who had sat down on the opposite sofa and was concentrating on following the English conversation. His hand was swathed in what looked like a compression bandage that reached up his forearm.

'What did they say about your hand?' Nathan asked grudgingly.

'It is not broken but very swollen. A lot of bruises, they say. They tell me to bathe it and rest it and keep it up.' He raised his arm to demonstrate with a glum expression. 'No piano for a few days.'

Nathan nodded and turned his attention back to Eric who had sat down next to Gabriel.

'So you're not being charged then?'

'Not yet anyway,' said Hannah, appearing with a tray bearing two teas and two coffees. 'Apparently the public prosecutor will have to study the case. If he's lucky it seems he might get away with a suspended sentence or a fine. For Gustave, it'll be a very different story, I imagine. *Salut* Gabriel. I'm glad nothing's broken.'

'Me too.' He thanked her for the coffee and Nathan saw him try to catch her eye.

'I think it's about time you told us about your part in all this,' Nathan said to him. 'The policeman said you phoned them to tell them about the rendezvous between Eric and Gustave. And then about our little rescue attempt too. How and why were you involved? And why, in God's name, didn't you tell us?'

Gabriel lifted his coffee cup to his mouth and drank a mouthful, taking his time.

'I was not allowed to say.' He put the cup down carefully on the saucer. 'I shall try to explain. The police wanted me to give them information. They did not want me to – what do you say? – warn you.' He paused, looking round at them. 'I have been in prison. You know this. When I came out the police asked me to listen to what is going on. On the street. In bars. In houses. Like I did for the crooks last time, but this time for them.'

'So you were a police informant?' said Hannah.

'Yes, exactly. It can be difficult when you come out of prison. If the police believe you are on their side, they can make it easier for you. You understand? So I hear things and then I tell them. They already knew about Gustave and his crimes but could get... *aucune preuve.*'

'No proof,' offered Hannah. 'So you were enlisted to help them get it?'

'Yes. They wanted to catch him...' He cast about for the words.

'In the act?'

'Yes. They heard that he has come to this *arrondissement* and has started asking questions about Eric. So they decide to watch and wait and asked me to see what I could find out.'

'Wait a minute,' said Nathan. 'If you were reporting back to the police, who was it that was giving Gustave information about this household, for example that Hannah was Eric's daughter?'

'Mark,' said Gabriel. He turned and looked apologetically at Eric. 'I am sorry, Eric. Mark has debts and needs money. He was seen meeting with Gustave and Robert. He is a fool.'

Eric swore violently in French, then apologised to Hannah.

'He's going to be an unemployed fool very soon,' he said.

'And probably prosecuted too,' added Nathan.

'Is Natalie all right?' asked Gabriel.

'The police took her home then dropped me off,' said Hannah. 'She was in remarkably good spirits. I guess she might have a reaction once she's got over the relief of being rescued.'

'Virginie will probably fuss over her so much she'll make Natalie wish she was still back there,' remarked Eric flippantly.

'Not with those thugs,' Nathan said with feeling.

'Really, *Papa*.' Hannah got up and started clearing the empty cups away. Eric watched her and a slow smile spread over his face.

'So you completely ignored my instructions then?' he said. 'Don't play the cavalry, I said, and what did you do?'

'We did. I know.' She grinned. 'But we did it pretty well, don't you think?'

'You've never done as you're told,' he said with a touch of pride. The next minute he was on his feet and putting his arms around her in a fierce hug. She looked astonished.

'Hey, watch the cups.'

'We did do pretty well,' muttered Nathan, more to himself than anyone else, 'but it's just as well the police arrived when they did.'

He looked across at Hannah but, released by her father, she had now turned and was leaning over, talking earnestly to Gabriel. It looked like she was arranging to see him. He'd left it too late, after all.

*

Gabriel made a weak effort to tidy up, putting a used coffee cup and plate in the sink in the kitchen, shaking the scatter cushion on each of the armchairs and tossing them back into what he hoped was an artistic position. In the glossy interiors magazines they made a big point of how you used cushions, didn't they? A girlfriend he'd once had was always buying those things and kept saying how the two of them should cultivate some look or other. She'd driven him crazy with it. Would such a thing impress Hannah? She was artistic. She was cultured too. Still he rather doubted she'd care. After all, that was why they got on so well: they shared similar priorities and image wasn't one of them.

He looked round the tiny apartment, wondering what else he could do. She might arrive any moment now and he was nervous. Eric had offered that Gabriel could stay for dinner that evening. Apparently, Hannah and Nathan had talked him into ordering a Chinese take-away since neither of them felt up to going out or cooking. Eric was a bit precious about food. If it wasn't French, he turned his nose up at it, but he had reluctantly agreed.

'Join us, why don't you?' he'd said. 'Better to have some company after a day like this. And you can't work.'

The latter was certainly true. But Gabriel couldn't imagine staying in that apartment all evening while Eric made light of the trauma they'd all been through and produced forced jocular conversation. Eric was a decent man and he meant well, but, God, he could be frustrating. All things considered their day's exploits had been a success, but the rest of them were walking on eggshells and Eric was oblivious to it: the silences, the looks and so many things left unsaid. What Gabriel wanted now more than ever was to get away. It was time to move on but he wanted some kind of sign from Hannah. He needed to know her decision; he needed to know that she would be with him.

Had Nathan told Hannah how he felt? It didn't look like it. She had said to Gabriel on the quiet that she'd like to come and see him, maybe before dinner?

'Unless you want to rest and get an early night?' she'd added solicitously.

'No. No. Come, please.' He'd smiled foolishly and realised that Nathan was watching him. 'I was thinking of asking you. We could have a drink. Talk. Whenever you're free, I'll be there.'

So now here he was, waiting on her visit. He checked in the fridge: there was still half a bottle of Chardonnay there. He got two glasses out and went back into the sitting room and sat down at the piano. His left hand felt solid and heavy and the bandage was tight and made him itch but he played a favourite tune with his right hand and even that helped. Music was always his balm when he felt stressed.

He was about to try another when he heard footsteps outside and a brief light tap on the door. He was quickly up and flinging it open.

''annah, come in.'

She smiled and his heart felt a little lighter. She had that effect on him.

He moved towards the kitchen. 'I've got some Chardonnay. Have a glass with me.'

'Thank you.'

He glanced back and saw her looking round. She was smiling again. She walked to the piano and began leafing through his music and he felt a wash of relief. It felt like a sign. If he could just get her to promise tonight that she was ready to move to France to be with him, he knew everything would be all right.

298

Chapter 21

Eric was in the kitchen making himself yet another coffee when he heard footsteps on the stairs and froze. It was Sunday morning and both Hannah and Nathan had not long gone out. Separately. Nathan had been the last to go and Eric had told him to leave the door unlocked.

'It's time we got back to normal,' he'd said.

But he didn't feel normal yet and hearing the steps now triggered a moment's panic until he saw Natalie appear at the top of the staircase.

'*Chérie*,' he said, going to embrace her and kissing her on both cheeks. 'I'm so relieved to see you. You look well. A bit tired perhaps. Are you all right? Did they hurt you? Coffee? I'm just making some.'

'Please.' She followed him back into the kitchen. 'I'm OK but they were rough with me. The young guy wasn't so bad but the other two were bastards. That Robert hurts people just for the fun of it. He's sick. Everyone arrived just in time.'

'I suppose the police told you what it was all about?'

'Yes. You were involved in a burglary with that horrible man.' She paused, eyeing him up warily. 'And someone died.'

'But I didn't do it.'

'No. They said. So what's happening with you? *Maman* said that you'd probably end up in prison.'

'She wishes.'

'But you're not are you? All because of something that happened nearly fifty years ago?'

'She was exaggerating.'

'So you're not being prosecuted?'

Eric shrugged it off. 'There may be some charges to answer but, like you said, it was all a very long time ago and we were fighting a war.'

'But you weren't fighting, were you?'

'Fighting comes in many forms, Natalie, especially when your country is occupied. But you're right: what I did that night was not a good thing and it wasn't for my country. I've regretted it ever since.' He produced a smile. Natalie was looking uncomfortable. She wasn't used to hearing him talking like this. 'Here's your coffee. Let's go and sit and you can tell me what's been happening.'

Natalie put her cup down on the coffee table and flung herself down on one of the sofas with a heavy sigh.

'I'm exhausted. I haven't had a minute to myself since I was rescued. What with a visit to the hospital and questions from the police. Then *Maman*.' Natalie rolled her eyes. 'She kept asking questions and telling me off for keeping her in the dark. As if I knew anything to tell her anyway. It's not as though I wanted to be kidnapped.' Natalie fixed him with a meaningful look. 'She's very cross with you, *Papa*.'

'Of course she is darling. But you know this would never have happened if you'd gone away like I told you to.'

Natalie grunted, and dropped her head down, looking up at him through her lashes.

'I'm sorry. But you can't blame me. You should have explained properly why. It's not much fun going away by yourself.'

'No. I suppose not.' He relented. 'And it's not your fault. I shouldn't have done lots of things. Anyway, I'm relieved it

300

all worked out in the end. I'm sure you don't want to talk about it. I know I don't.'

'Where are the others?'

'They've gone out. I've decided to have a party tonight. I know it's last minute but Nathan tells me they've got to get back to work next week. He'd half-planned to book a flight today but I told him he wasn't in a fit state to travel.'

Natalie sat up straighter, suddenly more alert. Eric wasn't surprised: Natalie loved a party as much as he did.

'So they're both staying over?' she demanded.

'Just a day or two. I'm not sure exactly. Hannah's not been very forthcoming this morning but when I said I wanted to have a party she offered to go and get some food in. I'll need some help.'

He fell silent. There would be no Jeanne there to help tonight. If he asked her she'd come, he knew, but only from kindness and he didn't want that. She was moving on and he'd resolved to let her go. He liked her very much but they weren't a match and he was beginning to suspect he didn't have one. Maybe he was getting too old for that now.

'I'd like to see Hannah and Nathan,' Natalie was saying. 'I ought to thank them for coming to my rescue. To be honest, I was a bit of a cow with Hannah when she first arrived.'

Eric was pulled out of his reverie and looked across with raised eyebrows. He almost laughed until he saw her face.

'Why?'

Natalie sniffed and looked down. 'I kind of thought she was trying to take over our family. Well, you really. Take over you. I was sort of jealous.'

Eric shook his head. 'You had no need to be jealous. You're both precious to me. So is Elizabeth but she doesn't seem to need me.'

Eric frowned. He thought of Hannah's recriminations

301

about him not being in touch, about not telling her anything, and it occurred to him now that his two younger daughters genuinely did seem to need him and he felt a pang of guilt and tenderness towards them both.

'It's not a contest between you, you know,' he said gently. 'You're both quite different but that's just who you are. I love you both the same. I'd like to think you could get on with each other, so maybe it would be a good thing if you met up later.'

They both fell silent. Eric picked up his coffee and savoured a long draught.

'It looked like Nathan got hurt,' said Natalie suddenly. 'I hope he's all right.'

'He's fine. Just bruised and sore.'

'What's he like? I mean, as a person?'

'Nathan? Well, he's English of course.' Eric shrugged and realised that he didn't know Nathan very well. There had been so many other things going on. 'He's been very helpful. Seems smart. Can be quite witty.' He sighed. 'He's got it bad for Hannah though, I know that. It seems they were an item for a while but they fell out a few weeks ago. His fault, he says.'

'Oh? Then he should tell her.'

Eric shook his head. 'It's not that easy. You see, now she's met Gabriel.'

'Yes, of course, Gabriel.' Natalie's expression darkened. 'He is rather gorgeous. And he thinks the sun shines out of her. I saw.' She hesitated, examining her father's face. 'I think maybe she fancies him too. What do you think?'

'Me darling? I don't know.' Eric drank more coffee and put the cup down. 'Gabriel was here yesterday afternoon and Hannah went down to see him last night but she seemed reluctant to talk about it.' He looked across at Natalie sharply. 'Don't tell either of them that I told you this, will you?'

Natalie shook her head and picked up her coffee.

Eric's thoughts turned to the party and the people he needed to ring. A lot of them wouldn't be out of bed yet.

'You will come to the party, won't you?' He noticed Natalie was looking more serious than usual. 'Are you up to it, Nat?'

'I am. In fact, I'll help.'

*

'Do you do much cooking?' Eric said, out of the blue. 'I mean, at home, normally?'

Nathan turned his head. It was still early on the Sunday evening and the two of them were in Eric's small kitchen, getting things ready for the party. Hannah had returned from her shopping trip that morning laden with food and she'd spent most of the afternoon sorting out dishes, cooking and laying things out. It was becoming difficult to know where to put anything down and a lot had already gone through to the dining table. Nathan had been out buying drinks, both alcoholic and non-alcoholic and they had seen each other little and certainly not to talk. Not that he'd tried exactly.

Now she had gone out again, saying there was someone she had to see but not specifying who it was. The two men had been exhorted to finish preparing the hors d'oeuvres and canapés while she was out, to which end she had offered some suggestions. But Eric, it seemed, had ideas of his own and was now cutting dates in half, putting small spoonfuls of cream cheese on them and ramming a walnut quarter into the top of each one.

'Yes and no,' Nathan replied to him now. 'I like to potter in the kitchen sometimes. But I won't poison you if that's what you're worried about.' Nathan had been toasting small triangles of sliced bread and was now cutting thin slices of

303

duck pâté to put on each one, garnishing the top with a piece of green olive.

Eric smiled. 'No, it wasn't. I suppose what I really meant was: do you like cooking?'

'Yes, when I've got the time and it's for someone else, not just for me. It never seems worth it just for me. What about you?'

Eric paused, reflecting. 'I suppose I'm lazy. I like good food. But I don't have the patience to produce it and my mind always seems too full of my work to spend the time.' He hesitated again. 'To be honest, I've been spoilt by women who have usually cooked for me. And living somewhere where there are wonderful restaurants close by, there's not much incentive I'm afraid.'

'There's only so many hours in a day,' said Nathan. 'You have to choose your priorities.'

Eric looked at him and nodded slowly. 'That's right. You do. I like to spend time with my friends more than I want to spend it in the kitchen.' He smiled. 'I hope we can be friends, Nathan. I realise it's not easy at the moment for you because of Hannah. But I hope we can stay in touch. You must come to Paris again.'

'Thank you. I'd like that.'

Nathan thought it unlikely he would, however, not to see Eric anyway, but he appreciated the offer. Right now, he just wanted to get this evening over with and feel well enough to get on a plane and go home. Seeing Hannah with Gabriel had brought his own priorities into sharp focus and he needed to get back to England and think some things through. He wasn't sure he could keep working for Timothy Blandish while Hannah did. Maybe it was time to move on. There again she would probably be leaving anyway, to travel with Gabriel.

His thoughts were interrupted by Eric calling a greeting in his loud, booming voice.

'Natalie, you've come. Good. Nathan, I know you've seen Natalie but you haven't properly met, have you?'

'Not properly, no.' Nathan turned. 'We exchanged a few words back in that godawful flat.' He wiped his fingers on a cloth and stuck out his hand. '*Enchanté*,' he said.

'*Moi aussi*,' she said with a smile.

'That means you too, doesn't it? Sorry, my French is very basic.'

'Nat's English is quite good,' said Eric. 'Speak slowly and you'll be fine. Right. Now you're here Natalie, you can take over doing these while I try ringing a couple of people I couldn't reach before. I've nearly finished.'

He wiped his hands off and left the kitchen.

Natalie looked around. 'What am I doing exactly?'

'He was cutting those dates in half and putting cream cheese on top.' Nathan pointed. 'Like those.'

'*D'accord.*'

'When you've finished those, there's a list there of other possible hors d'oeuvres that Hannah wrote out. The ingredients are all here somewhere.' He waved a hand vaguely around the kitchen worktops then towards the fridge, and smiled. 'But if you want to do something of your own choice, please do. Hannah has gone out so we can do what we like.'

Natalie nodded and smiled distantly, washed her hands and started cutting a date.

'I want to thank you for coming to rescue me,' she said in attractively accented English. She glanced in his direction. 'It was courageous.'

He shrugged and wished he hadn't. His right shoulder was very sore.

'I'm not sure about that but I am glad you're all right.'

'I want to thank Hannah too,' she said. 'Where has she gone?'

'I don't know.'

They worked in silence for a few minutes. Natalie finished the last few dates and read the list Hannah had left on the side then sniffed and turned to Nathan.

'Would you like a coffee?' she offered.

'I'd love one.'

She busied herself priming Eric's filter machine then leaned against the units as it bubbled through.

'So, you and Hannah,' she began. 'What is this? Are you a couple?'

He laughed. Even to his own ears it sounded hollow.

'No, we're not. We're friends.'

'So... why are you here exactly?'

'Me? Because... because I thought Hannah might be in trouble. I was worried.'

'And you came all the way to Paris because you are worried?'

'Yes.'

'Then I think you like Hannah a lot.'

Nathan sighed. 'Look, I don't want to talk about this.'

'Perhaps this is your problem. I want to help. I do. You don't look happy and I think I owe you because of yesterday. So tell me: what is the problem? Does Hannah not like you?'

'OK, look. We *were* a couple, very briefly. I thought she liked me. Maybe more than like. But then I was stupid.' To Natalie's enquiring expression, he added. 'I was jealous. I told her I wanted to finish it and we broke up. You understand broke up?' Natalie nodded. 'Now I realise I was wrong but it's too late.'

Natalie shook her head. 'It isn't. You tell her you were stupid and wrong. You tell her how you feel.'

306

'But she's met someone else.'

'Gabriel.'

'Yes. How do you know?'

'I saw them together before this *histoire* started.' Natalie leaned forward. 'So you just let him take her and you don't fight? You don't tell her how you feel? That, my friend, is not clever. Perhaps she is waiting for you to tell her? Perhaps she only likes him because he makes her feel like a princess? This happens.' She raised her eyebrows with a pointed look at him then moved away to pour the coffee.

Nathan shook his head. It sounded simple but it wasn't. There hadn't been the right moment for it and there wouldn't be now. He was pretty sure Hannah's decision was already made.

'It's too late for that,' he said.

'Not yet, it isn't,' she replied. 'Milk?'

*

'It's Hannah, isn't it?' said a man's voice. 'I think we met at the last party. And I hear you're Eric's other daughter.'

Hannah turned to see a middle-aged man with a beard smiling at her. He had a deep voice and his accent was thick – German perhaps – so she took a minute to understand what he'd said.

She offered a smile in return. 'Yes, I'm Hannah. I'm sorry, I forget... you are?'

'Elias Babler. I am a sculptor.'

'Yes, I remember now.' He leaned closer, clearly struggling to hear her. The volume of chatter and laughter was high. She raised her voice. 'Are you enjoying the party?'

'Yes, yes, of course. Eric's parties are always good. But you're leaving us, I understand. I am sorry. Hopefully you will

307

come and visit us again. Eric shouldn't keep these secrets from us – beautiful daughters he's never mentioned before. Are there others?'

He winked, offered another smile and was gone, working his way back through the crowd to the kitchen where all the booze had been left out. She snorted. Beautiful indeed. Then she thought of his comment about "others". She hadn't thought of that before. How naïve. Her father had been around, she knew that, and he *was* secretive. Maybe there was another daughter, or even a son, somewhere she'd never heard of. Oh, for God's sake, what a thought. She tried to shrug it away; she had enough on her mind right now.

It was evident already that Eric hadn't told his friends about the kidnap yet and all its ensuing troubles. He undoubtedly would, once he knew where he stood with the judiciary. In any case, it would hit the papers sooner or later. But whether the story he then told would bear much resemblance to the facts was doubtful. They'd have been embellished and adapted. Never let the truth get in the way of an entertaining story, that was his policy.

She glanced towards the top of the stairs. Someone had arrived but it wasn't the person she was expecting to see. It was her half-sister and Hannah moved across to greet her. There hadn't been much chance for them to speak since the dramatic rescue attempt.

'I've been hoping to see you,' she said in French. 'I missed you earlier. I understand you helped getting the food ready.'

'Not much really,' said Natalie. 'But I did want to see you and Nathan – to thank you for coming to find me. Nathan said you were determined to get me out, in case they...' She shuddered. 'And you were right: Robert had no intention of letting me go. Not alive. He's a pig.'

308

'I know. He tried to grab me too but I managed to get away. I felt guilty afterwards when they came for you.'

Natalie looked at her quizzically and shrugged. 'That's hardly your fault.' She looked down at the floor and fidgeted. 'I was horrible to you when you first arrived and I'm sorry. I was kind of jealous. I thought he was my father and I didn't want to share him with you. You seemed so... in control and I never feel like that.'

'In control? Me?' Hannah laughed. 'Neither do I. In fact I was jealous of you too so I think we're quits.' She hesitated. 'We should be friends.'

'Friends.' Natalie managed a half-hearted nod and a smile but looked doubtful. 'Is er... is Gabriel here?'

'No, not yet anyway.'

'I gather his hand's all bandaged up and he can't play. He'll hate that.'

'He does.'

Natalie's eyes narrowed. 'You have seen him then.' She paused. '*Papa* says he's a bad guy who's now a good guy and trying to do the right things. But he would say that, wouldn't he? He's a glass half-full kind of person. What do you think of Gabriel? Now you've stolen him away,' she added bitterly.

'I haven't stolen anyone. But I'm sure my father's right. He's just made some mistakes. Like everyone.'

Natalie regarded her searchingly. 'Well I like Gabriel too. Maybe when you've finished with him, you could pass him back?'

Hannah frowned. 'I didn't take him from you, Natalie. And as for passing him back? He's not a toy. He makes his own choices. We all do - the best we can.' She hesitated. 'It's not always fair, you know. Sometimes you end up feeling cast off, diminished. Believe me, I know. You just have to move on. It'll all work out when you meet the right person.'

'Now you're playing the big sister. I don't need your lofty advice, thank you.'

'Fine. Please yourself. I was only trying to be helpful.'

Hannah started to turn away but Natalie caught her arm.

'My father says this party's a celebration of me being rescued and a farewell to you and Nathan. I see Nathan's over the other side of the room. Have you two fallen out?'

'No. Why?'

'Because I think you should talk to the guy. Just talk to him. He deserves that at least. Anyway, I need a drink.'

Hannah frowned as Natalie left and weaved her way through the throng towards the kitchen. She glanced towards the top of the stairs again. Jean-Pierre, the bar owner, had just arrived. He saw her and nodded an acknowledgement but was hijacked by a woman in a velvet jumpsuit who slipped her arm through his in a familiar way. A few minutes later, the two of them had joined the crowd around Eric in the middle of the room.

Nathan was at the table, grabbing a couple of canapés, and Hannah walked over to join him. She picked up one of her father's date concoctions and took a bite. It wasn't bad.

'It's going well,' she remarked. 'Not that I ever doubted it. He's an expert at parties, the old rascal.'

Nathan flicked a look towards her father who was telling a story to the rapt gathering around him. He produced a wry smile then looked back at Hannah. 'I've never heard you refer to him like that before.'

'This trip has been a learning curve.'

'He's not a bad guy.'

'I know. He's just... Perhaps I've finally allowed myself to see him the way he is.' She shrugged. 'I still love him.'

She ate the other half of the hors d'oeuvre. 'Mm, good,' she muttered.

'I notice that you keep looking towards the stairs. Are you expecting Gabriel?'

She shrugged. 'He did say he'd come.'

'Perhaps he feels too awkward with his hand the way it is. He's used to playing for events like this. It must be difficult.'

She regarded him shrewdly. 'But I guess it's difficult for you too. You can't understand most of what's being said. I'm sorry I've neglected you. I've been kind of... preoccupied.'

'It's OK. I manage. A lot of people here speak enough English to have a short conversation when they realise I can't speak French.'

'You seem to have made an impression on Natalie anyway.'

'On Natalie?' He looked surprised and turned to look across to where the girl was standing by the kitchen door. He turned back, fixed a lingering look on Hannah and opened his mouth to speak, then closed it again.

Hannah frowned at him.

'She wanted me to talk to you. She was behaving rather oddly, I thought.'

'Was she? Right. I guess that's maybe because... well, we got kind of talking earlier and, er...'

'Hannah?' Eric's voice boomed out over the babble of chatter, insistent and demanding. 'Come over. I want you to meet Juliette. She can't stay long.'

Hannah apologised to Nathan and slipped away. It was another of Eric's many friends, a woman who painted icons, and she proceeded to talk at length about them and their symbolism and even delved into her shoulder bag to produce photographs of some of her best pieces. By the time Hannah managed to get away, Nathan was immersed in a group of people who seemed to be including him in the conversation. He was managing all right, she decided.

She glanced towards the stairs again, feeling dislocated and edgy. Maybe her plans weren't going to work out after all. People made promises all the time but often didn't deliver on them, people you thought you could rely on.

She finished her glass of spritzer and wandered into the kitchen to get a refill. The party was gathering energy and volume but it lacked music which just made her think of Gabriel again. She was certain now that he wouldn't come but perhaps it was better that he hadn't: it could have been awkward in the circumstances.

The evening dragged by. She grabbed a few canapés at intervals, rearranged or topped the plates up when they became bare or untidy, and started to drink neat wine, more perhaps than was wise, but she didn't feel like being wise tonight.

And she was more than a little tipsy when, at twenty to eleven, Béatrice walked up the stairs to Eric's apartment. She paused at the top and looked around. She wore a figure-hugging iridescent satin dress with a fish tail, and her strawberry blonde hair was swept up into a beehive. Her pose – slightly turned and hand on hip with her head thrown back – was perfect theatre. She was a woman who knew how to make an entrance and half the room, including Eric, took notice and turned to look at her. Conversations stopped.

'Eric,' said Hannah, pointedly using his name and pushing forward to take his arm and pull him away from his latest entourage, 'let me introduce you to Béatrice. Béatrice is an actress whose done some wonderful performances – you've probably seen her on stage. She also runs the most delightful and select tea rooms in Paris. Béatrice, this is my father, Eric Dechansay. He's a brilliant artist and a wicked man.' She grinned. 'And he hosts the best parties. I've been wanting you both to meet.'

Eric stepped forward, reached out for Béatrice's hand and

kissed the back of it ostentatiously. He kept hold of it and covered it with his other hand.

Béatrice smiled. 'What a pleasure to meet you,' she said coquettishly. 'I've heard so much about you.'

'Really? How flattering.' He began to lead her towards the kitchen. 'Let me get you a drink and you can tell me all about yourself. I want to know everything.'

She laughed. 'Oh Eric, my dear man, a lady never tells *everything*. I'll have a pink gin please.'

Chapter 22

Nathan was already up when Hannah went into the kitchen at eight twenty on the Monday morning. She had showered and dressed but he was still in his night shorts, his cotton dressing-gown hanging loosely round his shoulders. He pulled it around him as she came in and vaguely tied the belt. There was a smell of coffee and she noticed the filter jug was half full and he had a cup and saucer and an empty plate on the worktop beside him.

'Morning,' she said. 'Been up long?'

'A bit. I didn't sleep much so coffee and a croissant seemed more appealing. The table's still covered in stuff from last night.'

'This isn't much better,' she grunted and walked over to fill the kettle. 'I should have stayed up later and cleared some of it, I suppose. I wish he had a breakfast bar.'

'How did you sleep?'

'Not great. No sign of my father yet?'

Nathan shook his head. 'Did Béatrice stay over? They seemed to be hitting it off very well.'

Hannah threw a pointless glance towards the stairs as if Béatrice might suddenly appear there. 'Do you know: I don't know and I don't really want to.'

'You introduced them.'

'I did. I had a hunch he'd like her. She's flamboyant and

unexpected and just a little over the top. What's more, she's nearer his age than his recent girlfriends so they have some common references.'

'You think it'll last then?'

'I have no idea.' The kettle boiled and she poured water on the teabag in a cup then looked round again to check they were still alone. 'Underneath all the crazy stories and posturing, I think he's quite lonely. Anyway, it's up to them now.'

She swirled the teabag round in the water then pulled it out and dumped it on a plate. She leaned back against the unit wearily and sighed.

'You disappeared last night,' she said. 'I assumed you'd gone to bed.'

'I went for a walk. Night air, clear my head, that kind of thing. It got very hot and congested up here. I went to bed when I got back. I'm not a big party animal, you know that.' He hesitated. 'What about you?'

'I stuck it out for a while but I don't have my father's stamina for parties. I don't know what time it finished. It seemed to go quiet around three.'

Nathan nodded. He finished his coffee and refilled the cup, tipped some milk in and stirred it round and round. He straightened up, then leaned back against the unit again staring at her but saying nothing.

'I was thinking of ringing Timothy as soon as he's in,' Hannah said into the silence. She glanced up at the clock on the wall. 'I guess we both need to speak to him.'

'Don't ring yet.'

Hannah looked at him quizzically and he fidgeted his weight from one foot to the other.

'I... I wanted to talk to you last night but it was so crazy here, you couldn't hear yourself think. And then I wasn't sure...

315

I mean, I thought your mind was made up and I shouldn't interfere... But then I was thinking about it all night and what with what Natalie had said... I mean, she was right.'

'Natalie? What are you talking about? Nathan, you're not making any sense. Right about what?'

'About telling you.'

Hannah stared at him.

'I love you, Hannah.' He shook his head despairingly. 'I've been stupid. So stupid. Almost as soon as I'd said those things to you, I knew it was daft. Desperate really. I was jealous and scared and I think I was a coward too. I almost thought I'd rather be alone than cope with someone cheating on me again. No, it's OK – you don't need to protest – I know you weren't. I was just stupid. Blinded by my own stupidity in fact.' He pushed himself away from the unit and came to stand in front of her.

'Nathan, I...'

'No, let me speak. Please. I've missed you so much. Even the arguments. Then when I stopped to think about it, I kind of thought you could do better than me. I'm not musical or creative like you. I was scared you'd get bored with me and I didn't want to go through that again.'

He took Hannah's hand and stroked across the back of it with his thumb, then raised his eyes to her face again.

'I know Gabriel is all the things I'm not but I couldn't let you go off with him without telling you how I feel. Natalie said I should and she was right. I'd like you to reconsider. Because I love you Hannah and I want to have you back in my life. Please think about it before you do anything rash. He might not make you happy – he's footloose, unpredictable, you know that – and I would do my best to make you happy, I swear I would.' He paused. 'Please reconsider.'

He stopped speaking suddenly, his eyes searching her

316

face. Still he held her hand and Hannah looked down at it then back up at him.

'But I'm not going off with Gabriel,' she said, frowning.

'You're not?'

'No. That's what I went to tell him yesterday. It was a difficult conversation.' She looked down at their hands again. 'I like him a lot. I can't pretend I wasn't tempted. But we're not as alike as I wanted, or perhaps he wanted, to think. And when it came down to it...' She shrugged. '...I guess I knew I hadn't got over you.'

'Me?'

'Yes, you. I've missed our time together too.' She smiled wryly and prodded him gently in the midriff. 'Yes, even the arguments. And it became clear when you got hurt during the fight. I was so scared when I saw you on the floor, bleeding. I thought you were unconscious and it made me feel sick. Desperate. Honestly, I forgot about Gabriel completely. Isn't that terrible?'

'Not to me.' Nathan put his free hand to cup her face, leaned forward and gently kissed her on the lips. 'So, I'm forgiven then?'

'Yes, you're forgiven. Anyway I understand why you reacted that way. It's scary being in love with someone. It's a leap of faith, isn't it? I feel like that too. It's like diving into unknown waters and hoping you don't hit anything on the way down.'

'And that you'll be able to come up for air again too.'

She grinned. 'Exactly.' She disentangled her other hand and wrapped her arms round him. 'I love you too,' she murmured into his shoulder.

When Eric walked into the kitchen a few minutes later they were still wrapped round each other in a long and passionate kiss.

'Am I missing something here?' he remarked languidly.

*

'Nathan, so nice of you to get in touch.'

Timothy's voice in Nathan's ear dripped with sarcasm. After a brief argument, Hannah had agreed to let Nathan ring the office in Oxford to explain why neither of them had yet returned to work. As she admitted herself, Timothy was not the easiest person to talk to, even in the office; he was worse still on the phone. The distance between them and his lack of control always made him spiky. He wasn't a bad employer but he didn't believe in employer/employee dialogue. He talked; you listened.

Nathan opened his mouth to speak but Timothy was talking again.

'Daphne tells me you've been involved in some escapade in Paris. Why am I the last person to know? And why didn't you keep me informed? You do realise that you have work to do here? I don't pay you to go swanning off to Paris.'

'I'm sorry, Timothy. It wasn't really like that but it is a long story, too long to tell you over the phone. We'll explain everything when we see you. Suffice to say that Hannah's father had got himself into a serious mess and needed help.'

'And I suppose you two were the only ones who could sort it out?'

'Well, in a way, yes. That's how it worked out. Anyway, I got a bit hurt but I'm getting over it now so I promise we'll be on a plane tomorrow morning and back at work on Wednesday.'

'I'm going to expect a full explanation.'

'Of course, sir.'

'Hurt?' said Timothy on an afterthought, gruff now. 'Are you all right?'

'Yes, a bit beaten up but I'll be fine to work by Wednesday.'

Timothy grunted, expressed a muted concern and closed the call.

'What did he say?' said Hannah anxiously.

'He can't wait to see us back. He says he's missed us dreadfully.'

'He didn't say that.'

'How do you know?'

'Because I know Timothy and because I could hear your side of the conversation.'

'Well, why did you ask then, smarty pants? You could work it out for yourself. We've got some explaining to do.'

'Your bruises will help to mollify him.' She put a hand up and fingered the swelling on his cheek. 'Though I think they are starting to go down a bit.'

'Ow.' Nathan grabbed her hand.

'Baby,' she accused him. 'They don't seem to hurt you when you kiss me.'

'No, they don't.' So he did.

*

It was late morning when Hannah ventured outside into the courtyard. Béatrice, who had indeed stayed the night, had long since left for home and her precious tea rooms, and Eric had gone down to the studio to work, complaining loudly that he'd have to find a new studio assistant now. And it was a pain breaking them in, he said. He'd had a phone call from Mark first thing to say he had to go to the police station to answer some questions – though he was carefully vague about what –

319

and would be late. Eric told him not to bother coming in; he was sacked anyway. The ensuing conversation was brief. Then Eric rang Florence and told her not to come in for a couple of days. She could take it as paid leave and she was thrilled.

'I swear that girl won't last long either. She's got no passion.' His voice rose. 'She doesn't care. I'll be looking for two assistants soon.'

'You could try doing a little less,' Hannah ventured. 'Most men your age are retired or at least thinking about it. Why not ease back a bit?'

'Artists don't retire,' he roared. 'You should know that.' He'd tapped his head. 'There's always something else here that has to be got down on paper or on canvas or wherever. Always. When there isn't, shoot me.'

She didn't bother to argue; she knew he was right. Artists, writers, musicians, they never retire. Creativity is the engine of their day.

She stood outside Eric's front door now and paused. Nathan had fallen asleep on the sofa so she thought she'd go for a walk and get some fresh air. She had only been in Paris two weeks but it felt like an age and it would be strange now to go home. She had a desire to wander, to savour the last sights and sounds of the place, but she wanted to go alone. She had been on an emotional rollercoaster and she still felt giddy.

The meeting with Gabriel in his flat the previous evening had been painful. He'd been so certain that she was going to accept his offer to stay with him that it hadn't been easy to let him down. He'd said some things that had hurt and she'd not been slow to retaliate. They hadn't parted well but he had promised that he'd come to the party, then didn't.

She looked across to his front door, reluctant now to see him again and repeat the same painful arguments, but it was closed; there was no sign of life. In fact it seemed very quiet, unnaturally so. Something about it sent a shiver up her spine.

'*Mademoiselle Dechansay?*'

Hannah turned. Violette was tottering towards her, an envelope in her hand.

'This is for you,' she said, thrusting it at her. She jerked her head towards Gabriel's apartment. 'He's gone but he asked me to give you this.'

'Thank you,' said Hannah, frowning.

Violette turned to totter back.

'Gone?' said Hannah after her. 'Gone where?'

Violette paused. 'I've no idea. Perhaps that'll tell you.' She pointed towards the letter and retreated to her garden.

Hannah sat on the wooden bench outside her father's apartment and tore the envelope open. There were two sheets of paper inside. One was a letter; the other was a sheet of manuscript paper filled with Gabriel's frenzied music notation. She unfolded the letter and began to read.

My darling,

I am so sorry for the things I said yesterday. My disappointment made me cruel and you didn't deserve that. Please try to forget what I said; I didn't mean it.

My darling Hannah, it has been such a pleasure to know you. I shall always treasure our short time together and I will love you always. I have enclosed a copy of the piece I composed for you – something to remember me by. I shall think of you every time I play it. I have decided to move on. It's time. Hopefully I can find somewhere where the police don't find out who I am. I don't want to spend the rest of my life being an informer.

Nathan is a good man. I think I knew deep down what you were going to do that day in the kidnappers' flat. When you

321

rushed to Nathan's side as he lay on the floor, it was clear
where your strongest affections lay. I watched you fuss over
him and I knew. I just didn't want to admit it to myself.

Be happy.

Yours always,

Gabriel.

Hannah folded up the letter then glanced over the music
composition, folded that up too and rammed them both back in
the envelope and put it in her bag. She sat staring into space
for several minutes then got up and walked. She walked
without purpose, strolling past shops and offices, restaurants
and tiny pavement cafes, the hurly-burly of the Parisian traffic
not even registering on her consciousness. The city throbbed
with life and purpose but she barely noticed.

She had passed the Montparnasse cemetery and was still
walking away from the centre when she saw a large fire
burning in the front yard of an elegant three-storey house.
Workmen appeared to be remodelling the interior of the house
and the fire was consuming chunks of wood and scraps of old
wallpaper.

The gates of the yard stood open and she stopped and
stared. The heat of the fire burned at her cheeks even as she
stood on the pavement. The workmen were inside: she could
hear voices and one of them was whistling. On a sudden
impulse, she pulled the envelope out of her bag, stepped
forward and threw it onto the fire, quickly, rashly, then
watched it start to curl up and go brown before breaking into
flames.

Tomorrow they would be on a plane and going home. It
was going to be a fresh start. Daphne would be thrilled to hear
that she and Nathan were back together and Hannah was
excited too. But there would be challenges ahead. Compromise

was never easy and they would still argue. What they didn't need was emotional baggage so the letter and the music had to go.

She looked round, tried to figure out where exactly she had walked to, and turned to head slowly back.

Chapter 23

The studio was quiet. Some of Eric's artist friends liked to play music while they worked or listen to the radio but he preferred it like this. When it was quiet and everything was going well, he almost felt like he could get inside the painting on his canvas; he lived it; he breathed it. Without any outside distraction he was at one with it and seemed to know intuitively what he should do next.

But it *was* quiet. Strangely so and he wasn't used to it.

He looked up and glanced around. It was Tuesday morning and he was putting the last few touches to the commission for Sean, his American client. It had gone remarkably well, considering. The need over these last couple of weeks to forget the chaos of what was going on around him had at times only made him concentrate harder and he was cautiously pleased with it.

But the studio felt echoing. No assistants. No-one arguing or pottering around or asking advice. It had been a long time since it had been this empty. And Nathan and Hannah had left for the airport that morning so there was no-one upstairs either.

'I'll ring you when I get home,' Hannah had said before they left. 'I'd like to stay in touch. You will, won't you?'

'Of course,' he'd said and he'd meant it but they both knew he wouldn't. Hannah would ring two or three times, not get hold of him and would eventually give up. 'Come back and see me,' he said brightly. 'Next time will be less eventful. We can catch up.'

He looked at her luggage. She was carrying a large portfolio case and he was sure she hadn't had that when she arrived.

'What's in there?'

Hannah hesitated, looked at Nathan, then smiled sheepishly.

'It's the lady in the blue dress. I know you said to scrap everything that was damaged but I think I can mend it. Truly. It's doable and it's too lovely a painting to throw away. When it's done, I'll come back to visit you and bring it with me.' She glanced at Nathan. 'We'll both come. Or you could come and see us.'

Eric had been nonplussed, almost emotional, and gave her a quick final embrace.

'Thank you. I was a bit... well, hasty when I said that. I'd love you to be able to restore it. And I will. I'll come.'

And now they'd gone. The apartment felt quiet too. Hannah and Nathan had been chatty and laughing and quite different people in the last twenty-four hours. Nothing had been said but clearly something had been resolved between them. And it had come as a surprise to hear that Gabriel had left but Eric hadn't asked any questions. The world was full of people like Gabriel who struggled to stay in one place or to make any long-term connections. Was it restlessness or fear? We all hide behind something, he reflected. Even now, with all that had come out these last few days, there were still episodes in his life he chose to forget, episodes that it was better no-one knew about. He pushed the thought away.

His thoughts turned to Béatrice instead. She'd been a surprise, no question, a good surprise. They had arranged to go

325

out for a meal together that evening and he was looking forward to it.

He put his brush down and got up suddenly, feeling a need for more coffee. He poured himself a cup and walked to the window, looking down into the courtyard, then turned back and surveyed his studio. Slow down, Hannah had suggested. He supposed he could. The police were still saying that he might come out of the whole sorry business of the robbery with a fine or simply a caution. So much time had passed, they'd said, and his part in it had been small. Then he had – inadvertently – helped them catch Gustave. They'd impressed on him how lucky he was and he knew it, and they'd warned him not to get into any more trouble or there'd be consequences.

Of course, he hadn't mentioned the book he'd stolen from the house that night, the little one with the beautiful botanical illustrations that Hannah had always cherished so much. He'd spotted it on one of the bookshelves there and hadn't been able to resist slipping it into his pocket. It seemed a bit late to return it now. Embarrassing in the circumstances too.

No, he was going to draw a line under it all and start fresh. But not in the country, no. He was a city man at heart and he'd go mad if he didn't paint. What he needed was a new studio assistant and, since none of his friends knew anyone who was interested, he'd have to advertise.

He put down the coffee, found a piece of paper and started drafting an advert.

A Crack in the Varnish

Kathy Shuker

Hollywood actress, Esther Langley, has a home in the hills of Provence, an old converted abbey where she keeps her precious art collection. Now she has four paintings in need of restoration: one modern work, fire-damaged, and three crumbling old masters. It looks like a straightforward job for an experienced art restorer like Hannah Dechansay, and who wouldn't relish a few months in Provence?

But living and working on Esther's estate isn't easy. It's a tortured household, haunted by a tragic death. There's guilt and recrimination in the air and relationships soon start to unravel. Was the death an accident? Everyone has a different version to tell. There's something sinister going on and everyone, it seems, has something to hide.

Available as an eBook and in paperback, both standard and large print.

For more information about Kathy's books, please visit:
www.kathyshuker.co.uk

Milton Keynes UK
Ingram Content Group UK Ltd.
UKHW041852260324
440144UK00004B/227

9 781916 893054